HEAT RISES

ALSO AVAILABLE FROM HYPERION

Heat Wave

Naked Heat

HEAT RISES

RICHARD CASTLE

HYPERION
NEW YORK

Library of Congress Cataloging-in-Publication Data

Heat rises / Richard Castle.—1st ed.
   p. cm.
  Fictitiously attributed to Richard Castle, a character on the
ABC television show, Castle.
    ISBN 978-1-4013-2443-8 (hardback)
1. Women detectives—New York (State)—New York—Fiction.
2. Journalists—New York (State)—New York—Fiction.
3. Murder—Investigation—New York (State)—New York—
Fiction. 4. New York (N.Y.)—Fiction. I. Castle (Television
program)
  PS3600.A1H425 2011
  813'.6—dc22
     2011018735

Hyperion books are available for special promotions and pre-
miums. For details contact the HarperCollins Special Markets
Department in the New York office at 212-207-7528, fax 212-
207-7222, or email spsales@harpercollins.com.

Book design by Shubhani Sarkar

FIRST EDITION

10 9 8 7 6 5 4 3 2 1

SUSTAINABLE FORESTRY INITIATIVE Certified Fiber Sourcing www.sfiprogram.org

THIS LABEL APPLIES TO TEXT STOCK

We try to produce the most beautiful books possible, and we
are also extremely concerned about the impact of our manufac-
turing process on the forests of the world and the environment
as a whole. Accordingly, we've made sure that all of the paper
we use has been certified as coming from forests that are managed, to ensure the protection of the people and wildlife depen-
dent upon them.

To Captain Roy Montgomery, NYPD.
He made a stand and taught me all I need to know
about bravery and character.

HEAT RISES

ONE

The thing about New York City is you never know what's behind a door. Homicide Detective Nikki Heat pondered that, as she had so many times, while she parked her Crown Victoria and watched police cruiser and ambulance lights lick the storefronts on 74th off Amsterdam. She knew, for instance, the plain door to the wine shop opened into a faux cave done in soft beige and terra-cotta tones with stacked bottles nested in wall grottos fashioned of river stones imported from France. Across the street, the door of what had once been an FDR-era bank gave onto a staircase that spiraled downward to a huge array of indoor batting cages that filled with tween MLB hopefuls and kid birthday parties on weekend afternoons. But on that morning, just after 4 A.M., the most nondescript door of all, the frosted one without a sign, only a street number above it in gold and black foil stick-ons from a hardware store, would lead to one of the more unexpected interiors of the quiet block.

A uniform posted in front of the door shuffled to keep warm, silhouetted by the industrial-grade crime scene unit work light from inside that transformed the milky glass into the blinding *Close Encounters* portal. Nikki could see his breath from forty yards away.

She got out, and even though the air bit her nostrils and made her eyes teary, Nikki didn't button her coat against it. Instead she fanned it open with the back of her hand by rote, making sure that she had clean access to the Sig Sauer holstered underneath. And then, cold as she was, the homicide cop stopped and stood there to perform her next ritual: a pause to honor the dead she was about to meet. That

1

small, quiet, private moment lived as a ceremonial interval Nikki Heat claimed when she arrived at every crime scene. Its purpose was simple. To reaffirm that, victim or villain, the waiting corpse was human and deserved to be respected and treated individually, not as the next stat. Nikki drew in a slow breath, and the air felt to her the same as that night a decade ago, a Thanksgiving eve, when she was home on college break and her mother was brutally stabbed to death and left on the kitchen floor. She closed her eyes for her Moment.

"Something wrong, Detective?" Moment gone. Heat turned. A taxi rolled to a stop, and its passenger was addressing her from his backseat window. She recognized him and the driver, and smiled.

"No, Randy, I'm good." Heat stepped over to the cab and shook hands with Detective Randall Feller. "You keeping out of trouble?"

"Hope not," he said with the laugh that always reminded her of John Candy. "You remember Dutch," he said, making a head nod to Detective Van Meter up front in the driver's seat. Feller and Van Meter worked undercover in the NYPD Taxi Squad, a special anti-crime task force, run out of the Special Operations Division, that roved New York's streets in customized yellow cabs. The plainclothes cops of the Taxi Squad had a foot in the old school. They were generally tough asses who took no crap and did what they wanted and went where they wanted. Taxi Dicks roamed freely to sniff out crimes in progress, although with more scientific policing had lately been assigned to target their patrols in areas where robberies, burglaries, and street crimes spiked.

The cop at the wheel rolled his window down and nodded a wordless hi, making her wonder why Van Meter had bothered to open it. "Careful, Dutch, you'll talk her ear off," said Detective Feller with the Candy chuckle again. "Lucky you, Nikki Heat, getting the middle-of- the-night call."

Dutch said, "Some folks have no manners, getting killed at this hour." Heat didn't imagine Detective Van Meter paused a lot for reflection before meeting a corpse.

"Listen," she said. "Not that I don't like standing in twenty-five degrees, but I've got a vic waiting."

"Where's your ride-along?" said Feller with more than a little interest. "The writer, what's his face?"

Feller, fishing again. Just like he did every time they crossed paths, testing to see if Rook was still in the picture. Nikki had been on Feller's radar since the night months before when she escaped from a hired killer in Rook's loft. After Heat's battle with the Texan, he and Dutch were in the first wave of cops who raced to her aid. Ever since, Feller never missed a chance to pretend he didn't know Rook's name and take a sounding on her. Heat rolled with it; she was no stranger to interest from men, even liked it if they didn't cross a line, but Feller . . . In the Rom-Com he'd be more Com than Rom; the joshing brother rather than the love interest. Detective Feller was funny and good company but more for beers in the cop bar than Sancerre by candlelight. Two weeks ago she'd seen him come out of the men's room at Plug Uglies wearing a sanitary tissue ring around his neck, asking everyone if they'd also like a lobster bib.

"What's his face?" repeated Nikki. "He's off on assignment." And then to send the message, she added, "He's back at the end of this week, though." But the detective read something else in her voice.

"That a good thing or a bad thing?"

"Good thing," Heat said a little too abruptly. So she flashed a grin trying to reset her tone. "Real good." And then, to convince herself, she added, "Really good."

———

What Nikki found on the other side of the door was not an urban shrine to oenology with artfully stacked green bottles, nor did she hear the ping of an aluminum bat followed by the thud of a ball into padded netting. Instead, a throat-catching mixture of incense mixed with vapors from a harsh cleaning solvent rose up to greet her as she descended a flight of stairs to the basement. Behind her, Detective Van

Meter moaned a low "Whoa," and as Heat rounded the landing to make her turn down the last flight, she heard Dutch and Feller snapping on gloves. Van Meter muttered to his partner, "I catch an STD down here, I'll sue till I own the damn city."

At basement level they arrived at something that only charitably could be referred to as a reception area. The crimson painted-brick walls behind the Formica counter and the Internet catalogue chairs reminded her of a small, private gym lobby, and not a very high-end one. Four doors were spaced along the far wall. They were all open. Three led into dim rooms, lit only by the spill of harsh radiance from the CSU light stands set up to illuminate the lobby during the investigation. More light, punctuated by strobe flashes came from the far doorway, where Detective Raley stood watching the activity, latexed hands by his side. He saw Nikki out of the corner of his eye and stepped out to her.

"Welcome to Pleasure Bound, Detective Heat," he said.

Copsense made Nikki scope out the other three rooms before entering the crime scene itself. She knew they'd have been cleared by Raley and the uniforms who responded first, but she poked her head in each doorway for a quick glance. All she could make out in the murkiness were the shapes of equipment and furniture of the bondage trade, and that each chamber was themed. In order: a Victorian boudoir, an animal role-play parlor, and a sensory deprivation room. In the coming hours these would be swept by CSU, and forensic evidence gathered, but for now she was satisfied with her survey. Heat took out her gloves and walked to the far doorway, where Feller and Van Meter waited deferentially behind Raley. This was her case, on her turf, and unspoken etiquette dictated she go in ahead of them.

The corpse was naked and bound at the wrists and ankles to an X-shaped vertical wooden frame known as the St. Andrew's Cross. The structure was bolted to the floor and the ceiling in the center of the room, and the dead man's body sagged downward, bent at the knees, his buttocks hovering above the linoleum. The bulk of his weight, which Heat put at almost 250 pounds, now unsupported by muscle, strained the wrist straps high over his head and pulled his arms into a taut Y.

Detective Feller whisper-sang the chorus of "YMCA" until Nikki scalded him with a glance. Chastened, he folded his arms and looked away at his partner, who shrugged.

"What have we got, Rales?" said Heat to her detective.

Raley consulted a single page of notes. "Not much, as of yet. Check it out." He swept the room with his arm. "No clothes anywhere, no ID, no nothing. After-hours cleaning crew made the discovery. They're not English speakers, so Ochoa's doing the honors in the office getting their statement. Prelim, though, is they say the place closes about one, sometimes two, that's when they come in. They were doing their usual janitor stuff, figuring they were all alone, and came in here, to the, ah . . ."

"Torture chamber," said Nikki. "The rooms are themed. This one's for torture and humiliation." She read his look and said, "I worked vice once."

"So did I," said Raley.

"I worked it harder." Heat arched a brow and watched him blush. "So nobody else was here at the discovery. Did they see anyone leaving?"

"Negative."

"There's a bubble for a surveillance cam in the lobby," said Van Meter.

Raley nodded. "On it." And then he turned to Nikki. "There's a locked closet in the manager's office where the cleaners say she keeps the recorder."

"Wake up the manager," said Heat. "Tell her to bring in the key, but don't tell her about the body. Just say there was an attempted break-in. I don't want her making calls on the way here, and I want to see her reaction when she finds out."

When Raley stepped out to make the call, Heat asked the CSU technician and the police photographer if they had looked for any clothing or a wallet or ID anywhere else on the premises. She knew what the answer would be—these were professionals—but the bases had to be covered. The obvious, if thought to be too obvious, was what got overlooked and left holes in an investigation if you started assuming and stopped checking. They confirmed no clothing, ID, or other personal effects on their initial sweep.

Detective Feller said, "How about Dutch and I cruise the neighboring blocks, see if anyone who's up saw anything?"

Van Meter nodded. "At this hour not many people around, but we can hit the diners, garbage collectors, delivery trucks, whatever."

"Sure," said Detective Heat. "Appreciate the assist."

Feller gave her the puppy eyes again. "For you, Nikki? C'mon." He took out his cell phone and knelt to get an angle of the dead man's face with its camera. "Won't hurt to show this around to see if anyone knows him."

"Good thinking," she said.

On his way out Detective Feller paused. "Listen, sorry if I was out of line with the Village People thing. Just breaking the tension, you know?"

As much as she couldn't abide disrespecting a victim, she looked at him and read his embarrassment. As a veteran NYPD detective, she knew it was just misplaced cop humor and not meant to be callous. "I don't even remember it," said Heat. He smiled, gave her a head nod, and left.

———

Lauren Parry knelt on the floor beside the victim, and as she filled in each box in her report, the medical examiner recited to Nikki, "OK, so we have a John Doe, late forties, approximately two-fifty to two-fifty-five." The ME pointed to her nostrils. "Obvious smoker, definite drinker."

It was always tough with the Does, thought Nikki. Without a name to go on, you were hobbled at the starting gate. Precious time in the investigation would be spent just figuring out who he was.

"Preliminary TOD . . . ," Lauren Parry read the thermometer and continued, ". . . eight to ten P.M."

"That long ago? You sure?" Heat's friend looked up at her from the clipboard and stared. The detective said, "OK, so you're sure."

"Preliminarily, Nik. I'll run the usual tests when we get him down to Thirtieth Street, but for now that's a good window for you."

"Cause of death?"

"Well, you just want every little thing, don't you?" said the ME with a twinkle behind her deadpan. Then she grew pensive and turned to consider the corpse. "COD could be asphyxiation."

"The collar?"

"That's my best first guess." Lauren stood and indicated the posture collar biting into the man's neck, drawn so tight by the strapping at the back it caused his flesh to roll over its edges. "Certainly enough to restrict the windpipe. Plus the broken blood vessels in the eyeballs are consistent with choking."

"Let's rewind. Best first guess?' " asked Heat.

"Come on, Nikki, you know I always tell you first shot is preliminary." Then Lauren Parry looked back at the body, pondering again.

"What?"

"Let's just mark it 'choking' as a prelim until I do my autopsy."

Nikki knew better than to press Lauren for conjecture, just as her friend knew not to push her for speculation. "That's fine," she said, all the while knowing that her pal from the Office of the Chief Medical Examiner was mulling something.

Lauren opened a plastic drawer in her kit for some swabs and resumed her testing while Nikki did what she always did at a death scene. She clasped her hands behind her and slowly walked the room, occasionally squatting or bending, eyeing the corpse from all angles. This wasn't just a ritual, it was a fundamental procedure to clear her head of all conclusions and projections. The idea was to open her mind to impressions, to just let in whatever came in and, most of all, simply to notice what she was noticing.

Her sense of the victim was that he wasn't a physically active person. The sizable roll of soft fat around his midsection suggested a lot of sitting, or at least an occupation that didn't involve movement or strength like sports, construction, or other manual labor. As with most people, the skin on his upper arms was pale compared to his forearms, but the contrast wasn't great; no farmer's tan. That told her not only that he was indoors a lot, but that he either wore long sleeves most of the time or didn't likely tend a garden or play golf at a club. Even this long after summer there would be more residual tanning. She stepped close to examine his hands, being careful not to breathe on them. They were clean and soft, underscoring her feeling about his indoor life. The nails were neat but not manicured; she usually saw that among middle-aged men who were wealthy or young urban groomers who were more fit. The hair was sparse up top, befitting the age Lauren had fixed, as were the strands of white mixed in with its dull, iron filings color. The brows were wildly bushy, sometimes an indicator of a bachelor or widower, and his salt-and-pepper goatee gave him an air of academia or arts and letters. Nikki looked again at his fingertips and made note of a bluish tinge that looked to be within the skin itself and not topical like from oil paint or ink stains.

Bruises, welts, and abrasions were everywhere, front, back, and sides. Torso, legs, and arms. In keeping with her open-mind approach, the detective tried not to ascribe the marks to a night of sadomasochism. Possible, even likely, given the setting, but not for certain. There were no obvious cuts, punctures, bullet holes, or bleeding she could see.

The rest of the room was immaculate, at least for a torture dungeon. The CSU vacuuming and print dusting might yield some forensic evidence, but there was no visible trash, cigarette butts, or any clues such as a conveniently dropped hotel matchbook with a killer's room number on it, like you saw in old movies on TCM.

Again, keeping an open mind, Nikki refused to conclude there even was a killer in the classic sense. A homicide? Possibly. Murder? Still just possibly. The door had to be left open for an accidental death from a consensual torture session gone too far, resulting in a panic flight from the dom in the relationship.

Heat was sketching her own diagram of the room layout, something she always did as a personal companion to the one filed by the Crime Scene Unit, when Detective Ochoa came in after his interview of the cleaning crew. He had a sober tone as he quickly greeted Nikki, but softened when his gaze fell on the ME.

"Detective," said Lauren with a little too much formality.

"Doctor," he replied, matching her reserve. Then Nikki caught Lauren taking something out of the side pocket of her suit and slipping it into his hand. Detective Ochoa didn't look at it, just said, "Right, thanks," and stepped across the room, where he turned his back and fastened his watch to his wrist. Nikki could do the math on where The Oach was when he was awakened by the dead body call.

Seeing these two go through this charade of non-intimacy gave her a twinge. She lifted her pen above her diagram and paused, reminded of how not long ago she and Rook had similarly conspired to low-key their affair—also fooling no one. That was back in the summer heat wave, when he was a ride-along journalist researching Nikki's homicide squad, and ultimately Nikki, for the feature story he was writing for *First Press*. Having her picture on the cover of a respected national magazine was a mixed blessing for the publicity-shy Heat. Bundled with the annoyance and unhappy complications of her fifteen minutes came some unexpectedly hot times with Jameson Rook. And now, some form of a relationship. Well, she thought— something she had been doing a lot of lately—not so much a relationship but a . . . what?

After the heat of their romance ratcheted up and rose to even greater intensity, something else happened over time and togetherness. It deepened into what began to feel to Nikki like a Real Deal that was headed somewhere. But where it ended up heading was off a cliff into an abyss where it was suspended midair.

He had been gone four weeks now. A month of Rook disappearing on his investigation of international arms smuggling for a *First*

Press exposé. A month off the grid while he bounced around mountain villages of Eastern Europe, African seaports, airstrips in Mexico, and God knows where else. A month to let Nikki wonder where the hell they were with each other.

Rook's communications sucked and that didn't help. He told her he would be going deep undercover and to expect some radio silence, but come on. Going all this time in isolation without so much as a phone call was chewing at her; wondering if he was alive, rotting in some warlord's jail . . . or what? Could he really be out of communication this long, or had he simply not made a good enough attempt? Nikki denied it at first, but after days and nights of trying not to think the thought, she now struggled with the notion that perhaps the charm of Jameson Rook, the rogue globetrotter, was wearing thin. Sure, she respected his career as a two-time Pulitzer-winning investigative journalist, and knew intellectually what came along with all that, but the way he blew out of Dodge, the way he blew out of her life, so easily had her questioning not just where they stood as a couple but where he stood with her anymore.

Nikki looked at her own watch and wondered what time it was where Jameson Rook was. Then she looked at its calendar. Rook had said he would be back in five days. The question for Nikki was, by then where would they be?

———

Heat mulled resources and decided it would be more productive for her to wait for the manager of the underground sex club to arrive and unlock the video closet. That way she could free up her own pair of detectives to snag some uniformed officers and canvass the neighborhood on foot. Since the taxi team had volunteered to hit the diners, all-night workers, and delivery guys, she charged Raley and Ochoa (collectively and always affectionately known as "Roach") to concentrate on finding an ID or a wallet. "You should do the usual scans. Trash cans, Dumpsters, subway grates, under apartment stoops, or anyplace else that's a handy place for a dump and run. Not a lot of doorman buildings in this neighborhood, but if you see one, ask. Oh, and check out the Phoenix House up the block. Maybe some of our friends in recovery were up and heard or saw something."

Roach's cell phones chimed about two seconds apart. Heat held up her own mobile and said, "That's a head shot I just e-mailed you of our vic. If you get a chance, flash it, you never know."

"Right," said Ochoa. "Who doesn't love to have a picture of a choking victim shoved in their face before breakfast?"

As they started up the stairs to street level, she called after them, "And make note of any surveillance cams you see with a street view. Banks, jewelry stores, you know the drill. We can drop in and have them do a playback when they open for business later this morning."

―――――

Detective Heat had to shake off a foul mood after dealing with the manager of Pleasure Bound. Nikki doubted the woman had been awakened by Raley. On the contrary, Roxanne Paltz vibed having been up all night, heavily and severely made up and arriving in a tight vinyl outfit that creaked whenever she moved on the chair in her office. Her granny glasses had blue lenses matching the tips of her spiky, bleach-damaged hair, which gave off the unmistakable scent of cannabis. When Nikki told her the real reason they were there, the dead man in her torture chamber, she lost color and reeled. Heat showed her the picture on her cell phone, and the woman nearly got sick. She sat down unsteadily and drank a sip of the water Nikki gave her from the cooler, but after she recovered, said she'd never seen the guy.

When Nikki asked if she could have a look at the surveillance video, it got contentious, and Roxanne Paltz was suddenly all about constitutional rights. Speaking with the authority of someone who had been hassled for running a sex trade business, she cited just cause, unlawful search, client confidentiality, and freedom of expression. Her lawyer was on speed dial, and even though it wasn't even six in the morning, she called and woke him up, Nikki having to deal with her raccoon mascara glower while she parroted back his certainty that no cabinets could be unlocked or video screened without a judge's warrant.

"I'm just asking for a little cooperation," said Nikki.

Roxanne sat there listening to the attorney on her phone, nodding and nodding, vinyl creaking with each head bob. And then she hung up. "He says to go fuck yourself."

Nikki Heat paused and gave a slight smile. "Judging from some of the equipment you've got here, this would probably be the one place I could actually do that."

———

The detective knew she would get the search warrant and had just ended her call downtown to get the wheels turning on one when her phone vibrated in her hand. It was Raley. "Come topside, I think we got something."

She arrived back up on the sidewalk expecting sun, but it was still dark. Nikki had lost a sense of time and place down there, and she reflected that that was probably the whole idea.

Detectives Raley, Ochoa, Van Meter, and Feller stood in a semicircle under the green canvas canopy of the corner grocery across the street. Crossing 74th to meet them, Nikki had to pause so she didn't get run over by a delivery guy on a fat-tired bike. She watched his trailing breath as he passed, with somebody's order-in breakfast bouncing in the wire basket, and figured maybe she didn't have the hardest job in the city. "Whatcha got?" she said as she stepped over to the crew.

"Found some clothes and a shoe wedged in the space between the two buildings here," said Ochoa, training the beam of his Streamlight Stinger in the wall gap separating the grocery and the nail spa next door. Raley held up a pair of dark trousers and a black tasseled loafer for Heat and then slipped them into a brown paper evidence bag. "Spaces like this? Classic place to stash," said Ochoa. "Learned that in Narco."

"Give me the light, Crime Dog, think there's more here." Raley took the mini from his partner and squatted in front of the gap. A few seconds later he pulled out the mate to the other loafer then said, "Well, what do you know?"

"What?" Ochoa asked. "Don't be a dick, what is it?"

"Hang on a sec. If you weren't packing on the weight, you could have done this instead of me." Raley twisted his shoulder to get a better angle for his reach into the narrow opening. "Here we go. Another collar."

Nikki expected to see something in a leather gimp rig with sharp studs and stainless steel D-rings, but when Raley finally stood and held it up in his gloved hand, it wasn't that kind of collar at all. It was a priest's collar.

––––––

In 2005 New York City funded eleven million dollars to modernize the NYPD's high-tech capability by building the Real Time Crime Center, a computer operations hub that, among numerous capabilities, provides crime reports and police data to officers in the field with startling immediacy. That is why in a city of eight and a half million people it only took Detective Heat less than three minutes to get a likely ID on the victim in the torture dungeon. The RTCC accessed records and spit out a missing persons report filed the night before by a parish rectory housekeeper for a Father Gerald Graf.

Nikki assigned Roach to stay and continue their canvass while she made the drive uptown to interview the woman who filed the MPR. Detectives Feller and Van Meter were off their shift, but Dutch offered to help Roach continue knocking on doors. Feller appeared at her car window and said if Heat didn't mind the company, he'd be happy to ride shotgun with her. She hesitated, figuring this was about Feller engineering his opportunity to ask her to catch a drink or dinner later. But a veteran detective was reaching out to help with a case on his own time, and she couldn't say no to that. If he tried to bend it into a date offer, she'd simply deal with it.

Our Lady of the Innocents was on the northern border of the

precinct, mid-block on 85th between West End Avenue and River-side. At this early side of the morning rush hour, a five-minute drive, if that. But as soon as Heat pulled onto Broadway, they caught a red in front of the Beacon Theater.

"Glad to finally have some time alone with you," said Feller while they waited.

"For sure," said Nikki, who then hurried to steer the topic away. "Appreciate the assist, Randy. Can always use another pair of eyes and ears."

"Gives me a chance to ask you something without the whole world around."

She looked up at the light and considered breaking out the gumball. ". . . Yeah?"

"Any idea how you did on your exam for lieutenant?" he asked. Not the question she expected. Nikki turned to look at him. "Green," he said and she drove on.

"I don't know, seemed like I did all right. Hard to know for sure," she said. "Still waiting for the results to be posted." When the department's civil service test was offered recently, Heat had taken it, not so much out of a burning desire for the promotion, but because she wasn't sure when it would be given again. Budget cuts from the economic crisis had hit New York as much as any other municipality, and one response the year before had been to cut back on raises by postponing the scheduled rank advancement tests.

Detective Feller cleared his throat. "What if I told you I hear you aced it?" She gave him a side glance and then concentrated on the driver of the bread delivery truck who had stopped to double-park in her lane without flashers. While she hit her blinker and waited for the passing lane to clear, he went on. "I know this to be a fact."

"How?"

"From some inside sources. Downtown." He reached for the dash-board. "Mind if I back off the temp? Starting to bake in here."

"Help yourself."

"I try to keep myself connected." He turned down the knob one click, then decided on one more before he settled back in his seat again. "Not planning on riding in back of that cab forever, ya hear what I'm saying?"

"Sure, sure." Nikki made her swing around the bread truck. "I, um, appreciate the info."

"So when you get by your orals and all the other hoops they make you jump through—like teach you the secret handshake, or whatever—do me a fave? Don't forget your friends on your way up."

Whoomph, there it is, thought Nikki. She felt a little embarrassed. All this time thinking Feller wanted to date her when maybe what he really wanted was to network her. She replayed her mental picture of him at the cop bar clowning in his ass gasket lobster bib and wondered if the jester in him was all in fun, or if he was really just a skilled glad-hander. The more he talked, the more that picture emerged.

"When you get your gold bar, it's going to be a piece of good news in your precinct for a change. And you know what I mean."

"I'm not sure I do," she said. They hit another red at 79th, and unfortunately this was a long one.

"Not sure, that's a laugh," he said. "I mean Captain Montrose."

Nikki knew full well what he meant. Her skipper, her mentor, Captain Montrose, was under increasing pressure from One Police Plaza over his performance as commander of the Twentieth Precinct. Whether it was the bad economy, increased unemployment, or a reset to the dark days of the pre-Giuliani disorder, crime statistics were edging up throughout all five boroughs. And worse, they were spiking in election season. Gravity rules, so in response, the shit roll was all downhill to the precinct commanders. But Heat could see her captain was taking an extra pounding. Montrose had been singled out, called down separately for extra meetings and ass chewings, spending as much time at HQ as he did in his office. His personality darkened under the pressure, and he had grown atypically remote—no, more than remote, secretive. It made Nikki wonder whether something else was going on with him beyond precinct perf stats. Now what bothered

Heat was that her boss's private humiliation was Out There as department gossip. If Feller knew about it, others did, too. Loyalty made her deflect it, back up her boss.

"Listen, Randy, who isn't getting squeezed these days? I hear those weekly CompStat meetings at 1PP are brutal for all the skips, not just mine."

"Seriously," he said with a nod. "They should put a drain in the floor to let the blood run out. Green."

"Jeez, it just turned." Nikki pressed the accelerator.

"Sorry. Drives Dutch crazy, too. I tell ya, I've got to get my ass out of that cab." He powered down his window and spat. When he closed it again, he said, "This isn't just about the performance figs. I have a bud in Internal Affairs. Your man is on their radar."

"Bull."

"No bull."

"For what?"

He made an exaggerated shrug. "It's IA, what do you think?"

"No. I don't buy it," she said.

"Then don't. Maybe he is clean, but I'm telling you he's got his neck on the stump and they're sharpening the ax."

"Not maybe. Montrose is clean." She made a left onto 85th. A block and a half ahead, she could see a cross on the church roof. In the distance, across the Hudson, the apartments and cliffs were pinking from the rising sun. Nikki switched off her headlights as she crossed West End Avenue.

"Who knows?" said Feller. "You get rank, maybe you'll be in position to take over the precinct if he goes down."

"He is not going down. Montrose is under pressure, but he's straight as they come."

"If you say."

"I say. He's unassailable."

As Nikki got out in front of the rectory, she wished she had made the drive alone. No, what she wished was that Feller had just asked her for drinks, or bowling, or for sex. Any one of those, she would rather have dealt with.

She reached for the bell, but before she could press it, she saw a small head through the stained glass window in the door and it opened, revealing a minute woman in her late sixties.

Nikki referred to her notes from the RTCC message. "Good morning, are you Lydia Borelli?"

"Yes, and you're with the police, I can tell."

After they showed ID and introduced themselves, Nikki said, "And it was you who called about Father Graf?"

"Oh, I've been worried sick. Come in, please." The housekeeper's lips were quaking and her hands fluttered nervously. She missed the doorknob on her first attempt to pull the door closed. "Did you find him? Is he all right?"

"Mrs. Borelli, do you have a recent photo I could look at?"

"Of Father? Well, I'm sure somewhere . . . I know."

She led them over thick rugs that muted their footfalls through the living room and into the pastor's adjoining study. On the shelves of the built-in above the desk several photos in glass frames were perched between books and knickknacks. The housekeeper took one down, swiping her finger along the top of the frame to dust it before she handed it over. "This is from last summer."

Heat and Detective Feller stood beside each other to examine it. The shot was taken at some sort of protest rally and showed a priest and three Hispanic protesters, with arms linked, leading a march behind a banner. Father Graf's face, frozen in mid-recitation of a chant, was definitely the same as the one on the corpse at Pleasure Bound.

The housekeeper took the news stoically, blessing herself with the sign of the cross and then lowering her head in silent prayer. When she was done, blood vessels showed through her temples and tears streamed down her cheeks. There were tissues on the end table near the couch. Nikki offered her the box and she took some.

"How did it happen?" she asked, staring down at the tissues in her hands.

Fragile as the woman appeared, Heat thought better of giving her the details at that moment about the priest's death in a BDSM torture and humiliation dungeon. "We're still investigating that."

Then she looked up. "Did he suffer?"

Detective Feller squinted at Nikki and turned away to hide his face, suddenly making himself busy replacing the photo on the shelf.

"We'll have more details after the coroner's report," answered Nikki, hoping her dodge was artful enough to be bought. "We know this is a loss for you, but in a while, not just now, we're going to need to ask you a few questions to help us."

"Certainly, anything you need."

"What would be helpful now, Mrs. Borelli, is if we could look through the rectory. You know, search through his papers, his bedroom."

"His closet," said Feller.

Nikki moved forward. "We want to look for anything that would help us find out who did this."

The housekeeper gave her a puzzled look. "Again?"

"I said, we'd like to search the—"

"I heard what you said. I mean, you need to search again?"

Heat leaned closer to the woman. "Are you saying someone searched here already?"

"Yes. Last night, another policeman. He said he was following up on my missing person report."

"Oh, of course, sometimes we cross signals," said Nikki. That could well be the case, but her uneasiness was growing. She caught a look from Feller that said his antenna was up, too. "May I ask who this policeman was?"

"I forgot his name. He said it, but I was so upset. Senior moment." She chuckled and then stifled a sob. "He did show me a badge like yours, so I let him roam free. I watched television while he looked around."

"Well, I'm sure he filed a report." Nikki flipped open her spiral reporter's notebook. "Maybe I could cut through some red tape if you described him."

"Sure. Tall. Black, or do I say Afro-American these days? Very pleasant, had a kind face. Bald. Oh, and a little birthmark or mole or something right here." She tapped her cheek.

Heat stopped writing and capped her stick pen. She had all she needed. The housekeeper had just described Captain Montrose.

TWO

Detective Heat wasn't sure which she would prefer, to come into the station house and find Captain Montrose in his office so she could ask him about his visit to the rectory the night before or to find his executive chair empty and be spared the meeting for a while. As it happened, that morning, like so many others, she was the one to flick the lights on in the Homicide bull pen. The skipper's office was locked and dark behind the glass wall that gave him a view of the squad room. Her feelings upon seeing his office empty answered her question about preference; it disappointed her. Nikki wasn't a procrastinator, and especially when a subject was uncomfortable, her instinct was to get the noise out early and then deal.

She told herself this was all about nothing, and all that was needed was to clear the air. On its face, the captain's stop at Our Lady of the Innocents was not inappropriate. A missing persons report for a resident of the precinct gave legitimate cause to speak to the woman who filed it. That was standard police procedure.

What was not standard was for the commander of the precinct to handle a call that usually fell to a Detective-3, or even an experienced uniform. And to conduct a search—alone—was, again, not unheard of but still unusual.

An hour before, Heat and Detective Feller had gloved up and made their own walk through the premises and found no signs of struggle, breakage, bloodstains, threat mail, or anything out of the ordinary to their eyes. The Evidence Collection Unit would be more thorough, and, as they waited for ECU to arrive, Nikki was relieved that Feller had the discretion not to say anything, even though it was all over his face. She knew what he was thinking. Montrose, taking heavy fire from his bosses and under potential investigation by Internal Affairs for allegations unknown, had deviated from standard procedure and solo snooped the home of a torture vic the night he died. When she dropped Feller off at the 86th Street subway stop all he said to her was "Good luck . . . *Lieutenant* Heat."

Especially since she was the first one in the bull pen that morning, Nikki would have preferred to have been able to catch Montrose early and get him alone. In the break room she speed-dialed him from her cell phone while she poured milk on her cereal. "Cap, it's Heat. 7:29," she said to his voice mail. "Give me a callback when you can." Short and uncluttered. He'd know she would only call if it was important.

She carried her cardboard bowl of Mini-Wheats back to her desk, and while she ate in silence. Nikki felt the weight of the month of mornings she had faced without Rook. She looked at her watch again. The hands had advanced, but that damned calendar hadn't budged.

She wondered what he was doing at that moment. Nikki envisioned Rook sitting on an ammo crate in the shade of a Quonset hut at a remote jungle airstrip. Colombia or Mexico, by the itinerary he had sketched out before he kissed her good-bye at her apartment door. After she locked up, she raced to her bay window and waited there, watching vapor trail from the tailpipe of his waiting town car, wanting one last glimpse of him before he dissolved. She felt a glow inside at the memory of him stopping just before he got in the backseat. Rook had turned and blown a kiss up her way. Now that picture had faded to a feeling. The vision was replaced by her imagined one of Rook in rough country, swatting mosquitoes, jotting names of shadowy gun runners in his Moleskine. He was no doubt unshowered, beardy with sweat moons. She wanted him.

Heat's phone buzzed with a text from Captain Montrose. "@1PP. In touch when I get sprung." True to form, he was stuck downtown at headquarters for his ritual precinct commander accountability meeting. It made Nikki reflect on the downside of her impending promotion. One rung too many and your head shows over the parapet and becomes a big, fat target.

———

Thirty minutes later, just after 8 A.M., the Homicide bull pen was standing room only as Detective Nikki Heat walked her squad, plus a few extra attendees she had pulled in from Burglary and patrol, through the few details she had on the case so far. She stood in front of the big Murder Board and used magnets to slap two pictures of Father Graf at top center of the white enamel. The first, a death photo taken by CSU, was of much better quality than the cell phone snap she had taken herself. Beside it, she posted his protest march photo, cropped and enlarged to show only his face. "This is our victim, Father Gerald Graf, pastor of Our Lady of the Innocents." She recapped the circumstances of his death and used a dry-erase marker to circle the times of his disappearance, estimated death, and discovery on the timeline she had already drawn across the board. "Copies of these photos are being duped for you. As usual, they'll also be up on the computer server, along with other details, for access from your cells and laptops."

Ochoa turned to Detective Rhymer, a Burglary cop on loan, who was sitting on a filing cabinet in the back. "Hey, Opie, in case you wondered, that's the typewriter with all the blinky lights."

Dan Rhymer, an ex-MP from the Carolinas who had stayed in New York after his army hitch, was accustomed to the needling. Even back home they had nicknamed him Opie. He put some butter on his Southern accent. "Laptop computer, huh? Goll-lly. No wonder I couldn't toast my possum samwich on that thing."

During the chorus of "whoa"s Nikki said, "Excuse me? Anyone mind if I talk a little about the investigation?"

"Oo, frosty," said Detective Sharon Hinesburg. Nikki chuckled along until she added, "Trying out your new command mode for lieutenant?" The barb didn't surprise Heat, it was the realization that her pending rise was out of the house rumor mill and in the air. Naturally, it came from Hinesburg, an only modestly gifted detective whose main talent was for annoying Heat. Someone must have once told Hinesburg her outspokenness was refreshing. Nikki thought that person had done the detective a disservice.

"What do we have on cause of death?" said Raley, snapping things back to business for Heat and falling on the grenade Hinesburg had lobbed.

"Prelim puts us in a gray area." She made eye contact with Rales, who gave her an almost imperceptible nod that spoke volumes about camaraderie. "In fact, we can't even officially class this as a homicide until after the autopsy. Nature of the death left open lots of doors for accidental. You've got potential health issues of the vic, intent of the practitioner . . ."

"Or killer," said Ochoa.

"Or killer," she agreed. "Father Graf was a missing person, which pushes the likelihood of foul play." Involuntarily, her gaze ran to Captain Montrose's empty office, then back to the squad. "But this is the time for us to keep open minds."

"Was the padre a freak?" Hinesburg again, subtle as always. "I mean, what the hell is a priest doing in a kink dungeon?" Not the most delicate phrasing, but not the wrong question.

"That's why our direction for now is going to be to work the BDSM angle," said Heat. "I still need interviews with the housekeeper and others at the parish about the priest. Relationships, family, enemies, bad exorcisms—might as well say it—altar boys, you never know. Everything's on the table, but what's right in front of us is the sex torture. Soon as we get our warrant, which should be soon, Detective Raley, go screen that security tape. Let's see when he came in there and with whom."

"Not to mention, in what condition," said Raley.

"Especially that. And pull stills of everyone who came and went before and after, right up to the first responders." Her marker squeaked

"Security Vid" in neat block letters on the whiteboard. When she was done underlining it, she said, "While Raley's on that, let's try to find out if our victim had a history in the lifestyle. Ochoa, Rhymer, Gallagher, Hinesburg—you'll be canvassing the clubs and known Doms, masters, mistresses."

"Yes, *sir*." Hinesburg saluted, but she didn't get any laughs. The others were already on their feet, heading to work.

Minutes later, Nikki hung up her phone and called across the bull pen. "Ochoa, change of plan." She crossed over to his desk, where he was going over a printout of clubs in Manhattan's infamous Dungeon Alley. "ECU called in from the rectory. The housekeeper is saying it looks to her like things have been moved around and items are missing. I've got the manager of Pleasure Bound and her lawyer waiting for me in Interrogation, so why don't you head on up there and see what's what."

Hinesburg caught Heat's eye. "If I ask nicely, any chance I can forgo the kink circuit and handle the rectory?"

Since Hinesburg seemed to be back-door apologizing for her snarky episode, Nikki weighed the benefit of responding in kind and siphoning off some of the tension. "You have a problem with that, Oach?"

"Let me see . . . ," Ochoa held up his palms as if balancing a scale, ". . . church or sex dungeon, church or sex dungeon." He dropped his arms. "Light a candle for me while you're there, Sharon."

"Thanks for that," said Hinesburg. "And I apologize I busted you for sounding all bitchy. I didn't realize you were dealing with . . . ," she tilted her head conspiratorially at Heat and said, ". . . other issues." When Nikki gave her a puzzled look, the detective held up the morning edition of the *Ledger*, folded open to "Buzz Rush," the celebrity gossip section. "You mean you haven't seen this?"

Heat's eyes actually blinked at the picture. Right under a photo of Anderson Cooper at a charity function was a quarter-page candid shot of Rook and a stunning woman coming out of Le Cirque. The caption read, "Happy client? Eligible superstar journalist Jameson

Rook and his lit agent Jeanne Callow are all smiles after a swank *tête-à-tête* at Le Cirque last night."

Ever the sensitive one, Hinesburg said, "Thought you said Rook was off doing an article on arms dealers." Nikki heard the words but couldn't take her eyes off the photograph. "Coldest winter since 1906, and she's sleeveless. When he said he was going to be chasing guns, betcha didn't think they'd be like those."

––––––

They needed her in Interrogation. Nikki walked there on autopilot, still reeling from the knockdown punch. She couldn't grasp it, didn't want to believe it. Rook was not only back but out on the town while she waited for him like some Gloucester sea captain's wife pacing the widow's walk, searching the horizon for a mast. No beard, no sweat moons, he was scrubbed, shaved, and had his Hugo Boss sleeve laced through the elbow of his hot gym-rat agent.

Detective Raley caught up with her at the door to the Observation Room as she was preparing to go in, and Heat shoved Rook out of her head, even though she still felt brittle from the shock. "Not so good news on the security cam," said Raley. He was holding a banker's box with a Chain of Evidence form taped to the side.

"I assume that's the tape, right?"

"Tapes, yes. *The* tape, no. When I unlocked the cabinet, the one in the deck had run itself out and the label was dated two weeks ago."

"Lovely," said Heat. "And nothing from last night?"

"These tapes haven't recorded anything for several weeks. I'll check, but we'll be lucky if we see anything."

Nikki pondered briefly. "Screen what you have here anyway and pull faces. You never know, we may see Graf there and connect him with someone."

Raley disappeared up the hall with his box of tapes. Nikki continued into Interrogation.

––––––

"You already asked my client that question," said the old man. Simmy Paltz poked a finger bent from arthritis on the legal pad on the table in front of him. He looked to be a hundred, all skin and bones, withered and leathery. He wore a 1970s Wemlon tie in a big knot, but Nikki could have fit a hand right down to her wrist in the gap created between Simmy's pilled collar and his rooster neck. He seemed sharp enough though, and certainly a hard-line advocate. Heat guessed one way to keep your costs down in a small business was to retain your grandfather or great uncle as counsel.

"I wanted to give her time to rethink her answer, let her memory do its work," replied the detective. Then Nikki directed herself to Roxanne, who was still wearing the same vinyl and contempt as she had in her office at six that morning. "You're absolutely certain you had no dealings with Father Graf?"

"Like what, in church? Don't make me laugh." She sat back and nodded in satisfaction to the old dude. "He wasn't a client."

"Did anyone else have access to the locker with your security tapes?"

"Ha," from the lawyer. "Fat lot of good your warrant did." His eyes looked huge to Nikki behind the smudged eyeglasses that covered half his face.

"Ms. Paltz, who had keys?"

Roxanne looked to her attorney, who gave the go-ahead nod, and she answered, "Just me. The one set."

"And there are no other tapes, Roxanne?"

"Who is she," said the lawyer, "the Homeland Security?"

Roxanne continued, "Truth is, that plastic bubble in the ceiling does the job of keeping everyone in line anyway. Far as the clients know, it's on and they behave. Sort of the way when you call customer service and they say, 'This call may be monitored.' Their way of saying watch your mouth, asshole."

Heat turned a page of her notepad. "I'd like the names of anyone who was there last night, say from six o'clock on. Dommes, doms, clients."

"Bet you would," said the lawyer. "Pleasure Bound is a discreet business protected by rights of privacy and client privilege."

"Excuse me, Mr. Paltz, but last I heard, client privilege may protect lawyers and doctors, but not people who dress up and play doctor." Heat turned again to the manager. "Roxanne, a death took place on your property. Are you going to cooperate, or shall we close you down while we assess the public safety and health concerns at Pleasure Bound?" Nikki was only sort of bluffing. A shutdown, if she got it, would only be brief, but her assessment of the state of the business—old paint, cheap furniture, shopworn fixtures, neglected security surveillance—told her Roxanne operated on a thin margin and that even a week without clients would put a hurt on her. She was right.

"All right. I'll give you her name," she said after another nod from the lawyer. "Fact is, I only have one dominatrix at present. I lost my other two a couple of months ago to the higher-end places Midtown." Roxanne Paltz made an audible shrug with her vinyls. "I tell you, the bondage business is a struggle." Nikki instinctively waited for Rook's wisecrack. Same as she had so many times during his absence. What would he blurt? Knowing him, something like "That would make a catchy ad slogan." She pictured a match turning Rook's Le Cirque photo to ashes.

After Roxanne gave her the name and contact number of the domme, Heat asked about clients. "That's all on her," answered the manager. "She pays me to use the space, sort of like a hairdresser. The client bookings are her deal."

"For the record, Roxanne, can you account for your whereabouts last night between six and eleven?" Nikki widened the time frame since she hadn't gotten the official from Lauren Parry yet.

"Yes, I can. I was at dinner and then the movies with my husband."

After Heat wrote down the name of the restaurant and the movie, she asked, "And your husband can vouch for this?"

Simmy Paltz nodded. "You bet I can."

Nikki Heat looked from the old coot to Roxanne and made another note, this one mental. A reminder not to assume. Not in New York City.

Hadn't she just learned that painful lesson from Rook?

———

She called Detective Ochoa to find the domme while Roxanne and her husband were still in Interrogation, so they wouldn't have a chance to tip her off. Heat had given them some mug arrays of violent sex offenders to pore over, knowing it was busywork but the kind of busy that would keep them out of her way. Ochoa was only a few blocks from Andrea Boam's address in Chelsea, and just fifteen minutes later he rang back to report that her roommate said Ms. Boam had been away on vacation since the weekend. Nikki asked, "Did the roommate say where?"

"Amsterdam," said Ochoa. "The city, not the avenue."

"Imagine that. Amsterdam. For a dominatrix."

"Yeah," he agreed. "Sounds like a busman's holiday, if you ask me."

"Do a follow-up with Customs to run her passport, just to make sure she went," said Heat. "Smells like a solid alibi, though. Any luck with the priest's picture?"

"*Nada*. But. Canvassing these clubs isn't a total loss. Mostly, I've been interviewing submissives, and it's doing wonders for my self-esteem."

———

Heat was eager to know what was up at the rectory, but Lauren Parry texted her that the autopsy was complete on Father Graf, so she waited until she got to her car on her way to the coroner's before she called Detective Hinesburg.

"What's going on, Nikki?" asked Hinesburg.

"Just driving down to the OCME wondering what you discovered in the last hour and a half." Heat didn't do so well at keeping the irritation out of her voice, but it annoyed her to have to chase her detective down for a simple update. One of Sharon Hinesburg's dubious qualities was that a fair amount went over her head, and if there was any sting on Heat's comment, she didn't seem to notice.

"What are you going to say to that writer bastard?" said Hinesburg. "Guy screws with me, he doesn't get an encore, hear what I'm saying?"

Heat wanted to shout loud enough to make her ear bleed. Instead, she counted to three and calmly said, "Sharon? The housekeeper?"

"Right. Mrs. . . ." Pages flipped.

"Borelli," prompted Nikki. "What did Mrs. Borelli tell you about the missing objects?"

"Quite a bit, really. She's something else. Treats the job like a mission. Knows every inch of this place like she was running a museum." On the other end, Hinesburg turned more pages. "So the bottom line so far is a missing medal from a jewelry box."

"What kind of medal?"

"A holy medal of some kind." There was muffled talk as Hinesburg covered the mouthpiece, then came back on. "A St. Christopher medal."

"And that's the only thing she says is missing?" ask Heat.

"So far. We're still doing inventory together," Hinesburg added, making sure to sound busy. "But the other thing is, Mrs. B. says things are a little off here. Small things. Drawers with shirts and socks not stacked neatly like she does, books slightly out of alignment, a china cabinet closed but not closed all the way."

Nikki was beginning to get the picture and it was no small thing. It was sounding like someone had done a search of the rectory for something, and it was methodical, not a tear-apart job like she saw most of the time. This was starting to feel careful. Professional, maybe. Her thoughts ran to Montrose. Would he have done a search like that?

"Sharon, keep an inventory, even though Evidence Collection is doing the same. Include a list of anything that's moved or broken. However minor, understand?" Heat scoped the dashboard clock. "Doesn't look like I can get up there for a while, so do a sit-down with Mrs. Borelli, if she's up to it. Get anything about Father Graf that raises a flag. Unusual habits, arguments, visitors, you know what to ask."

There was a pause. "Sure, sure," came Hinesburg's distracted reply. Heat regretted not sending Detective Ochoa like she'd planned. Lesson learned. She made a decision to stop by personally to conduct her own interview of the housekeeper.

———

Traffic was miserable all over the city. More people in more cars was a reliable by-product of any sort of weather, especially a bitter cold morning dipping to single digits with a swirling wind. It also made parking a challenge. The "Sorry Full" signs were out at all the NYU Med Center garages adjacent to the Office of the Chief Medical Examiner. On her cruise up First Avenue Detective Heat could see even the courtesy spots at the entrances were already taken by other cop cars. At 34th she circled back to her secret weapon, the fenced-in Bellevue Hospital lot sandwiched under the FDR. It meant a block's walk in the arctic blast, but it was her only choice other than circling. The lot manager was too snug in his kiosk to step out when he saw her pull up. All she saw was fingers through his frosted window waving her in.

Before she got out of her car, Heat stared at her smart phone. She scrolled through e-mails again. No, she hadn't gotten one from Rook and missed it. Once more, she told herself, only once more. Heat pushed send/receive and watched the icon swirl. When it was done all it said was that she was still in emotional limbo.

By the time Nikki ascended the short flight of steps into the OCME lobby, she had no feeling in her cheeks and her nose was a faucet. Behind the reception desk, Danielle gave Heat her usual sunny hello and buzzed her through the security door. When she entered the small squad room the NYPD maintained for visiting cops, three of the four cubicles were occupied by detectives speaking on phones.

They had the thermostat cranked and Heat shed her overcoat. She looked at the parka mound on the back of one of the chairs and had opted for a hanger on the empty coat tree when her cell vibrated.

The number on the ID wasn't familiar, but the prefix was. The call was coming from One Police Plaza. In his text, Montrose had said he was at HQ. Nikki didn't want to get into it with him while sharing such close quarters with her brother officers but figured she would at least make contact and set up their next call. "Heat," she said.

"Is this the famous Nikki Heat?" She didn't know his voice, but it was all smiles and, for her taste, overblown for an opening line from a stranger.

She adopted the neutral tone she used on telemarketers. "This is Detective Heat."

"Not for long, I hear," said the caller. "Detective, it's Zach Hamner, Senior Administrative Aide here in Legal. I'm calling to personally congratulate you on your lieutenant's test."

"Oh." She wanted to step out into the hall, but in deference to the grieving families and her own sense of decorum, Nikki maintained a strict personal policy against using her cell phone in the public areas of that building. So Heat sat in the empty chair and hunched into the cubicle, knowing it didn't afford much privacy. "Thank you. Sorry, but you caught me a little off guard here."

"Not a problem. You not only scored well, Detective, but I see that your record is outstanding. We need good cops like you to rise in the department."

She cupped her hand around the mouthpiece. "Again, Mr. Hamner—"

"Zach."

"—Zach—I appreciate the kind words."

"Like I said, not a problem. Listen, the reason for the call is that I want to make sure you drop by and say hello when you come downtown to sign for your copy of the results."

"Um, sure," she said and then had a thought. "That's at Personnel. You're not from Personnel, though, are you?"

"Oh, hell, no. I'm upstairs with the Deputy Commissioner of Legal Matters. Trust me, it all goes through my desk, anyway," he said with an air of self-importance. "When can I expect to see you?"

"Well, I'm at the ME's now. I'm on a case."

"Right," he said, "the priest." The way he said it pinged Nikki with the strong impression Zach Hamner liked to show off his knowledge of everything. The guy with all the answers. The quintessential Essential Man. What did he want from her?

She mentally rolled through her schedule. Autopsy . . . Montrose, hopefully . . . squad meeting . . . the rectory . . . "How's tomorrow?"

"I was hoping for today." He paused, and when she didn't reply to that, he continued, "I've got a full load tomorrow. Let's meet early. Breakfast. You can sign docs after." Feeling more than a little steamrolled, Heat agreed. He gave her the name of a deli on Lafayette, said he'd meet her at seven, and hung up after one more congrats.

———

"Any word from the world traveler?" asked Lauren Parry. She looked up at her friend from her computer in the dictation office adjacent to the autopsy room. The ME wore the regulation protective moon suit, and, as usual, it was decorated with flecks of blood and fluid. She read Nikki's reaction and picked up her plexi-shield mask off the chair beside her. "Sit?"

"I'm good." Heat, who had just put on the clean coveralls issued to visitors, leaned against the back wall of the narrow anteroom and stared through the glass at the tables lined up in front of her. The near one, Mat #8, held the sheeted body of Father Gerald Graf.

"Liar," said her BFF. "If that's what good looks like, never show me bad."

Nikki returned her gaze to Lauren. "OK, let me amend that to say, I will be good. I guess."

"You're scaring me, Nikki."

"All right, all right, then . . ." Heat filled Lauren in on her morning surprise: Rook's triumphant return to Gotham to celebrate the completion of his assignment—a celebration that he had not included her in—and to add insult to injury, he still hadn't even called to say he was back.

"Ouch." Lauren's brow furrowed. "What do you think that's about? You don't think he . . ." She stopped herself and shook her head.

"What?" said Nikki. "Hooked up with someone else? You can say it. Don't you think I've already wondered that?" Nikki cleared away some dark thoughts. "Left long enough, you imagine all sorts of things, Laur. And then a month later you open the newspaper and see them come true." She came off the wall and stood straight. "Enough. He's back. We'll sort it all out." Her doubt was unspoken but loud. "Happy for you and Ochoa, though."

That brought Lauren up short. And then she smiled. Of course there was no hiding her romance from Nikki. "Yeah, it's good with me and Miguel."

As they both walked to the door, Nikki said, "I could learn to hate you, you know."

———

Two other medical examiners had customers on the first and third tables and, as Nikki entered the autopsy room, she silently repeated the mantra she had learned from Lauren on her rookie visit years ago. "Breathe through your mouth, it'll trick your brain." And, as always, Heat thought, almost . . . but not quite.

"A few hard-and-fast findings and then a few anomalies to show you," said ME Parry as they approached Graf's body.

"Time of death window turns out to be as thought. Eight to ten. I'd call it closer to the late end of that."

"TOD could be nine-thirty?"

"Ish." She curled the page around the top of her clipboard, exposing supine and prone templates of a human body on which she had made notations. "Marks and indicators. Already covered the eyeballs, the neck, here and here." She indicated each with her pen as she shared with Heat. "Multiple abrasions and contusions. Painful but none fatal. No broken bones. All pretty much consistent with the B and D experience."

Nikki was starting to think this may have been a session gone wild, after all, but kept her mind open.

"Three little discoveries worth testing for any significance," said the ME. She led Heat across the room to one of the storage cabinets. She slid the glass door aside and took one of the blue cardboard evidence buckets off the shelf. Nikki remembered how, after his first visit, Rook saw one and said he'd never buy a bucket of chicken again. Lauren took a small plastic vial out of the bucket with "GRAF" on the bar code and gave it to Nikki. "See that speck?"

The detective held it up to the light. In the bottom of the container was a dark spot about the size of a bacon bit. "Found that under a fingernail," Parry continued. "Under a microscope it looks like a piece of leather, but it doesn't match the leather on the wrist restraints or the posture collar." She returned it to the bucket. "Gonna lab that puppy."

She then walked Nikki down to the dehumidifying closet where they placed victims' clothes to dry, to preserve DNA for testing. Sheets of brown paper separated bloodstained clothes that hung there from numerous victims. At the nearest end, Heat could see Graf's black clothing and his white Roman collar. "Funny thing about that collar. There's a tiny bloody smear on it. Odd, considering that for all the abrasions on him, no skin was broken above his shoulders or on his hands."

"Right," said Nikki considering the possibilities. "That could be blood from an assailant, or killer."

"Or dom or domme, who knows yet?" Lauren was right. It could have been from foul play but just as easily from a practitioner with a cut from the torture session who stashed the clothes and ran in panic. "We'll also ship that down to Twenty-sixth Street for DNA testing."

Next Lauren called in one of the orderlies, who helped her roll the priest's body on its side, exposing his back. It was a thatch-work of whip welts and bruises, the sight of which caused Nikki to draw a deep breath through her nose, which she immediately regretted. She held it together, though, and leaned close when the ME pointed to a geometric bruise pattern on the small of his back. "One of these contusions is not like the others," said Lauren. Her eye for those details had helped Heat on numerous cases. Most recently, by spotting the marks left by a ring worn by a Russian thug who killed a famous real estate developer. This lower-back bruise was about two inches long, rectangular, and with evenly spaced horizontal lines.

"Looks like a mark made by a small ladder," said Heat.

"I took some stills that I'll e-mail you with my report." Parry nodded to the orderly, who gently returned Graf to lie faceup and then left the room.

"Sweet anomalies," said Nikki.

"Not done yet, Detective." Lauren picked up her clipboard again. "Now, cause of death. I'm going with asphyxia by strangulation."

"You hesitated this morning, though," Nikki reminded her.

"Right. The signs were there, as I told you. The obvious being the circumstances, the leather collar, eyeball hemorrhaging, and so on. But I balked because I saw other indicators that could mean acute myocardial infarction."

Heat said, "The bluish color I saw near his fingertips and on his nose?"

"Excuse me, who's the ME here?"

"I get the significance, though. A heart attack could eliminate homicidal intent."

"Well, guess what? He did have a heart attack. Turns out it wasn't fatal, he was choked before it could be, but it was a hell of a footrace to see which would kill him first."

Heat looked at the sheeted corpse. "You did say you smelled cigarettes and alcohol."

"And his organs proved all that. But." She gave Nikki a look of significance and raised the sheet. "Take a look at these burns on his skin. These are electrical burns. Probably from a TENS," said Lauren, referring to a transcutaneous electrical nerve stimulator, a portable electrical generator used in torture play.

"I've seen TENS," said Nikki. "I came across them in Vice."

"Then you also know they warn against ever using it near the chest." She lowered the sheet to expose Graf's torso, where the electrical burns were intense, especially near his heart. "Looks to me like someone wanted to put a big hurt on him."

"The question," said Nikki, "is why?"

————

They rode up together to the first floor. Heat said, "Got a question for you. You ever seen anything like that before?"

"TENS burns as severe as those? Not like that." As they reached the door to the NYPD office, Lauren said, "Know who I hear had some? That actor's kid who was always in trouble and got killed in '04 or '05."

"Gene Huddleston, Jr.?" said Nikki.

"Yeah, him."

"But he was shot to death. Some drug deal, right?"

Lauren said, "Right. It happened before I started here, but conversation was that he also had TENS burns all over. He was one wild kid. They figured it was part of his freak."

The NYPD office was empty. Nikki got her coat off the hook, but before she left, sat down at one of the computers. She logged on to the department server and requested a digital copy of the case file for Gene Huddleston, Jr.

————

As Nikki made her way through the vestibule to the precinct lobby, a woman standing near the blue velvet rope that cordoned off the wall of honor roll photos and plaques took a step into her path. "Excuse me, Detective Heat?"

"That's me." The detective stopped but made a quick check of the woman's rising hand. Someone had decided it was open season on cops this year, even in police stations, and Heat's natural caution kicked in. But all the woman held was a business card. It read, "Tam Svejda, Metro Reporter, *New York Ledger.*"

"I was wondering if I could have a few moments to ask you a couple of questions."

Heat returned the reporter's smile politely but said, "Look, I'm sorry, Ms. . . ." She looked at the card again. Nikki had seen her name in the byline but wasn't sure how to pronounce it.

"Shfay-dah," came the assist. "My dad's Czech. Don't feel bad, it stops everybody in their tracks. Go with Tam." She gave Nikki a warm grin, revealing a perfect row of gleaming teeth. In fact, her whole look was one-off supermodel: highlighted blonde with a great cut, wide green eyes that showed intelligence and a hint of mischief, young enough to get away without much makeup—probably not yet thirty, tall and slender. It was a look you'd associate more with a TV reporter than the pencil press.

"Good. All right, Tam works," said Nikki. "But I'm just here for a minute and then I'm on my way out of here. I'm really sorry." She took a step toward the inner doors, but Tam moved with her. She was taking out her reporter's notebook. A spiral Ampad, same as Heat used.

"A minute will do nicely, then I won't keep you. Are you classifying Father Graf's death murder or accidental?"

"Well, I can keep this short for you, Ms. Svejda," she said with flawless pronunciation. "It's too early in our investigation to comment on any of that yet."

The reporter looked up from her notes. "A sensational murder—a parish priest gets tortured and killed in a bondage dungeon—and you really want me to go with just that? A stock 'no comment?'"

"What you print is up to you. This is a young investigation. I promise when we have something to share, we will." Like any good interrogator, Heat found herself gaining information even when she was the one being questioned. And what she was learning from Tam Svejda's interest in the Graf case was that Nikki wasn't the only one who felt something more than just another homicide was going on.

The reporter said, "Got ya," but without missing a beat added, "Now, what can you tell me about Captain Montrose?" Heat studied her, knowing even her next "no comment" had to be carefully delivered. Tam Svejda would be writing this, not she, and Nikki didn't want to inspire some reporter-ese about circled wagons or tight-lipped cops. At last Svejda said, "If this is uncomfortable we can go off the record. I'm just hearing a lot of not so flattering things, and if you can steer me in my investigation, you could be doing him some good. . . . If the rumors are untrue."

Detective Heat chose her words. "You really don't think I'd dignify rumors, do you? I think the most productive thing I can do is to go in there and get back to my job working Father Graf so I can get you some solid information. Fair enough, Tam?"

The reporter nodded and put her notebook away. "I must say, Detective, Jamie did you justice." When Nikki furrowed her brow, she explained, "In your cover story, I mean. Meeting you, seeing how you handle yourself. Rook sure got you right. That's why Jamie gets the covers and the Pulitzers."

"Yeah, he's good." Jamie, thought Nikki. She called him Jamie.

"Did you see his picture in our morning edition with that piece of work, Jeanne Callow? That bad boy sure gets around, doesn't he?"

Nikki closed her eyes a moment and wished Tam Svejda would be gone—*poof!*—when she opened them. But she wasn't. "I'm running late, Tam."

"Oh, you go ahead. And say hi to Jamie. If you talk to him, I mean."

Heat had a distinct feeling she had more in common with Tam Svejda than a reporter's notebook. Quite possibly it was a reporter.

———

When Detective Heat got back to the bull pen, Captain Montrose was slouched in his office chair with the door closed, his back to the squad, staring out his window down to West 82nd Street. He might have seen her drive into the precinct lot below him, but if he did, he made no move to greet or look for her. Nikki made a quick scan of the While You Were Outs on her blotter, saw nothing that couldn't wait, and felt her heart race as she walked to his door. When he heard her knock on the glass, he beckoned her in without turning. Heat closed the door behind her and stood looking at the back of his head. After five eternal seconds he sat upright and swiveled in his chair to face her, as if willing himself out of some trance and down to business.

"You've had quite a day already, I hear," he said.

"Action-packed, Skip." He gestured to the visitor chair and she sat.

"Wanna trade? I spent my morning wearing the dunce cap at the Puzzle Palace," he said, using the less-than-flattering cop slang for One Police Plaza. And then he shook his head. "Sorry. I promised I wouldn't complain, but it's got to come out somewhere."

Nikki's gaze went to the windowsill and the framed photo of him and Pauletta. That was when she realized Montrose hadn't been staring out the window but at the picture. It had been almost a year since a drunk driver killed her in a crosswalk. The pain of his loss was borne stoically, but the toll was written on his face. Suddenly Nikki wished she hadn't initiated this meeting. But she already had.

"You called about something?"

"Yes, about the priest, Father Graf." She studied him, but he was passive. "I'm working the BDSM angle first."

"Makes perfect sense." Still just listening.

"And there are indications of a search at his rectory and an item or items missing." She regarded him more closely, but he gave nothing back. "I have Hinesburg up there on it."

"Hinesburg?" At last a reaction.

"I know, I know, long story. I'll do my own follow-up to back-stop her."

"Nikki, you're the best I've ever seen at this. Better than me, and that's, well, that's pretty damn good. Word's around you might be getting yourself a gold bar soon, and I can't think of anyone more deserving. I gave my recommendation, which might not be your best calling card the way things are going."

"Thank you, Captain, that means a lot."

"So what did you need to talk to me about?"

Heat tried to toss it aside and sound casual. "Just touching base on something, actually. When I went to the rectory this morning to confirm ID on the vic, the housekeeper said you had been there last night."

"That's correct." He rocked slightly in his executive chair but held her look. Heat could see the smallest flash of steel in his eyes and felt her resolve crumbling. She knew if she uttered the question she wanted to ask, it would start something in motion she would never be able to call back. "And?" he said.

Free fall. Nikki was in absolute free fall. What was she going to say? That with all his erratic behavior, the rumors about Internal Affairs—and now pressure from the media—she wanted to make him justify himself? Heat was one question away from treating him like a suspect. She had thought through everything about this meeting ex-cept one thing: her unwillingness to spoil a relationship over rumor and appearances. "And I just wanted to ask for your take. And see if you learned anything while you were there."

Did he know she was BS-ing? Nikki couldn't tell. She just wanted out of there.

"No, nothing useful," said the captain. "I want you to pursue the line you're on, the bondage thing." And then, signaling that he knew exactly why she was asking, he added, "You know, Nikki, it might seem unusual for me, a precinct commander, to personally respond to an MPR. But as you'll soon learn if you get your promotion, the job becomes less about the street and more about appearances and gestures. You ignore that at your peril. So. A high-profile member of my precinct, a church pastor, goes missing, what am I going to do? Sure not going to send Hinesburg, am I?"

"Of course not." And then she noticed him playing with the Band-Aid on his knuckle. "You're bleeding."

"This? It's fine. Penny bit me this morning while I was combing out a mat in her paw." He stood and said, "That's the way it's been going for me, Nikki Heat. My own dog turned on me."

———

The walk back to her desk made Heat feel like she was underwater in lead shoes. She had come within a whisper of destroying a relationship with her mentor, and only his orchestration of the awkward meeting kept her from doing that. Mistakes were only human, but Nikki was all about not being the one to make mistakes. Anger filled her for allowing herself to be distracted by gossip, and she resolved to focus on getting back to doing what she did, solid police work, and to avoid getting swept up in the sharp blades of the rumor mill.

On her monitor an icon flashed, alerting her that the case file she had requested from Archives had arrived. Not so long ago a requisition like that would have taken at least a day, or a personal visit to expedite delivery. Thanks to the department's computerization of all records, as spearheaded by Deputy Commissioner Yarborough, who'd brought the NYPD technology up to this century, Detective Heat now had the PDF of the 2004 investigation mere minutes after putting in for it.

She opened the file detailing the murder of Gene Huddleston, Jr., errant son of an Oscar-winning national treasure whose only child descended from wealth and privilege in a tragic spiral into a life of alcoholism, got kicked out of two colleges for sex scandals and drug abuse, then graduated to dealing and, finally, violent death. First she scanned for any photographs of the TENS burns Lauren Parry had mentioned, but found none on her first pass. Out of habit, she clicked on the roster page listing the investigators on the case to see if she knew any of them. Then she saw the name of the lead detective and felt a flutter in her diaphragm.

Heat slumped back in her chair and just stared at the screen.

THREE

The first thing Heat did after she clicked the tiny red square and closed the Huddleston file was call Lauren Parry. She tried not to think too much about it first, because she might hesitate and then hold back. That was the death of good police work. Gather facts but trust your hunches. Especially the ones about which facts to gather.

"So soon?" said Lauren when she picked up. "You leave something here? Tell me you didn't leave your keys. I've had that happen, and you don't want to know where I've found them."

"You're right, I don't." Even though she had her end of the bull pen to herself at the moment, Nikki looked over her shoulder before she continued. "Listen, I saw how busy you all were down there in B-23 this morning—"

"Yeah, yeah, what do you need me to fast track?"

"The priest collar. The one with the bloodstain. Can you push it to the head of the class for me?"

"You on to someone already?"

In her mind's eye, Heat kept seeing the bandage on Captain Montrose's finger. She wanted to say she hoped not, but answered, "Who knows? As much to eliminate as anything." Nikki heard papers rustle before the ME answered.

"Sure, I can expedite. It still takes time, you know."

"Then let's get this party started."

"Then I'll be burnin' rubber." Lauren chuckled and continued, "While we're talking, I just shipped my report over to you." Nikki checked her monitor and saw that the e-mail was parked there for her. "Heads up on an additional note I added. CSU did an evidence vacuum of the torture room—a few hairs, you can imagine—but they also came up with what looks like a sliver of fingernail." Nikki replayed her survey of the dead priest while he was still on the frame and recalled that his nails were not broken. Her friend underscored that. "I just did a double-check of the body, and neither his fingernails or toenails show signs of chipping."

"So it could be from whoever worked him over," said Heat. "Assuming it's not a holdover from another session." That possibility might not make it court-worthy, but it could open an investigative lead. Before they hung up, Lauren offered to push that test up the chain as well.

———

"How's it going in here?" she asked as she entered the audiovisual booth, a converted supply closet, where Raley was screening the security video from Pleasure Bound.

"Rockin' it, Detective," he said without looking up from his monitor. "That place isn't as busy as you'd think, so I'm flying through these tapes."

"This is why you're King of All Surveillance Media." She came around behind his table and leafed through the stills her detective had printed out so far. "Any hits on Father Graf?"

"Zip," he said. "Speaking of which, check out the guy on the leash in a gimp mask with a zipper mouth. It's like watching the outtake reel from *Pulp Fiction*."

"Or *Best in Show*," said Heat, examining it. Other than the cleaning crew and Roxanne Paltz, Nikki didn't recognize any of the dozen people whose faces Raley had captured. She set the stack down beside the printer. "I want to run these past the housekeeper up at the rectory. How soon until you finish?"

He paused the deck and turned to her. "Excuse me, but is this how one addresses the king?"

"OK, fine. How soon until you finish . . . sire?"

"Gimme twenty."

She looked at her watch. Lunch hour, for those who were fortunate enough to actually have one, had come and gone. She asked Raley what kind of sandwich he wanted and told him she'd be back in fifteen minutes. In the hallway, she smiled when the door closed and she heard his muffled shout, "Hello? I said twenty!"

Andy's Deli would have delivered, but Nikki was in the mood for a walk, even in the cold. No, especially in the cold. The day had put her head in a vise, and something primal howled to be outside and moving. The wind had begun to diminish, taking a fraction of the ache out of the winter air, but after dropping all day to four degrees, it was still plenty bitter, and the sensation of it invigorated her. Rounding the corner at Columbus she heard a loud crack behind her and turned. A big SUV was inching forward from 82nd for a right as well, and one of its monster tires had shattered an ice patch in the gutter, hurling frozen chips up onto the curb. Heat looked to see who still drove those big-shouldered gas hogs in the city, but she never got a look. The throaty engine gunned, and the SUV fishtailed into traffic and was soon swallowed by its own fading roar.

"Penis car," said a passing mail carrier, and Nikki laughed, loving New York and all its intimate strangers.

While the counter man at Andy's made a pair of BLTs for her, Nikki checked her phone and e-mail again. Nothing from Rook since she had last surfed—right before she ordered. She got two extra honey packets for Raley's iced tea from the condiment bar and checked her cell again. Then she thought, Screw it, and pressed Rook's speed dial. It never rang, just dumped straight to voice mail. While she listened to his announcement, not yet even sure what she wanted to say, a man beside her waiting for a tuna on rye flipped open his newspaper and Nikki was confronted once again by Rook and his doable agent grinning outside Le Cirque. Heat hung up without leaving a message, paid for the lunches, and hurried back out into the freezing cold, cursing herself for caving in to chasing a guy.

———

Sharon Hinesburg always wore her emotions on her face, and when Heat breezed into the rectory unannounced, the detective looked like she had just opened the fridge and gotten a whiff of curdled milk. Nikki didn't care. Misplaced sensitivity had led to one bad call assigning Hinesburg to handle this venue in the first place. She wasn't going to compound her lapse by worrying about Bigfooting her subordinate.

The decision to take charge was validated by the briefing she got. After several hours on-scene, the best Hinesburg could offer was a rehash of the information Heat already had learned both from her own chat with the housekeeper and the call from the evidence crew about the missing holy medal and disturbed clothing drawers. Nikki had the not unsupported impression that Detective Hinesburg's main activity had been to sit with Mrs. Borelli and watch *The View*.

She didn't lash out at her detective, though. Hinesburg was, and always would be, Hinesburg. Heat decided there was no sense misplacing her anger, which was at herself for not getting to this interview until the afternoon thanks to reporters, department politics, and worries about her boss.

"I hope you don't mind, Mrs. Borelli," Nikki began as they sat down at the kitchen table, "but we need to ask some questions while things are still fresh in your mind. I understand it's a difficult time, but are you up for this?"

The rims of the wiry old woman's eyes were swollen and red, but the look in them was clear and full of strength. "I want to help you find whoever did this. I'm ready."

"Let's review the period leading up to the last time you saw Father Graf. And I apologize if you have already been over this with Detective Hinesburg."

"No, she didn't ask me about any of that," said Mrs. B.

Hinesburg made a show of flipping a page of her pad. "You told me you last saw him yesterday morning at ten or ten-fifteen," she said, citing information that was already in the missing persons report.

But Nikki only smiled at the old woman and said, "Good, let's start there." After Heat spent a half hour quizzing her about Father Graf's last hours and days, through a series of questions doled out in small bites, a timeline emerged, not only of the previous morning but the weeks leading up to the pastor's disappearance. He had been a man of habits, at least in the early part of his days. Up at 5:30 for his morning prayers, opening the doors to the church at 6:30, on the altar next door for Mass at 7 A.M., breakfast served by Mrs. Borelli promptly at ten minutes to eight. "He'd smell the bacon and keep the sermon short," she said, comforted by the memory.

The rest of a typical day involved parish administration, visits to the sick, and meetings at a handful of community groups he served on. The housekeeper affirmed that he followed his pattern his last few days. Well, almost. "He had taken to longer lunches away in the afternoons. And was late for supper a few times, which was not like him."

Heat drained her coffee cup and made a note. "Every day?" she asked.

"Let me think. No, not every." Nikki waited while the woman thought and then wrote down the days and times she recalled while Mrs. B. poured her a refill.

"What about his nights?"

"He always heard confessions from seven to seven-thirty, although not many customers these days. Changing times, Detective."

"And after confessions?"

The housekeeper's face pinked and she rearranged the sugar bowl and creamer on the tabletop. "Oh, he'd read sometimes or watch an old movie on TV or meet with a parishioner if someone needed counseling—drugs, abused women, that sort of thing."

Nikki sensed a dodge and asked another way. "Was there any time that he wasn't working? What did he do for recreation?"

Her face reddened a bit more and she said to the creamer, "Detective, I don't want to speak ill of him; he was flesh, as we all are, but Father Gerry, he liked his drink and he would spend his evenings most nights having his Cutty at the Brass Harpoon." Another note to follow up on. If he had been a regular at a bar, even if it didn't lead to suspects, it meant friends, or at least drinking buddies, who might have some insights into a side of the padre the old woman wasn't privy to.

Nikki then got to the awkward question she knew had to be asked. "I told you this morning where we found the body." Mrs. Borelli nodded in a small, shameful way. "Do you have any indication that Father Graf was . . . involved in that lifestyle?"

For the first time, she saw anger in the woman. Her face grew stony and her eyes were riveted on Heat's. "Detective, that man took a vow of celibacy. He was a holy man doing God's work on earth and he lived a life of poverty, chastity, and obedience."

"Thank you," said Nikki. "I hope you understand, I had to ask." Heat then switched gears, studying the pages she had generated, and said, "I notice yesterday, the day you last saw him, as well as the day before, he left immediately after breakfast instead of conducting his usual meetings and office work. Any idea why he changed pattern?"

"Mm, no. He didn't say."

"You asked him?"

"Yes. He told me to butt out. Joking but not joking, either."

"Did you notice any changes in his mood?"

"I did. He was sharper with me. Like the butt out joke. The Father Gerry I knew would have said that and I'd have laughed. And so would he." Her lips drew tight. "He was definitely on edge."

Heat had to come at it again. "And you have no idea where this tension came from?" When she shook no, Nikki asked, "Anybody argue with him? Threaten him?"

"Not the past few days, as I recall."

Odd answer from the woman who seemed to recall everything about him. Nikki made a note to come back to that one later. "Any problems at the church?"

"There are always problems at the church," she said with a chuckle. "But nothing out of the ordinary."

"Any new people around? Strangers, anyone coming by at odd times, anything like that?"

She rubbed her chin and shook no again. "I'm sorry, Detective."

"Don't be silly," said Nikki. "You're doing fine."

Fatigue and the stress of a traumatic day were starting to draw the old woman under. Before she faded, Heat opened the manila envelope of stills Raley had pulled from the security cam at Pleasure Bound. The housekeeper seemed glad for the change of tasks. She cleaned her glasses and studied each of the faces carefully before shaking her head and turning the next page. About halfway through the array, Heat noticed her react to one—not a large reaction but a hesitation. Nikki flicked a look at Hinesburg, who nodded; she'd caught it, too. "Something, Mrs. Borelli?"

"No, not so far." But she looked at the photo one more time before she turned it facedown and flipped to the next. When she finished the stack, she said none of them looked familiar. Nikki had a feeling Mrs. Borelli might be going to confession soon.

They quit the kitchen, and Heat asked if Mrs. Borelli would mind walking her through the rectory so she could see firsthand the things that had been disturbed. "Where did the missing St. Christopher medal live?"

Before the housekeeper could reply, Sharon Hinesburg said, "The bedroom," striving for relevance.

"Before we go up there," said Mrs. Borelli, "I want to show you something." She beckoned for them to follow, leading them into the study, where she gestured to a cabinet that doubled as the TV stand. "I told your CSI folks about this. After they got here, I looked around and found this cabinet door cracked open just a smidge. And take a look inside." Nikki was about to stop her from pulling it open, but she could see that the door and its glass front had already been dusted for prints. There were two shelves inside. The lower was filled with books, a mix of paperbacks and hard-bounds. The shelf above was completely empty. "All his videos, gone."

"What sort of videos were they?" asked Heat. She noticed that the

TV rested atop a dinosaur VHS player, and to its side sat a compact portable DVD unit with red, yellow, and white cords jacked to it.

"A bit of everything. He liked documentaries and someone gave him the Ken Burns *Civil War*, that's gone. I know he had *Air Force One*. 'Get off my plane,' over, and over, and over . . ." She shook her head, no doubt banking that as a fond recollection of the dead pastor, then looked back to the empty shelf. "Let's see, there were also a few PBS things, mostly *Masterpiece Theater*. The rest were personal, like videos people took at weddings and gave to him. Also some videos he shot at some of his protest marches and rallies. Oh! The pope's funeral! He was at the Vatican for that. I suppose that's gone, too. Would that be valuable, Detective, would someone want to steal that?"

Nikki told her anything was possible and asked if she would write down a list of all the videos she could recall, just for a complete record or in case, by some unlikely chance, any of them showed up in someone's possession or at a flea market.

The crew from the Evidence Collection Unit was nearly done upstairs, and so the three of them were able to go through the whole house, except for the attic, where the ECU was still at work. One of Detective Hinesburg's observations had been correct, and that was that Mrs. Borelli was a housekeeper who took her job as a mission. She knew where everything went because she was the one who put it there and made sure it stayed clean, dusted, and in place. The anomalies were subtle and would have been lost on the casual visitor. But for the woman who went so far as to square the edges of stacked undershirts in bureau drawers and to align gleaming shoes on the closet floor, with tassels front, any disturbance was a Disturbance in the Force. With the guidance of her schooled eye, it was clear to Detective Heat that someone had definitely given the rectory a once-over. And that with the low degree of disruption to the house, it sure felt like a professional job.

That opened a whole new front. It certainly cast major doubt that the death of the priest had been a dominance session gone awry.

Nikki knew better than to get ahead of the investigation, but the whole torture thing, combined with a search of the rectory, was pointing less toward a sexual proclivity and more toward someone trying to find something out. But what?

And what was Captain Montrose's search about the night before?

Heat met up with the lead ECU detective, Benigno DeJesus, coming out of Father Graf's bathroom, where he had just logged and bagged meds from the cabinet. He recapped his findings, which corresponded to Mrs. Borelli's: the missing videos, moved clothing, doors slightly ajar, and the absent holy medal. "Something else we found," said DeJesus. Atop the priest's dresser he indicated the dark brown velvet box, hinged open to expose the tan satin liner.

"This where the St. Christopher was?" asked Nikki.

"Yes," said Mrs. Borelli from behind her. "It meant so much to Father."

The ECU detective lifted the empty box off the dresser. "Got something a little unusual." Heat knew and liked Detective DeJesus and had worked scenes with him often enough to read his understatement. When Benigno said something was a little unusual, it was time to pay attention to Benigno. "Underneath the doily." And when Heat hesitated, he added, "It's OK, I've dusted, logged, and photographed."

Nikki lifted the lace runner that covered the bureau top. There was a small scrap of paper under it, right under the spot where the St. Christopher's case had been resting. DeJesus tweezed the strip and held it up for her to read. It was a handwritten phone number. Heat asked, "Mrs. Borelli, are you familiar with this number?"

The ECU man slipped the paper into a clear plastic evidence pouch and laid it on his open palm for her to see. She shook her head. "What about the handwriting," asked Heat, "do you recognize it?"

"You mean is it Father Graf's? No. And it's not mine. I don't know this writing."

Heat was jotting the phone number onto her spiral when one of the other ECU techs appeared in the doorway and nodded to

DeJesus. He excused himself to the hall and reappeared shortly. "Detective Heat? A moment?"

————

The attic had one of those pull-down wooden staircases that tele-scoped into the ceiling. Nikki ascended it into the loft where De-Jesus and the technician who had summoned him were crouched in a pool of portable light beside an old mini-fridge. They parted to give her a view as she joined them. The tech said, "I noticed the dust pattern on the floor indicated this had been opened recently, but it's not plugged in." She looked inside and saw three square holiday cookie tins stacked on the white wire shelves.

DeJesus snapped open the lid of the top one for her. It was filled with envelopes. The ECU detective took one out for her to examine. Like all the others, it was a parish collection envelope. And it was filled with cash.

Benigno said, "This might be worth some study."

————

At the end of the day Detective Heat gathered her squad in the bull pen for an update of the Murder Board. It was a ritual that served not only as a chance for her to recap information, but also as an opportunity for Nikki and her crew to bounce theories.

She had already logged Father Graf's moves on the timeline, including the notation of the unaccounted for hours the day preceding and the day of his disappearance. "There's nothing on his calendar that helps. If we had his wallet, we could run his MetroCard to see what subway stops he made, but that's still missing."

"What about e-mails?" said Ochoa.

"Right there with you," said Heat. "Soon as Forensics finishes with his computer, why don't you pick it up and start reading? You know everything to look for, don't need to tell you." She tried not to let her gaze sweep to Hinesburg, but she did, and registered the pissy look before turning her back to print "Graf's e-mails" on the board.

Raley made his report. At Heat's direction, he had gone to Pleasure Bound to show copies of the stills to Roxanne Paltz, who made ID of the three dommes who worked there, two past and one present. As for the men, the manager either didn't know or wouldn't say. Afterward, on his own initiative, Detective Raley had walked the area near the underground dungeon, flashing the stills at local retail shops and to doormen. "I didn't get any hits," he said, "but I may have gotten a nice case of frostbite. Windchill's down below zero today."

The canvass of Dungeon Alley had also come up empty. Detectives Ochoa, Rhymer, and Gallagher covered the main BDSM clubs stretching about twenty blocks from Midtown to Chelsea, and none of the workers or guests they encountered said they recognized the photo of the priest. Detective Rhymer said, "It could mean someone's lying or it could mean Graf was discreet."

"Or he wasn't in the lifestyle," said Gallagher.

"Or," added Nikki, "we haven't talked to the right person yet." She told them about the slip of paper that was hidden under the lace runner. "We ran a check on the phone number. It was for a male strip club."

"Male strip club? Who did you run the check with—Rhymer?" When the laughs died out Ochoa continued, "You deny it, Opie, but it's always the wholesome ones."

Raley chimed in. "Don't listen to him, Opie. Miguel's just mad 'cause you only put a buck in his thong last time."

Heat declared that since Raley and Ochoa seemed the most knowledgeable, they could have the detail of going to the strip club to show Graf's picture. After Roach took a chorus of ribbing from the squad, she finished her recap of the missing items at the rectory. Detective Rhymer, who was on loan from Burglary, wondered if the videos got stolen because they had sex tapes in them. "If the priest was into something . . . unpriestly . . . maybe there was something embarrassing to someone else who was on the video."

Heat acknowledged that could be so and jotted it under "Theories" on the board as "damning sex video??" That notwithstanding, Nikki said that some things made her want to broaden the scope of their investigation. No sooner had she said the words than behind the squad she saw movement from the glass office. Captain Montrose got up from his desk and stood leaning against his door frame to take in her briefing.

"Starting tomorrow," Heat said, "I want to dig deeper into the parish. Not just to look into the parishioners who could have motives, but also any of the other activities Father Graf could have been involved in. Clubs, immigration protests, even charity drives and fund-raisers."

Then she told them about the stash of money in the attic, which came to about a hundred fifty thousand. All in bills under a hundred, all in parishioner collection envelopes. "I'll reach out to the archdiocese to see if they had any knowledge or concerns about embezzlement. Whether it's skimming, or an inheritance, or, I don't know, a secret lotto win—however that money came to be in his attic—we can't rule out the possibility that someone wanted to get it and tried to force him to say where it was. But," she cautioned, "it's too soon to run for that piece of candy, because there are other things to look at as well. Let's just say it's one of many reasons to open this case wider." Then she relayed the findings of the autopsy. "What was particularly striking was the degree of electricity the victim took before he died. TENS, in mild doses, get used in some torture play. But his burns, the heart attack, this did not look like play."

The room fell silent, the quietest that bull pen had been since Nikki had arrived to turn the lights on that morning. She knew what each squad member was going through. Each was reflecting on the last minutes of Father Gerald Graf's life on that St. Andrew's Cross. Heat looked at them, knowing that even in this group of smart mouths, there was no amount of cop humor that would overcome the compassion they felt for another human's suffering.

Mindful of the collective mood, Nikki resumed quietly. "Like any assault, perps use pattern behavior. I'm already looking into other assaults like this, especially involving electrical means."

"Detective Heat." All heads turned to the voice at the back of the room. For many, it was the first they had actually heard that voice in a week.

"Captain?" she said.

"I'd like to see you in my office." And before he stepped inside it, he added, "Right now."

———

Nikki wheeled her leg around, caught him on the back of his upper calf, and he went down. Don landed hard on the blue wrestling mat in the gym and said, "Jeez, Nikki, what's eating you tonight?" She extended a hand to hoist him up, and midway through the lift, Don thought he'd get cute and flip her. But he telegraphed his move with his eyes and she cartwheeled to his weak side, still holding his hand, twisted his thumb, rolled him on his stomach, and parked a knee on his back.

That afternoon, when she had gotten the text from her onetime personal combat trainer and now regular sparring partner, Nikki declined Don's offer. Her day had been a meat grinder, and all she wanted to do was get home and sink into a bath, hoping an early bed would let her escape the burden of the case, and of Rook, in sleep. But then came that last meeting with Montrose. Heat came out of there feeling caged, frustrated, and above all, conflicted. First thing she did was grab her cell phone and text the ex–Navy SEAL that she wanted a workout after all.

Poor Don was on his feet about two seconds before Heat dropped him again.

The meeting had been with a Montrose Nikki didn't know. He closed his door, and by the time he had walked around behind her to his desk, he had accused her of losing focus on the case. She listened but couldn't take her eyes off the Band-Aid on his finger, wondering whose blood was on that priest's collar if it wasn't the priest's.

Don went to the corner of the gym and toweled the sweat off his face. Nikki hopped on the balls of her feet in the center of the mat, energized, eager to resume.

Her captain had said, "We agreed this afternoon that you'd keep working the bondage line on this case. What happened? Did you eat some funny mushrooms for lunch and get it in your head to change it up?"

Who was this man, she wondered, talking to her like that? Her mentor, advisor, and protector all these years. Not so much the father she never had but certainly the uncle.

Don tried to fake her out. He shook his arms loose, going all rubbery, working on the tightness to catch her sleeping. But then he lunged, going low with his left shoulder to her waist, trying to straight-out tackle her. She sidestepped and laughed when he caught nothing but air and landed on his face.

"I started getting information that opened my thinking, Captain," she had told him, all the while wondering what to tell him and what to hold back—something that had never occurred to her to do with this man.

"Like what? Talking to all his parishioners to see who thought his sermons lacked humor? Interviewing the members of his Knights of Columbus? Going to the archdiocese?"

"There's that money we found," she said.

"There's the agreement we had," he said. Then Montrose had calmed a little, and a glimpse of the old the skip came to visit. "Nikki, I'm accountable for supervision here and I see you spinning your wheels on side shows. You are a great detective. I've told you before. You're smart, intuitive, you work hard . . . I have never seen anyone better than you at finding the odd sock. If there's one aspect of a case or a crime scene that doesn't ring true, seems slightly out of whack, you see it." And then that phase was over. "But I don't know what the hell to make of what you're doing today. You're half a day late to interview a key witness, and that's after your poor judgment sending Hinesburg. That's right, I said it, your poor judgment."

Don's feet bicycled the sky on his flight over Heat's shoulder. She rounded her back and dropped on one knee as she released him, keeping her head down and tucked toward her tummy in the follow-through. Twisted that way, she couldn't see him land. But the floor shook.

"I agree I should have been to the rectory sooner." Heat had halted there, saying no more about it. She reflected on her OCME round trip, heavy traffic included, getting delayed by that phone call from the administrative assistant at 1PP, and of course, that file she stopped to read about the old homicide. But to go further, to explain herself, would only be to sound defensive. This was hard enough. Hard enough trying to pretend she hadn't seen what she saw in that file. That the lead detective on the 2004 Huddleston murder had been Detective First Grade Charles Montrose.

"Yes, you should have been there but you weren't. That's not like you, Detective. Are you distracted by all this business of your promotion?" Then after he had let that work on her, he leaned forward on his blotter, hands clasped so she couldn't avoid seeing the Band-Aid right there. And then he lobbed out, "Or is it that you were too busy with other things? Like blabbing to newspaper reporters."

Station House Privacy Rule #1: There is no privacy in a station house.

"Let me assure you of one thing, Captain. The extent of my conversation with that reporter was basically different ways to say, 'No comment.'" She held his gaze so he could see the truth written on her. In that moment, she also made a decision. She concluded that this was not the meeting to ask him about the old Huddleston case. For now, as far as her boss was concerned, she had never even asked for that file. Whatever storm this was, she just hoped it would pass so she could focus on the work and operate in the open again in her own house.

"Make sure you keep it that way," he had finally said. "I know what the press can be like. Especially the Gotcha Press. You don't think I have them all over me? And the community pressure? And the jerkoffs downtown? I'll tell you what I don't need, Detective Heat, and that's one more reason for someone to climb up on my ass, and it better not come from you." His tone had been measured, which made his words sting all the more. "Know this. I will pull you off the case if you don't focus. Stay on the BDSM path and nothing else. Am I clear?"

She had no words and only nodded.

When she reached for the doorknob, he added, "Blow this case and it'll be bad for me. Bad for you, too."

Heat left wondering if that was advice or a threat.

———

Don, who had asked her to spar that night, had made an additional invitation. And that was to sleep together. They had a history of that, but it had become a dimming one. Somewhere along the line, years back and without much fanfare, Nikki's Brazilian jujitsu trainer had become her trainer with benefits.

When it started, they were perfectly matched for that. Neither was in a committed relationship; they liked each other, were intensely physical, and equally happy to let their grappling go no further than the gym or the bedroom. Their sex was occasional, energetic, and mutually passionless. It all changed for Nikki when Rook came into the mix. It wasn't even about serial monogamy for her so much as something else. Something she couldn't—or wouldn't—exactly put into words. Since the heat wave, Don and Nikki had confined their wrestling to the mat. He had floated invitations from time to time, which she had declined without explanation, also part of their unspoken rules.

That night, after the drubbing she gave him, before they parted for their respective locker rooms, he asked her again. And this time, for the first time in a long time, Nikki was tempted. No, more than merely tempted. She came very close to a yes.

On the walk back to her apartment, she sorted through her feelings. Close as she had come to saying, "My place," she had taken it right up to the line in her imagination and declined. The month without Rook had been a long one emotionally and physically. She could have easily had a night with Don, and neither he nor Rook would have had a say in her choice. But her no came from the same place as all the ones that preceded it. But why? Was she in a committed relationship now with Rook? She might have answered that differently before he went away. And certainly it loomed as a bigger question after the Le Cirque shot and all it meant. The issue for her was what kind of relationship, if any, she would have with Rook when—if—they did see each other again. Sleeping with Don that night would have been revenge sex. Which Don sure wouldn't care about, even if he knew. But she would. That wasn't her reason, though. Her no to Don had been about postponing a definition.

Or perhaps it was more transparent than that. Maybe she knew the last thing she wanted was to have one more complication added to the stress of her life. Hell, of her day. What she needed was a night of letting go, of lightening up.

She already had the bath in mind, lavender bubbles for sure. One more thing would give her the head break she needed. On Park Avenue South, Nikki stopped at the newsstand at the end of her block and snatched up tabloids and celebrity mags. Hok, the news vendor, gave her a special hello, the one with the wink he started giving Heat the day she was on the cover of *First Press* with Jameson Rook's exasperating story, "Crime Wave Meets Heat Wave."

Counting out the change for Hok, who smiled brightly when he got exact change, Nikki smelled fumes from an idling engine. "Hok, how do you stand that?" He made a face and fanned the air in front of his nose. She looked in the direction of the exhaust. It was coming from a big SUV a few paces down the sidewalk. She turned back to give the vendor his coins when the phrase "penis car" entered her thoughts. She turned again toward the SUV. It certainly looked the same as the one she had encountered on her walk to Andy's Deli—graphite gray with wide tires—but something was different. The plates. She had clocked those plates as Jersey. This had New York State tags. Hok offered her a plastic bag, which she waved off. She stepped from the newsstand and was surprised to see that the SUV was gone. Nikki stepped to the curb in time to see its headlights disappear as it backed down the street against traffic and disappeared into a side street.

Backward?

Nikki turned in a circle, getting a look at her surroundings. She saw nothing unusual. Nothing else unusual, that is. She was only a block from her place. Heat unfastened her coat, took off the glove on her right hand, and started walking with her eyes and ears on alert.

Her street was quiet. No cars at the moment, and in the stillness of the sub-zero night, she paused briefly to strain her hearing for any sense of a low engine rumble. Nothing. She moved quickly up her front steps to the vestibule, keys already in hand.

Vestibule, clear.

Heat unlocked and let herself in. Following an instinct not to get trapped anywhere, she bypassed the elevator and climbed the stairs to her floor, pausing occasionally to listen and then moving upward.

On her floor, she swept the length of the hallway in both directions. It was empty. She let herself into her apartment, threw the deadbolt behind her, and exhaled. Nikki quizzed herself. Was this paranoia? Stress response at the end of an exponentially crap day? Or did she have a tail? And if so, why? And who?

At the hall closet, looking for a hanger for her coat, she heard a noise from around the corner in the kitchen. A small sound. Perhaps the squeak of a shoe?

Heat unholstered her Sig. Holding it in her right hand, she moved forward, carrying her coat in her left. Nikki stopped, drew a slow breath, mentally counted three, then whipped the coat around the corner. She followed it in a low crouch with her gun braced in both hands, calling, "Police, freeze."

The man wrapped up under her coat stopped struggling with it and raised his hands up inside it. Heat knew before he even spoke. Nikki pulled the coat off his head, and he smiled sheepishly. "Surprise?" said Rook.

FOUR

"Drop your hands, Rook, you look ridiculous," said Heat. "What the hell did you think you were doing?"

"Racing to your loving arms. At least I thought I was."

"I could have shot you, do you know that?" she said as she holstered her Sig.

"It just occurred to me," he said. "That would have put a damper on my homecoming. Not to mention meant a ton of paperwork for you. I think we're both better off you didn't." He made a step from the kitchen to embrace her, but when she crossed her arms, he stopped. "You saw the paper."

"Of course, I saw the damn paper. And if I hadn't, half of New York City was very happy to keep shoving it under my nose. What the hell is going on with you?"

"See, this is why I came over. So I could explain this face-to-face."

"This ought to be good."

"OK," he said. "My agent and I had a very important business dinner last night. A major studio has optioned my piece on Chechnya for a movie." When Nikki didn't seem so excited by that, he continued, "So . . . since I had *just* gotten back to town . . . we went to dinner so I could sign the contracts. I had no idea anybody was going to take a picture."

"And when exactly did you 'just' get back?" she asked.

"Yesterday. Late. I trailed that money and the arms shipment all the way from Bosnia to Africa to Colombia to Mexico."

"Good for you," said Heat. "Now, that covers the last thirty days beautifully. What about the last thirty hours?"

"My God, once an interrogator . . ." He chuckled and met an ice wall. "I can tell you about that."

"I'm all ears, Rook."

"Well, you know about the dinner."

"At Le Cirque, yes, go on."

"The rest is simple, really. Mostly I crashed. I think I slept thirteen, fifteen hours straight. First real bed in weeks." He was talking faster then, eliminating pauses that made him vulnerable. "And after, I've been writing like crazy—phone off, TV off—writing. Then I came right here."

"You couldn't call?" Nikki hated the cliché even as it flew out of her mouth, but then decided if ever anyone had license to say it, she did right then.

"See, that's what you don't know about me. This is my process, you know, to sequester myself. Get it all down while it's still fresh in my head and my notes still make sense to me. It's how I work," he said, equal parts explanation and justification. "But this evening when I finally saw the newspaper, I knew how you'd feel, so I dropped everything to rush to you in true ain't-no-river-wide-enough fashion. All right, maybe instead of a handmade raft it was a taxi, but doesn't that count for anything?"

"Not so sure it's enough." She picked up her coat and draped it on the back of the bar stool, buying time to sort her thoughts out. The fact was, for Nikki, it did not erase the month of isolation and the emotional burrs and raw abrasions that came with her journey. But the grounded side of her, the grown-up of the pair, was looking at the horizon to the days and weeks and whatever that came after this moment.

Rook cleared his throat. "There's one more thing I need to say to you. And I know there's no way we can move forward until I get this out."

"OK . . ."

"I want to apologize to you, Nikki. Not just, 'hey, sorry,' but really. Apologize." He paused, either to let her absorb it or to find his way, then he went on, "This is all still new to both of us. You and I came to each other with full lives, past baggage, careers, the works. Both of us. And this trip of mine, this was the first time since we got together that you're seeing what my real work is like. I have the advantage of having gone on ride-along, so you—I get your life, inside and out. Me, I'm an investigative journalist. If I'm doing it right, I'm spending big stretches of time in places nobody else has the balls to go and under conditions most reporters wouldn't put up with. That explains why I fell off the radar on my story. I told you I might before I left. But it's no excuse for not calling you when I got in the clear. The only explanation I can give may sound flimsy, but it's the truth. When I come off assignment, I have a routine. I sleep like the dead and write like the devil, in seclusion. It's the way I've always done it. For years. But now—I realize something's different now. I'm not the only one involved.

"Now, if I could take back the past twenty-four hours, I would, but I can't. What I can do, though, is say when I look at you now and see the hurt in you—the hurt I caused by being insensitive—I see pain I never want to bring to you again." He let that sit there, then said, "Nikki, I apologize. I was wrong. And I am sorry."

After he finished, they stood there like that, facing off in her front hall, silently looking each other over from barely a yard away— one hoping the rift was behind them, the other trying to decide— when the warmth that suddenly stirred inside Nikki swelled and made a decision of its own. It took control, radiating within her until the spreading heat rose and wouldn't be stopped, making the "right here, right now" bigger—and more powerful—than anything else.

Rook sensed it in her, or maybe was feeling it in himself, too. It didn't matter—any more than who flew to the other first, open mouth on open mouth, hungrily reaching, searching to get closer, closer. Without looking, she one-handed her holster onto the counter. Still kissing, pressing himself to her, his fingers undid her blouse.

When they finally gasped for air, every breath became a shared lust, giving as well as taking; a quest of passion, of sealed lips and urgent tongues. He started to lead her to the bedroom by small steps backward. But Nikki had one more takedown in her that night. She rolled Rook over the back of the sofa and landed on top of him. He reached behind her, drawing her by the small of her back to him. She pressed forward, going with him. Then Nikki rose onto her knees and began to unbuckle his belt.

And then it was all about breathlessness again.

———

Nikki slept afterward, allowing herself a luxurious drift into the ozone, sinking deeply into the couch cushions, her naked thigh draped over Jameson Rook's magnificent ass. She awoke slowly about an hour later and lazed a few moments watching him as he sat at the counter working on his laptop in only his untucked shirt and Calvins. "I didn't even feel you get up," she said. "Did you sleep?"

"Too wired to be tired. Don't even know what a time zone is anymore."

"Does sex help your writing?"

"Sure doesn't hurt." He stopped and rotated to face her with a grin, then went back to his computer. "But I'm not actually writing-writing. I'm just downloading and saving some attachments I e-mailed myself. Won't be a sex—I mean sec. . . . Or do I?"

"You e-mail yourself? Rook, if you're lonely, I could e-mail you."

He continued working keystrokes as he explained. "I always back up my iPad docs and smart phone notes by e-mailing them to myself. That way, if my iPad takes a dip in a swamp or my phone gets confiscated by some former Eastern Bloc gun runner . . . or I leave it on the R Train like an idiot . . . I don't lose all my work." With a flourish, he double-tapped the track pad. "Done."

After they made love again, of all places, in the bedroom, Heat and Rook held each other in the dark. A trickle of sweat ran across one of Nikki's breasts and she wondered—his or hers? She tracked the sensation of its slow, meandering course between them and smiled. After a month apart, how wonderful to be close enough that she couldn't tell whose sweat was whose.

————

When they both decided they were hungry, she wondered aloud who was still delivering after midnight, but Rook was already at his suitcase fishing out a pair of sweatpants. "You're not going out," she said. "10-10 WINS said it's in minus temps tonight." He said nothing, just handed Nikki her robe and led her to the kitchen. He opened the door to the refrigerator and came out with a half dozen takeout trays.

"Rook, what did you do?"

"Hit SushiSamba on the way over." He set a container of each on the counter. "Let's see, got your Samba Park roll, your BoBo Brazil, your Green Envy . . . ," he paused to purr like a tiger, ". . . your tuna sashimi."

"Oh my God," said Nikki, "and you got yellowtail ceviche?"

"Do I know you? Margarita, señorita?"

"*Sí.*" She laughed, remembering how long it had been since she'd done that.

Rook set the pitcher he had mixed on the tiles and, as he salted two glasses, said, "Consider the potential irony. Four weeks surviving nighttime jungle landings in the cargo bays of unmarked planes, multiple detentions by corrupt border guards, getting roughed up in the trunk of some paranoid Colombian drug lord's El Dorado by his crackhead flunkies, only to be gunned down in my girlfriend's apartment."

"No laugh, Rook, I was feeling jumpy. I think someone was following me tonight."

"Seriously? Did you see who?"

"No. And not a hundred percent sure about it."

"Yes, you are," he said. "Should you call Montrose?"

There was a time that's exactly what she would have done. Detective Heat would have let her captain know and then vehemently declined his offer to park a cruiser out front (which he would have done anyway, ignoring her protests). It wasn't the uncertainty about the tail that stopped her, though. It was the uncertainty in the face of him questioning her judgment and leadership. Plus her own awkwardness dealing with the captain with so many suspicions swirling. "No," she said. "It's too weird with Montrose now. Kind of tense."

"With Montrose? And you? What's going on?"

The day had been such a grind, and this respite was such a welcome oasis, she said, "Way too much to get into now. I'm not shutting you out, but can we leave it until tomorrow?"

"Absolutely." He held up his glass. "To reunions."

They clinked *salut* and sipped. The taste of a margarita would always remind her of the first night they had sex in the summer heat wave. "Hope you learned your lesson about sneaking in here without a heads-up."

"You gave me a key. And what kind of surprise would that make, if I called?"

"The surprise would have been yours if I'd had company."

He served the food, placing the cut rolls of sushi on her plate and then his with chopsticks. "You're right. That would have surprised me."

"What?" she said, "You mean, surprised if I had been with someone?"

"You wouldn't be."

"I sure could."

"Could, yes. Would? No. That's not who you are, Nikki Heat."

"A little presumptuous." She ate some of the ceviche, and as she tasted the citrus and cilantro, relishing how it made the fish even fresher, Nikki reflected on how close she had come to bringing Don home with her that night. "And how do you know that's not who I am, Jameson Rook?"

"It's not about knowing. You can never really know someone. It's really about trust."

"Curious. We've never really defined our . . ."

". . . Exclusivity?" he said, finishing for her.

She nodded, "Yeah, that. And yet you trust me?" He chewed a Green Envy and nodded back. "And what about you, Rook, am I supposed to trust you?"

"You already do."

"I see. And how far does this trust extend?" she asked, chopsticking a dab of wasabi for her next victim. "What about travel? What's it called? The Hundred Mile Rule?"

"You mean the one that says you can do whatever—meaning whoever—you want if you're more than a hundred miles away? The variation on the 'What Happens in Vegas' Rule?"

"That's the one," she said.

"Since you brought it up, the places I've been, situations do present themselves. Do they ever. And yes, I absolutely subscribe to the Hundred Mile Rule." She set her chopsticks on the side of her plate, parallel to each other, and studied him. He continued, "But here's the thing. According to Rook's Rule, no matter where I am in the world, a hundred miles or a thousand, Mile Zero starts here." He poked two fingers on his chest.

Nikki thought a moment, then picked up a piece of sushi with her fingers. "When I finish this Samba roll? I want you to pretend Mile Zero is a beach in Fiji. . . . And we're on it alone." She popped it in her mouth in one bite and flicked her eyebrows at him while she chewed.

———

The next morning "brisk walk" took on a literal meaning as she and Rook picked their way over ice patches on the way to the subway in minus-two degrees Fahrenheit. At least the smack of cold in her face helped wake her up. Heat had to tear herself out of that toasty bed with him to make her breakfast meeting on time. He helped by getting up with her and brewing coffee while she showered. When she stepped out, he was packing up gear so he could get to his loft in

Tribeca and a day of writing. The deadline for his arms smuggling article loomed, and he told her that on its heels he owed the proof-read galleys for his ghostwritten romance novel, *Her Endless Knight.*

"I feel like I just had one of those," she said as they kissed at the stairs leading down to the 6 train at 23rd.

"Any complaints?"

"Only one," said Heat. "It is about to end."

Nikki made one more survey of Park Avenue South and was satisfied she wasn't being followed. And as Rook stood holding the cab he had hailed, waiting in the street while he watched her, his pause confirmed Nikki's suspicion that his early rise to get to work was an excuse to escort her without saying so. The sidewalk rumbled like distant thunder below, and she could hear the screech of the subway braking as it slowed at the station. She gave him a head nod and hurried down to meet it.

———

The deli Zach Hamner had chosen couldn't have been more convenient. The Corte Café storefronted her subway exit on Lafayette between Duane and Reade, right across the street from the Municipal Building and, just behind it, One Police Plaza. Heat pushed through the glass door behind a trio of construction workers who tossed their hardhats on a table and swarmed the counter, calling out orders for breakfast burritos and ham & eggs on a kaiser. She didn't know Hamner, but the skinny guy in a black suit and gold tie at a window table was a good candidate. He stood to wave at her with one hand; he held his BlackBerry to his ear with the other. As she stepped over, he said into his phone, "Listen, I gotta go, my breakfast meeting is here. OKlater-bye." He set the phone on the table and extended a hand. "Detective Heat, Zach Hamner, sit, sit."

Nikki took the chair across from him and noticed he had ordered for her. Coffee and a plain bagel with two plastic pots of cream cheese. "Coffee should still be hot," he said. "It gets jammed in here, and I didn't want us to spend our whole morning in line behind the construction goons." At the table beside them, a hardhat with a brush mustache looked up from his Sudoku, buck-snorted, and then went back to his puzzle. If Zach Hamner noticed—or cared—he didn't let on. "Anyway, glad you could make it. Hope it wasn't too much of an inconvenience."

She felt the side of her coffee cup. It was cool. She tried not to begrudge the extra hour she might have had with Rook, not to mention getting a jump on her case work. "I'm an early riser," she said. "Plus you were pretty insistent."

"Thank you," he said, making Nikki wonder if there had been some unintended flattery in her tone. "I reached out to make sure we had the opportunity to connect early in your process. Not just to let you know we're here—that Legal is here—if you need an assist along the way, but also because we think it's important to have a relationship with the up-and-comers of the department."

Heat was getting the picture fairly quickly. . . . How could she not? Zach, this—what did he say his title was?—Senior Administrative Aide to the Deputy Commissioner for Legal Matters, was a career networker. One of those functionaries who ate and slept the job, basked in the reflected glory of his boss, and drew power from the proximity he forged with the upper ranks. Hence the royal we. She decided he probably kept a picture of Rahm Emanuel taped to his bathroom mirror so he could see it when he shaved.

"You should know I have briefed the deputy commissioner on your stellar test score. I also slipped in a copy of that magazine piece on you. He's quite impressed."

"That's nice to know." She tore off a bite-sized piece of bagel and, as she smeared some cream cheese on it, continued, "Although, you know, if we do only get fifteen minutes, I hope those were mine."

"Interesting. I assumed that you had maintained a close relationship with the press." If he only knew, thought Nikki. She flashed on the wake-up surprise she had given Rook that very morning. Hamner continued, "From the article, I got the impression you knew just how to handle that reporter."

"It's a skill I've learned to develop," said Heat, suppressing a smirk. "But I'm not one for the limelight."

"Oh, please, we're grown-ups here," he said. "Ambition isn't a dirty word. Not at this table, I assure you." Clearly, she thought. "Your decision to take the lieutenant's test, was that not ambition?"

"In a way."

"Yes. And we are thankful you did. We need more Nikki Heats. And fewer bad apples." He sat back in his chair and jammed his hands deep in his pockets, studying her reaction as he added, "Tell me what's going on with Captain Montrose."

Nikki felt her small bite of bagel pushing against the inside of her sternum. Whatever agenda Heat had perceived for this meeting, pure networking wasn't it. She didn't yet know how much weight Zach Hamner carried, but caution led her to choose her words carefully. She sipped some cold coffee and said, "I've been hearing that Captain Montrose has been going through a rough patch over there." Nikki hitched a thumb behind her right shoulder in the direction of 1PP. "But I'm at a loss to understand it. Maybe after so many years working together, my experience with him has been different." Heat thought about leaving it at that, but there was a distasteful undercurrent of something hungry and cunning coming off the young lawyer. In spite of Nikki's unsettling feelings about whatever was going on with the Cap, her loyalty was strong and something about seeing all the dorsal fins break the surface lately made her add a little pushback. "With all due respect?"

"Please."

"If you invited me to breakfast hoping I would give you some dirt or to go on record and disparage my commander, you're going to be disappointed. I deal in facts, not innuendo."

Hamner cracked a grin. "You're good. No, I mean that. Well handled."

"Because it's the truth."

He nodded and leaned forward, casually pressing his forefinger into a cluster of sesame seeds on his plate before he nibbled them off.

"But we all know, especially a veteran detective knows, there are many truths. It's really just another value, isn't it? Like discretion. Hard work. Loyalty." His BlackBerry vibrated on the table. He looked at his screen, made a sour face, and pressed a button to silence it. "The thing about loyalty, Detective Heat, is that critical times come where a reasonable person has to be objective. Take a hard look at truths. To make sure old loyalties aren't suddenly misplaced. Or blinding." Then he smiled. "Or, who knows? To see if it may be time for some new ones." He rose to go and gave her a business card. "The office number rings to my BlackBerry after hours. Let's fly close."

———

It was still early for her squad to be in for shift, so Detective Heat speed-dialed their mobiles on her walk from the deli to HQ. The oystery clouds rolling in from New Jersey began to issue ice pellets that stung her face and bounced off the interlocking brickwork of the walkway between the Municipal Building and police headquarters. Halfway there Nikki stopped for shelter under the Tony Rosenthal sculpture and listened to the frozen rain tinking like handfuls of rice off its red metal discs while she made her calls.

The male strip club didn't open until eleven, so her plan was to split up Roach, assigning Ochoa to concentrate on getting Father Graf's computer from Forensics to check his e-mails and Raley to run a check on the priest's phone records. However, when she reached him, Ochoa reported that he and Raley had already hit the club the night before. "You were still behind closed doors with Montrose and we didn't want to disturb you since it looked like you were having such a good time in there." The detective paused to let his dry humor land then continued, "So we dropped by One Hot Mess at happy hour to see if we could get some momentum in the case."

"That's a load. You two just wanted an excuse to walk on the wild side." She could have just said what she felt and expressed her genuine appreciation for their initiative, but that would have been a breach of UCRAP—the Unspoken Compliments and Relationship

Avoidance Protocols observed among cops. So Heat said the opposite. As if she meant it.

"I did it for Raley," he said, responding in kind. "My partner, he's a curious pony who will not be broken." They'd had some success. After showing Father Graf's photo around, one of the strippers recognized him. The Nekked Cowpoke (whose name and spelling, he pointed out, had for the price of a lap dance been legally parsed to avoid trademark infringement) said the priest in the photo had been in the club a week before and had gotten into a shouting match with one of the other dancers. It was so heated the bouncer kicked the padre out.

"Did your cowpoke hear what they were arguing about?" asked Heat.

"No, that must have come before they threw down. But he did hear one thing before the bouncer intervened. The dancer grabbed the priest by the neck and said he'd kill him."

"Bring him in for a chat. Now."

"We have to find him first," Ochoa replied. "He quit three days ago and cleared out of his apartment. Raley is doing a trace now."

Her next call was to Sharon Hinesburg. She had been with Heat when Mrs. Borelli hesitated over one of the surveillance stills, so she got the call to work on finding an ID of the man. When Nikki reached Detective Rhymer, she told him to pass word to Gallagher that the two of them were back on the bondage beat. She wanted them to generate a list of freelance dominatrixes that they missed the day before. "I don't want any to slip through the cracks just because they didn't have relationships with the clubs in The Alley," she explained.

"This is a surprise," Rhymer said. "I thought we were going to work more lines than just the BDSM angle."

"New orders for now" was all she said, but as she flipped up the back of her collar and stepped out into the cascade of ice pellets, she wondered what resources she was squandering by following Montrose's edict. Her phone rang as she cleared the double-wide guard shack outside the lobby. Raley had scored a recent gas-and-electric hookup for the male dancer. His new apartment was in Brooklyn Heights, just over the bridge from where she stood. Nikki told Rales she'd be done in fifteen minutes and to pick her up in the Roach Coach on their way over.

———

At Personnel, Heat signed her request for examination results, checking the boxes for both e-mail and hard copy. Digital Age or not, there was something about having the document in hand that reassured her. Black-and-white still made it real. The clerk stepped away and returned a short time later to slide a sealed envelope across the counter to her. Nikki signed the receipt and stepped away with the aura of being too cool to rip into it right there in the office. That delay of gratification vaporized precisely two seconds after she got in the hall and tore it open.

"Excuse me, Detective Heat?" In the lobby Nikki turned to the woman she had passed who was getting on the elevator as she stepped off. She had never met Phyllis Yarborough, but Nikki certainly knew who she was. She had glimpsed the Deputy Commissioner of Technological Development at department ceremonies and, just over a year before, on *60 Minutes.* That was when Yarborough had celebrated the fifth anniversary of the Real Time Crime Center by giving a rare on-camera tour of the data nerve center she had helped as an outside contractor to design and now oversaw as a civilian appointee to the Police Commission.

The deputy commissioner was in her early fifties, a coin flip between handsome and attractive. To Nikki's view, attractive won the day. It was the smile. A real person smile—the kind you see more on entrepreneurial CEOs than government officials. Heat also noted that while many ranking women armored themselves in power suits or St. Johns upholstery, Phyllis Yarborough's business style was accessible and feminine. Even though she was wealthier than wealthy her suit only looked expensive. A tailored Jones New York cardigan and pencil skirt Nikki could have afforded, and seeing it on her, thought seriously about getting.

"Your name's come up a few times lately around here, Detective. Are your ears burning?" After she extended a hand to shake Nikki's, Yarborough said, "Do you have some time to come up to my office for a cup?"

Nikki tried not to look at her watch. The other woman read her and said, "Of course, you're probably on a tight schedule."

"Actually, that's quite true. You know how it is, I'm sure."

"I do. But I hate to miss this chance. Do you have three minutes for a quick chat?" She side nodded, indicating the two chairs across the lobby.

Nikki considered, then said to the deputy commissioner, "Of course."

When they sat, Phyllis Yarborough looked at her own watch. "Keeping myself honest," she said. "So. Nikki Heat. Do you know the reason your name has been popping up? It's in your hands, right there." When Nikki looked down at the envelope resting on her lap, the administrator continued, "Let me put this in context for you. In this year's Promotion Examination for Lieutenant over eleven hundred detectives took the test. You know how many passed? Fifteen percent. Eighty-five percent of the applicants flunked out. Of the fifteen percent that passed, you know what the highest score was? Eighty-eight." She paused. "Except for you, Detective Heat." Nikki had just seen her score and felt a small butterfly to hear it repeated. "You scored a ninety-eight. That is what I call flat-out exceptional."

What else was there to say? "Thank you."

"You're going to find out it's a mixed blessing, doing so well. It puts you on the radar as a rising star. Which you are. The downside is that everyone with an agenda is going to try to get their hooks in you." Just as Nikki reflected on her breakfast, Yarborough spoke her thoughts. "Expect a call from Zachary Hamner. Oh, I see from your face he already has. The Hammer's not a force for bad, but watch your back. You will be quoted." She laughed and added, "The damn thing is, he quotes accurately, so be double warned."

Nikki nodded and thought, The Hammer, huh? Perfect.

"I have my agenda, too, I just don't pretend otherwise. Know why transparency's a beautiful thing? Transparency means no shame. So I'll be shameless. There's a future up the ranks for a smart detective who has her heart in the right place. Prepare yourself, I might even court you to work with me."

This woman, as powerful and as busy as she was, had the quality of making Nikki feel like she was the only one on her mind that day. Heat wasn't naïve; of course the deputy commissioner was pushing an agenda, same as The Hammer had, but rather than feeling wary, Nikki felt engaged, energized. These were the same qualities of leadership that had made Yarborough a dot-com fortune years before in private industry. Heat said, "I'm certainly open to seeing where this all goes. Meantime, I'm flattered."

"This isn't just because you scored a ninety-eight. I've had my eye on you since your magazine article. We are two women with a lot in common." She read Nikki's expression and said, "I know, I know, you're a cop, and I'm a civilian—and an administrator, at that—but where I really connected with you in that article was when I read we are both victims of family murders." Heat noticed she used the present tense, a sign of one who knows the pain that never heals.

Looking at Phyllis Yarborough, Nikki found herself peering into a mirror image that bore the imprint of a distant agony. The kindred spirits out there never fail to recognize the sear of fate in each other and in it an invisible brand marking the nexus of their upended lives. For Nikki, it had been her mother, stabbed to death a decade before. Yarborough's loss was her only daughter back in 2002; roofied, raped, beaten, and dumped on a beach in Bermuda, where she had been on college Spring Break. Everyone knew the story. It was inescapable in the mainstream news and then milked beyond its shelf life by the tabloids long after the coed's killer confessed and went to prison for life.

Nikki broke the brief silence with an affirming smile. "Yet we go on."

The deputy commissioner's face brightened. "Yes, we do." And then she looked deeply into Nikki, as if taking her measure. "It drives you, doesn't it? Thinking about the killer?"

Heat said, "I wonder about him, if that's what you mean. Who? Why?"

"Do you want revenge?"

"I did." Nikki had given it lots of thought over the years, and said, "Now it's not so much revenge as justice. Or maybe closure. What about you?"

"Academic. My accounts are settled. But let me tell you what I've learned. Hopefully, it helps you." She leaned closer to Nikki and said, "There is justice. But there is no such thing as closure." Then she made an exaggerated show of looking at her watch. "Well now. I'm ten seconds away from not being a woman of my word." She rose, and as Nikki stood, they shook hands again. "Kick some butt out there today, Nikki Heat."

"I will. And a pleasure meeting you, Deputy Commissioner."

"Phyllis. And let's make sure this is just our first meeting."

Heat left One Police Plaza with the second business card she had been given in a half hour. It felt like the one she would actually keep handy.

———

A firefighter came out of the Engine 205 station house on Middaugh Street in Brooklyn Heights and trotted, hunched against the frozen rain, to his pickup truck at the curb. Detective Raley said, "Whoa, whoa, hold up, here. Guy looks like he's pulling out."

Detective Ochoa gave the Roach Coach some brakes and turned the rearview mirror so he could see Nikki in the backseat. "See what I put up with on a daily basis? 'Turn here, stop there, look out for the homeless guy . . .' It's like I've got the Felix Unger dude from *Two and a Half Men* as my talking GPS."

"Go before somebody takes it," said Raley as the pickup left.

After Ochoa parked, the three detectives sat in the Crown Vic with the blades on intermittent so they could observe the apartment house where the male stripper had just moved. It was a 1920s eight-story brick building surrounded by scaffolding for its renovation. No workmen were in sight, which Raley said could have been due to the extreme wintry weather.

"Figures a male stripper would move in across from a firehouse," said Ochoa. "In case he needs a pole to practice on."

"What's his name again?" asked Heat.

Raley consulted his sheet. "Horst Meuller. He's from Hamburg, Germany. My witness at the strip club says when Meuller started, he danced in a World War I getup as The Red Barin'. Now he does a Eurotrash strip in silver lamé as Hans Alloffur." He half-turned to Nikki. "All these guys have theme acts, you see."

"Tell her the name of that one stripper last night." Ochoa chuckled. "You're gonna love this."

"Marty Python," said Raley.

Nikki shook her head. "I won't even ask."

The super let them in so they didn't have to warn Meuller by buzzing his intercom. They took position outside his door and Ochoa knocked.

"Who is there?" came the accented voice from inside.

Raley held his shield to the spy hole. "NYPD to speak with Horst Meuller."

"Of course. Just a moment, please."

Nikki could smell the stall and was already down a half flight of stairs by the time she heard Meuller's deadbolt snap into place on his door, followed by Roach-kicks to the wood. She sailed through the vestibule and out onto the sidewalk, looking for the fire escape. "That way!" called Ochoa out the open third-floor window.

Heat's gaze followed Ochoa's gesture to the far end of the building, where the male dancer was sliding down and around the corner pole of the scaffolding, toward the sidewalk. Heat called for him to freeze, but he somersaulted off the last rung, landing on both feet. Meuller slipped and almost fell on the icy walkway but quickly got his balance and started to run, his long, blond Fabio hair fluttering behind him.

As Detective Heat took off after him, Raley blasted out the front door calling coordinates for backup on his walkie-talkie as he joined the foot chase.

Footing was treacherous with about an eighth-inch of ice granules down and more falling. When Meuller bolted across the intersection at Henry Street, an auto parts delivery truck slammed its brakes to avoid hitting him and skidded helplessly sideways, crashing into a parked car. Heat didn't cross Henry to pursue him. His side of the street was open sidewalk. Hers was largely restaurant and retail with numerous awnings overhanging the way, which meant she had a shot at running on concrete instead of ice.

By the next intersection, she was parallel with him. Heat made a fast street check over her left shoulder. The road was clear except for up the block, where she clocked the Roach Coach coming around the corner with its gumball lit. Slowing to keep from falling, she jogged across the intersection, calling, "NYPD, Meuller, stop!"

He turned, startled at the closeness of her voice, and when he did, his momentum pulled his center of gravity out from over his feet and he stumbled. Meuller would have fallen flat, but he grabbed the railing of some concrete steps leading up to the promenade to some high-rise apartments and only went down on one knee. He was just hoisting himself up when Heat leaped, grabbed the railing, and vaulted herself over, landing on top of him and taking him down.

The snap she heard as Meuller went down was followed by a *"Scheiss!"* and a moan. He writhed, groaning on the concrete stairs as Heat cuffed him. By then Raley had arrived and they brought him to his feet.

"Careful," said Nikki, "I think I heard something break."

"Ja, my collarbone, why did you do that to me?"

Ochoa had the Crown Victoria double-parked with the back door open, and they led their prisoner to it. "Why did you run?"

Horst Meuller never answered. The bullet ripped through the collar of his shirt, and Heat and Raley were sprayed with blood. He dropped again but didn't moan. Or make any sound.

Heat called, "Down, down, everybody down!" and hit the deck, covering Meuller's body as she brought up her Sig, scanning the apartment promenade, the high-rise, the roof across the street. On the other side of the fallen dancer, Raley had his weapon out and was doing the same; even as he called in the 10-13, shots fired.

On Henry Street, an engine thundered and tires spun, whining for purchase in the ice. Heat ran in a low crouch for cover beside Ochoa at the Roach Coach, but it was too late. The SUV spun its tires and sped off, driving over the curb as it turned onto Orange and out of view.

Heat recognized the SUV. She called it in as graphite gray with heavy-duty tires, but that was the best description she could give. This time, it had no license plates.

FIVE

The two paramedics in the back of the ambulance were still working on keeping Horst Meuller from slipping away when the uniform buttoned up the rear doors and it rolled from the scene. Nikki Heat stood holding her breath against its issue of diesel exhaust and watched it lumber off in the sleet, following the same route the SUV had not a half hour before. A block down Orange Street, at the perimeter of the crime scene, the siren kicked on, a sign that, at least for the moment, there was still a life on that gurney.

Detective Feller handed Heat and Raley each a cup of coffee. "Can't vouch for it, it's from the Chinese place over there. But it'll warm you up."

Raley's assist call had drawn a swarm. First on the scene had been the crew of New York's Bravest from the 205 up the block. If the dancing German pulled through, he would owe it to his firefighter neighbors for slowing the bleeding within minutes. Cruisers from the Eighty-fourth Precinct and the neighboring Seventy-sixth were first cops on-scene, followed immediately by Feller and Van Meter in their undercover taxi. With their roving status, it was typical for Taxi Squad cops to be first responders to officer assist calls, and Ochoa threw a barb at the pair for letting the home blue-and-whites beat them.

Dutch Van Meter winked to his partner and lobbed one back. "Oh, by the way, Detective, how'd you do apprehending the vehicle after your pursuit?"

Ochoa had come up empty. The chase was perfunctory at best given the shooter's head start, and they all knew it. But he had given it his best effort, able at least to follow the wide tracks in the freshly fallen sleet until he lost them on Old Fulton Street, which was more heavily traveled. He drove the Roach Coach on a honeycomb of the neighboring streets on his way back just to make sure, but no SUV.

On the other side of the yellow tape, the first TV news minicams were setting up. Nikki saw a lens pointed at her from under a blue Gore-Tex storm cover and heard her name. She rotated to present her back to the press line and once again grumbled a mental curse about her magazine cover.

Feller took a sip of his own coffee and made a face. "So none of you saw the shooter?" Steam rose as he poured it out into the gutter. Heat, Raley, and Ochoa all looked at one another and shook their heads.

"It was one of those split-second things," said Raley. "We're all focused on our prisoner, you know, and out of nowhere, bang."

"More like boom," said Ochoa. All nodded in agreement. "I make it a rifle."

"Boom," said Van Meter. "Not much to go on."

Heat said, "I know the vehicle." They all turned to look at her. "I saw it yesterday. Twice. Once in the afternoon on Columbus on the way to Andy's and then last night in my neighborhood."

"What's this, Detective?" Heat turned. Captain Montrose had come up behind her. He must have read their surprise, and explained, "I was on my way to 1PP for a meeting and heard the ten-thirteen. Now, am I to infer that you were being tailed but you didn't report it?" He didn't wait for an answer. "I could have called in protection."

"I wasn't sure. And I didn't want to draw resources without more certainty." Heat left out the part about how the strain between them made her hold back.

The old Montrose would have taken her aside for a chat. But New Montrose snapped at her right there in front of her colleagues. "That's not a call for you to make. I'm still your commander. My job isn't yours . . . yet." At that, the captain turned and crossed the sidewalk to confer with the CSU team gathered around the bullet hole in the service door of the high-rise.

An ass-kicking in front of the family is an uncomfortable thing for everyone, and in the dead air that followed, the other detectives busied themselves trying not to make eye contact with Heat. She turned her face upward into the sleet and closed her eyes, feeling the hundred little stings of the sky falling.

––––––––

When she got back uptown, Nikki made a quick stop to do an appearance check outside the door to the bull pen, where the fluorescent overheads created a poor man's mirror in the window of Montrose's dark office. It wasn't about vanity; it was about dried blood. At the shooting scene in Brooklyn Heights, EMTs had given her wipes to clean her face and neck, but her clothes were another story. The emergency shirt and slacks she usually kept folded in her desk file drawer were still at the cleaners following a latte mishap, so the rust-colored spray on the collar of her blouse and in the V pattern down the front where her coat had been open would have to do. While Nikki made her appraisal, she heard Detective Rhymer's soft drawl coming around the corner from the squad room.

Heat couldn't hear all he was saying, just snippets because he was speaking in hushed tones. She picked up phrases like "... wheel spinning and make-work ..." and "He said, 'Screw it, life's too short ...'" and then "... Heat's more worried about her freaking promotion ..."

Listening in was tantalizing but made Nikki feel skeevy, like she was in a soap. What had Phyllis Yarborough said a few hours before? Something like "transparency means no shame"? So Heat turned the corner to face whatever she would face.

What she found was Detective Rhymer leaning in gossip mode with Sharon Hinesburg at her desk. Both sat upright in their rolling chairs when they saw her walk in. "Damn, look at you," said

Hinesburg, hopping to her feet. "Who took the bullet, you or the dancer?" She was extra loud, the way people get when they're diverting attention. Or hoping to.

Nikki ignored her and gave a puzzled look to Rhymer. "Are you and Gallagher done working your list of dommes already?"

He rose, too, albeit more tentatively. "Not quite. We came back so I could drop Gallagher off."

Nikki scanned the room and didn't see his partner. "What, is he sick?"

"Gallagher, he, ah . . . He requested a reassign back to Burglary." The detective turned to Hinesburg as if he'd find some help, but Sharon was letting him deal his own hand. The whispers Nikki had just overheard sufficed for her to do the math. Another day talking to dominatrixes felt like a waste to Gallagher and so he booked out. Apparently with some opinions expressed about Detective Heat on his exit. "You know," continued Rhymer, "we had some cases hanging that needed some attention, and he must have just felt, you know, obliged to mind them."

Heat knew it was bull but didn't expect Opie to throw in his partner. This latest piece of unrest created by her coming promotion tasted bitter, but she set it aside. Her immediate concern was that she was suddenly down one investigator. "In that case, I'm glad you hung in, Ope."

"I'm here, Detective." But then he couched it. "Long as I can be, that is."

———

At the Murder Board a few minutes later Heat selected a new marker color and printed the dancer's name in the upper left corner where there was plenty of white space. "Probably doesn't feel like it to him, but it's Horst Meuller's lucky day," she told the squad. "The slug they pulled from that door was a .338 Magnum."

Raley said, "Any brass?"

She shook no. "My guess is he either never threw the bolt since it was one shot, or if he did, the casing ejected into the vehicle and left with him."

Ochoa let out a low whistle. ".338 Mag. Man . . . Hunters use those loads to drop grizzlies."

"And, apparently, pole dancers," said Heat. "I want to find out why. Detective Rhymer, dig deeper on Horst Meuller."

"I thought you wanted me to check out the freelance dommes," he said.

Nikki stopped herself and for the hundredth time thought about her contentious meeting with the captain and all the lines of this investigation he had closed down. She clenched her teeth and reversed herself, trying not to choke on her own words. "Stay on the BDSM canvass. When you finish, let me know. Then we'll see where we are with Meuller."

"Are you sure Meuller was the target?" asked Raley. "If that SUV was tailing you, seems like maybe you're the one who got lucky this morning."

"As a trained sleuth that possibility did not escape my notice," said Nikki, tugging at her bloodstained collar and triggering a laugh from the squad. Heat turned to the board and sketched a looping arc from Meuller's name to Father Graf's. "What I really want to do is see what the connection is, if any, between these two victims. Hopefully, our dancer will survive and be able to shed some light. Meanwhile, let's treat these two incidents as related."

"By interviewing random dominatrixes?" said Detective Rhymer.

His instincts were right; it was her orders that were wrong, and she knew it. But she followed the edict. "Dommes for now, Opie. Clear?"

"What about the money in the cookie tins?" asked Raley. "Want me to contact the archdiocese, see if they have any suspicions about the padre doing some skimming?"

Once again, Heat came nose first against one of the brick walls Montrose had put up. It was an obvious trail to follow; why had the captain obstructed it? "Leave that to me for now," she said.

Hinesburg reported that she had no hits yet on the man in the surveillance photo Father Graf's housekeeper reacted to. "Which only means he may not have a criminal background."

Nikki said, "I'll call Mrs. Borelli and press her. But keep working it and all the other stills." Heat opened the folder of surveillance pictures and took one out. It was of a man and a young woman coming down the stairs into the lobby of Pleasure Bound. The woman was laughing with her face turned up at her companion, but his was obscured by a Jets cap. Nikki posted it on the board with a magnet. "Had a thought about this one. See on his arm there, the tattoo?" First Raley and then the others rose to gather closer. The tatt was of a snake coiled around his left upper arm. "Real Time Crime Center keeps a data bank of scars and tattoos. Why don't you have RTCC run it, Sharon. See if you get any matches."

"Detective?" said Ochoa. "I know that woman."

Raley said, "Something you want to tell us, pard? You in the lifestyle and holding back?"

"No, seriously. I talked to her yesterday. Know that domme who's over in Amsterdam? Whatsername . . . Boam? Andrea Boam?" He tapped the picture with his pen. "That's the roommate I talked to."

"Pay her another visit," Nikki said. "Let's see what this roommate knows about charming snakes."

———

Heat had to wade through a dozen messages on her voice mail from people who had seen her on the TV news at that morning's shooting scene and hoped she was OK. One was from Rook, who also insisted on treating her to a non-takeout dinner, "in a sit-down restaurant like a respectable woman." Zach Hamner left word, as did Phyllis Yarborough. Nikki appreciated the sentiments but could see how easy it would be to keep up with all the bonding outreach from 1PP and never get her work done. She saved the messages to answer later. Lauren Parry down at OCME, however, got an immediate callback.

Lauren began, "I just want you to know that I am going to be seriously pissed if I come in here some morning and find you laid out on one of my tables."

"I'd hate that, too," said Nikki. "I'd want a week to diet first."

"Yuh, right," her friend laughed, "like you'd need to, woman of steel." Nikki could hear keystrokes and pictured the ME in the cramped dictation office, at the desk that looked out onto the autopsy room. "OK, interesting discovery about that fingernail they vacuumed up in the torture room. It wasn't a fingernail after all, but tested out as hardened polyester."

"Plastic? That looked like a fingernail?"

"Exactly like a fingernail clipping. Even the same color. But know what it actually was?" Lauren, always happy to put on a show, said, "Wait for it . . . A piece of a button. Little crescent-shaped sliver broken off a button."

"So no DNA help."

"No, but if you find the button, we can always match it."

The detective didn't see a lot of hope there. "What else you got?"

"Something inconsistent came out of the ECU sweep at the rectory. I'm looking at the meds they collected from the victim's bathroom chest. There is a vial of adefovir dipivoxil. That's a reverse transcriptase inhibitor used to treat HIV, tumors, cancer, and hepatitis-B. The thing is, Nikki, the priest had none of those conditions. And none of it showed up in his tox screening."

A true odd sock, Heat thought as she finished jotting down the list of diseases. "But it was his prescription?"

"Made out to Gerald Francis Graf, ten milligrams. The pill count says it was full."

"Who's the doctor?" Nikki wrote Raymond Colabro on her spiral Ampad.

"And a heads-up," Lauren added. "The DNA test is still in process on that blood on Graf's collar."

"What about that little speck you showed me in that vial?"

"As I thought, a flake of leather from a laminate. But it's not consistent with any equipment at Pleasure Bound, including the other studios, or any of the devices in their storage locker. I've ordered more forensic testing to ID its source. When we get a hit, I'll call you." Before she hung up, she added, "And remember, Detective Heat, you show up on my autopsy table? I'll kill you."

———

The first thing the old lady said when she saw Heat was "Good Lord, is that blood?" Heat had managed to do a commendable wet paper towel job on her coat in the precinct restroom but skipped the blouse. Her neck was wrapped by a scarf, and she had her coat fastened all the way up, but some of her collar must have been visible. Mrs. Borelli seemed less put off by the idea of blood and more focused on the laundry mission. "Give me a half hour, I can get that out for you."

Career caregiver, thought Nikki, smiling at her. "Thank you, but I won't be that long." Heat adjusted the scarf to conceal the stain.

When they reached the kitchen, the housekeeper said, "You're going to roast in that coat. If you're leaving it on for me, don't." Nikki kept it on anyway and sat at the table where there was a cup of hot coffee waiting for her and homemade pizzelles resting on the saucer.

Ms. B. still seemed fragile, so the detective decided not to jam her right off about the picture. Instead she began by saying, "I dropped by to see if you can clear something up. Yesterday we collected prescriptions from Father Graf's medicine cabinet, and among them was something called adefovir. What's confusing is he had none in his system and had none of the diseases it would be prescribed for."

"I don't know what he had in that cabinet. I cleaned in there, but personal is personal, and it doesn't get any more so than a medicine chest."

Nikki nibbled a pizzelle. It was extraordinary. If heaven were made of vanilla, that is what it would taste like. For Nikki, this was lunch. She finished it off and said, "I wanted to ask if perhaps the adefovir was yours."

"No. And trust me, last thing I need is another pill to swallow."

"Fine then. As long as I'm here," said Heat, suddenly feeling like her last name should be Columbo—why not? she was certainly wearing the coat—"I want to ask if you had any new thoughts about the pictures I showed you." When the woman shook no, Nikki handed her the photos again and asked her to give them a second look. She cleaned her glasses on her sweater and surveyed them. This time she went through the stack with no reaction to the one she had hesitated over before.

"Sorry," she said and handed the array back across the table. Nikki was trying to figure an approach that wouldn't traumatize her even more, when Mrs. Borelli said, "Oh. I did have one other thing to mention to you. I thought of it this morning and was going to call you, but here you are." She seemed overwhelmed by circumstances. "You asked if Father Gerry had any trouble with anyone."

"Please, go ahead." Nikki flipped to a clean page.

"We had a priest here a while back. There were accusations that he had been . . . improper with two of the altar boys on a weekend field trip. Now, I don't know what happened, and neither did Father Graf, but as the pastor, soon as he heard about it, he did the right thing and reported it immediately to the archdiocese. They transferred Father Shea and started an investigation. But one of the boys' parents, Mr. Hays, filed a lawsuit—which was fine, who wouldn't? But he also harassed Father Graf."

"Harassed how?"

"Phone calls at first, and then showing up here at the rectory, unannounced. He kept getting more and more irate."

"Did he ever get violent or threaten Father Graf?"

Mrs. Borelli tilted her head side to side. "He got loud. Shouted a lot, blaming him for letting it go on, and then accused him of trying to whitewash it. But he never threatened, until about three months ago."

"What did he say, Mrs. Borelli? Did you hear his exact words?"

"I did. It was the one time he didn't shout. He was calm, you know? Scary calm. He said . . . ," the old housekeeper tilted her head back as if reading the words on the ceiling, " '... I'm done talking. Your church may protect you but not from me.' Oh, and he also said, 'You don't know who you're dealing with.' " She watched Heat writing the quotes down then continued. "I apologize for not thinking of it yesterday. Part was because Mr. Hays hasn't been around since then, so I let it go. And also yesterday I was a little, you know..." She said it with a shrug and played with the crucifix around her neck. The poor woman looked drained. Nikki decided to let her rest.

But first she got the name and address of the irate man from the parish registry, as well as the name of the accused priest. At the front door she reassured the housekeeper that she had done the right thing in sharing the information and added pointedly, "It's always helpful to speak up no matter when your memory brings a detail to mind." Then she handed the photo array back to Mrs. Borelli and left.

———

The blue-and-white that had followed her to the rectory was waiting with its engine idling when she came out. Heat walked over to the driver, a mean-looking career uniform whose nickname around the Two-oh was The Discourager because when they posted him at the entrance to crime scenes nobody dared cross the line. "Harvey, don't you have something better to do?" she asked when he powered his window down.

"Captain's orders," he said with a voice accented by sandpaper and gravel.

"I'm heading to the precinct. I'll be taking West End instead of Broadway."

"Don't you worry, Detective, you won't lose me." He said it casually, but the fact was The Discourager was exactly the pit bull you wanted to have your back. She handed him the small bag of pizzelles Mrs. Borelli had given her. When he looked inside it he damn near smiled.

———

Later that afternoon, back in the bull pen, Detective Heat wheeled her chair over from her desk and stared at the Murder Board hoping it would speak to her. It didn't happen in every investigation, but with uncanny frequency, if she was focused enough, quiet enough inside, and alert to the right questions to ask herself, all the disconnected facts—the squiggled notes, the timeline, the victim and suspect photos—they wove together in a harmonious voice that spoke to her of the solution. But they did it on their schedule, not hers.

They weren't ready yet.

"Detective Hinesburg," she said, still facing the board. When she heard the footfalls draw up behind her, Heat stood and pointed to the blue printing that said, "Graf Phone Records." There was no check mark beside the notation. "Wasn't that your assignment?"

"Yeah, well, in case you hadn't noticed, I've got a number of assignments to clear."

"When?" was all Nikki said. It was all she had to. Hinesburg saluted in a way that irritated the piss out of Heat and returned to her desk. Heat turned back to the board, this time not seeing anything on it, just needing someplace to look while she let her temper subside.

Raley hung up his phone and crossed over with the cap of his pen in his teeth and a notepad in his hand. "Got some info on the Mad Dad," he said, referring to the altar boy's irate parent. "Lawrence Joseph Hays. One aggravated assault in '07 against a neighbor with a barking dog, in his neighbor's apartment building. Charges suddenly dropped at the request of the complainant. Doesn't say why."

"That's his only prior?"

"Affirm."

Heat said, "We should pay him a visit this afternoon."

"That'll be tough. I already called his office to set a meet—didn't say why, of course. He's in Ely, Nevada, on business." Before Nikki could ask, he said, "I was wondering where it was, too. Ely's like this teensy dot on the map in the middle of the desert."

"What kind of business is he in?" she asked.

"He's the CEO of Lancer Standard."

"The CIA contractors in Afghanistan?"

"The one and only," said Raley. "Black helicopters, freelance commandos, and saboteurs for hire."

Heat said, "Ely must be their training center."

"I'd tell you you're right, but then I'd have to kill you."

"Hilarious, Rales. Find out when Hays gets back. I want to talk with him myself."

———

Ochoa called in to report that his visit to the domme's roommate was fruitless. "Got here, and she'd cleared out. Building super said she rolled out a couple of suitcases last night."

"Did she leave a forwarding?" asked Heat.

"Not that lucky, I'm afraid. I did call the hotel in Amsterdam her roommate listed with Customs, just in case she knew where she was headed. Front desk says Andrea Boam is still checked in but hasn't been around for two days. He thinks she and some guy hooked up." He chuckled. "Interesting choice of words, considering she's in bondage."

"Nice to know if we don't clear this case, Miguel, at least you've got some material for the Christmas talent show." Heat saw the lights flicker on in Captain Montrose's office and a small butterfly beat its wings in her chest. "Look, I have to go. But Forensics is done with Graf's computer. When you get back, see what you can find on it."

Detective Heat kept herself at a discreet distance but saw that Montrose was back but he wasn't alone. He was behind closed doors with two serious suits she didn't recognize. It did not look like a happy gathering.

———

Later, after they had spent some time going through Father Graf's computer, Roach came over to Heat's desk in tandem. "So what do you make of the suits?" said Ochoa. "Internal Affairs?"

Raley said, "My money's on Men in Black. If there's a big flash of light, put on your sunglasses."

To Nikki, the look and the soberness screamed IA. But there was enough gossip floating around the Twentieth without adding to it, so she kept it on point and asked what they'd learned from the computer. Roach led her to the timeline on the Murder Board. "First thing we learned," said Ochoa, "was that priest needed a new computer. That fossil took ten minutes just to boot. First we opened up his History and Bookmarks."

"Always telling," Raley added.

"Nothing shocking there. A few Catholic sites, Public Television, online booksellers—all mainstream, no erotica. According to his recommendations and recent purchases, he was nuts for mysteries . . ."

". . . Cannell, Connelly, Lehane, Patterson . . ."

"There were other favorite sites," Ochoa continued. "A number of charities and human rights organizations. One Chinese, most Latin American."

Raley said, "That's where we might have some traction. We opened up his Outlook to check his calendar."

"He never used it," Ochoa chimed in.

Raley picked it up with "So we checked out e-mails. He had a message about an urgent meeting from an activist group he was involved with, *Justicia a Guarda*." Nikki's gaze went to the picture at the top of the board, of Graf at the protest rally.

"Literally, 'Justice to Guard,'" translated Ochoa. He pointed to the timeline. "The meeting was ten-thirty the morning he disappeared."

"Right," said Nikki. "The housekeeper said the last time she saw him, Father Graf broke routine and left right after breakfast for somewhere unknown."

"I think now we know," said Raley.

"It took him two hours to get to a meeting? That's another time gap," she said. "Either way, the folks at *Justicia a Guarda* may have been the last to see Father Graf alive. Boys, take the Roach Coach and go see what they know."

Just after 6 P.M., Rook breezed into the bull pen and turned in a circle.
"My God, I have been away too long. It's like coming back to visit my old grammar school. Everything looks smaller."

Nikki rose from her desk and made a quick check of Montrose's office, but he had shut the blinds for his IA meeting long before. "Rook, do you even own a phone?"

"You know, there's a pattern here. Nikki Heat is a woman who doesn't love surprises. Duly noted. Remember that on your thirtieth birthday, OK?"

He held out a garment bag to her. "What's that?" she asked.

"At the risk of offense, another surprise. On the news it looked like you might need a change of clothes. Something a little less, shall we say, Type-A Positive?" He handed her the garment bag by the hanger loop. "There's a Theory store down Columbus. This may be a little stylish for taking down cold-blooded killers, but they'll just have to adjust."

She wanted to hug him but let her grin say it. Then, what the hell, she kissed his cheek. "Thanks. I love surprises."

"Woman, you have my head spinning." He took a seat in his old chair from his ride-along days. "We don't have to go now if you're busy."

"Busy hardly describes it." She looked around to make sure she wasn't broadcasting. "Things are even tougher between me and Montrose." She drew closer and whispered, "He's got Internal Affairs in there for some reason. Plus, I had one of my borrowed detectives from Burglary transfer out today. In a huff."

"Let me guess. Rhymer. What a weasel. I never bought that whole Opie act."

"No, Rhymer's solid. His partner, Gallagher, quit."

"In a snit?"

"Stop it."

"Or I'll get hit?"

"Count on it."

"No . . . kidding?" While they chuckled, his cell phone rang. He made a puzzled look at his caller ID. "Don't let me hold you up, I'll take this." As he left the room, she heard him exclaim, "Oh my God. Is this Tam Svejda, the Czech who loves to bounce?"

––––––

He took Nikki to Bouley in Tribeca, still one of the greatest meals in a city of great meals. Roach phoned just as they were entering, and Heat and Rook stopped while she took their call in the vestibule—not the worst place to wait, surrounded by walls that were decorated by shelves of aromatic fresh apples.

Between drink orders and bread selection she briefed Rook on the main points of the Graf investigation, including some of the problems she was having with Captain Montrose. She left out his link to the old Huddleston case, since even she didn't quite know what to make of it. Plus she was in public. They had an alcove to themselves, but you never knew. He listened intently, and she enjoyed watching him suppress his urge to blurt premature theories based on his writer's imagination instead of facts. He did interrupt when she told him Raley and Ochoa had just left the headquarters of *Justicia a Guarda*.

"Those are militant Marxists," he said. "Not your warm and fuzzy Kumbaya demonstrators at all. A few of them are ex-Colombian FARC rebels who'd be happier with rifles instead of picket signs."

"I'll have to look into that part," and Heat got out her notepad. "Roach says, according to the office staff there, Father Graf was a staunch supporter of their cause, and they're mourning him. Even though one of the leaders threw him out of the meeting the other morning when he showed up drunk." She pondered a Graf connection with armed rebels. "How violent are they, I mean here in New York?"

"Probably no more than, say, the IRA back in The Troubles." He tore off a piece of raisin bread. "They're fresh on my mind because

I witnessed some assault rifles and grenade launchers being delivered to them in Colombia."

"Rook, you were in Colombia?"

"You'd know that if you ever asked me how my month was." He dabbed a fake tear from his eye with his napkin. Then he grew pensive. "Do you know Faustino Velez Arango?"

"Sure, the dissident writer who disappeared."

"*Justicia a Guarda* are the dudes whose small army broke him out of his political prison and snuck him underground last fall. If your priest was mixed up with those guys, I'd start taking a hard look at them."

Nikki finished her cosmo. "You had me worried, Rook. I thought we were going to go the whole night without a wild, half-baked theory."

On their walk back to his loft it had warmed just enough for rain to mix with the ice pellets. The cruiser that was following them pulled alongside, and The Discourager lowered the passenger window. "You two sure you won't take a ride?" She thanked him and waved it off. Heat could accept protection, but not a chauffeur.

She opened a bottle of wine while he flipped on the eleven o'clock news. The reporter live on the scene of a manhole explosion in the East Village said, "When the rain came down, it washed road salt away and it corroded a junction box, causing the blowout."

"And the itsy bitsy spider went up in about a gazillion pieces," said Rook. Nikki handed him his glass, then killed the TV during the teaser for the shooting in Brooklyn Heights. "I can't believe you don't want to see it. Do you know what some people do just to get on the news?"

"I lived it all day," she said, slipping off her shoes. "I don't need to see it at night." He opened his arms wide, and Nikki nestled herself into him on the sofa, burying her nose into the open throat of his shirt, breathing him in.

"How are you going to work things out with Montrose?"

"Hell if I know." She sat up, cross-legged on the cushion beside him, taking a sip of her wine and resting her palm on his thigh. "I don't even know what to make of him, he's so not Montrose to me. The attitude, and the behavior—that's the tough thing. Searching the rectory, roadblocking my case. I don't get it."

"Or is it that you do get it and you're afraid of what it might mean?"

She nodded, more to herself than to him, and said, "I thought I knew him."

"That's not the issue. Do you trust him? That's what's important." He took a sip, and when she didn't answer, he said, "It's like I said last night. You never really know someone. I mean really, do I know you? How well do you know me?"

Tam Svejda, the bouncing Czech, came to her mind. Again. "Right. I guess you can't know everything about someone. How can you?"

"You're a cop. You could interrogate me."

She laughed. "Is that what you want, Rook? For me to grill you? Break out the rubber hose?"

He jumped to his feet. "Stay right there. You gave me an idea." He went to his reading nook to the side of the living room. From behind the bookcases, she heard keystrokes and then a printer fire up. He returned with some pages. "Ever read *Vanity Fair*?"

"Yeah. Mostly for the ads."

"On the back page each month they interview a celebrity using a standard questionnaire they call The Proust Interview. It comes from a parlor game that was all the rage back in Marcel Proust's era as a way for party guests to get to know each other. I guess this was pre–Dance Dance Revolution. Proust didn't invent it, he was just the most famous one to play it. This is a version floating on the Internet." He held up his pages with a sly grin. "Wanna play?"

"I'm not so sure. What kind of questions are they?"

"Revealing, Nikki Heat. Revealing of who you truly are." She reached for the pages but he pulled them back. "No previews."

"What if I don't want to answer some of them?" she asked.

"Hmm." He tapped the rolled pages against his chin. "Tell you what. You can skip answering any question if . . . you take off an article of clothing."

"You're kidding. You mean like strip poker?"

"Even better. It's strip Proust!"

She mulled it over and said, "Shoes off, Rook. If we're going to do this, we're going to start even."

"All right, here we go." He flattened the pages on his thigh and read, " 'Who is your favorite author or authors?' " Nikki blew an exhale and frowned, thinking. Rook said, "Playing for your blouse. No pressure."

"I'll go with two. Jane Austen and Harper Lee." And then she said, "You have to answer, too."

"Sure, no problem. I'll say a certain Charles Dickens and toss in Dr. Hunter S. Thompson." He went back to the pages. " 'Name your favorite hero in literature.' "

Heat reflected and shrugged. "Odysseus."

"Mine, too," said Rook. "Pinkie pull." He held out his little finger and she hooked hers onto it and they tugged and laughed. "Nobody gettin' nekkid yet. Try this. 'Who is your favorite poet?' "

"Keats," she answered. For 'Ode on a Grecian Urn.' "

Rook replied, "Seuss. For 'One Fish, Two Fish.' " He went back to the page for his next question. " 'How do you wish to die?' " They both looked at each other. Then Nikki took off her blouse. He had similar sentiments and took off his sweater.

"I told you I may not want to answer some of these."

"And therein lies the game, Detective Heat. Moving on to " 'What musician has impacted your life the most?' "

"Most impactful musician . . . ," she said, pondering. "Chumbawamba."

"You're kidding. Not Bono? Or Sting, or Alanis Morissette, or— really? Chumbawamba? *Tubthumping* Chumbawamba?"

"As a matter of fact, yes. When my high school drama coach told me a freshman couldn't play Christine in *Phantom*, a song about getting knocked down and getting up again resonated very strongly with me." Still does, she thought. "What about you?"

"Steely Dan for 'Deacon Blues.' And James Taylor for everything, especially 'Secret O' Life.'" Then Rook palmed his forehead, "Oh, oh, no, wait! I forgot AC/DC."

Heat made a buzzer sound. "Ambivalent reply, Rook. Points off, pants off." After he complied, he looked at the questionnaire, made a little head shake, and turned to the next page.

"Whoa, whoa, penalty flag," Nikki said. "You can't skip questions, let's hear it."

He shuffled back and read, "'What qualities do you look for in a woman?'" Rook paused. "Minefield, I'm not answering that." After she made him take off his shirt, he said, "This is not how I saw this game going," and he turned to the top of the next page. "Payback time. 'What qualities do you look for in a man?'"

"I can answer that. Honesty. And a sense of humor."

"Uncanny how I have the quality of being both honest and funny. Like if you asked me about your clothes and said, 'Hey. Does this blood make my ass look fat?' I'd tell ya."

"Are you stalling because you're losing?"

"Fine." Next he read, "'Who would you have liked to be?' All right, I'm going to answer this one first. A backup singer for Aretha Franklin. The sequined dress could be an issue, but that would be my other life. You? Who would you be?"

She didn't hesitate. "Meryl Streep." He gave her a sympathetic look because they both knew she gave up her theater major when her mother was killed.

"Moving on. 'What is your present state of mind?'"

All Heat could do was think about the turmoil she was experiencing. She didn't answer and took her slacks off.

"My state of mind . . . ?" said Rook. "The Strip Proust tide is turning. Yay! Next question: 'What is your idea of misery?'"

"Pass. I don't like how these questions are going." As she unhooked her bra and set it on the coffee table, she said, "You have to answer, too, Chuck Woolery."

"Simple. Misery for me is what I felt after I hurt you by not calling after my trip."

"To coin a phrase, good answer," said Nikki. "Next?"

"Let's see . . . 'What is your motto?'" He dropped his head. "I don't have a motto. Who has a motto?"

"You've got a choice, underpants or socks."

"There. *That's* my new motto."

"Nice try," she said.

He slid out of his underwear, leaving his socks on. "Take that, Spitzer."

"I actually do have a motto," said Heat. "It's 'Never forget who you work for.'" And as she voiced the words, Nikki felt a creeping unease. It wasn't exactly shame, but it was close. For the first time it sounded hollow. Fake. Why? She examined herself, trying to see what was different. The stress, that was new. And when she looked at that, she recognized that the hardest part of her day lately was working to avoid confrontation with Captain Montrose. That's when it came to her. In that moment, sitting nearly naked in Rook's living room, playing some silly nineteenth-century parlor game, she came to an unexpected insight. In that moment Nikki woke up and saw with great clarity who she had become—and who she had stopped being. Without noticing it, Heat had begun seeing herself as working for her captain and had lost sight of her guiding principle, that she worked for the victim.

Right then Nikki resolved to call her own meeting with Montrose first thing the next day. And let the damned chips fall.

"Hello?" said Rook, bringing her back. "Ready for the next one?" She looked on him with clear eyes and nodded. "Here we go then. 'What is your ideal dream of earthly happiness?'"

Heat paused only a moment to think. Then she said nothing, but stood and slid out of her panties. Rook looked up to her from the couch with a face that she couldn't resist, so she didn't. She bent down, taking his mouth in hers. He met her hungrily and pulled Nikki into his arms. Soon, the rhythm of their bodies answered that last question. She didn't think about it but found her lips to his ear, whispering, "This . . . This . . . This . . ."

SIX

At eight the next morning Nikki sat at a window table at EJ's Luncheonette, blowing on her large coffee and waiting for Lauren Parry to pick up her phone. Instead of corporate jazz or Soft Hits of the Eighties and Nineties, the programming for anyone stuck on hold at OCME was a loop of short messages about New York City's municipal opportunities and services. Rather than Seal's "Kiss from a Rose" or Shania Twain's "Man! I Feel Like a Woman!" the mayor invited you to call 3-1-1 for all your information needs and some monotone DOT administrator extolled the virtues of Alternate Day, Alternate Side Parking. Where were Annie Lennox's "Sweet Dreams" when you needed them?

"I have a question for you," said Heat when Lauren finally came on the line. In the background she could hear the snap of gloves and the lid of a metal pail clanging open against a wall. "It's about that bruise on Father Graf's lower back. You recall it?"

"Of course. What about it?"

It had come to her in bed with Rook—appropriately enough—at dawn. Heat had been sleepless, mulling the confrontation she planned to bring to her captain in the coming hours. Next to her, Rook turned onto his side and Nikki rolled to face his back, using her fingertips to comb down the sprung hairs on his cowlick. He looked thinner to her than when he had left. His shoulder muscles revealed more cording, and even in the waxy light his ribs were defined by deeper shadows between them. Her eyes traced his vertebrae to the small of his back, where she saw the fading bruise. While they were drying each other from their shower, she asked him where he got it.

Rook told her that two weeks before, he had ridden by cargo ship from Rijeka, on the Adriatic, to Monrovia on the West African coast, where he witnessed what he considered a brazen daylight offload of black market arms. The dealer, who was on the wharf to supervise the transfer of thirty tons of AK-47 rounds, plus crates of grenade launchers, onto waiting trucks, kept glancing up from his Range Rover to the ship's navigation tower, where Rook was lurking, trying to be inconspicuous. But after the convoy lumbered off the pier, Rook went below to his crew quarters, only to be grabbed by three of the dealer's goons. They put a hood over his head and drove him for over an hour, to a plantation in the hills. There, they removed the sack but handcuffed him while he waited, locked in an empty horse stall in the barn.

At nightfall, he was taken to the great lawn beside the yellow plantation house, where the arms dealer, a former MI6 operative named—or at least using the name—Gordon McKinnon, was at a picnic table tossing back Caipirinhas under strings of fiesta lights shaped like red chili peppers. Rook decided not to let on how much he knew about McKinnon from his research . . . that the former British SIS man had amassed a fortune brokering black market weapons to embargoed nations in Africa . . . that the blood flow from Angola, Rwanda, the Congo, and recently Sudan could be traced to the drunken, sunburned, ginger-haired man right before him.

"Have a seat, Jameson Rook," he said, and gestured to a wooden stool across the table. "Oh, come on. I knew it was you when you boarded in Croatia." Rook sat but didn't speak. "Call me Gordy." Then he laughed, and added, "But I guess you damn well know that already, don't you? Huh, am I right?" He slid a tall glass across the rough timber to him. "Drink up, it's the best fucking Caipirinha on this whole fucking continent. Both my bartender and my cachaça are flown in from Brazil." Maybe he was too drunk to remember his guest's hands were cuffed behind him and he couldn't reach his glass.

"I read all your stuff. Not bad. Bono and Mick. Bill Clinton. Well done. But come on, Tony fuckin' Blair? And Aslan Maskhadov?

I've damn sure got more going than that bollocks you wrote about the damn Chechen. Maskhadov, hah! Only regret is I didn't sell the grenade that killed him." He tilted his glass back and some of it sloshed down his face onto his Ed Hardy shirt. His barkeep replaced the glass with a fresh one, and he continued, "Hey now, bottoms up. This is your last drink."

And then he stood, pointing the biggest handgun Rook had ever seen, an Israeli Desert Eagle .50-caliber, right at him. But then he pivoted, sighting to the left, firing into the night. The thunderclap report of the Eagle was followed immediately by hissing and a white-hot glow that filled the grounds with the brightness of frozen lightning. Rook turned to look behind him. In the searing brilliance he could see magnesium flares lined up along the fence posts across the great lawn. McKinnon fired again. His bullet struck another flare, which sparked to life, huffing and fizzing as it spun off the fence into a pasture, illuminating fleeing horses and a pair of Gulfstream IVs parked in the distance.

The arms dealer raised both fists in the air and war whooped to the Liberian sky. He polished off his drink and said in a hoarse voice, "Know what I love? Rockin' my own life. Did you know I have enough bloody cash to buy my own country?" Then he laughed. "Oh, wait, I already did! Are you aware, Rook, I have been given— are you ready for this?—diplomatic immunity? They made me minister of some shite or other here. Truly. I do what I want and nobody can touch me."

He brought up the Desert Eagle and stepped closer, training it on Rook again. "This is what happens when you poke it where it doesn't belong."

Rook stared into the gaping muzzle and said, "What was it that I rode up here in, a Range Rover? Have your valet pull it back up. Think I'm ready to go." McKinnon jerked his hand to menace him with the gun. "Put that damn thing away, you're not going to shoot me."

"No? What makes you think so?"

"Because you would have done it back in port and left me floating out to the Canary Islands. Because you put on this whole . . . show for me. Because if you kill me, who will write your story, Gordon? That's what you want, isn't it? Of course it is. And you gave me some great quotes. 'Rocking your life'? 'Minister of some shite'? Brilliant. It's tough to be a bad boy and have no fan club, isn't it? You didn't bring me here to kill me, you brought me here to make you a legend."

McKinnon rushed up to Rook, locking his elbow around his neck. "What's with you? Do you have some fascination with death that makes you think you can tease me? Huh? Huh?" He pressed the muzzle against his temple and stared at Rook with wild eyes dancing with the mad light of devil fire from the flares.

Rook sighed and said, "Still waiting for that Range Rover."

McKinnon set the gun on the table then pushed Rook backward off his stool onto the stone patio, where he landed hard on his hand-cuffs.

In the time it took Detective Heat to walk from EJ's on Amster-dam to the sidewalk in front of the precinct, Lauren Parry had called her back. "I just checked the photo of the bruise. It definitely could be from handcuffs. I'll do a test but hinged cuffs would definitely account for the ladder-shaped bruise at the small of his back." Then she asked, "What do you suppose it means?"

Heat said, "It means we hope it means something."

———

Captain Montrose told her he was busy when she knocked on the door frame and said she needed to talk with him. Heat came in anyway and pulled the knob behind her until it clicked. He looked up at her from some printouts. "I said I was busy."

"I said I needed to talk." Detective Heat, the immovable object.

Montrose stared at her from under a thick hedge of furrowed brow. "This is what my life's come to. Numbers. First they criticize my stats, telling me to step it up, pay my rent. Now they're sending me these." The captain lifted the thick spreadsheet off his blotter and let it drop with unmasked contempt. "Target numbers. Micromanaging me. Telling me how many Class C violations to write up this week for blocking sidewalks and littering. Class B summonses, too. Let's see . . ." He ran his finger along a row. "They want eight seat belt violations and six cell phone tickets. Not five, not seven. Six.

"I don't make my numbers, they do a number on me. So what's my choice, fluff my books? Do I tell the uniforms not to take certain robbery or assault reports so the stats don't work against me? If it doesn't get written down, it never happened. What do you know, a crime drop in the Twentieth!" He capped his highlighter and tossed it on the desk. It rolled onto the floor, but he made no attempt to stop it. "If you're determined to interrupt me, sit down." She took one of the guest chairs and he said, "So how are you going to brighten my already perfect day?"

Nikki knew where to begin. With her goal, simply stated so it wouldn't get lost. She said, "I want to open the Graf case wider."

"Did you complete the BDSM checks like I told you?"

"Not yet, but—"

He cut her off. "Then this meeting is over."

"Captain, with due respect, we're chasing a foul ball. Promising leads are surfacing and I feel hamstrung not being able to follow them."

"Such as?"

"OK," she said, "the money stashed in those cookie tins. Why would you tell me not to reach out to the archdiocese right away?"

"Because it's not relevant."

Nikki was struck by his sense of certainty. "How can you know that?"

"Are you questioning the judgment of your commander?"

"It's a legitimate question, sir." She made the "sir" carry respect. Nikki wanted her case back, not for him to dig in his heels to prove his rank.

"Your vic was killed in a bondage dungeon—work it."

"This feels like a roadblock."

"I said work it."

She decided to move along, hoping to find an open flank. "I also have a shooting victim with a connection to the priest."

"And to your negligence for not reporting the tail."

To Nikki this began feeling like her jujitsu sparring matches with Don. She raised a fact, the captain threw a feint. Heat didn't take his bait. "We can discuss that later, but let's not get sidetracked. Father Graf had the phone number of that strip club hidden in his room. Eyewitnesses saw him fighting with the dancer. I want to work that angle, but you have my investigation corralled."

"You'll make a fine lieutenant in this department," he said. "You're already learning how to shift blame."

"Excuse me, but I am doing exactly the opposite. I'm taking responsibility. I want you to let me run my case my way." Since Nikki had made up her mind the night before to reclaim her sense of mission, she pressed onward, making her scariest leap. . . . She addressed the elephant. "What is going on with you, Captain?"

He poked his finger hard enough on the spreadsheet to dimple it. "You know damn well what's going on with me."

"I wish I did. I get the pressure," she said, "I do. But there's a lot of other stuff I don't get. Things I've observed. Things I've learned. And, frankly, it worries me."

There was a sea change in that room. Her skipper's anger and irritation gave way to a steely wariness. He studied her with an intense concentration that made Nikki uncomfortable. His head was glistening, and behind him on the window that gave onto the street she noticed an aura of condensation forming on the glass, probably from his elevated body heat. It outlined Montrose like his own ghost. "Learned, like what?" he said.

Her tongue felt like it had a sock on it. "Your search of the rectory the night of Graf's killing, for instance."

"Asked and answered already." His voice was chillingly calm and his face had taken on a flat affect. "If you have more, let's hear it. Is there more?"

"Captain, let's not go down this road right now."

"What road? The one that leads to you implying I had something to do with his death?" Under his measured tone Nikki could sense the next wave of anger building pressure. "Is that what you think?"

When she hesitated, the interrogator in him kicked in. Nikki had always been impressed by how intimidating her mentor could be working a suspect against the ropes. Except now it was all on her. "You're already knee-deep, Detective, so you'd better bring it— unless you want to go on the record in a formal conduct review."

Heat ran down the short list in her mind. She looked at the fresh Band-Aid on his finger and pictured the blood on the priest's collar. Then she thought of the TENS scars on Graf and how similar electrical burns had also appeared in the 2004 case Montrose had investigated. And now the latest revelation, that the bruise on the small of the priest's back came from handcuffs . . . Yes, these raised lots of questions, and Nikki didn't like the way the scale was tipping as she weighed them. However, none of these proved anything. And she certainly couldn't voice them. Not without mortally wounding an already frail relationship. So she said, "Nothing worth discussing."

He slapped the palm of his hand on the desk and she jumped. "Liar!" In her periphery, Nikki saw heads in the bull pen turn their way. "It's all over you. Come on, Detective, lay 'em on the table. Or are you saving it for your new friends at 1PP?"

"Captain . . . no, I . . ." She trailed off, on the defensive now.

"Oh, or maybe you're holding it for the next article." He read her reaction and said, "You haven't seen it yet?" He reached to his briefcase and pulled out the morning edition of the *Ledger*. "Metro section, page three." He tossed the newspaper on the desk right in front of her. It was folded open to the story, a short item headlined, UPHEAVAL AT UPPER WEST SIDE PRECINCT. Reported by Tam Svejda. "You still claim you didn't talk to that reporter?"

"I didn't."

"Somebody did. And gave her details, including Gallagher bailing in frustration. I wonder who."

Rook's phone call from the bouncing Czech played itself back, but Nikki dismissed it as a possibility. There was no way she could imagine him doing that. "I have no idea."

"Bullshit."

"Captain, whatever else is going on here, I hope you know . . ."

But he stopped her, holding out the palm of his hand in the gulf between them. "We're done," he said. There was a gravity, a global finality in the weight of his words. Montrose stood. She sat looking up at him. How had this meeting slipped out of her grasp? Nikki had only wanted one thing when she walked in there, and it had dissolved in the toxic haze. "And if you have anything to discuss about this case, you bring it to me, not reporters, and especially not the sharks downtown. Tempting as it is to go polishing that gold bar, remember, you work for me."

"You don't need to tell me who I work for." Heat rose to face him, feeling herself reclaiming lost meaning from a mislaid motto. "There's a killer out there, and for the sake of his victim, I want to catch him."

"Damn it, Heat, not every victim is your mother."

Her old friend might as well have slapped her face. He knew her vulnerability, and that stung her all the more. But she didn't back off. Nikki absorbed it and spoke her guiding truth. "No, but every victim is somebody else's mother. Or their father, or daughter. A son, or a wife."

"I'm telling you. This time, let go of this."

She said, "If you know anything about me, you know I am not going to lie down."

"I could fire you."

"You'll have to." And then, as turnabout, she dealt him his own vulnerability card. "How will you explain that downtown? Because you must know I'm not the only one asking these questions."

His jaw muscles flexed. He tilted his head to her, leveling a challenge. "Are you saying I can't stop you?"

"You can't." Heat returned his stare, unblinking. "Make your call, Captain."

He pondered a moment. Then, unhappy but resigned, he said, "Go ahead then." And as she turned to go, he said, "Detective Heat. Watch your back. You may be poking into something you wish you had never gotten into."

On her walk across the bull pen, Hinesburg said, "Detective Heat, you got a sec?"

"Actually, Sharon, not the best time."

"I think you should make time." There was something in the way Hinesburg presented herself that felt different. The bluff of arrogance was muted. Replaced by an uncharacteristic urgency.

"All right. What is it?"

In answer Detective Hinesburg handed Nikki photocopies of Father Graf's phone records. There weren't many calls over the month, so Heat was able to scan the pages quickly. She stopped abruptly, however, when she hit the last page, covering the prior week . . . the one before Father Graf was killed. There were numerous calls to and from two phone numbers Heat recognized—because she had called them so often herself. They were the office and cell phone numbers of Captain Montrose.

Heat looked up from the page to his office. He was standing at the glass wall looking at her. Just as they made eye contact, Montrose snapped his blinds shut.

———

In fewer than five minutes Nikki had assembled her squad at the Murder Board. Detective Heat moved quickly before the captain had a change of heart about breaking the restraints he had placed on her investigation. She also wanted to energize her people by illustrating that this was a new day.

The revelation about Montrose showing up on the victim's phone records was huge, but Heat decided not to bring it up at an open meeting. She had collected the file from Hinesburg and told her that she would take it from there. It would mean another confrontation, but the captain had already turned off his lights and left, so it would have to come upon his return. As painful as the meeting with her embattled commander had just been, her next session could make that one look like high tea.

They all took notes while she reported that the bruise on Father Graf's lower back had likely been caused by handcuffs. "Isn't that consistent with the whole bondage-torture deal?" asked Rhymer.

"Could be," said Heat. "It could also be the best evidence that he was brought there against his will." Ochoa raised a forefinger. "Question, Miguel?"

"He was a big drinker. Plastered the morning he disappeared, according to his activist group. Have we checked records to see if he got cuffed for a Drunk and Disorderly over the last few days?"

"Good thought," Nikki said. "Sharon, when you get with RTCC on that snake tattoo, ask them to run this week's ten-fifty complaints and see if Graf shows up."

She assigned Ochoa to look up Dr. Colabro about the mysterious prescription. "Then I want you and Rales to make another visit to *Justicia a Garda*. I hear they have paramilitary connections. Find out who their leaders are and invite them in for a chat. Use the waiting room instead of Interrogation. I don't want them treated like suspects, but I want them on our turf, in a formal setting."

She put Detective Hinesburg on the found money from the rectory attic. "Reach out to Forensics and hustle along a complete workup on that cash. Everything. And Sharon? Like yesterday." Hinesburg arched a brow, taking that like the shot it was. Nikki couldn't give a rat's ass. She continued, "I want to pay a visit to the archdiocese later today to ask them if they had any accounting concerns from Our Lady of the Innocents. So whatever you can get before I go—get.

"Rhymer. You're off dommes. Dig into Horst Meuller. He's able to speak this morning, so I'm going to make a hospital call. Meanwhile, you learn all you can. Obviously any more on his connection to Graf, but also work history, financial, any connection to Pleasure Bound . . . Also run him through Interpol and Hamburg police."

Rhymer dotted a sentence on his pad and said, "Nice to see we're moving out of the horse latitudes."

"You and me both," she said. "Tell your pal Gallagher. If he wants to come back, I can let bygones be bygones."

———

From where she stood looking out a tenth-floor window of New York Downtown Hospital, Nikki could pick out the spot across the East River where the shooting had taken place the day before. A low range of buildings south of the Brooklyn Bridge blocked her street-level view of the exact location on Henry, but on their far side she was able to pinpoint the high-rise where it all went down. Ragged, bruisey clouds streaming trails of snow and frozen rain gobbled the top of the apartment building as she watched, darkening the neighborhood until it disappeared in a curtain of foul weather.

"Excuse me?" Nikki turned. A male nurse with a youthful face and surfer dude curls was smiling at her. "Are you waiting for Dr. Armani?"

"Yes, I'm Detective Heat."

He took a step closer and his smile widened. Nikki thought he had the most brilliant teeth she had seen since the Dawn of Bieber. "I'm Craig." He gave her a quick head-to-toe that was approving yet somehow not creepy. She bet Nurse Craig got laid a lot. "Dr. Armani is stuck on rounds. We're a teaching hospital, you know, and she is, well, she is definitely not one to be hurried." Craig said it with the intimacy of a patient lover.

"How long will she be?"

"If I had a nickel . . . But good news, she told me to personally escort you to Mr. Meuller's room." He flashed his teeth again. "My lucky day."

The uniform outside the door rose from his metal folding chair when Heat approached. She gestured for him to sit and he did. The detective turned to her guide and said, "I can take it from here."

"Craig," he answered.

Nikki said, "Yeah, I got that," and that seemed to please him no end. He walked on but not without a turn back to wave before he rounded the corner.

The dancer had his eyes locked on her the moment she entered the room. Because of his wound he couldn't turn his head, so Heat stopped at the foot of his bed to help him out. "How are you feeling?" He croaked out something she couldn't make out. Either it was in German, or the thick bandages framing his jaw made it hard for him to talk. "You got lucky, Horst. An inch or two lower, you wouldn't be here."

Heat had been briefed on the phone by his surgeon. The bullet had completely blown out his trapezius muscle but missed the carotid artery. If the shot had come from above, say from a rooftop or balcony, instead of from a car window, the trajectory would have been downward with fatal consequences.

"Lucky?" he said. "You break my collarbone and now this." Meuller paused and pushed the morphine button connected to his drip. "My dancing career is over. What do I do now?"

"You talk," she said. "Why did you run from us?"

"Who says I was?"

"Horst, you rappelled three stories down a scaffolding to get away. Why?" He couldn't turn away so he looked up at the ceiling. "Any idea who would want to shoot you?" He kept his gaze fixed above her. "Tell me about Father Graf."

"Who?"

"This man." She held the picture above him so he had to see it. "Father Gerald Graf." He pursed his lips and did a mild head shake, which obviously pained him. "Eyewitnesses saw you fighting with the priest at One Hot Mess. The bouncer intervened when you tried to choke him. You also threatened to kill him."

"I don't recall." With the accent, it came off sounding like Sergeant Schultz's "I know nuh-think" from *Hogan's Heroes*. And about as credible.

"I'm asking because he is dead now. Choked." She omitted the other details, holding them for corroboration, in case he decided to confess. "Is that why you ran, because you killed him?" He pressed his morphine button repeatedly and turned his eyes upward again. "Let's walk it back. What was your relationship with Father Graf?"

This time he closed his eyes. And kept them closed, the corners of his lids twitching from the effort to shut her out. "You rest up, Mr. Meuller. You'll need it. I'll be back to talk later."

Nurse Craig was fussing with meds on a cart outside the door, pretending he wasn't waiting for Nikki. "I'll be seeing you again, I hope," he said.

"Never know, Craig, it's a small hospital."

He looked around, flunking the irony test. Then he gestured toward the elevators and walked with her. "Sometimes I think maybe I should do some professional dancing." Nikki gave him a side glance and, even in the scrubs, figured he could.

"I hear there's big money for male nurses at bachelorette parties," she said and pushed the down button, hoping the car would arrive soon.

"Maybe. Wouldn't want to do the clubs, though. After seeing that guy, the stripper pole is bad for you."

"How?"

"I had to sponge bathe him this morning. You wouldn't believe all the scars. Looks like rope burns all over his legs and chest."

The elevator doors opened, but Heat didn't get on. "Show me."

Detective Heat didn't wait to get back to the Two-oh to deal with the discovery of TENS burns on the dancer. She got off the FDR at the 61st Street exit and took First Avenue uptown. At the first stoplight, she speed-dialed Captain Montrose's direct line. Four rings in, she could picture the lonely light blinking in the dark office, and sure enough, it dumped to voice mail. Nikki left her name and the time only, trying to keep the tightness out of her voice. She knew she would have to address his numbers on the priest's phone records, but she had planned that for the end of shift, when the office had cleared. But finding those marks from electrical burns on Meuller forced her hand. It was time to ask him about the Huddleston murder he had handled back in 2004. Heat didn't know its relevance, but experience had made her wary of coincidences.

Lost in thought, turning left onto 79th, she ran the tail end of the yellow and immediately saw police lights in her rearview mirror. For a split second her heart jumped—even cops get a *klong* if they think they're going to get ticketed—but it was The Discourager alerting traffic that he was shaving the light with her. He pulled his cruiser beside her at the next stop and she powered her window down. A mix of sleet and snow hit her sleeve. "Don't worry about me," he said, "I've got life insurance."

"Just keeping you on your toes, Harvey," she said with a laugh and pulled away. One more Montrose attempt. Nikki tried his cell. It didn't even ring, but went straight to voice mail. Heat left another brief message and tossed her phone on the passenger seat. She'd try again in five minutes, back at her desk.

She crossed Fifth Avenue for her cut across Central Park, taking the Transverse. As always, Nikki's gaze drifted to the right for an appreciative glimpse of one of her favorite buildings in the city, the Metropolitan. On that raw winter's day it looked to her like a brooding hulk, damp and icebound, hibernating among bare trees of a mean winter. The blare of car horns brought her to the rearview, where she saw a white step van, tagged with graffiti, lurch to a stop across the road behind her, blocking it. More horns. Then she could hear the double chirp of a siren and The Discourager's command voice on his PA. "Move the vehicle . . . now."

The 79th Street Transverse is a two-lane road cut like a narrow canyon ten feet below ground level across Central Park. An urban compromise, its submersion allows traffic to flow without spoiling the view. As the street lost elevation descending beneath the park's East Drive, Heat entered the shelter of the underpass and the Crown Victoria's wiper blades chattered across the dry windshield. As she emerged, a loud pop echoed in the tunnel and her steering wheel lurched in her hands. Not a flat tire, she thought. But instantly came another series of pops, and the rear of the car fishtailed in the slush. She took her foot off the gas and corrected as best she could on the icy road, but without air in any of her tires, it was more like skating than driving. Her car slid sideways until the front end smacked hard into the wall of rocks lining the road. At impact, Nikki lurched against her seat belt, and papers, pens, her cell phone—everything loose in the car—flew. Shook up but unhurt, Heat couldn't figure how she got four flat tires. She craned to look behind her. Since her car was diagonally across the road, she had to look through the rear side passenger window. Just as she made out the traffic spike strip lying across the underpass, the back window exploded. A bullet struck the side of her headrest, ripping it off the seat and shattering the driver's window beside her.

Nikki dove, flattening herself as far down as she could, clawing the two-way out of its bracket. "One-Lincoln-Forty, ten-thirteen, officer needs help, Seventy-ninth Transverse at East Drive, shots fired." She unkeyed the mic and listened. Nothing. She tried again. "One-Lincoln-Forty, ten-thirteen, Seventy-ninth Transverse at East Drive, shots fired, do you copy?" Silence. She was groping on the floor trying to find her cell phone when another bullet tore through the seat back and into the dashboard just above her head. If the shooter was a professional, the next one would be lower. She had to get out of that car, fast.

The angle of the skid worked in her favor; the driver's side door was away from the direction of the shots. She threw herself out onto the icy, wet pavement and rolled under the car door to shelter herself behind the front tire and the engine block. That's when the third bullet fractured the steering wheel.

With four flats the Crown Vic sat low enough that she could lie prone and get a view without having to gopher up and make herself a target. Heat drew her Sig Sauer and pressed her cheek down against the slush. Behind her in the underpass an SUV idled. Not the graphite gray, this one was navy blue. In the dimness of the tunnel, it was impossible to see how many there were. The driver's door stood open with the window down, so her guess was that the driver was also the shooter, using the window frame as a brace. She made a quick clock of the street behind her and got a bad feeling. There was no oncoming traffic. The Transverse cut across Central Park, connecting two busy avenues. The only way there could be no cars was if somehow both ends of the road had been blocked.

There was movement at the SUV when she looked back. A glint—probably reflection off a scope—shimmered briefly in the open window of the driver's door. Heat made an isosceles brace, pressed the butt of her gun on the ground, and squeezed. The sound was deafening as her shot reverberated under the chassis. Nikki didn't wait to see if she hit him. She was still smelling cordite as she duckwalked away, keeping the Crown Vic between herself and the SUV.

After twenty yards, the road curved and she was able to jog upright. The same high wall that trapped her down in canyon of the Transverse was serving as cover. Behind her she could hear the growl of the SUV engine and then a brief squeak of brakes. Her abandoned car was diagonally across the lane and would have to be moved unless the shooter wanted to chance coming on foot.

Nikki stepped up her pace, wishing to hell she had located her cell phone. She arrived at a point where the curve that had concealed her began to straighten out. She slowed to a walk and then stopped before rounding the bend and risking exposure. Lying down in the slush and pressing herself against the icy rocks of the wall, she crawled forward until she had a view of the straightaway.

What Heat saw chilled her more than the ice she was lying in. A hundred yards out, three men in ski masks and hooded rain gear were slowly walking a line across the road toward her. They all held rifles.

SEVEN

For Nikki Heat everything became about calculations. Panic had no place except to get her killed. As odds go, they sucked, but keeping her head would make the most of them. The TOs at every combat survival course she had ever taken had all drilled the same message. Put fear in your back pocket and train yourself to rely on your training. Assess, calculate, seek opportunity, act.

Her rapid assessment was simple: She was in the worst possible tactical position, trapped on a walled subterranean road midpoint between one shooter in a vehicle coming up behind her and three riflemen advancing on foot ahead of her. Heat's next appraisal was bleaker. There was an experienced air about the three men she was watching come toward her. They walked at an unhurried pace, with a military demeanor, weapons at the ready—alert but not tense. These were professionals who would not be fooled or spooked.

As they advanced three abreast, spanning the width of the road, she calculated her chances of putting a shot in each, left to right, from a distance of a hundred yards. *Pop, pop,* and *pop.* But while Heat weighed the riskiness of pulling off three successive kill shots with a handgun, they adjusted, as if reading her mind, to form a single file close to the wall and that opportunity evaporated. Nikki crawled backward before they could see her.

Around the curve behind her, she heard a revving engine and metal on metal as the SUV pushed her abandoned car out of the way. The sound was terrorizing in its implications. So she fought her fear and assessed. It meant that the shooter would come in the SUV, not on foot. What else? That he was probably alone. If he wasn't, his partner would have just driven her car out of the way for him.

Calculations: At pace, the three on foot would be there in twenty seconds. Sooner for the SUV.

Nikki looked upward, her eyes stinging from the sleet fall. The wall was about ten feet high, about the same as an average home ceiling. Leafless branches from park shrubs drooped down about two feet. She holstered her Sig, pulled her gloves out of her coat pockets, and started to climb.

The spaces between the rocks were barely wide enough for her to get a toehold, but she managed to find enough bite to boost herself up on her right foot and finger claw the rock above her head with her left hand. She reached up with her right for a jutting edge above, and in the transfer of weight, her shoe lost its grip on the icy rock and she landed on all fours on the frozen, soupy roadway.

Ten seconds lost.

Ten seconds until the three shooters rounded the bend and saw her.

The engine of the SUV stopped revving and purred. It was coming her way. Nikki was caught in a classic pincer movement.

Even if she were able to climb the ice-glazed rocks, there was no way to do it in ten seconds. With no opportunity to act upon, she made her own. In a split second of computing odds and physics, Detective Heat created what her training officers called a SWAG plan—acronym for Scientific Wild Ass Guess. She drew her weapon and started running toward the SUV.

The driver would be looking for her, so she had to come at him unexpectedly enough to startle and quick enough not to be a target. The midday overcast was so gloomy that she could see his headlight beams stabbing through the falling sleet and snow. Charging fast around the bend, Nikki dropped and rolled out right into the SUV's path, putting two rounds into the windshield and then stretching lengthwise between the front wheels, letting it drive right over her. By the time he braked, her head was under its rear bumper. She scrambled out from underneath and started running back toward Fifth Avenue.

Heat knew there was no room for the SUV to turn around, which was the core of her SWAG plan, to charge past instead of run from it. What she hadn't expected was for the driver to jam it in reverse and floor it to pursue her. The engine banshee whined and wheels threw slush as the rear end closed in on her. Losing a step of critical speed, Nikki turned and fired on the run at a rear tire. The shot missed and punctured the fender. She got off one more and the tire burst. The vehicle swayed wildly. The driver overcorrected, sending himself into a skid. His tires whirled uselessly in the slush and he smacked the rear end into the wall. Nikki kept moving, but when she heard the door unlatch, she turned, braced, and pumped four bullets into the driver's side window, shattering it. A head in a ski mask slumped against the windowsill, motionless.

Around the bend came the sound of feet slapping the wet road on the double. Heat would be a sitting duck if she made a run toward the entrance on Fifth. Once again she reversed field, moving toward her attackers, but stopped at the SUV. Nikki holstered, grabbed the roof rack, and climbed up on top of it. From that height, she was able to take hold of the bare branch of a shrub sagging down from the park. She pulled herself up the wall, hoisting the upper half of her body over it, the rocky ledge digging into her waist as her legs dangled.

A bullet hit the rock beside her left foot and sent out a spray of jagged chips. Nikki almost lost her grip on the shrub but held on, hooking her knee on the ledge. When she hauled herself up and over, she heard something hard strike the roof of the SUV with a resonant *bong*. She reached for her holster. It was empty.

Below, a protest of air wheezed from a shock absorber, and Nikki heard the thump of multiple boot soles on sheet metal. They were climbing up after her.

She got up and ran full speed. Her legs fought through waist-high shrubbery turned leafless and sharp by winter. The branches stung her thighs and whipped behind her as she plowed east paralleling the Transverse. A panic swell rose when she reflected on the sound back there. Boots on metal. They hadn't even paused to talk or check the driver, they just came. Fifth Avenue, if she could just get to Fifth Avenue.

At a break in the trees just before she reached the park's East Drive, Heat paused. This was an organized hunting party, and if she were organizing one, she would cover the target's escape route in case something went awry. Much as Nikki hated to give back her narrow head start, she crouched, panting in the thicket, to survey the tree line on the far side of the clearing. When she determined the best vantage point, she saw him. Through the visual clutter of sleet and snowflakes, a dark form huddled against a rock on high ground. She didn't need to see the rifle to know it was there.

Time to rethink. Blocked to the east, the other three would be closing in soon from the west. The Transverse cut her off to the south. But seven blocks north, near the reservoir, sat the NYPD Central Park Precinct house. It might as well be seven miles. What else was there? Heat envisioned a map of the park, and one word popped into her mind:

Castle.

There was a police call box near Belvedere Castle.

Detective Heat, wet, cold, and unarmed, reversed direction, bending her route slightly north as she moved parallel to the course of her three oncoming pursuers who, hopefully, would not expect her to backtrack their way.

She broke out of the woods on the footpath leading to the castle. Taking that trail presented a risk she accepted, trading exposure for the speed it would give her. There were no other footprints than hers as she sprinted in the new snowfall. Unfortunately, the weather had limited the population of runners and walkers that day—and darkened her hopes of getting help or access to a random cell phone.

The flakes had picked up intensity but not enough to cover her footprints. It wouldn't matter. These men would be able to hunt her anyway. The thought made her increase speed and cast a look over her shoulder. As she did, Nikki slid on a patch of ice. The hard landing knocked the breath out of her. Her kneecap radiated pain like it had been smacked with a hammer. While she collected herself, a frozen twig snapped deep in the woods she had just left. They were coming. She hauled herself up. Lungs searing, Heat raced onward.

Belvedere Castle was built in the 1860s as an observation tower overlooking Central Park's old reservoir. Its ornate turrets, arches, and main tower, masoned of granite and native schist, replicated the feel of Sleeping Beauty Castle right in Manhattan. Heat barely looked at it. Her focus was on a lamppost holding the police box on the far side. Nikki slowed to a jog, taking care not to fall on the ice that had formed on the brickwork of the courtyard. That's when the .50-caliber slug blew the police box clean off the post.

The crack of the rifle echoed off the face of the castle, sending waves rippling through the woods. Heat didn't wait for the follow-up shot. She hurled herself over the low stone wall rimming the courtyard. The next bullet ricocheted off the granite trim above her head as she crouched pressing her back against the stones. Nikki had to dig in her heels in the ice to avoid sliding four stories down the sheer rock cliff she was perched on. One slip would guarantee her a broken skull on the tumble down.

They would divide up to get her. She knew her hunters were disciplined and tactical, so two would fan out to flank her. The third would wait for them to reach their positions then come over the top for her. That bought Nikki time but little else. Even if she could survive a descent down Vista Rock, running across the white ground below in her dark clothes would be suicidal. The only difference between her and a target silhouette would be that she was flesh and not paper. No, she had to play the odds again; she had to take the fight to them.

But not all of them. That was her slim chance. If they had split up as she anticipated, one of them would be alone, nearby and waiting. Nikki inched on her butt laterally along the wall, careful to keep her footing. A fall would be the end of it. She reached a cluster of Chinese wintersweet and used the bare shrubs as cover when she periscoped up for a careful peek over the wall.

He stood alone presenting his side to her ten yards away, cradling his rifle, eyes fixed through his ski mask on the point where she had bailed over the wall. Heart pounding, she lowered herself and closed her eyes, summoning details of the image she had just seen. His position was in an open expanse of courtyard, no cover for her. To her left—and most appealing, behind him—was the pavilion . . . a roofed open-air patio bordered by low walls on three sides, with the fourth side open to the courtyard. Mindful that his partners could have her in their sights any second, she pulled herself farther along the rock ledge toward the back side of the pavilion. Along the way, she selected the largest loose rock she could find. It was about the size and heft of a shot put. Heat slid it in her side coat pocket.

Getting up and over the wall into the pavilion would be tricky. Huge icicles rimmed the entire roof, and their drips had frozen on the wall beneath them. She looked down. A slip now would be fatal. So would waiting.

Nikki stretched into a yoga pose, unfolding herself lengthwise along the top of the wall. Then, trying to avoid excess movement or noise, she slowly poured herself over the top and down to a rest in the patio area. Heat drew one long breath to quiet her pulse rate, then took off her coat.

She crawled to the wall closest to the courtyard and peered over. Her hunter was still there, but at this angle his back was to her. With the rock weighing heavily in the pocket, she tossed her coat over the cliff and screamed while she ducked.

Footsteps. Running her way.

But they stopped short of the pavilion. When they did, Nikki vaulted over the patio wall and caught him looking down the cliff at her falling coat. He heard her coming, spun, and tried to level the rifle at her. But she was already inside the muzzle with her left hand grasping the forestock, using it to pull him toward her as she brought her right fist up to his Adam's apple. He was trained in close combat, though, and he dropped his chin to shield his windpipe. Her fist struck his ski mask instead. He countered instantly, twisting his body in a hard pivot, using his hip and her grip on the rifle to twirl her off him.

Heat landed on the icy bricks, but still clutched the forestock. She yanked backward. His forefinger was stuck in the trigger guard, and she heard bone snapping as she pulled. A round fired as he fell backward beside her. The bullet struck the pavilion roof, knocking a sheet of ice and a row of icicles onto the courtyard around them. She got up, trying to take the weapon from him, but he scissored her legs at the knees, knocking her back down.

He got up on one knee, moaning as he shook his broken finger clear of the guard. Heat lunged for the rifle. She should have gone for him instead; he simply raised the weapon and, as her momentum carried her by, slammed her with his forearm, sending her skidding in the ice debris. With his right forefinger dangling loose inside his glove, he transferred the rifle to his left side and went for the trigger with his good hand. But just as he pivoted to aim at Nikki, she came at him, thrusting the sharp end of an umbrella-sized icicle deep into his gut. The weapon dropped from his hand and he clutched his wound, eyes flashing disbelief through the holes of his mask. Heat took the rifle in both hands and hammered the butt hard into his windpipe. He fell backward, fumbling at his neck, gurgling and bleeding out of his stomach on the snow.

Across the courtyard, one of the other hunters double-timed into view and hunkered down behind a rock. Nikki took the rifle and scrambled back inside the pavilion. She was still outnumbered, but at least she had a weapon.

Sirens approached. They weren't close yet, but they were coming.

Just as she positioned herself, resting the rifle on the top of the wall, almost braced for her holding action, a blur of two figures moved into the woods, fleeing.

Nikki's body began to tremble but she kept close watch. Only when the sirens grew loud and she could see flashing lights did she let down. Still clutching her weapon, Heat leaned back against the wall, looking upward at the castle that had been her salvation.

———

Time had first slowed down and then stood still for Nikki. The ensuing minutes had no definition. And strangely, no sequence. A psychologist might say she didn't shut down, she surrendered. After the tense ordeal of being hunted, shot at, evading, and then doing some hunting and killing of her own, Heat released control. For her it was the greatest luxury of survival.

Events lost their connective tissue and for Nikki Heat they kaleidoscoped. One moment, a face swam into view, reassuring her. Next, latex-gloved hands pried the rifle from her grip and slid it into plastic. Her own leather gloves came off, revealing palms wet with ice melt and blood. She found herself sitting in the back of an ambulance without recalling the journey. Did she walk there? Bushes parted in slow motion as her two assailants fled. Wait, that was before . . . She hallucinated Elmer Fudd standing there. Elmer Fudd with earflaps and jumbo binoculars hanging from his neck and snowflakes collecting on his eyebrows. Coffee in a cup rippled from her quaking hands. An EMT shined her penlight across her eyes and nodded, pleased. She pulled the blanket snug around her shoulders. Where did the blanket come from?

When the two shooting investigators from downtown joined her in the rear of the ambulance, Heat tossed back the rest of her coffee to spike her sharpness. She willed herself into the moment and walked them through the whole damn deal. They took notes and asked questions. Questions for clarification at first, and then the same questions asked a different way to see if her answers matched. She had been through this waltz before and so had they. Her answers were clear; they danced politely. But their goal was different than hers. They wanted to determine if she had killed according to policy. She wanted to capture the bastards, and this interview was something to get through so she could get back to work and do just that.

Elmer Fudd wasn't a hallucination, after all—although he had a different name. The old man wearing the binoculars and the L.L.Bean hunter's cap was actually Theodore Hobart. A birder who had spent the morning in the castle tower waiting for an eastern screech owl to return to its cavity in a tree near the Turtle Pond, Hobart witnessed the siege below and called 911 on his cell phone. Heat thanked him for saving her. He blushed and plucked the feather of a red-tailed hawk from the breast pocket of his Barbour coat and gave it to her. To Nikki it felt like a rose.

Zach Hamner pulled up in a black Crown Vic and strode to the suits from downtown. Heat watched them confer briefly, one of the detectives gesturing toward the pavilion and the other to the woods where a K-9 dog was leading his partner into the brush. On The Hammer's walk to the rear of the ambulance he stared over at the body under the tarp. "Nice to see you made it, Detective," he said, standing on the bricks and looking up to her.

"Feeling good about it myself." Nikki folded her arms tightly inside the blanket, not much up for a handshake with the lawyer.

"The boys say it's going to go down as a righteous kill. Your story checks out with the bird-watcher, too."

Heat tried to like him but wasn't having much success. She said, "So you can relax. No liability for the department?"

"None so far," he replied, not reading any of her subtext. Nikki wondered where all the men with a sense of irony had gone in this city. "Sounds like you were quite the hero. That's not going to hurt things for your promotion."

"Given the choice, I'd rather do it the old-fashioned way," said Heat.

He said, "I hear ya," but he was looking away as he did, more interested in the form under the tarp.

"Who was he?"

"Male Hispanic, twenty-eight to thirty. No ID. We'll run prints."

"You see any of them?" Nikki shook her head. "Any idea who they were?"

"Not yet."

He studied Nikki and could not miss seeing her resolve. "They say the SUV down in the Transverse is gone. No sign of the other guy, the driver you say you shot." Then he said, "These guys were pros."

It always annoyed her to have office functionaries roll up after the action and play cop. All she said was "Tell me."

He looked at his watch and then around the crime scene. "By the way. Where the hell's your boss? Where the fuck is Montrose?"

———

The Hammer irritated her, but he wasn't wrong. Precinct commanders always showed at every major incident involving their people. Captain Montrose didn't make Belvedere Castle. He wasn't in his office when she got back to the Two-oh, either.

Everyone knew of her ordeal, and all eyes fell on her as she entered the bull pen. In any other profession Nikki would have been forced to spend the rest of the day being pestered by sympathetic coworkers milking every detail of her story out of her and pushing her to share her feelings. Not in Copland. Ochoa set the tone when she reached her desk and he sidled over, checking the wall clock. "About time you rolled in," he said. "Some of us have been working this case."

Raley pivoted on his office chair to face them. "I hope you have a good reason for keeping us waiting."

Heat thought a moment and said, "I made the mistake of taking the park. The Transverse was a killer."

Detective Ochoa had a ball of kite string in his hand. He set it on her blotter. "What's this?" she asked.

"Old trick. Tie one end of it to your gun." He winked and clucked his tongue.

Then the three paused five seconds, letting the silence express the friendship. Marking the end of the interval, Raley stood. "Ready to hear what we've got?"

"Am I ever," said Heat. She wasn't just seeking solace in work, Nikki now had highly personal stakes in jamming this case even harder.

Lancer Standard, the CIA contractor, had finally called Raley back to set an appointment with Lawrence Hays, who was due back tomorrow from his desert training facility in Nevada. "Weird," he said. "His secretary said that he would only meet with you. By name, he specifically mentioned Detective Heat. I never brought you up."

"Pushy, but it just means he's done his homework," said Nikki. "He's a military type and probably wants to deal with the leader of the squad."

Ochoa said to his partner, "Man's busy. Can't waste time on a loser like you."

"Loser?" said Raley. "Partner, you are talking about the King of All Surveillance Media, now including hard drives."

"Whatcha got, sire?" asked Nikki.

"I took another look through Father Graf's computer and found a link to a second e-mail account that didn't forward to his Outlook. I accessed it and found only one folder. It's labeled 'EMMA.' There were no saved e-mails in it, nothing in the inbox. Either it was inactive," Raley speculated, "or it's been purged."

"Call Mrs. Borelli at the rectory," said Heat. "See if that name means anything to her." She cast another glance at the dark office across the pen. "Any Montrose sightings?"

"*Nada*," said Hinesburg, joining in as she crossed over. "And his cell is dumping to voice mail. What do you think it means?"

"Cap's been off the charts lately, but I have to say this has me shaking my head." Nikki recalled his warning an hour before her ambush to watch her back, and wondered if it was more than sage advice. The salacious hunger in Hinesburg's eyes alerted Nikki that this was not the forum for thinking out loud about her boss, and she moved on. "Anything on the money in the cookie tins yet?"

"Oh, yes, and get this," she said. "The serial numbers trace to cash used in a DEA sting years ago."

Ochoa asked, "How does a stash from a fed drug deal end up in a priest's attic?"

"Do we know who the DEA deal was with?" said Heat.

"Yeah, an Alejandro Martinez." Hinesburg consulted her notes. "He cut a plea bargain for a deuce in Ossining and he's out. Clean jacket since his release in '07."

Nikki crossed over to the board and started to write his name next to the notation for the found money. "Let's see how clean this Alejandro Martinez is. Bring him in for a chat."

They had just scattered to work their assignments when a familiar voice called from the door to the bull pen. "Delivery for Nikki Heat?"

Jameson Rook stepped in toting dry cleaning on hangers looped over his hand. "You know, I can't just drop everything and keep coming here every time you get all bloody."

Heat looked at the clothes from her closet, then at Rook, and then to Roach, arching a brow at them. Ochoa said, "We figured, you know, that he'd want to know how your day was going."

Rook asked, "Did you really stab him with an icicle?" When she nodded, he said, "Please, tell me you said 'Freeze,' because that would be only perfect." Rook was grinning, but there was worry behind it. He put his free arm around her waist. "Detective, you doing OK?"

"Fine, I'm just fine. I can't believe you did this." She took the clothes from him.

"Think they match. . . . You seem to have this sort of practical monochromatic thing going in your closet, not that I judge. All right, I judge. We need to take you shopping."

She laughed and pulled a couple of items from the selection he'd brought. "These will do just fine." She kissed his cheek, forgetting herself in a rare office display. "Thanks."

"I thought you had protection. What happened to your Discourager?"

"Poor Harvey, you should have seen him. Mortified. In all his years he never got blocked like that."

"How ... discouraging. Whatever's going on, you need better. When I went by your apartment, there was a car sitting up the block watching, I know the look."

Nikki got a fresh chill and draped the clothes across the back of her chair. "How do you know it was watching?"

"Because when I walked up to it, he sped off. I yelled stop, but he kept going."

"The yelling stop, that never works," said Raley.

"Did you see him, get a description?" Ochoa had his pad open. Then he said, "You didn't get a description, did you?"

"No," said Rook. And then he took out his Moleskine notebook. "But would a license plate help?"

———

"Got it," said Raley, hanging up the phone. "Vehicle you saw was registered to Firewall Security, Inc., a domestic protection division of ... are you ready? ... Lancer Standard."

"We should get on them. Get over there right now," said Rook. "These have got to be the guys who ambushed you. It adds up, the surveillance, the military tactics, let's go."

Nikki finished putting on her clean blazer and said, "First of all, there is no 'we' or 'let's,' Rook. Your ride-along days are through. And second, there's nothing to go on. Third, if they are up to something, I don't want to let on that I know...."

Rook sat down. "When you get to the fifteenth reason, let me know. I believe this is like Little League; isn't there a mercy rule?"

She put a hand on his shoulder. "You're not totally wrong. Of course this guy Hays and Lancer Standard have my attention, but let's go about this the right way."

"Did you say 'let's'? Because I heard 'let's.'"

She laughed, shoving him so he spun a rotation in the chair. Then Nikki felt Ochoa's presence, standing in the middle of the bull pen, ashen. The smile left her face. "Miguel?"

The detective spoke in a voice so low it would not have been audible if the room hadn't gone completely silent. "Captain Montrose. . . . He's dead."

EIGHT

Special Investigations owned that city block and would control it for as long as they pleased. Rook, who liked Montrose and knew how much the captain meant to Nikki, had wanted to come along for support, but she said no. She knew what it would be like. Immediates only. And she was right. Even Heat and Roach had to park outside the yellow tape and walk; that's how tight that crime scene was. The press called Nikki's name as she passed, but she kept her eyes front, ignoring them—especially Tam Svejda, who hopped sideways along the no-go line, shouldering her way between reporters and making desperate pleas for a comment.

There was a lull in the precipitation, but the afternoon sky hung low and sullen. The three detectives strode wordlessly, crunching over pellets of sidewalk salt toward the middle of 85th, where strobes were flashing in front of the rectory of Our Lady of the Innocents.

Nikki recognized the shooting suits from the castle. The pair clocked her as she approached, gave a nod, then went back to their business. Heat had never seen these two before in her life, and now here they were again, crossing paths the second time that same day.

Montrose's Crown Victoria sat parked in front of a fire hydrant and was ringed by portable isolation barriers of white plastic sheeting stretched on aluminum frames. Nikki stopped on the sidewalk a car length away, not knowing if she had it in her to proceed. Cameras inside the barrier flashed like lightning punching against the gloom. "We can do this, if you'd rather," said Ochoa. She turned and saw the sadness behind his cop mask. Beside him, the skin around his partner Raley's lips was white from pressing them together so hard.

Nikki did what she had done so often on this job. She put on her armor. There was a switch inside her, the one that sealed off her vulnerability, like triggering a fire door in the Met. For the space of one long breath, which was all it took, she made the silent acknowledgment she always made to honor the victim she was about to meet, threw the switch, and she was ready. Detective Heat said, "Let's go," and entered the crime scene.

The first thing she took in was the quarter inch of ice and frozen slush coating the entire top of the car, notable because there was a clear circular patch about the size of a DVD on the roof above the driver's seat. Raising herself up on her toes, she saw the dimple of the bullet's exit point. She bent forward to look through the back window, but it was like trying to see through a shower door. Then the shooter from Forensics took another picture inside the car, and the slumped body formed a horror movie silhouette.

"Single head shot," said the voice. Nikki rose up and turned from the rear window, and one of the suits, Neihaus, was on the curb with his pad.

"You have positive ID this is Captain Charles Montrose?" was the first thing she said. When he nodded, she asked Neihaus to say it. "You're absolutely certain Charles Montrose is the victim?"

"Yes, I have matched him to his ID. But speaking of, you knew him, right?" He tilted his head toward the open passenger door, and she felt her stomach swim. "Going to need confirmation, you know that."

"That's him." Detective Ochoa rose up from his crouch at the open car door and walked back toward them. He showed his palms to Nikki and shook his head slightly, signaling Don't. And for the hundreds of victims she had seen in the hundreds of awful ways people can die and what it does to their bodies, and for the traumatic day she had had already, Nikki decided there was no point testing her armor.

"Thank you, Detective," she said in a formal tone.

"No problem." His face said anything but.

Nikki shifted gears, asking Neihaus, "Who found him?"

"Guy from a cleanup crew looking for a parking place to get in the Graestone." In near unison, Heat and Roach looked up the block. A commercial van from On Call, a smoke and water damage recovery company, was double-parked at the rear service gate of the prestigious Graestone Condominiums. Detectives Feller and Van Meter were interviewing a man in coveralls. "Says he was mad he couldn't find a spot while some jerk had parked at the hydrant, and he was going to give him some shit. Surprise."

"How about witnesses?" She had to ask, even knowing that if anybody had seen or heard anything, a 911 call would have preceded the accidental discovery by the van's driver.

"None so far. We'll canvass, of course, but you know . . ."

"Did you ask the housekeeper if he had some reason to be here at the rectory?" Nikki asked. "Her name is Mrs. Borelli. Have you talked with her?"

"Not yet."

"You want some extra manpower?" said Heat.

"I know this is your skip and your precinct, Detective, but this one's ours." Neihaus gave them his most assuring look. "And don't worry, this is family. Commissioner's going to give us any resources we need."

"You go over the car yet?" said Raley.

"No note, if that's what you mean. Forensics is on latents, that'll take a while. His weapon's down on the front floor mat. Nothing unusual in the vehicle on first go-over. Trunk's got the standard-issue kit, vest and whatnot. Oh, and two canvas grocery bags of canned dog food. Must have had a pooch."

"Penny," said Heat, her voice cracking as she continued, "a dachshund."

On their walk back to the Roach Coach, Feller and Van Meter hailed them and they stopped. "Sorry about the captain," said Feller.

"It's fucked up" was Van Meter's take.

"You get anything from the On Call driver?" asked Nikki.

Feller shook his head. "Just the details of the discovery. No unusual activity."

Nikki said, "You know what? No way this is isolated. Whatever's going on here, I don't know what it is except that it is bigger than we suspected."

"I hear that," said Ochoa.

"Bunch of paramilitary types come after me in the park, trying to kill me . . . ," she said. "Guys with no history or connection to me, at least not from the one I put down. Now, a couple of hours later, Montrose is dead. . . ."

"In front of Graf's rectory? I'm sure not buying coincidences," agreed Raley. "Something's up."

Detective Feller said, "Look, I know how you felt about him, it's a big loss, I'm sorry for you. All of you. He was a good man. But . . ."

"But what?" she said.

"Come on, let's be objective. With all respect, you're too close," said Van Meter. "Your skipper was under huge pressure. 1PP had his nuts in a vise, his wife dies . . ."

Feller picked up his partner's point. "It's no secret how unhappy the man was. Nikki, you know this is going to come down as a suicide."

"Because it is," from Van Meter. "You're going all Area 51. He ate his piece."

The urge to scream at them overwhelmed Nikki, but instead she sought her cop's detachment, and when she had reclaimed it, she let herself examine what they were saying. Was it possible with all those pressures—plus all the strange behaviors she had witnessed—that the Cap had taken his own life? Her boss, who had snooped the rectory and had so obviously worked to cut off her investigation, was slumped in his car with a bullet in his head. And people were sure it was suicide?

Was it suicide?

Or was he involved in something? Could the captain have crossed over and gotten into something dirty? No, Nikki dismissed those thoughts. She couldn't imagine the Charles Montrose she knew doing anything like that.

Detective Heat shivered. She didn't know what was going on, but she knew one thing. Standing there on the snow, deep in the coldest winter in a century, she saw herself on the tip of an iceberg. And all around her in the water were sharks.

———

The purple bunting was already hung above the main entrance to the precinct when they got back. Of course, business in the house was still being conducted, but the air was somber. On the trip through the lobby to Homicide, Heat noticed that the uniforms wore mourning bands across their shields. Conversations everywhere she passed were hushed and had the odd effect of making the ring of telephones sound louder. Captain Montrose's office remained empty and dark. There was also a seal on his door.

Detective Rhymer gave her an interval to settle at her desk before he came over. After they shared brief condolences, he handed her a file. "Just came in. An ID of your dude from the park."

Detective Heat flipped open the cover and a mug shot of the rifleman she had stabbed at Belvedere Castle stared back at her. Sergio Torres, DOB February 26, 1979, was a shoplifter turned car radio thief who did enough jail time to hook up with Latin gangs on the inside. That relationship earned him a few new stretches stacking time for carjacking and assaults. She closed the file on her lap and stared into the near distance.

"I'm sorry," said Rhymer. "I should have waited."

"No, no, it's not that," said Heat. "It's just . . . This is not sitting right. I mean, Torres had no military background. I saw this guy in action. He had skills. How does a gang banger get trained like that?" Her phone rang.

It was Rook trying her again. It must have been his tenth call. And for the tenth time, Nikki didn't pick it up, because if she did, she'd have to talk about it. And once she did that, it became real.

And once it became real, it was all over. And Heat couldn't afford for it to be all over right now.

Not in front of everyone else. Not while she was going for lieutenant.

"Hey?" said Ochoa. "Timing sucks, but before all this went down I set a meet with *Justicia a Garda* and they're here. Want me to try to push it to tomorrow?"

Heat gave it serious thought. No, she had to power forward. Keep paddling or risk sinking. "No, don't cancel. I'll be right there. . . . And Miguel? Thanks for stepping in like that, ID-ing the captain."

"Before you thank me you should know something," he said. "The God's truth? I couldn't look."

———

"Thank you for coming," said Nikki as she entered the waiting room. She was met by silence. A man and woman, both about thirty, sat across the table from Detective Ochoa, arms folded, without so much as a glance her way. Heat couldn't help but notice that they also still wore their coats, another nonverbal cue.

As soon as Nikki sat, the woman, Milena Silva, spoke. "Mr. Guzman and I are here as hostile participants. Also, I am not only one of the directors of *Justicia a Guarda*, I have a law degree, so you have fair warning before you begin."

"Well, first of all," began Heat, "this is just an informal meeting . . ."

"In a police station," said Pascual Guzman. He looked around the room, clawing fingertips through his Che beard. "Are you recording this?"

"No," she said. It bugged her that they were trying to run her meeting, so she pressed on. "We invited you here to help give some background on Father Graf, to help us find his killer or killers."

"Why would we know anything about his killers?" said Guzman. His co-leader put her hand on the sleeve of his olive-drab coat, and it seemed to calm him.

Milena Silva said, "Father Graf was a supporter of our human rights work for many years. He marched with us, he organized with us, he even traveled to Colombia to see firsthand the abuses of our people at the hands of the oppressive regime your government supports there. His death is a loss to us, so if you are thinking we are involved in his killing, you are mistaken."

"Maybe you should look at your CIA." Guzman punctuated his shot with a pointed nod and sat back in his chair.

Heat knew better than to level the playing field by engaging in polemics with them. She was more interested in Father Graf's last hours and, especially, if there was any bad blood in the movement, so Nikki kept to her own agenda. "Father Graf was last seen alive at your committee offices the other morning. Why was he there?"

"We don't have to share the confidential strategies of our group with the police," said the woman with the law degree. "It's a First Amendment right."

"So he was there for a strategy session," said Nikki. "Did he seem upset, agitated, acting out of the ordinary?"

The woman fielded that one, too. "He was drunk. We already told your *cobista* here." Ochoa's face revealed nothing at the insult and he remained quiet.

"What kind of drunk? Falling down? Disoriented? Happy? Nasty?"

Guzman loosened the knit scarf around his neck and said, "He became belligerent and we asked him to leave. That's all there is to know."

Prior experience told Nikki that when someone declared that that was all there was to know, the opposite was true. So she drilled down. "How did he show his belligerence, did he argue?"

Pascual Guzman said, "Yes, but—"

"What about?"

"Again," said Milena Silva, "that is confidential under our rights."

"Did it get physical? Did you fight him, have to restrain him?" When the two didn't answer but looked to each other, Heat said, "I am going to find out, so why not just tell me?"

"We had an issue—" began Guzman.

Silva chimed in, "A private, internal issue."

"—And he was irrational. Drunk." He looked to his companion and she nodded to go on. "We were . . . passionate in our disagreement. Shouting became shoving, shoving became punching, so we made him leave."

"How?" She waited. "How?"

"I . . . threw him out the door."

Nikki said, "So it was you who fought with him, Mr. Guzman?"

"You don't have to answer that," said Milena Silva.

"Where did he go?" Heat asked. "Did he have a ride, get a cab?"

Guzman shrugged. "He went away is all I know."

"This was about . . . ," Heat looked at her notes, "ten-thirty A.M. Early to be drunk. Was that common for him?" This time they both shrugged.

"Your organization is well armed back in Colombia," said Heat.

"We have the spirit to fight. We are not afraid to die, if necessary." It was the most animated she had seen Pascual Guzman.

"I understand some of your members even attacked a prison and helped Faustino Velez Arango escape." The pair exchanged glances again. "Yes, I know Faustino Velez Arango."

"Dilettantes and Hollywood stars pretend to know our famous dissident writer, but who has read his books?"

Nikki said, "I read *El Corazón de la Violencia* in college." Ochoa regarded her with an arched brow. She continued, "How much of that . . . fighting spirit . . . did you bring here?"

"We are peaceful activists," said the woman. "What use would people like us have for guns and rifles here in the United States?"

Heat wondered the same thing, only not rhetorically. She placed the mug shot of Sergio Torres on the table between them. "Do you know this man?"

"Why?" asked the lawyer.

"Because he's a person I'm interested in knowing more about."

"I see. And because he's Latino and a criminal, you ask us?"

Guzman stood and tossed the photo. It fluttered halfway across the coffee table and landed facedown. "This is racist. This is the marginalization we rise up to fight against every day."

Milena Silva stood, too. "Unless you have a warrant to arrest us, we are leaving."

Nikki was done with her questions and held the door for them. When they were gone, Ochoa said, "You read *El Corazón de la Violencia?*"

She nodded. "Lot of good it just did me."

———

The remainder of the afternoon she spent using her focus on work to fend off the malaise that had settled like a toxic fog in the halls of the Twentieth Precinct. In any other field, after the startling death of a leader, business would have closed for the day. But this was the New York Police Department. You didn't clock out for sadness.

For better or worse, Nikki Heat knew how to compartmentalize. She had to. If she didn't put an airtight lock on her emotional doors, the beasts pounding on the steel plates to get out would eat her alive. The shock and sadness, they were to be expected. But the raging howls she worked hardest to silence came from guilt. Her last days with her mentor had been contentious and full of suspicions; some voiced, some merely contemplated—her own dirty secrets. Nikki hadn't known where it was all leading, but she had clung to a tacit belief that there would be a resolution that would make the two of them whole again. She never imagined this tragedy cutting short the story Nikki thought she was telling. John Lennon said life was what happened while you made other plans.

So was death.

Blunt as they had been back at the crime scene, Nikki took the advice of Feller and Van Meter and sat down to unpack the facts of the Montrose death without prejudice. Detective Heat got out a single sheet of paper and penciled details. Making her own private Murder Board on the page, she especially focused on the captain's strange new behaviors in the days ramping up to this dark one, logging them all: the absences, the agitation, the secretiveness, his obstruction of her case, his anger when she insisted on doing the sort of investigative work he had trained her to do.

Heat stared at the page.

The questions lingering in the back of her mind stepped forward and raised their hands. Clean or dirty, did Captain Montrose know what the stakes were? Was he trying to protect her? Is that why he didn't want her looking into the Graf murder too deeply? Because if she did, a bunch of armed guys were going to try to stack her garbage in the park? Were they CIA contractors? Foot soldiers from drug cartels? A Colombian hit squad? Or someone she hadn't even landed on so far?

And did these guys go for him next?

Nikki folded her sheet of paper to put in her pocket. Then she thought a moment, took it out again, and crossed over to the squad's Murder Board to write it up there. No, she was not buying the suicide. Not yet.

———

"This is an official call," said Zach Hamner, making Heat wonder what their other conversations had been. "I just received a formal complaint from an organization called . . ." She could hear papers rustling on his end and helped him out.

"*Justicia a Garda.*"

"Yes. Nice pronunciation. Anyway, they are alleging harassment and racist statements based on a meeting you had with them earlier today."

"You can't be taking this seriously," she said.

"Detective, do you know how much money the city of New York paid out over the last decade in claims against this department?" He didn't wait for her reply. "Nine hundred and sixty-four million. That's pocket change short of a billion with a B. Do I take claims seriously? You bet. And so should you. You don't need something like this coming up right now. Not with your promotion pending. Now, tell me what happened."

She gave him a brief recap of the meeting and the reason for it. When she was finished, The Hammer said, "Did you have to show the mug shot of the gang banger? That's the inflammatory part."

"Sergio Torres tried to kill me this morning. I will damn well show his picture to everyone connected to this case." When Hamner said he got it, she continued, "And one more thing. Conducting an investigation is hard enough without outsiders second-guessing my case work."

"I am going to chalk that up to your obvious stress from the day you've had. By the way, our condolences on the loss of your commander." Nikki couldn't shake her memory of The Hammer standing outside the ambulance that morning whining, "Where the fuck is Montrose?"

She figured one push-back was enough for this call, so she let it go. "Thanks."

"Where do you go from here?" he asked.

"Back to what I was doing. Finding out who killed Father Graf. And maybe my boss."

Zach's chair creaked. He must have sat up. "Hold on, wasn't that a suicide?"

"We'll see," she said.

———

Rook met her with a cocktail when she opened her apartment door. "I hope you're up for a mojito. This is a recipe I picked up in a dive bar near a beachside landing strip in Puerto Rico."

She traded him her coat for the drink, and right there in the entryway, they raised their tall glasses up in a toast. But Heat and Rook didn't clink right away. Instead they held each other's eyes a long moment, letting the intimacy of their stillness speak. Then Nikki set her glass down on the foyer table, saying, "First things first," as she folded her arms around him and they hugged.

"I figured after your day, you would be in the mood for some red meat," he said when they moved into the kitchen.

"Smells amazing."

"Roast beef tenderloin—simple-simple—just salt, pepper, and rosemary, plus the usual sides, mashed potatoes, brussels sprouts."

"Comfort food. Rook, you don't know what this means right now. . . . Oh, yes you do." And then she took another sip. "You don't have time to do this, what with bringing me clothes and trying to write your article."

"Done! E-mailed it off two hours ago and came over here to take care of you. I was going to make kabobs, but after your morning in the park, I figured skewers would be too darkly comic, even for me."

"And yet you mentioned them."

"What can I say? I'm an enigma inside a conundrum inside a condom." Nikki started to laugh but caught herself. Her face became drawn and she sat at the counter. She stayed there, perched on the bar stool, through her mojito and a glass of a surprisingly perfect red from Baja California, while Rook carved and served. He transferred the place settings from the dining table to the counter and they ate there, the informality of it relaxing her. She was hungry but only managed a small portion, choosing instead to fill him in on things she hadn't told him about her difficulties with Captain Montrose. He told her she didn't have to talk about it if it was painful, but it wasn't, she said, it was therapeutic, a chance to let out the burden she carried.

Nikki had already told him just before strip Proust that there had been tension with Montrose, but this time she told him the details. She shared the unsettling suspicions that arose in her beyond the captain oddly showing up at Graf's the night he was killed: how he obstructed her case in every way, plus the blood on the priest's collar that coincided with the bandage on his finger. And then there was the baffling recurrence of TENS burns . . . on Graf, on the male dancer, and on a victim in an old murder case Montrose had worked when he was a Detective-1.

Rook listened intently without interruption, interested in her story but more eager to let her download and relieve the pain she bore. When Nikki finished, he asked, "The suspicions you had, did you share them with anybody? Internal Affairs? Your new friends downtown?"

"No, because they were only, you know, circumstantial. He was in a world of hurt already. You open that lid, it's Pandora's Box." Her lower lip quivered and she bit on it. "I opened the door a crack about it with him this morning. He kind of boxed me into it, and let me tell you, it hurt him. It really hurt him." She tilted her head back and squinted, refusing to let herself cry, then continued, "I'm ashamed to admit it now, but there was a part of me, this morning in the park . . . ?"

He knew where she was going. "You wondered if he could have been part of it?"

"Only for a second, a second I hate myself for, but he gave me this warning at the end of our meeting. It had to cross my mind."

"Nikki, there's nothing wrong with thinking things. Especially in your work, come on, it's what you do."

Her head bobbed in acceptance and she forced a thin smile.

"Did you ever get an ID on your attacker, the Human Popsicle?"

"You are a sick man, Jameson Rook."

He bowed theatrically. "Thank you, thank you."

Then Heat told him about Sergio Torres. How his rap sheet was the legacy of an ordinary gang banger but he was trained like a soldier.

"I don't get it," said Rook. "How does a mundane metropolitan miscreant master menacing military methods and maneuvers? Mystifying."

". . . Yeah . . ." Nikki cocked an eye at him. "I was sort of thinking the same thing . . ."

"Have you looked into whether he was connected to the Mara Salvatrucha gang? The MS 13s supposedly called a hit on all NYPD cops about a year ago," he said. "And, breaking news from my recent arms trip, the cartels are giving paramilitary training to MS 13 gangsters to fight their drug war in Mexico."

"I'll check that out tomorrow." She slid off the bar stool and excused herself. A few seconds after she disappeared down the hall, she called out, "Rook? Rook, come here."

When he reached the bathroom, she was standing near the window. "Have you been in here since you got here?"

"I think the answer is evident in the lowered toilet seat. No."

"Look at this." She stepped to the side, indicating water drops from melted ice dotting the windowsill. She pointed to the latch. It was unlocked. "I always lock that." She grabbed a flashlight from the cabinet under the sink and shined it on the latch. A minute abrasion in the brass tongue gleamed where it had been jimmied. It was nothing Nikki would have noticed had it not been for the droplets.

Together they made a survey of the apartment. Nobody was hiding and nothing was missing or out of place. Mindful of the careful snoop somebody had performed at the rectory, Heat took extra care to notice the little things. Nothing was disturbed. "You must have scared him off when you came in, Rook."

"Ya know, my days of droppin' in unannounced may be over."

They locked up and went downstairs to tell The Discourager, who was parked across the street. "Want me to call it in?"

"Thanks, Harvey, but I'll do it in the morning." The last thing she wanted then was an evening of bright lights and forensic dusting. It wouldn't kill Rook and her to use the other bathroom for one night. "Just wanted to give you the heads-up."

Rook said, "Hey, Harvey, don't you ever sleep?"

The veteran cop looked at Heat. "Not after today, I don't."

———

Nikki took what she insisted was a well-deserved bubble bath in the guest tub while Rook did the dishes. He waited for her in the living room, surfing ESPN, missing football season, glad MLB was days away from Pitchers and Catchers. At eleven, he switched off the TV. "You didn't have to do that for me," she said.

Nikki was in a robe, her hair wet, and looking comfortably

dazed by the hot bath. She folded into him on the couch, smelling faintly of lavender.

"I think we already know the lead story," he said.

"Yup. Precinct Captain dies in apparent suicide." She turned to him, just inches away. The relaxation left her face. "They'd be wrong. He never would have done it."

"How can you be sure?"

"Same reason I knew he didn't kill Graf."

"Which is?"

"He was Captain Montrose."

The instant she said it, the doors to all the compartments Heat had so carefully closed off flew open. The seals broke, and a day of emotion—from the flight for her life in Central Park to the trauma of Captain Montrose's death—rushed out to seize her. Rook watched the wave take her. She quaked and her eyes dripped tears. Then she cried out, throwing her head back in a release that startled even her. He opened his arms, and Nikki grabbed him desperately, clinging to him, shaking, sobbing and sobbing, as she had not in ten years.

NINE

When Heat came out from her shower the next morning and found Rook on his computer at her dining room table, she came up behind his chair and placed a hand on each of his shoulders. "There's something not fair about a world where you get paid all that money for a job you do in your underwear." At her touch Nikki felt the tension melt from his muscles. He dropped his hands off the keyboard, bringing them around behind her, gently gripping the back of her thighs. Then he rocked his head backward, resting it between her breasts, and peered up at her.

"I could lose the underwear if it would make you happy," he said.

"That would make me very happy, but I just got a text that I've got a drug dealer coming in to be interviewed." She bent to kiss his forehead. "Plus I have my oral boards today. Last hurdle before the lieutenant promotion."

"I could help you with that. The orals." She just stared at him, and he turned to her with a face of innocence. "What?"

"Tell me, Rook, is there a single word in the dictionary a guy can't turn into something salacious?"

"Quatrain. Big points at Scrabble. Zip when it comes to double entendre, and I have tried. Oh, how I've tried." Then he said, "With all that's happened, couldn't you get a postponement?"

"I could." It was all on her face. Nikki was not going to let down. "But I won't." She gestured to his MacBook. "I thought you finished your arms smugglers piece. Is that your next bodice ripper, Miss St. Clair?"

"Nothing so lofty."

"What is it?"

"Rather not say just yet." He closed the lid and stood to face her. "Bad luck." Then Rook drew her to him and they kissed. He was tender and gentle, comforting. "You doing OK this morning?"

"No, but I'll get through."

"There's French Roast on." Rook made a move toward the kitchen, but she clung to him and held him in place.

"Thank you for last night. You were . . . a friend."

"Anytime, anywhere, Nikki Heat." And they kissed again.

She dressed while he poured her coffee and squeezed them both some juice. Nikki reappeared looking puzzled and holding up her cell phone. "Want to hear something odd? I just checked my office voice mail. One of the messages was from the travel agent I referred Captain Montrose to. She said she can't believe the news, especially since she just talked to him yesterday. He booked an island cruise."

"Yesterday?" When she affirmed, he clapped his hands once and said, "John le Carré!" He read her bewilderment and added, "You know John le Carré, right? *Spy Who Came in from the Cold, Constant Gardener* . . . Oh, and *A Perfect Spy*—transcendent, best ever! But . . . John le Carré's first novel was *Call for the Dead*. This secret agent is found. Suicide, they say. But that theory unravels because he left a wake-up call the night before. See the logic? Who leaves a wake-up call if he plans to kill himself?"

"Right," she said. "And who books a cruise? Especially Montrose." She frowned. "Now? And alone?" She had started to mull the oddness of that when he interrupted.

"I'll be dressed in two seconds."

"For what?"

"To come with you," said Rook. "We have to get to work. This suicide theory is full of holes. Oo, sorry. Poor choice of words, forgive me, but I'm getting fired up."

"Well, take a breath. We went over this. Your ride-along days are over. I can't have you tagging along now. There's too much going on."

"I won't be in the way." Her stare forced him to admit, "Much."

"Not happening. Besides, it's too complicated now. I'm under a lot of attention and it might appear unprofessional."

"Why? Lieutenants have boyfriends, too."

"Maybe, but not working cases with them." She watched his jaw flex. "Why is this such a big push for you?"

"Because of yesterday. I want to keep an eye on you."

She moved close and held him. "Rook, that is so very . . ."

". . . Sweet?"

"I'll go with stupid."

———

The seal was off the door to the glass office, and the two Men in Black from Internal Affairs were waiting for Heat when she entered it. "You can close that," said Lovell, the angular one with the sharp, pterodactyl features, who was seated behind the desk. His partner, DeLongpre, had perched on the bookcase, strategically in Lovell's eye line and slightly behind the guest chair so they could trade signals. Nikki noticed the hefty one had carelessly shoved the framed photos of Montrose's wife aside to make room on the shelf for his ass.

"We have some questions for you about your commander," began Lovell when she took her seat.

"You mean there's something you don't know? You spent enough time working him over."

Lovell smiled patiently. "Just because we're IA doesn't make us the enemy, Detective Heat, you ought to know that."

Then DeLongpre said, "So let's dial down the snark factor," making himself sound exactly like the enemy. Or the bad cop to Lovell's good one.

"How can I help you?" she said.

They asked general questions at first: how long they knew each other, her view of his performance, how she would characterize his leadership over the years. Heat was truthful but guarded. These guys were in the business of looking for spiders in the basement, and

Nikki didn't want to further sully the captain's rep. Actually, she was glad for the opportunity to put it out that Montrose had been such an exemplary boss and, not insignificantly, a fine human being. But all that goodwill Nikki thought she was building ended up leveraged against her.

Lovell said, "Sounds like you had a great relationship."

"We did."

"Then what happened?" He tilted his head back and scrutinized her over his hooked Triassic Period nose. When she didn't reply, he said, "Come on, he lost it. What was it about, and when?"

Nikki had conducted enough interrogations of her own to know when she was getting channeled. "I don't know if I feel comfortable with those exact words."

"Then choose your own," said Lovell.

DeLongpre added, "Because goodness knows we want you to feel comfortable."

"I don't know if I would say he lost it," she said. "It was more like a slow change. A little more tense, that's all. I cut him slack because of his wife getting killed." She didn't know which was stronger, her instinct to protect his memory or her mistrust of these two.

Lovell said, "Is that why you said to your squad yesterday . . . ," he read from his notepad, " 'Cap's been off the charts lately, but this has me shaking my head'?"

Who gave them that? Heat wondered. Although she had an idea. "That's out of context. I think I said it when he was MIA."

Lovell held the pad up and repeated, " 'Cap's been off the charts lately . . .' Sounds like plenty of context to me. I hear you two really tore it up in this office yesterday morning. Shouting, desk pounding . . . Well?"

"He was feeling pressure. The CompStat push, you know. Target numbers."

"Yeah, he told us about that, too. But why was he up your skirt?" said DeLongpre. Heat knew that was calculated to press a button, so she ignored it. But she had to answer. So she tossed them a bone.

"We had some disagreements about the case I'm working on." She was prepared to say little and leave it general. But they had other ideas.

"The priest, right? And you thought he was involved somehow in the killing, is that what set him off?"

Heat was stunned. As she grappled for a reply, DeLongpre jumped in. "He conducted a solo search of the rectory, correct? You found that suspicious."

Then Lovell hit her with "And he screwed with your case, blocking viable avenues of your investigation."

"Especially hinky, since the phone records established Montrose had a relationship with the vic," said his partner.

These guys were thorough. "If you know all these things, what do you want from me?"

"More." Lovell unfolded all six-two of himself from the chair and came around to sit on the front of the desk. He smoothed his skinny black tie and looked down at her from his perch. "We want to know what else you're holding."

"You expect me to dish dirt on my old skip?"

"We expect you to assist the department in its investigation, Detective."

DeLongpre said, "He was into something, let's hear what you've got."

She looked from MIB to MIB. They had positioned themselves so that following their conversation felt like watching a tennis match. "I don't have anything. No more than you already mentioned." Which was mostly true. The rest was unfounded and circumstantial, like the captain's finger cut.

In a singsong, DeLongpre said, "Bull . . . shit . . ."

She didn't turn his way but spoke her remarks calmly to Lovell. "I deal in facts. You want to spitball, call Detective Hinesburg in again. I'm going to apply myself to finding out who killed my commander."

"Find out who killed him?" When Lovell raised his eyebrows,

the lines in his vast forehead formed an inverted V. "Nobody killed him but him."

"You don't have proof of that."

"You just gave it," he said. The Internal Affairs man got off the desk and walked the room, ticking off each point on a finger. "Straight-shooting, tough-but-fair captain's wife dies a year ago and he goes around the bend. He starts to slip. Can't handle the pressure of the command, and the pack wolves at HQ descend on him, making him even more erratic. Maybe it's temptation, maybe it's anger at the system, he gets himself involved in something—we don't know what yet, but we'll damn sure find out—and when you . . . his protégée . . . called him on it and handed him his ass yesterday, he felt the walls closing in." Lovell snapped his fingers once. "He leaves your meeting and eats his gun."

Nikki shot to her feet. "Hold on, you're putting this on me?"

Lovell smiled, and deep vertical creases appeared on his cheeks. "Give me something that says it isn't."

"Till then," said DeLongpre, "live with it."

———

Heat was aware of someone standing over her and broke off her glazed stare following her floating screen saver. It was Ochoa. "Ran a check on the doc who wrote the weird prescription for Father Graf. Dude's bogus. Address is a mail drop. Nobody heard of him."

Nikki shook off the heavy residue of her IA meeting. "Is he licensed to practice in New York?"

"Was," said the detective. "A little bit tough, though. Seeing how he died at a nursing home in Florida ten years ago."

Her phone rang. Hinesburg was calling from outside Interrogation to tell her the drug dealer had arrived.

———

"I have never seen this man before in my life," said Alejandro Martinez. He slid the mug shot of Sergio Torres across the table to Heat. She noticed how delicate his hands were. Immaculately manicured, too.

"Are you positive?" she asked. "His rap sheet includes drug busts up in Washington Heights and the Bronx. Would have been about the time you got out of O-Town."

"I assure you, Detective, since I left the penitentiary I have not engaged in any narcotics sales or consorted with any criminals. That would be a violation of my parole." He chuckled. "Ossining has a lot of fine qualities, but I don't plan to return." Nikki took in this dapper man, sounding so refined, positively Continental—and wondered how much blood had gotten under those clear lacquered nails before he was finally busted. Watching him sit there, looking all soap opera *patrón* at sixty-two, with his distinguished gray temples and his Dries Van Noten suit complete with pocket square, who would ever suspect the scores of lives he had ruined and bodies he had disposed of in empty oil drums and lime pits?

"Life's been good for you since then, it appears," she said. "Expensive clothes, jewelry . . . I like the wristband."

Martinez pulled back the monogrammed cuff on his right wrist and extended his arm across the divide so Nikki could appreciate the pounded silver bracelet studded with gemstones. "Nice," she said. "What are these, emeralds?"

"Yes. Like it? It's from Colombia. I saw it on a business trip and couldn't resist."

"Did you buy that recently?" Heat wasn't jewelry shopping. She was laying groundwork.

"No, as I'm sure you know, the terms of my parole do not permit international travel."

"But you sure could afford a piece or two like that. Mr. Martinez, you seem to have plenty of money."

"My experience in Sing Sing brought me to reflect humbly on money and its use. In my own individual way, I try to use whatever wealth I have managed to save as a tool for good."

"Does that include your drug money? I'm thinking specifically about a few hundred thou you scored back in 2003 in Atlantic City."

The man was unruffled. "I'm sure I am not aware of what you're talking about."

Nikki reached over to the chair beside her and moved the open cookie tins of cash onto the table. "Does this refresh your memory?" For the first time since she came in the room, Heat saw the veneer crack. Not much, but his eyes flicked side to side. "No? Let me help you. This cash has been traced back to a deal brokered in your hotel suite at one of the casinos. The buyer was undercover DEA. He went in with a wire and this cash and was supposed to come out with a duffel of cocaine. Instead, he turned up in a Pennsylvania landfill three weeks later."

The twinkle of rogue charm left his eyes as they hardened. But still he said nothing. "Let's try some more show-and-tell." Nikki handed over a picture of Father Graf.

"I don't know this one, either." He was lying. Cool as he was, Martinez showed the classic stress tells . . . the blinks, the dry mouth.

"Look again, I think you do."

He gave the most cursory glance and slid it back. "I'm afraid I don't."

"Do you have any idea how this money ended up in his possession?"

"I would refer you to my prior answer. I don't know him."

Nikki told the ex-con about the priest's murder and asked him where he was that night. He pondered, fixing his eyes to the ceiling and swabbing a chalky tongue over his laminates.

"As I recall, I was out to dinner. Yes, at La Grenouille and then back to my apartment for the remainder of the night. I'd rented *Quantum of Solace* on Blu-ray. You could be a Bond Girl yourself, Detective."

Heat ignored the comment but made a note of his alibi. She collected the tins of cash to go. Then she sat them back down and opened her pad again. "And where were you yesterday between eleven A.M. and two P.M.?"

"Do you plan to convict me of every murder in New York City?"

"No, Mr. Martinez. I'll be satisfied with just two."

———

After Nikki returned the DEA cash to Property, she went back to the bull pen to check messages before she left for her orals. At the entrance, she stopped and stared in disbelief. Internal Affairs had boxed and cleared everything in Captain Montrose's office. It sat completely empty.

———

Late that afternoon at One Police Plaza, they called Heat's name. She put down the magazine she couldn't concentrate on and stepped into the examination room.

It was just as Nikki had pictured it when she had visualized the orals in her mental preparation. Heat had learned from others who had taken the boards what to expect, and there was the scene before her. She stepped into a fluorescent-lit, windowless classroom where five examiners—a mix of active duty captains and administrators—sat behind a long table facing a lone chair. Hers. When Nikki said hello and took her seat, the dynamic suddenly reminded her of the ballet school judges scene in *Flashdance*. If only she could get through this by busting a move.

"Good afternoon, Detective," began the administrator from Personnel who was moderating. Ripples of test anxiety stirred in Nikki. "Each member here will be asking you open-ended questions relevant to the duties of lieutenant in the NYPD. You may answer in any way you choose. Each of us will score your answers, then we'll combine results to determine the disposition of your candidacy. Do you understand today's procedure?"

"Yes, sir, I do."

And then it began.

"What do you see as your weakness?" asked the woman from Community Relations. A trapdoor if there ever was one. If you say you don't have one, points off for being cocky. Name a flaw that inhibits your ability to do the job, you might as well get up and leave the room then.

"My weakness," began Nikki, "is that I care so much about the job that I invest in it at the expense of my personal life. That's largely because I don't see this so much as a job but a career—or actually, a mission. Being a member of this department is my life. To serve the victims, plus my fellow officers and detectives . . ." The simple process of diving in and speaking from her heart calmed the stage fright inside her. The satisfied looks from the panel told her she was off on the right foot, too, and that didn't hurt her ability to keep her head.

Focused and relaxed as she had now become, the questions that came at her during the next half hour felt more like honest conversation than a make-break test. Nikki deftly fielded inquiries about everything from how she would specifically go about evaluating those under her, to her feelings about workplace diversity, to means to deal with sexual harassment, to command judgments such as when, and when not, to deploy vehicle pursuits.

As the session came near its end, one of the judges, a commander from Staten Island who from his body language she read as the sole doubter up there, said, "I see here that you killed someone the other day."

"I believe two suspects, sir. Only one has been confirmed."

"And how do you feel about that?"

Nikki paused before answering, knowing this was another tricky one. "Regretful. I value life, and that was . . . and always would be . . . a last resort. But if the play is dealt, I have to respond."

"Do you feel it was a fair fight?"

"Respectfully, Captain? If someone is looking for a fair fight, he'd better not draw on me."

The members shared nods and satisfied looks and passed their score sheets to the moderator. He looked them over and said, "We will, of course, have to calculate these, but I feel confident in saying you have done exceptionally well, Detective Heat. Combining this with your outstanding score on the written, I have a feeling good news is coming, and soon."

"Thank you."

The Personnel administrator said, "If I'm not getting ahead of the horse here, have you given any thought to commanding your own precinct?"

"Not really."

He grinned. "I would."

———

Promptly at nine the next morning, Detective Heat announced herself to the receptionist in the lobby of the Terence Cardinal Cooke Building in Sutton Place. To Nikki, the archdiocese headquarters was an odd place to be while tapering off a mild hangover and feeling blissfully sore following her night with Rook. He had insisted on a major celebration after her oral boards, and party they did. A pocket of warmth grew inside her as she reflected on how fortunate she was to have a man like him in her life, who always sought ways to escape to brightness amid the dark. Her face broadened into a dopey smirk, recalling how she had made Rook laugh by screaming "quatrain!" at a critical moment in bed.

An administrative aide in a brown three-piece suit, who introduced himself as Roland Jackson, was waiting on the nineteenth floor when the elevator opened onto the chancery offices. "Monsignor is expecting you." He carried an armload of fat manila pocket files in one arm and gestured with the other for her to precede him through the nearest door. "Detective Heat is here," he said as they stepped in.

They had caught the monsignor hurrying to put on his black suit jacket for the meeting. He was still flexing his elbow to adjust one sleeve as he came around to shake her hand, which he did with both of his. "Hi, Pete Lynch."

"Thanks for making the time, Monsignor." Nikki returned his warm smile. Thirsty as she was, Heat declined the coffee or tea offer, and the three of them took seats in the modest conversation grouping to the side of the monsignor's desk. "I understand this is in regard to Gerry Graf," Monsignor Lynch said. His countenance darkened. "It's a staggering loss. When something like that happens anywhere, it's deeply felt, but more so among our fraternity. You must know that. I hear you lost one of your own, too. He's in our prayers, as well."

She thanked him and then steered the conversation back to Father Graf. "As the man who administers the day-to-day affairs of the archdiocese, I wanted to get a sense from you of him as a pastor. Were you aware of any problems with him?"

"Such as?"

"Well, for instance, any financial irregularities in parish accounting? Conflicts with parishioners or anyone here? Inappropriate behavior . . . of any kind?"

"You can say it, Detective, you mean sexual?"

"I do." Nikki found herself studying the monsignor, then staring.

"None I am aware of." He broke off eye contact and removed his wire-framed glasses to rub the bridge of his nose between his thumb and forefinger. "Roland has the parish books there. Anything untoward?"

"No, nothing of the sort." Mr. Jackson patted the files on his lap. "His books always balanced, he was loved by the parish, and he was not involved in any personal scandals."

"What about the situation with the priest you removed, the one who they say molested those boys on the field trip?"

The monsignor's forehead gained a mild sheen, and a glance flicked between the two men. "Father Shea," prompted Roland Jackson without necessity.

"These behaviors are the scourge of our holy church now. As you mentioned, we removed that priest immediately, and he is in a counseling program isolated from any parish, especially children." Then Monsignor Lynch added, "He will probably face criminal charges— and should."

Nikki said, "I hear one of the parents threatened Father Graf, accusing him of complicity."

"You mean Mr. Hays." He replaced his glasses. "Can you begin to imagine the pain a parent endures when his innocent child is molested?"

"Unimaginable," she said. "I wanted to find out if you were privy to any specific threats against Father Graf made by Mr. Hays."

Jackson shuffled his deck of pocket files and found a printout of an e-mail. "About a month and a half ago, Father Gerry received this." He handed the page to Nikki. It was a full page, single-spaced rant laden with expletives and accusations. The last lines read, "You ever hear of a Tikrit Tune-up? I have, padre. You suffer until you pray to die and then you suffer some more. Lots more. The best part is when you call out to God for mercy and He looks down and spits upon your withered douche bag of a soul."

"Monsignor Lynch," said Heat, "this is not only direct and specific, but it's very much like the way he was killed. Didn't you take this seriously?"

"Of course, Detective, no threat would be dismissed out of hand. However, Mr. Hays was understandably agitated. Also, Father Graf wasn't the only one he sent notes like this to, so we had no cause to focus on him alone."

Roland Jackson backed him up. "Father Shea got one, of course, very similar."

"Even I got one," said the monsignor.

"Why didn't you report this to the police?" she asked.

"We were hoping to handle this as an internal matter."

Heat said, "And how has all that been working out for you fellas?"

Monsignor Lynch registered a weary sense of defeat. "Your point has been well made many times, Detective Heat, believe me. And, given the benefit of hindsight, well . . ." He lowered his eyes and then brought them back to her. "Do you have any idea what it is like to love an organization so much that it is like your family? But like any family, it has flaws that pain you, but you endure nonetheless because you trust in its greatness?"

"I think I have an idea," she said.

―――――

The cold blast when she came out the revolving door onto First Avenue numbed Nikki's face, and the wind was so strong that Heat had to shelter against the dark gray marble wall of the vestibule so she could make out Deputy Commissioner Yarborough over the scratchiness on her cell phone. "Is this a bad time, Nikki?"

"No, I'm just out here pounding the pavement."

"Well, if what I hear is true, you won't be doing that much longer. You're the talk of the building this morning after your oral boards. I have a feeling you're going to have bigger responsibilities than wearing down your Nine Wests in the cold."

A fire truck rolled by with full siren and horn. Nikki plugged one ear and turned to the wall. When it had passed, she said, "That's awesome. I have to admit, it felt like it went OK."

Phyllis Yarborough laughed. "Love the understatement. Let me tell you how I read it. I think you're not only going to get your gold bar, but with the sudden command void in your precinct, there's talk they may fast-track you to a captaincy so you can assume Montrose's job. Nothing's firm, but this is your heads-up to hang loose on your calendar. You may get the call anytime, think you can do that?" In the brief pause when Nikki's heart fluttered, the deputy commissioner said, "Don't worry, Nikki. We both know you're up for the task."

―――――

The Waterfront Ale House, the closest eats near the OCME, was at the start of lunch rush so Nikki Heat and Lauren Parry grabbed one of the high tops in the bar rather than wait for a table. For a saloon the food was surprisingly good and always adventurous. Both ordered from the chalkboard. Nikki had the porter onion soup, her friend broke out and said she'd try the elk burger.

After Heat filled her in on her exam results and the recent call from Phyllis Yarborough, Lauren congratulated her, but seemed muted. She said that in spite of the good news, she was worried about Nikki after her ordeal in Central Park. The detective glanced out the window to Second and The Discourager parked in his blue-and-white and reassured Lauren she felt secure enough. "And after lunch I'll be in the safest place in Manhattan. The Montroses didn't leave any relatives, so I'm going to 1PP to see what I can do to assist with the memorial service."

Their food arrived. The ME bisected her elk burger and asked, "No relatives? No kids?"

"The dog was their kid."

"What kind of dog?"

"Long-haired mini dachshund, just like yours." Heat pulled a strand of melty cheese from her spoon and could see the wheels turning in her friend. "Dr. Parry, before you get any ideas about Lola getting a big sister, the captain's neighbor has Penny and wants to keep her."

"Penny . . . ," said Lauren. "Tell me she isn't sweet."

"A prancing bundle of cuteness." Heat grew reflective. "It's one more thing that weakens the suicide theory. Cap doted on Penny. No matter what else was going on, no way he would just abandon her."

"Good luck trying to derail where this train is heading with that," said the ME. "This has momentum. A suicide disposition is all but signed and sealed."

Nikki studied her friend. "Is it me, or do I hear reservations?"

"I am a skeptic by profession. That's science."

"But . . ."

Lauren Parry set down the crescent of remaining burger and dabbed her mouth. "I don't like the bullet trajectory. It's in the realm, but for my taste it tracks forward and to the left too much. Plus it was a chin shot." They both knew that most shooters minimized a nonfatal miss factor by sticking the barrel in their mouths, hence the cop slang "eating your gun." She must have sensed

Nikki's thought process and added, "Yes, there was residue on his hand."

Heat pushed her soup aside and stared out the window, lost in thought.

———

She should have known something was off by the look on the lieuten-ant's face when she showed him her list. "I see . . . right. Just a moment, please." The department's funeral director went to a desk in the back of the small office suite and punched a number on his phone without sitting. While Nikki waited, she studied the Honor Roll of the Fallen—heroes remembered forever on tall brass plaques that lined the walls of the reception area. Framed pictures traced the history of memorial ceremonies for New York's Finest from sepia to black-and-white to Kodachrome to digital. She reviewed her list, which included suggested speakers, Emerald Society bagpipes, and a request for a helicopter flyover, since that was one of Captain Montrose's early units before he made detective.

Lieutenant Prescott returned. "Would you like to have a seat?"

"Is there a problem?"

Prescott's face grew solemn. "Detective Heat, I appreciate your volunteering to assist us with the service for Captain Montrose, but our planning doesn't go to anything as, well . . . elaborate . . . in this particular case."

"Is it the helicopter? I've seen it done, but that's only an idea."

"Frankly," he said with sympathy in his eyes, "none of it fits our planning." When she frowned, he added, "Well, perhaps a speaker. You, if you like."

Someone came in, and when she turned, Zach Hamner was there in shirtsleeves and tie. "You should have called me, Heat, I could have saved you a trip."

"Why are you part of this?" she asked but directed it to Prescott.

"I phoned him," explained the lieutenant. "In interpretive cases like this one, we consult with the commissioner of legal matters."

"I don't understand 'interpretive,'" said Nikki.

"Simple as this," said The Hammer. "A ruling needs to be made as to whether a Full Honors service is appropriate for a death that's not line of duty. Budget watchdogs like to sue if the city spends frivolously."

"Frivolously?!"

Hamner waved both hands in front of him. "Calm down, not my term, OK? But the people who sue use it, and worse. However, the fact remains, a Full Honors memorial for a suicide, not to mention for a cop whose suspicious activity may implicate him in a murder . . . ?" He shook his head.

"I can't believe I'm hearing this," she said. "We're talking about a veteran, decorated precinct commander. They haven't ruled it suicide yet. And where do you get this business of suspicious activity implicating him in a murder?"

"Why, from you. Yes, I got a prelim from your IA meet this morning."

Heat was floored. Her own words were being abused. "This is unacceptable. No Full Honors? What are you planning, Zach, a cardboard box and a shopping cart?"

Prescott stepped in to quell the storm. "We have a nice service level that includes a suburban mortuary near his home and an escorted ride with several motorcycles to the plot near his late wife."

"And this is the last word?"

Zach said, "It is unless someone else foots the bill."

"This is an affront."

"This is what happens when you take the coward's way out."

"Mr. Hamner . . . ," cautioned the lieutenant, but Nikki wouldn't be stopped.

"That's it," said Heat. "I know how to deal with this. I'm going public."

"You'll do no such thing," said Hamner. "If you go to the press, do you realize the damage that would do?"

"I can only hope so," she said and then left.

————

Back in the bull pen, Nikki was still fuming. She had unloaded over the phone to Rook on her way uptown to the precinct and thought she had calmed down, but announcing the slap against Montrose to the squad only rekindled her anger. The words of the monsignor from that morning about having faith in a family despite its flaws did little to quell her upset.

So Nikki Heat did what she always did under those circumstances: immersed herself in work. "I want Lawrence Hays the minute he gets back in New York," she said to Detective Raley. "He made a specific threat against Graf in writing and I want him, now." She gave him copies of the e-mail threat to distribute to the squad.

Raley read the e-mail. "Whoa. . . . On it."

Detective Ochoa said, "I may have something to make you feel a little better. I couldn't let go of why Father Graf's housekeeper, Mrs. Borelli, is being be so cagey about our mystery guest." He pointed to the unidentified man in the Pleasure Bound surveillance still. "So I ran her last name through priors."

"Great idea," said Sharon Hinesburg, whose responsibility it was to ID him, and who hadn't thought of it.

"Anyhoo," continued Ochoa as if Hinesburg hadn't spoken, "I got a hit on a Paul Borelli in Bensonhurst. Nothing big, a few busts for weed and disorderly conduct." He handed her the mug shot. It was a match for the man on the board.

"Her son?"

"Nephew."

"Still enough to embarrass his aunt. Pay him a visit." Nikki posted the mug shot on the Murder Board next to the surveillance photo. "Oh, and nice one."

"Yeah," said Detective Hinesburg. "Nice one."

————

When Nikki came home to her apartment and opened her front door, it banged into something after a few inches and stopped. "Oof," said

Rook on the other side. "Hang on a sec." Then he pulled it open wide. He was holding a screwdriver and standing beside a stepstool.

"What are you doing?" she asked.

"I have a surprise for you." He pointed above the door, to where he had mounted a wireless lipstick camera. "Huh? What do you think?"

"Rook, a NannyCam?"

"Correction: NikkiCam. After the fingerprint team left, I thought you needed some extra security, so I went over to the spy store on Christopher Street. I could spend hours in there. Mainly because I can see myself on every monitor." He struck a pose in the hall mirror. "I really am ruggedly handsome, aren't I?"

She stepped past him and looked up at the camera. "Not a bad installation."

"Oo, this is starting to sound like one of those porn videos where I'm the casual laborer." Rook smiled. "As you know, nothing casual about how I work."

"No, quite diligent. You're on my list for employee of the month." She kissed him and went to the counter to drop the stack of mail she had brought up along with the evening newspaper.

"What's your pref for dinner? Take out or go out?" When she didn't answer, he turned. Nikki's face had gone pale. "What?" Rook got up and stood beside her at the counter where she had unfolded the front page of the *New York Ledger*. When he saw the headline, he looked at Nikki but didn't dare interrupt her. Heat was too engrossed, too stunned by what she was reading.

TEN

INFERNAL AFFAIRS
Suicide Cop, Infighting Tarnish 20th

Insider Exclusive

By Tam Svejda, Senior METRO Reporter

Just how bad can it get for the NYPD's 20th Precinct? Yesterday this paper reported bickering and disarray within the station's Homicide Squad over what has been characterized as "a rudderless, wheel-spinning" probe into the shocking sex dungeon strangulation of a local priest. First it was the good father, now it seems it's his investigation that's choking.

Frustrated detectives were openly questioning the leadership of longtime precinct commander, Captain Charles Montrose. According to those familiar with the situation, the captain had recently become more of a part-time visitor than a full-time commander at his Upper West Side cop shop, spending increasingly more hours outside his office, and closing himself off from staff the few hours he was present.

Friction . . . and Heat

Sources agreeing to speak on condition of anonymity confirm the captain's absences were only one element that failed to get the investigation into Father Gerry Graf's murder out of the starting blocks. Montrose's disputed choices hamstrung detectives (led by magazine cover-cop Nikki Heat, whose dazzling rate of case clearance made her a rising star among hero-hungry commishes downtown). For instance, he banned Detective Heat and her ace squad from following promising leads, instead ordering them to pursue a grand tour of Dungeon Alley, even though it was a road that continually proved colorful yet fruitless.

Members of the 20th also recently witnessed an in-house throw down between Heat and Capt. Montrose over the stalled case, complete with desk pounding and finger pointing. "It was NYPD black and blue," said one insider who asked not to be identified.

Bad To Worse

The latest installment in this melodrama was written in blood. Yesterday police responded to a gunshot victim in a parked car. The man was none other than Captain Charles Montrose. Pronounced dead at the scene, he was killed by a single bullet wound to the brain from his own gun. The incident occurred at the curb of Our Lady of the Innocents—poetically, ironically, but not so coincidentally—the very parish of the murdered priest.

Buried Anger

The controversy surrounding a commander under fire, and now a probable suicide, has spilled out of the brick and concrete bunker on W. 82nd that houses the Two-Oh and rattled some windows a few miles south at One Police Plaza. NYPD toppers have reportedly balked at a Full Honors memorial service for the dead captain, leaving some in the ranks of The Finest angered by the lack of wisdom—and compassion—in a decision to dishonor a long career tarnished at its end, but preceded by decades of bravery, spotless service, and sacrifice.

Angry cops recognize the obvious. The climate of upheaval is not solving any cases. One source summarized it this way. "Whoever killed Father Graf is still out there. In an election year I sure wouldn't want to have to explain to the citizens of New York City why killers roam free while the brass picks fights over the size of a fallen veteran's funeral." Evidence points to one thing that's certain. The NYPD has one problem that cannot be buried.

Nikki started to pace. "This is not good, this is not going to help."

Rook said, "Last I checked the *Ledger* wasn't so much about helping anything except newspaper sales. Seems fine to me. OK, her writing's a little on the tabloidy side, but that's not so much a flaw as an editorial policy."

She mulled the tone Rook had used for "her writing." Nikki's antenna was already up about Tam Svejda, but she had refused to play the role of current girlfriend jealous of the ex. So then, Heat asked herself, why was she obsessing?

"I don't see the problem," continued Rook. "Yellow prose aside, it hits the mark, doesn't it?"

"That is the problem. She never names sources but clearly someone in the precinct is feeding her." And then she stopped pacing and nibbled her lower lip. "They're going to think it's me, you know."

"Who is?"

"1PP. The timing of this couldn't be worse after I lost it with Zach Hamner and threatened to go public."

"Did you?"

"No, of course not."

"Then don't worry."

"I guess," she said. And then read the article again.

––––––

Heat's money was on Sharon Hinesburg as the leak. When Nikki got there the next morning for the start of shift, bull pen chatter was all about the *Ledger* piece, and when she scanned the faces of her squad, the only one she could picture blabbing to the media was the only detective who wasn't in on the conversation . . . because she was over at her desk on a personal call.

One thing was clear under the volcano cloud of negativity. Nobody in that building had mixed feelings about Montrose's funeral. Roach had already opened an account at a local bank for donations, and everyone said they'd kick in. "Fuck 'em," said Ochoa. "If downtown won't give Skip a send-off, we will."

Nikki called the squad to the Murder Board to change the channel from gossip to work. "Detective Ochoa, where are we on Mrs. Borelli's nephew?"

"Paid a visit to Paulie Borelli yesterday in Bensonhurst, where he's a part-time chef at Legendary Luigi's Pizza."

"Luigi's Original?" asked Rhymer.

"No, Legendary. Luigi's Original is actually a copy."

"What about Paulie?" asked Heat.

"He says he never even met Father Graf. FYI, Paulie B. doesn't strike me as much of a churchgoer. He did cop to being a semi-reg at Pleasure Bound, but not the night of the priest's murder. He alibis out at an establishment in the Alley known as . . . ," Ochoa flipped a page in his pad and recited, "The Strung and the Restless."

There was laughter—the first Nikki had heard in that squad in a long time. She let it play out and then said, "In deference to Mrs. Borelli, we'll let it drop there." Compassion ruled. Nikki couldn't see increasing the old woman's mortification.

There was a stirring in the back of the room. Heads turned as a doughy-looking man in a white shirt with two gold bars entered the bull pen. "Oh," he said, "I see I've interrupted."

Heat took a half step toward him. "No problem, Captain, may I help you?"

He came up to join Nikki at the Murder Board and addressed the squad. "Probably best that you're all in one place for this. I'm Captain Irons. I've been assigned as the interim commander of this precinct. My mandate is to get things on an even keel here while the decision is made as to who should be the permanent replacement for Captain Montrose." He paused, and Nikki saw numerous eyes go to her, but she remained stoic and gave the temporary man her attention. "Now, even though I come from Administration, and it's been a few years since I was out here in the field, and I know I can't replace your old cap, I'll do my best to make this workable for everyone. Fair enough?" The room chorused a "fair enough" back to him.

Even though it was limp, he said, "Thank you for that." He turned
to Nikki. "Detective Heat? A moment?"

————

They met in Montrose's glass office and stood because it was still bare
following the instant purge by Internal Affairs. "Guess I'll have to
get some furniture, won't I?" He sat against the lip of the counter that
housed the heat register, and Nikki noticed how his soft belly forced
his shirt to spread between the buttons. "I know your rep. You're a
heck of a detective."

"Thank you," she said, "I do my best."

"Here's the deal. I have a shot here at turning things around,
direction-wise." Irons gave her a look of significance as she wondered
how else one turned things around except direction-wise. "Now, I
know you are involved in some holdover cases."

Heat put a mildly corrective spin on it. "Actually, I have an active
case. In fact, the meeting you . . . ah, joined . . . was about the case
I'm working now. The dead priest?"

"That's all fine, but that goes back burner. Effective now. I have
set a personal goal to show what I can do here. And, for me, that
means turning to a fresh page and running hard with cases that start
on my watch. Day one. Today."

"Excuse me, Captain Irons, but I was attacked in Central Park
by five armed men, three of whom are still out there, and I believe it
was related to the Graf murder."

"You believe? You mean like an assumption? A theory?"

"Yes, I know it's not the same as proof," she said, already feeling
herself on quicksand. "I'm working it hard now, sir. And since we
got off to a slow start already, I don't believe this is the time to put it
on the back burner."

"I understand your personal interest." It sounded dismissive because it was. He crossed his arms and studied his shoe shine, then said,
"The guy you killed, he had gang connections on his sheet, right?"

"Yes, but—"

"I've been reading all the departmental bulletins about gang initiations, some of which are to target police officers. I think I can work this out for both of us by turning this over to the gang task force. If you're a target, you can step aside from that case, be safe, and I get my investigative priorities met." He didn't wait for her to respond. "Now. Moving forward. I hear some patrol officers discovered a body in one of the pedestrian tunnels in Riverside Park about a half hour ago. Homeless guy. But if there's foul play, I want to be all over that. Top priority."

Detective Heat pondered a moment and smiled. "Then you want my best investigator on this. Sharon Hinesburg."

"Can you spare her?"

"I'll manage, sir."

He seemed happy. Nikki would be happier when she replaced him.

———

Detective Rhymer came to Heat's desk. "Just got back from a meet with our German dancer's agent. The guy's a sketch. A support system for a toupee working out of a fleabag office in Chelsea."

"Any beefs between the agent and the client?" she asked.

"Anything but. The rep told me Meuller was a steady client who worked hard, stayed out of trouble, and made him a lot of money. The only bump in the road was that Meuller's boyfriend died recently," said Rhymer. "Agent says after that, his top earner changed addresses and basically crawled in a hole. Didn't answer calls, like that."

"How did the boyfriend die?" asked Heat.

"Ahead of you. I checked it out. Natural causes. He had some congenital heart condition and the ol' ticker stopped ticking."

Over at his desk, Detective Raley hung up his phone so quickly he missed the cradle. He replaced it while he grabbed his coat and hurried over. "Lawrence Hays's private jet just touched down at Teterboro."

———

The New York headquarters of Lancer Standard comprised the top two floors of a black glass office high-rise on Vanderbilt a half block from Grand Central. It was the sort of building commuters passed every day hustling to and from trains without giving it much notice, unless they were clients of the custom shirtmaker on the ground floor or the gourmet gym in its basement.

"Is Mr. Hays expecting you?" asked the woman behind the counter in the reception lobby.

Detective Heat reflected on the nature of work done by this soldiers-and-spies-for-hire company, and then on the operative that Rook saw casing her apartment, and said, "I'm going to bet Mr. Hays already knows we're here." The receptionist invited them to have seats, but the three cops stepped away from the pink marble counter and stood. Roach had insisted they accompany Heat to this meeting. The Discourager, hunkered in his blue-and-white Radio Mobile Unit, may have had her back in transit, but Raley and Ochoa didn't want her walking into the offices of a CIA con- tractor alone.

It was only seconds before they heard a buzz and two very fit men held the wood-paneled door open to the security vestibule. As she passed the pair, Nikki could see their suits were tailored to ac- commodate shoulder holsters, which made her wonder if the custom shirtmaker twenty-six floors below was the beneficiary of his co- tenants' outfitting requirements. Before they could proceed, the lobby door needed to close behind them and lock. When the bolt shot, one of the minders pressed his thumbprint to a scanner and the door ahead of them slid open.

At the top of a carpeted spiral staircase they arrived at the pent- house floor and the anteroom of Lawrence Hays's executive suite. In a very matter-of-fact way, one of the escorts said, "I'd like to take your firearms."

"I'd like to see you try," said Ochoa, equally as matter-of-factly. There was no way Heat was going to give up her weapon, either, and she wondered how this would play out—three New York cops facing two running backs in a stare-down.

The door opened and Hays said, "Stand down, they can come in as is."

Heat recognized him from the Internet search she had done as well as from a *20/20* profile she had seen on Hays the year before, after he personally led a daring helicopter mission to rescue one of his contractors who had been kidnapped by the Taliban. He was Top Gun handsome but shorter than she'd expected. In the video profile he had laughed and described himself as "five-foot-eight of pissed off cobra," and he was all that, particularly with his alert eyes and that lean muscle flexing under his black polo shirt and tight Gap jeans.

Hays picked his travel duffel off the couch, tossed it beside his desk, and gestured for them to sit. He took the tan leather easy chair facing them, which complemented his sandy Steve McQueen hair and desert suntan. The relaxed throw of one leg over the other, the casual dangling of his aviators from the V of his shirt, and the heartland smile were winning enough to Nikki, but as she settled down between Raley and Ochoa, she reminded herself this was the man who might have killed—or arranged to have killed—Father Graf and sent a platoon of operatives to Central Park to cancel her day. Those were two items Nikki wanted to find out about. Or at least hear his answers and put them to the smell test.

"What can I do for you, Detectives?"

Heat decided to pull the rug on the laid back pose. "For starters, you can tell me how it felt to kill Father Graf."

The response from Hays was curious. No, bizarre. Rather than getting rattled, he lounged his head back onto the chair and smiled. As if narrating a nature video, he spoke to the ceiling. "And so the gal detective begins with a weak attempt to throw the interview subject off balance. Classic opening gambit, which is to say . . . ," he brought his head forward to look into her eyes and said, ". . . clichéd."

"You haven't answered my question, Mr. Hays."

"You've got to earn my answers, miss." And then, narrating again, he said, "Ouch. In the hole on the first Q! Frustrated by the response; distracted by the chaff of implied sexism. What will she do?"

Heat knew exactly what he was up to. Hays was employing some sort of mind game to fend her off and hijack the interview. Probably some counter-interrogation technique he taught in Ely, Nevada. She told herself to shut out his psychological noise and stick to her agenda.

"Where were you the night your pastor was killed?"

"Why?"

"Because I suspect you may have killed him and I want to confirm your whereabouts."

"Strategy Two employed," he announced. "Stepping it down from the absolute 'how did it feel' to the wimpy 'you may have.' Why, oh, why do they send me amateurs?"

"Your whereabouts, Mr. Hays."

"Where? Oh . . . about." He laughed. "About could be so many places. She will be a long time checking that."

Nikki decided to shift gears on him. She took out the picture of Sergio Torres and handed it over. "Do you know this man?"

"This is no man. This is a photograph." He cocked an eye at her. "Oh, tell me the glorified meter maid doesn't have a sense of humor."

"His name is Sergio Torres," continued Heat, "and I want to know if you have ever employed him as one of your contractors."

He nodded. "That I will answer." Hays waited until he had milked the moment. ". . . By saying that I do not confirm or deny personnel in my employ for reasons of their own safety. And national security." He laughed again and said to Raley, "You could ask Julian Assange."

Heat persisted. "So you have never seen him?"

"Mm, they all look about the same to me."

Ochoa tensed beside her. She pressed a gentle elbow against him and he settled.

Hays lifted his arm like a pupil. "May I ask one now?" She waited and he said, "Why are you asking me about this . . . *hombre*?"

"Because the same day he tried to kill me, one of your operatives was seen doing surveillance on my apartment." It was the first time she had seen him thrown. Not much, but the cobra eyes took a hit.

"Let me tell you something, Officer. If I was going to conduct surveillance on you, you'd never know it."

This time Heat provided the narration. She looked up at the ceiling and said, "Invulnerable mercenary general covers ass for sloppy work with bravado, even as he makes mental note to seek and terminate the stakeout driver." She lowered her gaze to him and said, "Rookie." While he was digesting that she took out the e-mail from the archdiocese and recited, "'You ever hear of a Tikrit Tune-up? I have, padre. You suffer until you pray to die and then you suffer some more. Lots more. The best part is when you call out to God for mercy and He looks down and spits upon your withered douche bag of a soul.'"

"He covered for that freak who touched my kid." The CEO swagger was crumbling. The lid was sliding off the parent's rage.

"You don't deny writing this?" she said.

"You're not listening! These guys spoil innocence and hide behind their cassocks and cover for each other."

Nikki held up the page. "Because this description is very much like how he died."

"Good. One less sanctimonious bastard protecting the child molesters of the world." He sat panting, leaning forward on his thighs.

Nikki stood. "Mr. Hays, I'd give you my card, but I am sure you have fully researched all the ways to find me. When you have an alibi for that night, you'd better give it to me. Or I'll be back and arrest you. At your . . . whereabouts."

———

They waited until they got out onto the sidewalk on Vanderbilt, all three detectives assuming the place would likely be wired for sound, maybe even picture.

"What was that guy on?" said Raley.

"All calculated, Rales. Psy-Ops smoke screen." Then Heat said, "I want you guys to dig away on Sergio Torres. Go back to his kindergarten if you have to. Girlfriends, gang members, cell mates, everyone. Find out who he's connected to and we've got our killer."

Ochoa looked up to the top of the black high-rise. "We were so close."

Heat said, "Not enough. Hays gave us nothing solid. He only said he was glad it happened—not that he did it."

"What about the e-mail, though?" asked Raley.

Nikki shook her head. "Any lawyer would punch holes through it because he never says technically he's going to carry it out. His verbiage is rhetorical. The threat's implied."

Ochoa said, "Tell that to Father Graf."

"We seem to be in the minority, but we all know this is a hell of a lot bigger than Father Graf, guys," said Heat. "There was the attack on me, plus whatever Captain Montrose was into."

"You don't think he was part of the killing, do you?" said Raley.

"In my heart, of course not. But we need to keep on this without letting up so we can see where it goes."

Ochoa said, "Too bad our new commander doesn't see it the same way."

Heat's phone buzzed. She checked the screen and it was a text from Zach Hamner. "Pls come to 1PP conf. rm on 10 in 30 mins." A rush of elation swept in Nikki's chest. She replied with a yes and said to Roach, "Keep the faith, boys. Remember, Irons is only interim."

———

Snow began falling in fat clumps, making Nikki's traffic experience getting downtown to Park Row a nightmare. If she had only taken the subway, it would have been a snap just to duck into Grand Central from the Hays meeting and grab a 4 or 5 express to Centre Street. Fifteen, maybe twenty minutes, and done. But with the rest of the shooting team that hunted her down in the park still at large, Raley and Ochoa persisted and she gave in, allowing The Discourager to drive her to One Police Plaza in his RMU.

Harvey wasn't much of a talker, which was fine with her; she was trying to clear her head for her big moment and could do without. The only conversation they had was when he offered to light up the bar on top of the cruiser when it looked as if she'd be late and she said no. He made up for it with assertive wheel work and liberal use of his horn. When Nikki got out in front of the Municipal Building on Centre, she was tense and fighting car sickness.

Heat reached the lobby of 1PP with ten minutes she never thought she'd have to spare. She needed that time to collect herself. After the promotion and swearing in, she might be called upon to speak to the committee and she didn't want to go in frazzled. Especially if, as Phyllis told her, they might be bumping her to captain and giving her a command, she didn't want to blather and make them rethink their choice. She wished Rook could be there, and the fact that she thought of him sharing that moment with her brought her a degree of calm. They could celebrate later. Brushing the snow off her coat, she looked for a quiet place to sit and think.

The seats where she had enjoyed her conversation with Commissioner Yarborough were open, but on her way over she stopped. Tam Svejda stood in her path. Her back was to Heat as she folded her notebook and shook hands with the public information officer. Nikki made a sharp turn to get to the elevators before she was spotted, but it was too late.

"Detective Heat? Nikki Heat, wait up." Nikki stopped and turned. The PIO gave her a cursory glance as he passed by and took the elevator car Heat had been waiting for. "How did you like the article?" asked Tam as she strolled over.

"Tam, I'm sorry but I have a very important meeting I can't be late for." Nikki pressed the button and added, "Not to be rude." Then she pounded the button twice more.

"Listen, this wouldn't be for attribution." The reporter opened her palms. "Look, Ma, no pen. Completely off the record. Any thoughts?"

"My one remark is I wish you would think a little about the damage you do with an article like that, especially to the reputation of a good man."

Childlike, as if she wasn't listening, Tam Svejda said, "Uh-huh. . . . But it was accurate, right? I mean I did ask you for help, but you said no."

"It's not something I do," said Nikki. The elevator opened and she stepped aboard.

"But this worked out just as well, right?"

"What did?"

"Jamie, of course. You couldn't talk, so you used Jamie."

Heat stepped off before the doors closed. "What are you talking about? Your source for that article was Ja— Rook?" Heat wondered if she was being played. She had figured Hinesburg or maybe Gallagher, or both, had leaked the story. In her disbelief she said as much to herself as to the reporter, "You got it from Rook?"

"Yeah, Jamie e-mailed me his notes, even. Oh my God, I thought you knew." Nikki was speechless and just stared. "Nikki Heat, no wonder you're such a great detective. You just got me to reveal my source." Tam slapped her own forehead with the heel of her hand. "Some journalist, huh?"

———

Rook. She needed to talk with Rook. But not then. She couldn't. As soon as Nikki rounded the corner into the hall outside the tenth-floor conference room, a uniform said, "Detective Heat?"

On her walk up, she answered, "Here."

"Go right in," said the officer, "if you're all set."

Nikki couldn't have felt less so. The trauma of the week was enough to put her gut on the spin cycle. Now, adding to her anxiety, came this staggering news that Rook had been the source of a leak to

Tam Svejda. And who was this reporter bimbo to Rook? With all these jagged fragments of distraction swirling in her head, making her very much want to turn and run, Heat put up her firewall. She focused on the promotion waiting on the other side of the door and, with it, her chance to take over the Twentieth and, finally, wrest control of the Graf case and run with it. She nodded to the cop and said, "Set."

————

There was no promotion committee waiting for her. There was only one person in the room and it was Zach Hamner, seated at the far side of the conference table, facing her as she entered. The other fifteen chairs in the room were empty, but she could see from the scattered evidence of coffee rings on napkins and the unaligned swivel chairs that there had been a big meeting there recently.

The next major tell that something was amiss was his flat expression. Plus, he didn't invite her to sit. Instead, he laced his fingers together on the tabletop and said, "Nikki Heat, you are hereby relieved of duty, until further notice."

Blindsided, Nikki felt herself coming undone. Her eyes fluttered, and she began to have the sensation of tumbling, of losing her balance after being hit by the force of the shock. As she tried to gain her equilibrium, the side door opened and Lovell and DeLongpre, the Men in Black from IA, came in and waited. The Hammer said, "Please turn over your shield and gun to these men."

ELEVEN

When Nikki rested a hand on the back of the executive chair in front of her for steadiness, it rocked on its swivel hinge and the result was only to increase her sense of disorientation. She had entered with confident strides to assume her promotion and all that came with it, but in the mere crossing of a threshold she found herself cast adrift. Veering into a sickening emotional slide, Heat went spinning like one of the cars she had passed on the way there: tractionless, grappling for control, hurtling for the inevitable crash.

Detective DeLongpre wanted her shield. Nikki willed herself to reclaim her center and straighten herself up. Then she complied. His IA partner, Lovell, stood on her other flank with his hand out. Heat didn't even look at him. She withdrew her Sig from its holster and handed it over, grip first, but with her eyes locked on Zach Hamner's. "What's this about, Zach?"

"It's about you being suspended from duty while you are under official reprimand. Clear enough?"

Implications crashed over Nikki all at once and she felt her knees weaken. "A reprimand . . . ? What for?"

"For starters, going to the media. You have a problem, you talk to us. You don't go outside the family."

"I didn't talk to the media."

"Bullshit. Yesterday you get all up in my ass about Montrose's funeral, and when you don't get your way, you threaten to go public. And then, this." He held up a copy of the *Ledger* that was marked up with comments in red ink. "This is the commissioner's copy."

"I was upset. I lost it." Nikki lowered her voice to convey the rationality he didn't witness the previous day. "But it was an empty threat. I never should have said it."

"The time to think was back then. You dragged this department down, you disgraced yourself, and you blew a once-in-a-career opportunity. You think you're going to get promoted now? You'll be lucky if you come out of this with a job chalking tires. How the hell are you going to be trusted to lead if you can't be trusted?" He let that sink in and said, "Look, these are the bigs. Ambition is not a dirty word. But never, ever, at the expense of this department, Heat. Because one thing that is not tolerated here is disloyalty. You betrayed us."

"I didn't do it."

"Someone sure did. Do you have any idea the problems you have caused us?"

Nikki thought carefully. Pointing to Rook wouldn't be much help and would only make the leak appear more orchestrated. Even Tam Svejda assumed Heat was utilizing Rook as a back channel. The Hammer would go there before she finished her sentence. So she repeated the truth. "It wasn't I."

"You stick to that, Heat. See how much it comforts you while you sit at home." Zach stood to go.

"But I'm on a case."

"Not anymore." And then The Hammer left the room with the two men from Internal Affairs.

———

Nikki was in such a daze, so lost in her own mind, that she meandered through the snowfall right past The Discourager's blue-and-white. Harvey called out to her from his driver's window, using the title she technically no longer bore. She turned back, wobbling on unsteady feet, feeling like she couldn't pass a field sobriety test, and got in. "Shit's really coming down," he said. It took Heat a second to realize he was describing the storm. "Even you couldn't see through it." He hit the wipers. They scraped heavy, wet clumps to the sides that stuck, but the windshield filled, becoming clotted again before the next pass. The weather was becoming just like her life. It just kept coming down. Nikki wanted to be out in it. She wanted to wander in the snow and disappear.

"Where to?" he said. "Back to your squad?"

His innocent question slapped her with the New Reality. Nikki Heat did not have a squad. She turned her face away, making a project of smearing the condensation from her passenger window so he wouldn't see the tears pooling. "Home," she said. "For now."

———

Rook raced to meet her, skidding on his socks as soon as she opened her door. "You are not going to believe what I just learned." If he had waited, maybe taken a breath, he would have sensed it, seen the damage, downshifted and cocked his head and asked what was up. Instead, she got his back, retreating to the laptop on her dining table, shooting power fists in the air and roaring, "Yesss!" Nikki drifted into her apartment behind him, not hearing or even feeling her own footfalls. The sensation was as if she were floating or, dare she say— suspended.

Nose deep in his MacBook Pro, Rook crackled with energy. "It's been eating at me. I remembered hearing something about Lancer Standard—Lancer Standard: Mercenaries to the Stars." He turned to her to laugh, but Heat startled him by slamming down the lid of his laptop.

"Why'd you do it?" she said.

He searched her, frowning. ". . . Nik?"

"You can quit the act. Tam Svejda told me."

He looked puzzled. "Tam? You talked to Tam? About what?"

She moved to the counter and came back brandishing the copy of the *Ledger*. "This. The article that just got me suspended because they think I leaked it."

"Oh, my God," Rook shot to his feet, "they suspended you?" He took a step to her.

"Don't!" She put up both palms to stay him and he stopped. "Just . . . keep away from me."

His mind was racing, so it took him a few seconds to piece things together, and by then, she was striding to the kitchen. He hurried to follow, catching up to her as she opened the fridge. "You really think I had something to do with this?"

"I didn't have to think it. I was told. By your bouncing Czech." She still had the newspaper in her hand and tossed it at him. By reflex, he caught it.

"Tam? Tam told you I sourced this?" Rook realized he still had the offending *Ledger* in his hands and tossed it into the other room. "No way."

"Great. Now you're calling me a liar?" said Heat.

"No, no, I believe you. I just don't understand why she would say that." He felt it all spinning out of control and said, "Nikki, listen to me. I did not leak this to her."

"Yuh, right. Like you're going to admit it now."

"How can you think it was me?"

Heat reached past the Sancerre and pulled out a Pellegrino. This was a time for a clear head. "For one, I've been looking at that prose you said was so . . . what did you call it? . . . tabloidy? Well, I smell a few Rook-isms in there. Calling the funeral issue a 'problem that cannot be buried' . . . What else? Oh. 'NYPD black and blue'?"

"Come on, I . . ." He stopped himself and looked like he'd tasted something foul.

"So those *are* your words." She ditched the water and got out the wine.

"Sort of. But I never shared. It sounds like synchronicity."

"It sounds like bull. Tam says you e-mailed notes to her."

"Nope. Did not."

Nikki pointed to his laptop over on the dining table. "What was that secret typing you've been doing?"

"All right, full disclosure. Yes, I have been writing up some notes for an article I plan to write on this Montrose thing."

"You what?!"

"See? That's why I didn't tell you. I wasn't sure how you'd feel about it after the cover piece I did on you."

"Rook, this is even more devious. You were hiding it from me because you knew damn well I'd be against it?"

"No. . . . Yes. But I was going to tell you. Eventually."

"You're digging deeper the more you talk."

"Look, I am an investigative journalist and this is a legitimate story."

"That Tam Svejda says you slipped to her."

"No."

"What else did you slip her?"

"Oh. Oh ho! Now I'm seeing what's happening here," he said. "This is the green monster rearing its head."

Nikki slammed the bottle down on the counter with a loud crack. "Do not minimize what I am going through by tagging me with some cheap label."

"I'm sorry, that was out of line."

"Damn right it was. Now it's my turn." The pent-up emotion from her week of agony spilled over. "Get your stuff and get the hell out of here."

"Nikki, I . . ."

"Now."

He hesitated and said, "I thought you trusted me."

But she was already storming down the hallway with the bottle in her hand. The last thing Rook heard from Heat was the locking of her bedroom door.

———

The next morning, even though she knew she had no reason to, Nikki got up at her usual early time, showered, and dressed for work. While she was in the shower, Raley and Ochoa left her a message of between-the-lines support. They knew about the suspension like everyone by now and had left what they called a Roach-mail. "Hey, uh, Detective, or . . . whatever I should call you now," said Ochoa.

Raley was on the other line and said, "Hey, partner, how about a little sensitivity? Hi, it's Roach calling. Do they let you get calls in the penalty box? Anyway your dirty coffee mug is still in the sink down here at the precinct."

"That's right," said Ochoa, "and if you think we're going to wash it for you, dream on. So if you want the mug, well, you know what to do. . . . See ya?"

She thought about calling back, but instead Nikki sat on the cushion of her window seat while she watched a sanitation crew remove the overnight snow from her street. It gave her something to do. As she idled there, Nikki wondered if she should roll some cell phone video, in case she got a chance to upload the latest viral of a parked car getting its fender peeled away by a city snowplow.

That would help her get her job back, all right. Leak video of a municipal embarrassment.

Her solitude was anything but peaceful. Zach Hamner's accusations insisted on visiting her perch in the bay window. He had called her disloyal. She dismissed that but then wondered, had she been? Nikki had done nothing deceitful, but the objective part of her—the part that was all about middle-of-the-night gut checks and self-reproach—wanted to pick at the wound. So she did. Heat asked herself, had she caused harm to others by her relationship with Rook? She hoped not. And then there was ambition. The Hammer had also scolded her about that, and she worried herself over whether her sense of entitlement to the new rank had emboldened her to threaten Zach to go public over the funeral.

What ate at her most was the trust issue. He'd said you can't lead if you can't be trusted. Nikki wasn't bothered by what that cockroach thought of her. But what gnawed at Heat was her own perception. Did she trust herself to lead?

Her phone jarred her back to the present. The caller ID was from 1PP. Nikki went for the green button so quickly, the phone slipped out of her hand, but she caught it before it hit the floor. "Hello? You there?"

"Nikki Heat, it's Phyllis Yarborough. Hope you don't mind me calling your personal number."

"About the only way to reach me today." Heat tried to make it light without putting any stink on it. Like she was taking it all in stride.

"I hear that," said the deputy commissioner. "May I tell you flat out, this sucks?"

Nikki laughed, and even though the call didn't sound like it was going to be the reprieve she had hoped for, she was glad for it. "You won't get much argument out of me."

"I just want you to know, if you weren't aware of it, the decision was not unanimous. There was one dissenting vote, and you're talking to her."

"Oh . . . I didn't know that. But thank you. That means a lot."

"Have to say, I'm not a fan of The Hammer anyway, and this time he did not disappoint. He called the meeting, he fanned the flames, he pressed for the sanction, he was obsessed." Yarborough paused. Nikki figured it was her turn.

"I do have to admit I understand Zach taking it as an affront, the way I lit into him about the captain's funeral."

"Oh, boo-hoo, he needs to grow a pair. I'll tell you something, Nikki, I not only don't believe you leaked this, I believe this is pure politics. Zach and his network of man weasels were fine when I was interested in grooming you for my team at RTCC, but there was a definite sea change after Captain Montrose died." She quieted her tone and added, "I am sorry about that, by the way, I know it's a loss for you."

"Thanks." Nikki's curiosity was piqued. "Why do you suppose the change?"

"Because if my candidate—that would be you, my dear—gets

fast-tracked to replace Montrose that weakens their power. Look who they put in there. Floyd the Barber. They don't want a precinct commander, they want a puppet."

"I appreciate you standing up for me."

"Considering the result, I don't think I did you any favors."

Nikki said, "I think working the street is safer than 1PP."

"That's politics, it's an ugly game."

"And one I don't care to play, thanks," said Heat. "Not why I swore my oath."

"Actually, that's why I called," said the deputy commissioner. "Since backstabbing isn't your favorite sport, I wanted to let you know that I'll keep my eyes open for you. I can't promise there won't be any more surprises, but maybe I can head them off, or at least I can warn you."

"Wow, that's very generous."

"You deserve it. So what's up for you? Daytime dramas? Scrap-booking?" When Nikki's pause was the answer, Yarborough continued, "Of course not. You're Nikki Heat. Listen, do what you have to do. But if you need anything, anything at all, please call me."

"I will," said Heat. "And Phyllis? Thanks."

———

About an hour later, impatient with exile in her apartment, unable to escape needling thoughts through daytime TV, Nikki bundled up. Even the process of getting ready was a confrontation with her unhappy situation: By reflex, she reached for her holster—empty—muttered a quiet curse, and, for the first time Heat could recall in ages, had to step out her door unarmed.

The best way to cover ground in Manhattan during a snow event is to go under it. As was her habit, Nikki picked up a 6 train at Park Avenue South and rode it down to Bleecker for a transfer to the uptown B. Waiting on the platform, she performed the straphanger's rite of leaning over the edge of the track every sixty seconds, scouting up the dark tunnel for the gleam of an oncoming headlight reflected on the tracks. It didn't make the trains come any faster, but it was something to do other than look for scurrying rats in the grime below.

Nikki did her headlight check, she did her rat check, and she also did a platform check. There had been no cruiser parked downstairs that morning—no Discourager to give a two-finger salute or bring coffee to. They had pulled her protection when they pulled her shield. Heat didn't clock any threat and got on her car for the ride uptown to the Twentieth, and was able to relax a bit.

But her inner demons got on with her and muscled into the next seat. Always a clear thinker who could slow things down and navigate the wildest distractions under fire, Nikki couldn't shake her thoughts free of how her whole life had been upended in a blink. What the hell was going on? She prided herself on being skeptical, not paranoid, but Heat seriously believed she was being railroaded. But why? And by whom?

It pained her that a few hundred words in an also-ran newspaper could get her kicked out. That damned article.

And Rook.

Her sharpest agony. She had invested in this guy. Waited for this guy. Felt something for this guy that went beyond the bedroom . . . or wherever else they took each other. Nikki did not give herself easily to a man, and this betrayal by Rook was why. Heat reflected on her answer at the oral boards about her greatest flaw and admitted her reply was a mask. Yes, her identification with her job was total. But her greatest flaw wasn't overinvestment in her career. It was her reticence to be vulnerable. Unarmed as she was—literally—she had been emotionally so with Rook.

That was the gut shot that had blown clean through her soul.

———

What the hell was she doing back there in the bull pen? The others weren't asking her that. Nikki Heat was asking herself.

When she had put on her coat and picked her way along the

unshoveled sidewalk heading from her apartment to the subway, Nikki had decided that she needed some things from her desk. Not knowing how long this suspension would last—or whether it would be permanent—there were materials she required and wanted at home. By the time she came up the steps from the B train under the American Museum of Natural History and trudged toward Columbus Avenue, she had convinced herself that entering her squad room was all about dignity. And that dirty coffee mug Roach had alerted her to.

The truth behind her visit was that the detective in Heat craved information. And what Nikki learned only served to deepen her suspicions about her reversal.

Right off the bat Roach drew her aside to a quiet corner. "WTF?" said Ochoa.

"Yeah, why'd you have to go and get yourself suspended?" added Raley. "Your timing sucks."

"Not so much that we care about you," said his partner, "but the Graf investigation's upside-down in the ditch with four wheels clawing sky."

"Do I even need to ask why?" Nikki knew from her meeting the day before.

"Because of the Iron Man," said Ochoa. Heat had a mental bet that would be the handle they'd give Captain Irons. She also bet they weren't the first. "He's pulling all resources into the dead homeless guy, even though it's gonna end up accidental OD."

"For all intents, this case is dead." Raley side nodded to the Father Graf Murder Board, which had been carelessly erased and hung there, suspended on the easel with only the ghostly streaks of Nikki's colored markers to hint at its prior purpose.

"It almost seems convenient," she said.

Ochoa chuckled. "Know how we're always pimping Rook over his wild-ass conspiracy theories?" Heat nodded even as she masked her pain at hearing his name. "Nothing compared to what Rales and I have been thinking."

"Any answers?" asked Heat.

Raley said, "Only one. On your time off, let us know what you need."

"On your 'time off,'" repeated Ochoa, complete with air quotes.

———

The only satisfaction she could draw from this disheartening news about the shelving of the Graf case was that Sharon Hinesburg was ordered by Captain Irons to go undercover as a homeless woman and had to spend the night in the Riverside Park pedestrian tunnel. "Let it snow," Nikki said.

On a whim—yes, a whim, she told herself—Heat logged onto her computer so she could print out a PDF of the Huddleston homicide file, the 2004 case then-Detective Montrose had run. Disbelief.

Her password didn't work.

Access denied.

Nikki phoned the IT department help desk. After a brief hold, the technician came back on and apologized. He said that due to her renewed classification, she was currently unauthorized to use the NYPD server.

After she set the phone back on its cradle, Heat realized how wrong she had been. She had mistakenly thought it wasn't possible to feel more shaken and alone. Stepping out into West 82nd Street, Nikki turned to face the icy wind rushing crosstown off the Hudson. But she knew that no matter how long she stood there, it could never dish out enough cold to numb her. She turned her back against the bluster and plodded toward the subway to go home.

"Lady-lady!" was the last thing Heat heard before the collision. She whirled in the direction of the shout a split second before the delivery guy and his bicycle smacked into her, knocking her down onto Columbus Avenue. They landed in a tangle—arms, legs, and a bike—surrounded by ruptured cardboard take-out cartons, broccoli in oyster sauce, smashed wontons, and a duck leg. "My order's ruined," he said.

Still down, with handlebars against her cheek, Nikki turned up from the gutter and said, "You were going the wrong way in that lane."

His response was, "Hey, up yours, lady." He jerked his bike off Nikki and raced away, leaving her and his lost order down in the crosswalk at the side of the avenue. For a split second as Heat watched the patch of filthy snow and sand under her face redden with her blood, she actually wondered if whoever killed Montrose had also sent the crazy delivery guy on the bike. Such was the rabbit hole of conspiracy thinking. When you actually stop and look around and wonder, who in the world can you trust?

————

When Rook opened the door, his expression was a mix of shock and vigilance. First he reacted to her face with its tributaries of dried blood fanning like tentacles from the spot in her scalp where Nikki held a wadded handkerchief. Then, out of experience, he checked the hall to make sure she wasn't on the run and being followed. "Nikki, jeez, what happened?"

She strode past him through his foyer and into the kitchen. He locked the door and joined her. Nikki held up a hand. "Shut up and don't say anything."

His mouth opened and then closed.

"I'm a great cop. I was on track to blow past lieutenant and make captain. I was going to be running the precinct. And, as a cop, one thing I understand is motive. And when I look for your motive in leaking that article? . . . I get nothing. It makes no logical sense. Why would you give your notes on a story that's your exclusive to somebody else? For sex? Please. I can tell, Tam's way too needy to be good in bed." He started to speak and she said, "Shut up. With no motive, I just don't know why the hell you would have done that. So I'm making the choice to believe you.

"I not only want to, I have to. Because whatever's happening on this case, it's kicked up to a new level and there's nobody I can trust except for you.

"Everything's caving in. I'm locked out and the murder investigation I have been moving heaven and earth to conduct is now in the Dumpster because the bumbling pencil jockey they replaced Captain Montrose with is basically Inspector Clouseau. Say nothing.

"Now . . . as I lay there minutes ago in the southbound lane of Columbus, mowed down by a wrong-way and rather unapologetic delivery bicyclist, shivering, bleeding, and taking stock of the new low my life had achieved, I thought, Nikki Heat, are you just going to lie there? And, tempting as it may be to while away my forced hiatus at Starbucks playing Angry Birds, waiting for 1PP to call and say sorry, that is not an option. I am too stubborn and too personally invested to let this case die. But—minor technicality—I am no longer an active member of the NYPD. No gun, no badge, no access to records, no squad. Oh, and people are trying to kill me. So what do I need? I need help. To press this investigation forward I need a partner. I need someone with experience, with balls, someone with top investigative skills who knows how to stay out of my way and isn't afraid to put in some sick hours. Which is why I am here in your kitchen bleeding on your custom slate flooring. OK, you can talk now. What do you say?"

Rook didn't reply. Instead, he turned her gently to look over the kitchen counter into his great room. And she beheld the Murder Board Rook had reconstructed in his loft. Not everything was there—for instance, no photographs—but the main elements were in place: the timeline, the names of victims and suspects, leads to track down. It needed a big update, but the foundation was all right there.

Heat turned back to Rook and said, "Well? Are you interested or not?"

TWELVE

While she sat atop the closed toilet lid in Rook's master bathroom, he bent over her, carefully drawing aside strands of hair to examine the cut. Nikki stared at her blood-caked face in the mirror and said, "This looks a lot worse than it is."

"Oh, if I only had a nickel for every time I said that in my life."

"To whom, Rook? Unsuspecting girlfriends catching you with someone in a bar?"

"You sully me with your tawdry assumptions." Then he added, "Usually, it was the bedroom." He turned to the mirror so Nikki could see his proud grin. "Once in an armoire. God, I miss high school." He moved to the counter and picked up the dish of warm, soapy water he had prepared.

"What do you think, Doctor? Stitch, or no stitch?"

Rook dipped a cotton ball in the solution and gently dabbed her scalp. "Fortunately, this is in the abrasion rather than laceration category, so no stitch. Although, when was your last tetanus shot?"

"Recently," she said. "Right after that serial killer worked on me with his dental picks out there in your dining room."

"We do have the memories, don't we, Nikki?"

Twenty minutes later, showered and dressed in a fresh blouse and pair of jeans that had been hanging in his closet, Heat appeared at the kitchen counter. "Transformation, complete," she said.

He slid a double espresso over to her. "You weren't kidding. When you get knocked down, you do get up again."

"Just watch."

———

"Can I tell you you're off to a good start?" Nikki called out while she gave his Murder Board a once-over. Rook emerged from the back hall of his loft carrying a plastic milk crate of office supplies and an aluminum tube easel to hold the giant presentation pad that was sitting in the guest chair, waiting to be invited to join the party. "Most of what we need to focus on is right here."

"Good notes, the writer's friend," he said. "I'm sure it's not as dense with possibility as a Nikki Heat Murder Board. It's like the branch office version. I call it Murder Board South."

"It's more than exists uptown right now." She told him about Captain Irons and how his ineptness had accomplished more than all the obstacles Montrose had thrown at her, effectively bringing the investigation into the priest's homicide to a whimpering halt. "So, basically, we are the Graf case right now."

"Let's make it count," said Rook.

They spent the next hour updating his old information with her new leads and persons of interest. He kept track of the board, partitioning sections for each major thread to investigate as well as restructuring the timeline to add recently discovered elements; she created index cards on the big four-by-sixes from Rook's crate of supplies, expanding status details and listing unresolved questions, all corresponding to the categories he had drawn on the whiteboard. Whatever noise had rained chaos down on their relationship fell away in their focus on the task at hand. From the start, and without much ceremony, the two fell into an easy and efficient routine. At last, when the board was current and the cards were coded and filed, they stood back to admire their progress.

Heat said, "We're not a bad team."

"The best," agreed Rook. "We finish each other's references."

"Don't get cocky, writer boy, now comes the hard part. There's no way with our limited resources and manpower to investigate every lead and every person we're looking at up there."

"No problem," said Rook, "let's just pick one and go arrest him.

That narrows the field. Or, even better, use the Gadhafi method and arrest everyone."

"You're bringing up a point we—meaning you—need to remember. I can't arrest anyone. Remember? No badge, no gun?"

He processed that and said, "We don't need no stinking badges. And as for a gun, what's a roving band of killers to you, as long as there's an icicle handy?"

Nikki held a pencil out to him, point first. "You'd be wise to remember that."

"Noted."

"Given we're only a two-horse carousel, we need to draw priorities." She set the presentation pad on the easel and tore off the cover, exposing a fresh page. "Here are the prime targets as I see them." Heat uncapped a marker and printed her A-list, giving Rook a rationale for each choice: "Sergio Torres . . . If he wasn't Graf's murderer, he's linked to the killer in some way—and his skills are too good for his rap sheet; Lawrence Hays . . . not only has the means and motive, he threatened Father Graf. And what were you so excited to tell me about Lancer Standard right before I tore your head off last night?"

"I remembered hearing something nasty about Hays's group, so yesterday I reached out to a source of mine at The Hague from a piece I did on Slobodan Milošević's, air-quotes, heart attack right before his verdict. Score. Check it out." He pointed to his laptop screen and quoted, " 'An international human rights watchdog group filed suit to have Lancer Standard brought to the World Court on charges of abuses by its contractors in Iraq and Afghanistan involving sex shaming, waterboarding, and . . . ,' wait for it: 'torture through use of transcutaneous electrical nerve stimulation, or TENS.' " He looked up at her and said, "And where have we heard of that before, boys and girls?"

"Nice one," she said. "Definitely has my interest." Heat continued with her A-list. "Horst Meuller . . . Our German male dancer threatened Graf, and he took a bullet for some reason. Even if it was intended for me, I want to know why he ran; Alejandro Martinez . . . That was his dirty druggy money stashed at the rectory, I want to know why; *Justicia a Garda* . . . militant with a violent revolutionary pedigree and, don't forget, Father Graf was last seen with them. Emma . . . I don't know who Emma is—never got a chance to find out—but Graf had a purged e-mail file with her name on it. Emma makes my list. Tattoo Man . . . A John Doe seen on security cam with one of the domme's roommates. A loose end I can't let go of. Captain Montrose . . . OK, two ways to look at him. First, his suspicious behavior before he died links to Graf. What was he up to and why? Second, his so-called suicide. I don't buy it." She capped the marker and stepped back from the easel.

"That's narrowing it down?" said Rook.

"Hey, you don't know the stuff I've left off. For instance, besides the physical evidence Forensics is running, I am very curious about two odd socks from the rectory: the prescription in Graf's medicine cabinet, and what's the significance of that missing St. Christopher medal?" She wrote "Rx" and "St. Christopher" on the board, then Nikki tapped her temple with the cap of the marker.

"Well, this is plenty to get started on," said Rook. "Nice job, you."

"You, too." And then she couldn't resist tossing a little barb. "By the way, Rook, I'm not going to be seeing any of this in the newspaper, am I?"

"Hey . . ."

"Come on, lighten up, I'm kidding." He looked at her askance. ". . . Well," she admitted, "half kidding." Rook considered a moment and grabbed her coat off the bar stool. "You're throwing me out?"

But then he grabbed his, too. "No, we're both going out."

"Where?" she asked.

"To fix the half that isn't kidding."

———

Riding up in the elevator at the Midtown offices of the *Ledger*, Heat insisted the trip was not necessary. "Take a joke and let it go. I told you I trusted you."

"Sorry. I can tell you still haven't made peace with believing me. I want both. Trust and belief. And peace."

Nikki shook her head. "Pulitzer, huh? For writing?"

The elevator let them out at the sixth-floor home of the Metro Section, a fluorescent-bright, open-plan sea of cubicles filled with men and women keyboarding at computers or talking into phone headsets, or both. Except for the fact that the space was about half a city block in size, the din of activity reminded Nikki of the bull pen at the Two-oh.

Tam Svejda gophered up at the far end of the room and waved both arms over her head as soon as she saw them. When they arrived at her corner cubicle, she yanked off her headset, sang out a "Hi-ee," and threw a big hug on Rook. Nikki both enjoyed and did not enjoy watching the Bouncing Czech kick her right heel up behind her during the embrace like starlets do when they greet the hosts on late night talk shows. Heat was relieved to get a simple handshake, however distracting it was to have Tam beam at Rook during it.

"I got so excited when you said the both of you were coming up. What's this about? Please tell me you have some more inside stuff."

"Actually, we're here about the other inside stuff," said Rook. "Nikki . . . Detective Heat says you told her you got it from me."

"That's right," Tam said.

Nikki arched a brow at him then turned away to survey the busy newsroom as Rook squirmed. "Well, that's a bit hard to imagine," he said. "Since we never spoke about any of this. In fact, when you asked me the other day on the phone, didn't I specifically say I couldn't give you any help?"

"That's true . . . ," said the reporter. That brought Heat's attention back to the cubicle.

Rook said, "Then how could you say it was me?"

"I," muttered Heat under her breath to the writer.

"Simple." Tam sat and swiveled to her computer. After a few keystrokes her printer started spitting out pages. She handed the first one to Rook. "See? This is the e-mail you sent me."

Heat moved close to him and they read it at the same time. It was an e-mail addressed from Rook to Tam. The subject line read, "The Two-oh, Inside." What followed was a single spaced, full page of notes detailing facts about the troubled Graf case as well as the controversial problems surrounding Captain Montrose. The next three pages finished printing and she handed them over to Rook, too. He just skimmed, but the last paragraphs were all about the conflict surrounding Montrose's funeral. Rook lowered the pages and felt Nikki's stare. He said, "This looks a lot worse than it is."

"Wanna bet?" said Heat.

———

Magoo was waiting for them in the vestibule of the loft when they got back to Tribeca. If Rook's computer guru wasn't college age, he was close to it, pear-shaped, about five-two, and had one of those sparse, curly beards, with only a promise of a mustache, that made Nikki wonder, why bother? His pale, earnest face was dominated by black-framed glasses with lenses as thick as they come, eliminating any doubt how Don Revert got the nickname Mister Magoo. The question, which would remain unasked, was why he kept it.

"You didn't waste any time getting here," Rook said as his consultant snapped open a hard-shell rolling equipment case and began to set up shop on the desktop in the office.

"You shine the Bat Signal in the sky, I must answer." Magoo pulled out cables and diagnostic equipment—small black boxes with meters—and set them beside Rook's laptop. During his setup, he looked up from time to time at Heat, treating her to glimpses of eyes made giant by his thick glasses.

"That's a nice case," she said, not knowing what else to offer.

"Oh, yeah. It's the Pelican Protector. Of course, I got it with the foam lid liner and padded dividers. As you can see, I can pretty much use the Velcro tabs to custom configure it for any load." Nikki was pretty certain that had just constituted foreplay.

Rook explained to his personal nerd the e-mail Tam Svejda

received and then showed him the hard copy. "The thing is, I never sent it." He said this as much for Magoo's information as for reiteration to Heat.

"Yessss," said Magoo. "Come check this out."

He and Nikki both came around to flank him, but Rook's laptop screen was filled with an intimidating string of code and commands that made no sense to either of them. "You're going to have resort to plain English, my man," said Rook.

"All right, how about, 'Dude, you've been owned.' Is that vanilla enough?"

"Getting warmer."

"OK, layman's terms. You know those ads on TV and radio for the services that allow you to subscribe to RDA? Remote desktop access?"

"Sure," said Nikki, "you pay a fee and they set you up to be able to access your work computer from anywhere. Especially geared for traveling businesspeople. You go online from a laptop in your room at the Cedar Rapids Holiday Inn and you can do work and transfer files on your office computer in New York or LA. . . . That it?"

"Absolutely. It's basically an access account that lets you make any remote computer you designate do what your other computer tells it." He turned from Heat to Rook. "Somebody broke into your laptop and installed their own RDA account."

"I've been hacked?" Rook straightened up from hunching over the desk and beamed at Nikki. "This is wonderful! . . . I mean, not so good for the computer but . . . Oh, man, excellent news. But also bad. It's complicated. I'll shut up."

Heat was focused on other ramifications. "Can you tell who installed this RDA?"

"No, it's heavily encrypted. Whoever hid this on the hard drive really has skills."

"Rook was out of the country recently, could it have happened then?"

Magoo shook his head. "This was installed the other day. Anybody been in your loft? Maybe you left your laptop somewhere un-attended?"

"Mm, no. I've had it with me at all times. Working at her place." The same thought came to Heat, but Rook voiced it. "The water on the bathroom windowsill. Whoever it was didn't break in to steal something. They broke in to probe me. Well, my computer. I feel so . . . violated."

"Listen," said Magoo, "I could try to break into it and see who it was. In fact, I'd love the challenge. But you have to know something. If I crack it, I may set off an alert to tell whoever it is that they've been busted. You want me to do that?"

"No," said Nikki. Then she turned to Rook. "Get yourself an-other computer."

———

Magoo left with a check that included a fee for his services plus the cost of a new, clean laptop he promised to return with inside the hour. As soon as the door closed, Nikki said, "I am so sorry I doubted you."

Rook made a small shrug. "I don't see it so much as doubting me. I think it was more like pouring sulfuric acid on my character and virtually shredding me as a human being."

She smiled. "So we're good now?"

"Way good." Then he said, "Damn. I am so easy."

She moved close and put her arms around him, pressing her groin against his. "Hey? I'll make it up to you."

"Count on it."

"Later."

"Tease."

"To work."

"Too bad."

———

Heat began with her Priority List on the presentation pad. First in order was Sergio Torres. She might not have had the assets of the NYPD at her disposal, but she did have resources at the FBI. A few months before, while tracking down the serial killer from Texas who duct taped her to a chair in that very room, Nikki had contacted the Bureau's National Center for the Analysis of Violent Crime at Quantico, Virginia. During the process of investigating that case, she had forged a friendship with one of the NCAVC analysts. Heat got on the phone to her.

The beauty of a professional relationship in law enforcement is that little needs to be said to conduct business. Nikki supposed it was the residue of the code, attributed to John Wayne, of "Never complain, never explain." Heat said she was working a case on her own and wanted to run a name without going through NYPD. "Mind if I ask your interest in the subject?" asked her analyst friend.

"He tried to kill me and I took him out."

"Give me everything you've got, Nikki," she said without pause. "We'll run this SOB so you even know his favorite ice cream flavor."

Heat fought off an unexpected well of emotion at the gesture and with coplike understatement thanked the analyst and said she'd be interested in whatever she learned.

Riding a sense of goodwill from the kindness of others, Nikki opened her cell phone to Recents and scrolled to Phyllis Yarborough's number from the call she had made that morning. "I'm taking you up on your offer. I need a favor."

"Name it."

"That guy who tried to kill me in Central Park the other day. His rap sheet undervalues his skill set. If it's not ethically compromising to you given my job status, I was wondering if you could run him through your RTCC database and see if anything pops."

As with her FBI contact in Quantico, Phyllis Yarborough did not skip a beat. "Give me the spelling of his name," was her reply.

———

Rook was already up and running on his new MacBook Air and jumped to his feet when she finished her calls and came into his office. "I have run down a very interesting piece of information on one of our players," he said.

"Do tell." Nikki sat in the guest chair and let herself melt into the soft cushions, feeling newly upbeat and admitting to herself she was enjoying this new work arrangement with Rook.

"I ran some Googles and Bings on some of the names we've got on Murder Board South. Not exactly Philip Marlowe gumshoeing bad guys in *The Big Sleep*, but it has its rewards. I can snack, for instance. Anyway, I had gotten around to checking out our human rights activists at *Justicia a Garda*. Milena Silva, as presented, is an attorney. However, Pascual Guzman . . . know what he did before he left Colombia? A college professor at Universidad Nacional in Bogotá. And what did he teach?"

Nikki took a stab. "Marxist philosophy?"

"Try computer science." Rook sat back at his desk and referred to his screen. "But Professor Guzman left the university. Why? It was in protest because he claimed the computer programming he was doing in his department was being used by the secret police to spy on dissidents." Rook punched the air with his fist and stood. "That's it. This is the guy who hacked my computer."

"But why?"

"OK . . ." He came around the desk, pacing. "Want to hear my theory? Guzman . . . and a cadre of radicals he recruited here in New York embraced violence too much for their friend and ally, Father Gerry Graf, who was fine with the protests but not with the bloodletting to come. They fight. Graf has to go. They kill Graf, done and done. But no. Here comes Detective Nikki Heat with all her smarts and tenacity and they say, Heat has to go. They try to bushwhack you in the park, thoroughly underestimating the heat that is Heat. And when that doesn't work, they try to take you out another way: hack me to get you in trouble with One Police Plaza and knocked off the case. Boom."

"Let's arrest them right now," said Nikki.

Rook's zeal deflated and he slumped down on the edge of his desk.

"When you say that, it's like you're saying my theory is crazy and unsubstantiated."

Heat smiled. "I know."

"Well, come on, doesn't it make sense?"

"Parts of it do. Especially Guzman being a computer guy. But . . . ," she paused, slowing down to model behavior for him, ". . . but it's all based on conjecture. Rook, have you ever thought of writing crime fiction instead?"

"Nah," he said. "I'm all about keeping it real."

––––––

They were planning their next moves when the impact of the severe winter cold charted their immediate course. The TV and radio news was all over a major breaking story at the power plant on the East Side, where one of the giant, ninety-five-foot-tall boilers that pumped thousand-degree steam through underground pipes and heated Lower Manhattan had exploded. A mechanic was injured and expected to survive, but the consequence was that there was a steam shutoff in the entire zone serviced by that plant. The spectacular TV helicopter pictures of the crippled plant went split screen as the anchor showed a map of the affected area which would be without steam for the next two or three days.

Nikki said, "Look, my apartment's right in the middle of the zone."

"Man," said Rook. "Gotta feel sorry for the buildings that don't have their own boilers 'cause the landlords are too cheap to upgrade from district steam, huh?" He chuckled and then read from her expression that she was living in one of them. "You're kidding. Oh, I am loving the irony, Nikki: No heat. And minus-degree temperatures tonight? Let's go get some of your clothes and lady-whatevers and bring them here."

"You'll use anything to get me to shack up here, won't you?"

"Steam failure, water hammer, act of God, I am above nothing."

––––––

It was already feeling cool in the lobby of Nikki's apartment building as they came in. The elevator doors opened and several of her neighbors got off with suitcases and overnighters. Some said they were bound for Upper West Side hotels; others were off to couch surf with relatives in Westchester County. When Heat and Rook were about to get on for the ride up, a hand parted the doors. It was Nikki's building super, a cheerful Pole named Jerzy. "Hello, Miss Nikki, and hello, you, sir."

"Going to get cold tonight, Jerzy," she said.

"Oh, very cold. Be glad you not have goldfish," he said. "Mrs. Nathan, she have to move her goldfish to Flushing."

Rook said, "Is it me or is there something sad about hearing goldfish and Flushing in the same breath?" When Jerzy just stared at him blankly, he said, "It's probably a translation thing."

"Anyway, Miss Nikki, I stop to tell you is all taken care of. I let the man from cable company in to fix cable TV."

By reflex, she almost said thank you, but stopped herself. Nikki had not booked any service call from a cable TV repairman. "Is he up there now?"

The super said, "I don't know. He went up an hour ago."

Heat stepped off the elevator back into the lobby and Rook followed. "Let's take the stairs, shall we?" As she led him on their climb to her floor, Nikki opened her coat and reached once again for the gun that wasn't there.

THIRTEEN

eat and Rook reached the landing at her floor and stopped to scope out the hallway, which was quiet. Rook whispered, "Shouldn't we call the police?" Nikki thought it over and knew deep down she should. But there was also a pride thing that kept her, an experienced cop, from pulling resources from actual crime responses in the middle of a city emergency for a suspicion that could be nothing.

"I am the police," she whispered back. "Kind of." Sorting through her door keys, she slipped the one for her deadbolt off the split ring. That way, she could both avoid jangle at the door and be able to insert a key simultaneously in each of her locks to make her entry quick and surprising.

Treading lightly up the hallway, staying close to the wall the whole way, they reached her door and stopped. Nikki hand signaled for Rook to stay where he was, then made a fluid dancer's move, crouching low under the surveillance hole, to the opposite side of the door and landed without a sound. She stayed low and listened at the jamb, then gave him a head shake. Rising up slightly and balancing on the balls of her feet so her leg muscles were coiled, Heat readied each key at the opening of its lock. She mouthed a silent three count, nodding her head to mark cadence for him, then ran the keys home, twisted the locks open, and threw herself low into her apartment calling out, "NYPD, don't move!"

Rook flew in right behind her, following the procedures he had observed back on his ride-along—keeping close but not in a line that made for an easy target, then fanning himself to the side so he could be her eyes there and protect her flank from a surprise.

There was no one in the foyer, the dining room, or the living room. As Rook followed her past the kitchen and down the hall to clear the two bedrooms, baths, and closets, he noticed that somewhere along the way she had grabbed her backup Sig Sauer. After they cleared the apartment, she returned the Sig to its hiding place in the cubby on the living room desk and said, "Hey, nice entry."

"Thanks." And then he gave her an impish grin. "If you like, I can demonstrate a few variations."

She rolled her eyes. "Oh yes, teach me, Rook. Teach me all the ways."

————

Jameson Rook was mighty pleased with himself about his trip to the spy store when the wireless monitor came out of the pantry and he played back the video from his NannyCam. He scrolled backward through the ghosty images, not having to go far, just about an hour, until he came to movement. A man in a cable company logo cap entered with a large toolbox, then left the frame as he roamed off into the hallway. "Great coverage," said Nikki. "You could work for C-SPAN."

But a moment later the man returned and moved to the living room, where he knelt and opened his toolbox in front of the TV. "Look at that," said Rook. "Dead center in the frame. I'm better than C-SPAN. I could work for C-SPAN2."

They zapped through the next fifteen minutes as the visitor worked at the cable box. When he was done, he fastened the snaps on his toolbox and left the apartment in the quadruple speed of video time-lapse. Rook hit stop and wandered from the counter over to the living room. "What do you know. It's like Freud said. Sometimes a cable guy is just a cable guy." He picked up the remote and said, "Unless it's Jim Carrey, and then—"

Nikki threw a tackle on Rook, on the way down running her

hand up his arm and stripping the remote from his grasp. When they both hit the floor, he said, "What the hell was that for?"

Nikki walked back to the counter, cradling the remote, and said, "This."

Rook picked himself up and joined her as she rolled back the NannyCam video and froze it on the face of the cable guy as he passed under the camera on his exit. The freeze was of the man Heat and her squad had been trying to ID and locate from the Pleasure Bound security video.

The man with the coiled snake tattoo.

———————

An hour later, after the bomb squad had cleared her building and those in the surrounding area, a hero in an eighty-pound blast suit emerged with the cable box and placed it in the Mobile Containment Unit on the trailer in the center of the street. When he was clear of the opening, his sergeant pressed a remote control button and the hydraulic actuator whirred, gently closing the armor-plated hatch and sealing the cable box inside.

Heat made her way to the cop who was being helped out of his protective suit by a detail from Emergency Services. As soon as he had his right hand free of his heavy glove, she shook it and thanked him. In spite of his nonchalant "Hey, you're welcome," his hair was sweat-matted to his forehead. The look in his eyes was enough to tell her that handling the real deal was never taken casually by those guys, no matter how much they brushed it off. As he described the bomb to her, Rook joined the circle, as did Raley and Ochoa, who had heard the call go out and dropped everything to get down there.

After his K-9 had sniffed the apartment and confirmed the cable box as a hit, he did his X-ray. The trigger device was a simple mercury switch poised to be detonated by battery when someone pressed the power button of the TV remote control. "What kind of explosive?" asked Nikki.

"Evaporation sample of the taggant was positive for C4."

Ochoa whistled. "Plastic explosive."

"Yeah, it most definitely would have spoiled somebody's night," said the man from the bomb squad as he took a long drink of water from a bottle. "They'll lab it, but, by my calc, it's going to test out as military grade. Not so easy to come by."

Rook turned to Heat. "Not from what I've learned over the last month. Especially if you have connections to the military—however unofficial."

————

Cementing his status as King of All Surveillance Media, Detective Raley took the NannyCam drive so he could pull the still frame of the cable guy and circulate it. Before they left, Heat cautioned him and Ochoa not to get themselves in trouble with Captain Irons. The two partners shared a look and scoffed. Rales said, "Hm, let's see . . . Iron Man or Detective Heat . . . Iron Man or Detective Heat . . ."

"Just be careful," she said.

"You, too," said Ochoa. "You're the one working with Rook."

————

It was after hours, and Heat figured Lancer Standard would be closed for the night, so she looked up Lawrence Hays's home address from the information Mrs. Borelli had given her out of the parish roster. "You really think you're going to get anything out of him?" said Rook after she gave their taxi driver the street number on West End Avenue.

"If you mean a straight answer to any of my questions, no. But I want to jam this guy. Keep the pressure on him. An over-the-top ego like his, you never know what'll shake out."

Heat had just finished pressing the intercom at the top of the stone steps of the town house near 78th when the voice behind them said, "Help you?" It was Lawrence Hays. He wasn't wearing a coat, so she figured he must have seen them approach on his security cams and come out a side door to surprise them. "I have an office, you know, you don't need to harass me at my home."

"Good evening to you, too, Mr. Hays. This is Jameson Rook."

"Yeah, I know, the writer. Doctor says I have an allergy to the press, so you'll pardon me if I don't shake hands."

"And I have one to blood, so it all works out," said Rook.

Before the macho sideshow escalated, Nikki thrust out the surveillance still she had of the cable guy from Pleasure Bound. "Have you ever seen this man?"

"This again?" said Hays. He angled the photo to the light, gave it a quick eyeball, and handed it back. "Nope. What's he? Some Craigslist stud who stuck you with the motel bill, Miss Heat?"

She ignored the distraction. "He tried to blow up my apartment."

"And a new HD flat screen," added Rook. "Using military grade C4. Mean anything to you?"

Hays smiled mirthlessly at Nikki. "Tell you something you don't seem to get. If I wanted to blow you up, you wouldn't be standing here. Right now there'd be pieces of you coming back down on Gramercy Park like confetti."

Heat said, "So you're saying you do know where I live, that's interesting."

"Tell you what I don't know. Is why you're on a holy crusade for some priest who not only protected that scumbag who messed with my kid—my kid!—but who was also aiding and abetting homegrown terrorists."

"Why," said Rook, "just because he was a social activist?"

"Wake up. Graf was neck-deep with those Colombian *revolutionarios*."

Nikki kept him going so he wouldn't lose his steam. "*Justicia a Garda*? Gimme a break, they're no terrorists."

"No? Have you seen them in action? How many of your men have these cowards killed and blown up? Use your head. If they'll attack their own government prisons just to break out their brainwashing socialist writers, how long do you think it is before that gig gets imported here?"

"Mr. Hays," said Heat, "are you saying some of your contractors were killed in Colombia by members of the organization Father Graf supported?"

"I'm not saying anything." Too late. He realized he had slipped and voiced an additional motive for Graf's murder and started walking it back. "For reasons of national security, I cannot confirm or deny the actions of my government consulting firm."

"I think you just did," said Nikki.

"Know what I think? I think you'd better get lost. Because something else I know about you, Nikki Heat, besides your address. You're not even a cop anymore. That's right." He started to chuckle, and said, "So get off my property. Before I call the police—the real police!"

They could still hear him laughing when he turned and slipped off into the night.

————

Heat woke up the next morning with Rook's face in hers. Kneeling beside the bed in his T-shirt and boxer briefs, all he needed was a leash in his teeth to look like a retriever waiting for his trip to the park. "What time is it?"

"Almost seven."

She sat up. "I slept that late?"

"I've been up for two hours," he said. "Phoning some of the noble characters I consorted with on my journey through the shadowy world of arms trafficking."

"Why?"

"It struck me in our afterglow last night. Oh, yes, it was an afterglow. . . . I got thinking about military grade C4. And then I started thinking, I bet I already know people—outside the military, I mean—who might supply it."

The sleep was slowly lifting from her. "You mean to Lancer Standard?"

"No, Hays would have his own source and wouldn't need to go

black market. I inquired about another organization we posted on Murder Board South."

"*Justicia a Garda.*"

"Correct. And what I just learned from a guy we shall call only T-Rex—hailing from the smuggler's port of choice, Buenaventura—is that a shipment of an unspecified nature left Colombia and was delivered three weeks ago, off the books, in Perth Amboy, New Jersey, to one Pascual Guzman." He held up his hand. "Come on, up top for the Rookster."

Instead of fiving him, Nikki sat cross-legged and frisked the fingers of both hands through her hair to wake up. "Did this T-Rex say it was C4?"

"Mm, no. T's exact words were, some kind of shipment, he didn't know what."

"Then we don't know squat. Unless we confirm it was C4."

"Shouldn't we at least talk to Guzman?"

Heat shook no. "First rule I learned from Captain Montrose about interrogations was, don't initiate a meeting blindly. Know what you want or are likely to get. What I know about Pascual Guzman is that he's a circumspect stone wall who will answer nothing at best, and at worst, light me up on the radar to Zach Hamner when he files another harassment complaint. We'll have to go at him another way."

Rook was unfazed. "I think this guy hacked my computer. Plus he admitted he had a smack-down with Graf the day he died. I think we should shake down Pascual Guzman and ask him about the secret shipment. He's smelling to me like our killer."

"Last night you were sure it was Lawrence Hays."

"I know. I get excited. Hays was the bright, shiny object of the moment."

Nikki said, "And what is Guzman?"

He hung his head. "Again, you chasten me with your need for reason."

———

Two hours later, Nikki had a cab drop them between Tenth Avenue and
41st, just blocks off Times Square. The forecast promised it would be
slightly warmer that day, but at 9 A.M. it was still under five degrees
and the shadows of the low sun ran long and chilly on the West Side
of Manhattan. While Roach worked the photo of the cable guy,
Heat's plan was to try to find him by locating the woman who appeared in the Pleasure Bound surveillance photo with him. According to the missing woman's landlord, Shayne Watson worked as a
prostitute in Hell's Kitchen. The former roommate of the dominatrix
was still off the radar, and Heat's agenda for the day was to hit the
streets and show her photo to other prostitutes, hoping to get a line
on her.

"I've got this one," said Rook. He took a photocopy of the surveillance shot and stepped up to a woman leaning against the wall and
smoking outside a diner. "Morning, miss." She looked him up and
down and began to step away. "Please, this will just take a second. I'm
trying to find one of your colleagues, a fellow prostitute and—"

The woman flicked her cigarette at him and it bounced off his
forehead. "Asshole. Calling me a hooker . . ." She hurried away, shouting something about calling the cops mixed in with more curses until
she rounded the corner.

As amused as Heat was by Rook's gaffe, she didn't have much
better luck. Sure, Nikki was better at spotting the working girls, having worked vice herself, but they smelled cop on her and either closed
up or just ran as soon as she approached. "This could take forever,"
said Rook.

"It's too early in the day for most of them to be out; we'll do better as we get more to talk to." That was fine to say, but Nikki was
still striking out at noon when the sidewalks started filling in front
of the hot sheet motels.

They ducked into a coffee shop to warm up and Rook continued
his skepticism about the plan. "All they do is run. And you don't
have any authority to stop them."

"Thank you for defining my newly impotent status," she said.

"I've got the solution," said Rook. "It's ingenious."

"This worries me."

"One word: Fishnets." As she began to wag no, he lowered his voice and pressed on. "You always talk about how you worked undercover in vice, right? Walk the walk. Put your stuff on the street. . . . Unless you have a better plan."

Nikki considered it awhile and said, "I suppose there's a cheesy clothing store around here somewhere."

"There ya go," he said way too loudly. "You'll make a great hooker." Nikki didn't have to turn to know the whole coffee shop was staring at her.

Rook rented a room for the afternoon at the Four Diamonds, which he observed was the only way that number of diamonds would ever be attributed to that establishment. It smelled of strong disinfectant and boasted unlimited ice, no doubt to go along with the unlimited nicotine burns dappling the bathroom counter and the nightstand. Nikki changed into her new clothes, and while she slathered on the makeup she had chosen, Rook called from the bedroom, "I feel like we're in *Pretty Woman.* I'd take you right now in the bubble bath except the cockroaches are still using it."

"What do you think?" asked Heat. She stepped out of the bathroom and posed, showing off her heavy makeup, hoop earrings, leopard-print Uggs knockoffs, ripped tights, and a lime green plastic raincoat.

Rook appraised her from his seat on the corner of the bed and said, "So, this is what your life has come to?"

———

Out on the sidewalk Nikki kept her distance from the other working girls up the block, giving them time to get used to her. Some of the women were territorial, seeing Nikki as an income threat, and gave her a hard time or moved along, wary of the undercover cop vibe that still came through the mascara and false lashes. Most were cordial, though. Introducing themselves, asking how she was getting by. Then, when she had their confidence, Nikki said she was looking for a lost BFF she was worried sick about. Out came the picture, which was studied and passed around, but got no response.

The hardest part was fending off the johns. Just telling them as they drove by—some whistling or patting the roof of their cars with open palms—that she wasn't interested didn't suffice. A few times she had to duck into the lobby of the Four Diamonds, and that took care of it. Once, though, a persistent guy, an intense construction worker who said he was off shift and had a big drive to Long Island, double-parked his pickup and followed her into the lobby. There, Rook appeared, announcing congratulations, that he was on the pilot of a new reality show, *To Catch a John*. Problem solved.

Nikki was standing on a corner with a few of the girls when her phone buzzed. It was Deputy Commissioner Yarborough. "Is this a bad time?"

"No, Phyllis, never a bad time for you." Nikki was glad this wasn't Skype.

"Just wanted to let you know I had them run Sergio Torres through the database. Sorry, but no hits beyond what appears on his rap sheet."

"Oh. Well, thanks for trying." It was hard to mask her disappointment.

Yarborough said, "Doesn't seem like Torres is your problem, anyway. Saw on the morning report you had a visit from the bomb squad." After Heat filled her in briefly on those events, the deputy commissioner asked, "Any idea who your perp is?"

"Not by name," said Heat. "He's a John Doe I've had my eye on in the Graf case. In fact, he's got a distinctive tattoo we ran through your RTCC but came up empty."

"I'll find the request and have them put it through again. And to make sure we turn over all the stones, I'll supervise the run myself."

Nikki was just thanking her when a horn blared and a carload of drunk frat boys shouted, "Aw-woo! Hey baby! Yo, skank!"

"Where the hell are you, Nikki?"

"Oh, just hanging with some friends. We're watching *Jerry Springer.*"

———

About four o'clock, when Nikki was discouraged, cold, and ready to pack it in, a young woman with a kind face and a greening bruise below one eye looked at the picture and said, "That's Shayna. Doesn't do her justice, but that's Shayn, for sure." Nikki turned the folded page over and asked if she recognized the man with her, the one with the coiled snake tattoo on his bicep. She didn't. But she had seen her friend recently. Shayna Watson was rooming at the Rounders Motel in Chelsea.

———

Sometimes they run, sometimes they hide, sometimes they just don't answer the door, hoping you'll go away. Shayna Watson slid the chain, opened up, and invited them in. She seemed drained of emotion—or self-medicated, Nikki couldn't determine which. But when the hollow-eyed woman moved some laundry off the bed so they could sit, Heat was relieved that this didn't look like it would be a fight.

Rook let himself fade into the background, leaving it to Nikki to connect. Mindful of her fragility, Heat spoke gently and steered away from any information that might spook her. For instance, omitting that this was part of a murder investigation entirely. Shayna Watson didn't need those particulars to tell Nikki two simple things. "You are in no trouble of any kind, Shayna, OK? I'm just looking for this man," she said, holding out the picture. "I'd like to know his name and where I can find him, then we'll be on our way."

"He's a bad dude," she said in a distant voice. "When Andrea . . . she's my roommate . . . left for Amsterdam, he made me steal her keys to the bondage place she works at. That's why I ditched my apartment. And I liked that place. I had to hide from him. Oh, God . . ." Her face paled and her brow knotted with worry as she surveyed the door, like she was playing out a private nightmare. "You found me. Do you think he will now?"

Nikki gave her a reassuring look. "Not if you help me find him first."

On their cab ride to Hunts Point, Heat decided this was not a mission to bluff through with mascara and spunk. She called the police. Protocol would have been to phone the Forty-first Precinct, since that's whose turf they were heading to. But that would require some awkward explanation of her departmental status unless she wanted to lie and pretend she was still officially on the job. So the police she called was Roach.

"The guy in the photo with the snake tattoo is named Tucker Steljess, no middle name yet," said Heat. She spelled the last name so they could run it and see if any priors or last known addresses spit out. "Rook and I are getting off the Bruckner now on our way to the address we got for him. It's a motorcycle repair shop on Hunts Point Avenue where it crosses Spofford. Don't have the street number, but you can dig it out."

"Will do," said Ochoa. "And you're quite the good citizen to phone in this tip."

"Hey, I support our local police," Nikki said. "Speaking of which, might do a courtesy heads-up to the Four-one."

"Raley's on it now. What's your plan?"

"I'm two minutes from the location. Good citizen that I am, Rook and I are going to observe until you arrive. Don't want this SOB slipping away."

Ochoa said, "Just watch your back, citizen. Let the pros handle this."

The winter darkness fell early, and from their window seats at Golden Dip'd Donuts, Heat and Rook watched lights shutting off across the street, in the back of the repair shop's garage. Then they saw movement. Wife beaters were out of season, so they couldn't get a positive ID of the snake tatt under the long-sleeved waffle tee, but Nikki's heart double pinged when the big man pulled down the corrugated rolling door and she eyeballed Tucker Steljess.

"He's going to leave," said Rook.

Heat speed-dialed Ochoa. "What's your ETA?"

"We're just clearing the RFK toll plaza."

"Subject's getting ready to go on the move," she said.

"We've already put it out on the air," replied Ochoa. "You should see units any minute."

When she hung up, Rook was already out the door, crossing the street. She cursed to herself and caught up with him outside the rolling door. "What do you think you're doing?"

"Slowing him down. You can't, he knows you. I can go in and play lost driver looking for directions. Or better yet, mid-life orthodontist seeking advice about Harleys versus BMWs."

Behind Rook, keys jangled. Steljess stepped out the office. And made Nikki.

He pushed Rook into her and they both staggered into the metal rolling door, which thundered and shook as they crashed into it. Steljess was rounding the corner when they recovered. Heat slipped Rook her cell phone and, as she ran, called out, "Hit redial. Tell Ochoa I'm pursuing eastbound on Spofford."

He had a block on her by the time she turned the corner. For a big man he was fast, but Nikki was faster. She poured it on and was soon gaining. Since she was unarmed, her strategy was to stay only close enough to keep him in sight until backup arrived, so she gave it enough tempo to tighten the distance yet lag far enough back to evade if he was carrying.

Steljess did what most fleeing suspects do, lost speed by looking back to see how he was doing, and soon Heat had a sweet twenty-five-yard pace to maintain. He didn't like the company and tried to slip the invisible leash. At Drake he made a sudden left, threading himself across the street through rush hour traffic. Nikki lost a few yards on him dodging cars but picked him up again as he ducked into the driveway of an auto salvage yard.

She stopped outside the gate and listened. This would be a good place to lose her, especially if he knew the layout and could use a back exit. It would also be a good place to make herself vulnerable if she blundered in unarmed. So she eased closer to the side of the open gate to hear if she could pick up any footfalls.

Heat caught the flash of motion in the convex mirror overhead, but it was too late. Tucker Steljess pivoted around the edge of the fence she was hiding behind, clutched the front of her coat with both hands, and swung his weight, lifting Nikki up off her feet and tossing her across the yard.

She landed back-first against a detached car door that was leaning against a metal paint locker. He threw her with such force that the steel locker tipped forward, landsliding small cans of paint and supplies down on top of her.

Nikki grabbed a paint can and threw it at him, missing, but his flinch gave her a precious second to clear the other cans off her so she could get up before he came at her. But he didn't come. Instead, Steljess was starting to crouch in what she recognized as a shooting position as he reached inside his down vest. She threw another can that hit him in the shoulder, but didn't deter him.

In fact, he smiled.

Heat saw the Glock clear his vest and felt stupid and helpless. In a futile move she clawed for the car door, hoping as a shield it would at least slow the bullet. As soon as Nikki pulled it over herself, she heard the crack of the gunshot.

FOURTEEN

S he didn't feel the bullet hit the door or her body. In the blink between synapses, in which Nikki wondered if she didn't sense it because she was already dead, she heard two familiar voices shout, "NYPD, freeze!" then three rapid shots followed by a body falling heavily against her improvised shield. As she lay there, pinned, feet pounded toward her. Then came the welcome sound of a gun being kicked and skittering away across asphalt.

"Clear." The relaxed voice belonged to Dutch Van Meter.

Detective Feller called, "Heat, he's down. You all right? Heat?"

Feller holstered his weapon and got her out from under the pile. Even though Nikki insisted she was fine, he made her sit down on a ratty office chair that was rotting in the yard beside a plastic tub of spent cigarette butts. Blue-and-whites from the Forty-first were pulling up outside the gate behind the undercover taxi. The emergency lights flashed into the entrance to the salvage yard, giving the night a surreal quality, especially as the colored lights strobed on Van Meter. Still holding his Smith & Wesson 5906, he stood up beside Tucker Steljess's body, after trying in vain for a pulse. He made a smooth sideways palm chop to his partner, signaling a flat line.

"Don't worry about me, fellas, I'm fine. I'm just the one who got shot at." Rook pulled himself up from his hiding place behind a corrugated cardboard carton labeled "Brake rotors—Fair to OK" in black marker. Rook was putting on a show of mock indignation, but Nikki knew the signs, having seen them . . . having experienced them herself. . . . He was shaken. Getting shot at does things to you.

In his statement to the incident commander, Rook said he had phoned Ochoa while he was on the run behind Heat, giving block-by-block scouting that Roach relayed over the radio. After following her across Spofford Avenue, he saw Nikki get pulled into the salvage yard. That was the last of his play-by-play. He pocketed her cell phone and snuck up to peek in the gate just as the paint locker spilled down on her. Without hesitating, he started out for Steljess, figuring he could blindside tackle him. But half the distance to him, just as Heat pegged the big man with a paint can, Rook saw the gun clear the vest. And then Steljess must have seen him out of the corner of his eye because he spun, starting to bring the Glock up in his direction. Not knowing what else to do, Rook took a dive behind some boxes just as he fired. The cops from the Forty-first, plus Raley and Ochoa, who were also in the semicircle around Rook, turned as one to look at one of the boxes. Indeed, there was a fat, nine-millimeter's worth of bullet hole in it.

Rook had thought both he and Nikki were finished, but then he heard Detectives Feller and Van Meter identify themselves, followed by three shots in quick succession.

When they were done with him, Rook joined Heat and Feller, who had already given their statements. Dutch Van Meter had fired the three shots and was still being debriefed. "Cake," said Feller. "This'll come down as righteous."

Nikki said, "Got to tell ya, if it hadn't been for you . . ."

"You're welcome," said Rook. He saw their amused expressions. ". . . What? If that box had been filled with air filters instead of brake rotors, I might not be standing here right now."

"In truth Rook did distract him enough to give us time to get in," said Detective Feller. "Wasn't the smartest play I've ever seen run, but effective."

Rook gave Nikki a look of vindication and said, "Thank you, Detective. And from now on, I'll never watch another episode of *Cash Cab* without thinking of you and Dutch. For me, the Mobile Shout-Out will forever be the Mobile Shoot-Out."

Feller turned to Nikki. "Couldn't have been a box of air filters, huh?"

"Seriously, Feller," she said, touching his shoulder. "Your timing didn't suck."

"Turning into our primary mission, Heat, saving your butt. This what you call suspension?"

"Don't know what you mean," Heat said. "I was just being a good citizen."

———

Raley and Ochoa gave them a ride back to Tribeca in the Roach Coach. As soon as they left the scene, Ochoa hopped on his cell phone to the precinct to get the results on the background check he had requested on Steljess. "Yeah, I can hold." Then he turned over his shoulder to Nikki. "You don't mind if I do this with you in the car, do ya? I know you're not doing any sort of police work, so if you happen to pick up any information, I trust you won't pay attention to it."

"Oh, absolutely," said Heat, returning his wink.

Raley gave it some gas as he steered onto the Bruckner and said, "What's the deal with you, Rook? I mean, you figure you have some sort of superhuman powers, you can just hero-stride into the line of fire and repel slugs?"

"Somebody had to spring into action, seeing how you gentlemen took your sweet time arriving. Tell me, if I looked on the floor up there, would I see some White Castle wrappers from your stop on the way?"

Nikki was amused by how easily Rook fell into the understated cop talk, trading barbs instead of overt compliments or thanks. But she wasn't feeling quite like being so oblique in her gratitude for what he did trying to save her. She slipped her hand over his and gave a squeeze. And then she let go and slid it up the inside of his thigh. They were still holding radar eye contact when Ochoa finished his call.

"As I said, pay no attention to this back there while I brief my partner, all right?" The detective finished jotting a note on his pad and turned to Raley. "Tucker Lee Steljess, male cauc, thirty-three, has a few assaults in his jacket. Mostly beefs in biker bars plus he recently got early release serving fifteen days of a forty-day sentence for breaking the front window of a liquor store. By the way, know what he used to break the window?"

Raley said, "I love it when you spice the story, pard. What did he use?"

"A pimp."

"Only awesome."

"Just wait. You ready? Digging back, Mr. Steljess was once a cop." Ochoa gave Nikki a quick glance over his shoulder. "That's right. Uniform for a long time before he finally made D-3, then worked undercover Narco in the Bronx." He consulted his notes again. "Reports are he was volatile and pretty much a loner. Nickname was Mad Dog. Service discharge says he, quote 'identified excessively with his undercover narcotics subjects' unquote. Also known to harass hookers. In spite of that stellar record, they cut him loose in '06."

"Go figure," said Raley.

Ochoa said, "But neither of you heard that." Then he handed his notes over the seat to Nikki.

————

The two of them said nothing on the elevator ride up to Rook's loft. They just stared at each other as they had in the backseat of the Roach Coach. The air between them flowed thick with a longing that had no words, and they both knew that to try to find them or speak them would only weaken the overwhelming magnetic pull each of them felt. They stood close. Not touching—that would break the spell, too. Just near enough to almost touch . . . just enough to each taste the breath of the other as the rocking motion of the ride brought them to almost brush bodies.

When he closed his front door, they threw themselves at each other. The force of the heat that engulfed them plus the wave of exhilaration from their close call propelled Heat and Rook into a dimension of sexual longing that was as unstoppable as it was primal. Gasping, Nikki pulled her mouth away from his and leaped up onto him, hooking her legs behind his. Rook flexed his leg muscles for balance and steadied himself, pulling her tightly to him. She pressed her face to his ear and bit. He moaned with surprise and excitement and turned her to sit up on his kitchen counter. As he undid her coat front, Nikki reclined herself backward onto her elbows so she could watch him, finally speaking. "Now," she said, "I need you right now."

————

"This is where petting leads," he said later.

"Petting? What century are you from?" She unfolded herself from their lazy, naked tangle on his couch and poured each of them another glass of wine from the bottle on the coffee table.

"Do not mock me because I am a wordsmith. Would you rather I called it groping? Because that's what you did in the Roach Coach, you know."

"Oh, I know." Nikki handed him his glass and they *tink*ed. "You say that like you've never been groped in a police car."

"Well, only yours." Her cell phone rang, and as she got up to retrieve it from her knot of a coat, he continued, "But if you have some notion about starting some sick sexual game where we do it in police cars, I'm all for it."

Lauren Parry said, "Hope I'm not interrupting sump'n-sump'n. Miguel says by the look of you two when he and Raley dropped you off, I should wait a decent interval. Actually, he called it an indecent interval." Nikki looked down at herself, not wearing a stitch, and Rook, just the same, his fine ass making its way down the hallway.

"No, we were just relaxing."

Her friend said, "Pants on fire."

"What pants?"

The two had a nice laugh about that, then Lauren said, "Listen, since I'm betting you don't have a pen anywhere on you, I'll give you a second to find one. I have some interesting off-the-record stuff to share. . . . Even though Detective Ochoa tells me you are anything but still involved in case work due to your suspension."

Nikki plucked a rollerball from one of the numerous coffee mugs that Rook had converted to pencil cups and scattered around his loft. One of the perks of sleeping with a writer. "I'm ready."

"First off," began the ME, "and this is why I really called, because I knew it would give you some peace of mind. . . . The bloodwork on Father Graf's Roman collar came in and it was a negative match for Captain Montrose."

"Yessss."

"Yeah, I thought that would be a lift. I'm already having them run Sergio Torres, and now I'll add this guy you took on tonight—*unarmed.*" Lauren put an underscore on the word that made it sound as boldly comical as it did insane. The objective view of her best friend wasn't lost on Heat.

"OK, I do have to admit I got a little sloppy. Still adjusting to the whole unarmed private citizen thing."

"Don't know what to say, Nikki. I'd tell you to get a hobby, but we both know what the chances are of that."

"Don't be so sure," said Heat. "Is vigilante considered a hobby?"

"You've been hanging out with Jameson Rook too long; you're starting to talk like him." Which gave Nikki the second reason to smile in that conversation. Lauren continued, "I also have lab results that came in on that little chip of leather. Remember that?"

Heat pictured it, looking like a tiny bacon bit in the bottom of the vial when Lauren had showed it to her in the autopsy room. "Sure, the fragment you found under Father Graf's fingernail."

"That's the one. It came back sourced from a commercial brand of leather."

"Bondage gear?" asked Nikki.

"No. The manufacturer may be familiar to you. Bianchi."

The brand was well known to Heat as it was to anyone who geared up for law enforcement. "It came from a police belt?"

Always precise, Lauren clarified, "Or a security guard's. It came from either a holster or a cuff case. You're the one who tipped me to the handcuff bruising on the victim's lower back, so, if you want to speculate, cuff case is a good bet."

"I wonder . . . that is, if you knew anyone who could possibly have a word with Detective Ochoa at this late hour of the night . . ."

"Go on," she said, enjoying Nikki's counter to her teasing about Rook.

"I wonder if a search of a certain dead ex-cop's home or his motorcycle repair shop would show an old Bianchi cuff case with a new scratch on it."

Heat heard the mouthpiece get covered and hushed voices. One of them was Miguel Ochoa's. "Will do," said Lauren when she came back on. "He and Raley will head to Steljess's place tomorrow first thing. Do you want me to also have him look at Captain Montrose's case and holster?"

Lauren's question was the one Heat was afraid to ask out loud. "I suppose. I mean, it would be nice to eliminate that possibility." And then, feeling disloyal to his memory, she added, "However remote." As Rook drifted back in the room with a robe on and carrying one for her, Nikki said, "And Lauren, as long as we're talking about the captain, would you mind if I pester you about one other thing?"

"Name it."

"I know they must have run his gun by now."

"That's right. It had been fired, but they never recovered the slug. It was a through-and-through and out the roof."

Heat recalled the dimple around the hole in Montrose's Crown Vic. "And that's that?"

"Of course not," said the ME. "The gun had his blood and tissue on it. Also his hand tested positive for powder residue and trace metals."

"How many bullets in the magazine?" asked Heat.

"Report said all but one . . . I think."

"Humor me, Ms. Parry. Would you ask Miguel to look into it himself? And by himself, I'm not saying I don't trust the testing. I'm just saying nobody comes close to a Detective Ochoa–quality job."

And then Nikki said with a tease, "And you must know what I mean by that, right, Laur?"

"Yes, I do," she said with a laugh. "He's a very thorough investigator." Lauren was still laughing when she hung up.

———

Rook ordered in some chicken scarpariello and a salad from Gigino's for them to share, and still hanging out in their robes, they ate a late supper at his counter while Nikki filled him in on the newest information from Lauren Parry.

"It all lays out, doesn't it?" He ticked each off on a finger. "Steljess caught on surveillance in the bondage dungeon, Steljess was a fired ex-cop, Steljess would have handcuffs and a cuff case, he sure had a gun, Steljess is our killer."

Nikki poked a grape tomato from their salad with her fork. "That's pretty definitive. Then tell me why he did it. And why did all the shooters come after me in Central Park? And what is this all about?"

"I got nuthin'."

She popped the tomato in her mouth and gave him a sly smile. "I'm not saying you're wrong . . ."

"When you say things like that to me, I call it a Kardashian. Know why? Because I'm looking for the but."

"However . . . ," she said, "it's still circumstantial. If Roach comes up with a matching fingernail gouge on the matching cuff case, that's at least a solid connection. Even that's still not proof. I need facts."

Rook served another piece of chicken onto her plate. "Whoever said facts are funny things? Dead wrong. Can't recall the last time I was ever amused by a fact. Now, intuition and conjecture . . . that's like filling the bouncy castle with laughing gas."

"Just so you know, I thoroughly agree that Steljess is our prime suspect." Her face clouded. "It's too bad he had to be taken out. I was hoping to sweat him. In my heart, I believe he killed Montrose."

Now it was Rook's turn to look doubtful. "It's not that I'm saying you're wrong . . . but why?"

Heat smiled. "Now you're thinking like a cop."

———

Heat woke up to an empty bed. Detective that she was, she felt Rook's side and the sheets were cold. She found him on the computer in his office. "You're shaming me, Rook. This is the third morning this week you've gotten up before I did."

"As I lay there watching the digits change on the clock on my nightstand, stumped and more than just a bit frustrated by this case, I got up and took a page from your book, Nikki Heat. I went out to stare at the Murder Board."

"And what did you learn?"

"That Manhattan is very noisy, even at four A.M. I'm serious. What's with all the sirens and horns?" She sat in the easy chair across from him, waiting, knowing he was ramping up to something. He had the look of the guy holding cards. That's why she always beat him at poker. "So I waited for one of the items on the board to jump out at me or connect to another. Didn't happen. So I went the other way. I asked myself, 'What don't we have?' I mean besides closure.

"And then it came to me. It was probably why I couldn't sleep in the first place—because it was a touchy area last night."

"Captain Montrose," she said.

"Exactly. You said he was always telling you to look for the odd sock. Nikki, he was the odd sock. Think about it. Nothing he did was like the man you knew. . . . Like the man anybody knew." She shifted in her seat, but it wasn't from upset at the subject, it was because energy was moving through her. She didn't know where Rook was going, but her experienced sense told her he was asking the right questions. "So with that in mind, I tried to figure out what he was up to. Hard to know. And why?"

"Because he had gotten so closed, so secretive."

"Precisely. Odd sock behavior. He'd lost his wife, so he wasn't talking with her, either. But guys, no matter how stoic we appear—unless we're moody loners, or those Queen's Guards at Buckingham Palace—have to talk with someone."

"Father Graf?" she asked.

"Mm-maybe. Hadn't thought of him. I was thinking more like some existing personal bond. A lifetime confidant. The mortgage buddy."

"Explain?"

"The one pal you can call, no matter what time of night it is and no matter what you've gotten yourself into, who would mortgage his house to save your rear, no questions asked." He saw her glint of understanding. "Tell me, who is a cop closest to?"

She didn't hesitate. "His partner." Nikki was just about to say the name, but he beat her to it.

"Eddie Hawthorne."

"How could you know about Eddie?"

"Writer's friend. A little thing called an Internet search engine. Got multiple hits on citations of valor for those two, both as uniforms and detectives. I figured if they found a way to stick together when they got their gold shields, they'd be tight."

"Eddie retired and moved away, though." A distant memory brought a smile to her. "I was at his retirement party."

"July 16, 2008." He indicated his laptop. "I loves me my Google." Then Rook pressed a few keys and his printer came alive.

"What's that, Eddie Hawthorne's cholesterol level?"

He took two pages from the tray and walked over to Nikki, handing her one of them. "It's our boarding passes. The car service picks us up for LaGuardia in a half hour. We're having lunch with Eddie in Florida."

Eddie Hawthorne pulled up in his Mercury Marquis as soon as they stepped from the terminal in Fort Myers. He got out and gave Nikki a big hug, and as they parted and looked at each other, Nikki's eyes gleamed as they hadn't in a long, long time.

He took them to a fish taco place two exits west of Interstate 75 off the Daniels Parkway. "It's local, it's good, and it's close enough to the airport so you don't have to sweat making your return flight this afternoon," he said.

They ate at a patio table shaded from the sun blare by a Dos Equis umbrella. The first part of the lunch conversation was reminiscence about their lost friend. "Charles and I were partners so long people didn't see us as two people after a while. I walked by our sarge once— all by myself, you see—and he looks right at me and says, 'Hi, fellas.'" The old cop laughed. "That's the way it was. Hawthorne and Montrose, the thorn and the rose, that was us, man. Damn, that was us." Eddie Hawthorne seemed more interested in talking than the food, which was excellent, and so Heat and Rook just listened, enjoying fresh grilled fish and shirtsleeve weather while he reminisced. When the subject turned to Montrose's wife, the laughter over glory days faded. "So sad. Never saw two people so close as he and Pauletta. It's a stunner for anyone, but man . . . It hollowed Charles out, I know it did."

"I kind of wanted to ask you a little about that, I mean the past year," said Nikki.

The ex-detective nodded. "Didn't think you flew all the way down here for the *horchata*."

"No," she said, "I'm trying to make sense of what went on with the Cap."

"You won't be able to. Doesn't make any sense." Eddie's lip quaked briefly, but then he sat up, willing some steel into his body, as if that would help.

Rook asked, "Did you have much contact with him since his wife was killed?"

"Well, you could say I made a lot of attempts. I flew up for her funeral, of course, and we sat up talking most of the night after the service. In truth, maybe more sitting than talking; like I say, I made attempts, but he went to stone in there." Eddie poked his heart with two fingers. "Who couldn't understand that?"

Nikki said, "It's not uncommon to sort of slide a rock over you for a time after you suffer a trauma like that. But after a period of intense grieving most people come out of the funk. And when they do, it's sort of startling, the new energy."

Eddie nodded to himself. "Yeah, how'd you know that?" Nikki felt Rook's hand touch hers under the table briefly. Hawthorne continued, "It was out of the blue, like three months ago. He calls and talks awhile. Old times small talk, that kind of stuff. More conversation than I'd heard from him in ages. Then he says to me that he's been sleeping poorly, tossing thoughts all night. I told him to join a bowling league, and he just says, 'Yeah right,' and keeps on about his insomnia.

"He asks me, 'Edward, you ever get bothered by any of the old cases?' And I said, 'Shit, man, why do you think I retired?' and we had a good laugh about that, but he came right back to it, like he was scratching at poison ivy. And he gets to the point, saying that he's been thinking more and more about The Job and how he's having doubts about his purpose. Even said—get this—wondering about how good a cop he was. Can you believe that?

"So he says he's been sitting up nights chewing on this one case we worked together, saying he was never satisfied we got it right, and the deeper the hole gets dug around him with all the administrative bullshit he has to deal with, the more he feels the itch to do something. Something to prove that he's still the cop he believed he was. I told him to open the Scotch and watch some Weather Channel, anything to get his mind clear, and he gets pissy with me, saying he thought that I of all people would understand the importance—the duty, he says—of getting it right. I didn't know what else to say to that except, let's hear about it then. Charles says he never believed it was a bad drug deal. It didn't figure for the victim and his priors to be in with that low end of a dealer, or in that part of town. And I said what I said back then, drugs is dangerous business; if they don't get you, the dealers will. And then I reminded him I always thought if it wasn't a busted deal it was a Latin gang initiation." There it was again, thought Nikki. The catch-all explanation for unsolved crimes. "But Charles, he said he was picking up pieces that smelled like a planned killing and a cover-up. He said he was looking for a revenge motive. Either way," he shrugged, "what are you going to do? You give it your best shot and don't look back. That's what I did, anyway. But he wasn't one to let anything go unfinished." The steel left him and his lip quivered again. "I dunno, maybe that's what finished him."

"The case," said Nikki. "What was the case that bothered him so much?" But she knew the answer before she asked it.

"The Huddleston kid," answered Eddie.

FIFTEEN

f Nikki couldn't have access to the Huddleston file, she would have the next best thing. She asked Eddie Hawthorne to walk her through the case. The ex-detective leaned far back in his plastic chair, and when his head left the shade of the umbrella, the sunlight that hit his hair made the black dye shine purple. His eyes worked back and forth as he searched his memory, and he exhaled loudly, girding himself for this unexpected heavy lifting. "Two thousand four," he said. "Charles and I were working Homicide out of the Four-one and got the call about a gunshot victim in a car over on Longwood. That zone was pretty much junkie central, you know? Joke among the uniforms was, you hit a perp with your baton and the crack vials come falling out like a piñata. Anyway, so Charleston and I roll, figuring this was just another garden variety crack whack.

"We reset that notion pretty quick, though, as soon as we drove up and clocked the M5. The only Beemers in that zip code belonged to dealers and we knew them by heart. So we got ready to check out the vic, figuring on a kid from maybe Rye or Greenwich who saw *Scarface* one too many times and made the mistake of coming to the big city to bypass his pharmacological middle man. Profile was right, too, when we saw the body. Very early twenties, expensive clothes, Green Day CD still blasting an endless loop on the custom sound system. But then it kicks up a notch when Montrose says he knows this kid. Not personally, but from TV. Wallet and registration both ID him as Eugene Huddleston, Jr., son of the movie star, and then it all starts to tumble in place for us. He'd been all over the news, especially *Access* and *ET*, for his drug spiral. Nothing like Charlie Sheen, but enough for me and my partner to paint the picture. And why wouldn't it make sense?" Eddie wasn't just being rhetorical. Nikki could see he was seeking her understanding. She gave a mild shrug, enough to acknowledge how it could happen, but mindful, too, that a detective follows evidence and doesn't lead it, which was probably the same homily that kept her captain awake in hindsight.

"How was he done?" asked Heat.

"Single head shot."

"How, face? Execution style in back?"

"Temple," said Hawthorne.

"Like a drive-up buy where the dealer sees the gourmet car and thinks fat wallet and puts one : . . here?" She pointed a finger pistol at Rook's left sideburn.

"See, that's where it started to fight our theory." Eddie put a finger to his own right temple. "Entrance wound on this side. Passenger side."

All these years later, Heat was back there in her mind with Montrose and Hawthorne, processing that first odd sock. "You sure he was done in the car?"

"No doubt. Brains and broken glass on the driver's side."

"The window was up?" Odd sock number two for Nikki; not inherently significant, just . . . odd. "What about the passenger window, open or closed?"

Eddie's eye rolled upward while he thought. "Closed, yeah for sure, closed."

"So whoever shot him was probably inside the car with him," said Heat.

"Riding shotgun," offered Rook. He saw their expressions, crossed his arms, and said, "All yours."

Nikki continued, "And I assume no prints?"

"None that did us any good. Just his clubbing and party buddies, a few girlfriends, and plenty of no-matches." Which meant no criminal records for the unknowns. "All the matched prints alibied out," he said, a step ahead of Nikki.

"Anything else about his body? No signs of beating?" She wanted to know if Eddie knew about the TENS burns.

"Not beating, per se. His wrists had marks like he'd been tied up."

"Or cuffed?"

He grew thoughtful. "Honestly, never thought of cuffs, but here's what we did attribute it to. We check out the neighboring buildings, of course, and we come upon this empty loading bay inside a low-rise industrial space. Old sign said it had been one of those textile rental places that supply uniforms and coveralls to hotels and construction. Door's unlocked and, inside, there's nothing in the whole place but this wood frame lying in the middle of the concrete floor."

Heat and Rook exchanged glances and Nikki said, "Describe it for me, Eddie."

"Simple. Like a wood pallet hammered together, kind of crudely, but in the shape of a big X—about seven feet long, three wide. And the thing of it is, it had straps at each corner."

"Like restraints," said Heat.

"Yeah, but improvised. I think they were tie-downs, like you'd get for strapping a kayak to your roof rack. Of course, this was the point when me and Rose totally fell out of the drive-up-drug-deal-gone-bad notion. Somebody took that kid in there and lashed him to that rig." When Hawthorne's face grimmed up, it was like he was seeing something unpleasant right then and there instead of years ago. "In addition to the chafing at the young man's wrists and ankles, he had these red marks like a bad sunburn. Only in blotchy areas all over his skin. I'm talking about his chest, his legs, his . . . his groin . . ." Eddie winced and said, "You get the idea. Charles and I worked it as best we could, but given the kid's history of drugs and drug busts and all the crazy and dangerous stuff he got into, it went down as a sour drug deal."

"What about the torture?" asked Rook. "Didn't that play in?"

"Oh, yeah." Hawthorne nodded. "OCME said it was electrical, something called a TENS. That just added credence to the bad drug deal theory, saying Huddleston wasn't a drive-up target of opportunity but was probably dealing regularly with a player who the kid shorted on money, and the torture and killing was payback to make him an example to others or to increase the dealer's status in the ranks."

"I'm not accusing, Eddie, I'm just asking this to get into the load Captain Montrose was carrying," said Nikki gently. "You guys didn't take it any further?"

"We wanted to, but the Huddleston family, they were begging for closure. They'd had enough, so pressure came from downtown to move on, especially since there'd been official disposition. And then Charles got his promotion and took over the Twentieth, so it fell away."

Heat handed him the mug shot of Sergio Torres. "This guy would have been doing some low-level dealing north of 116th and in the Bronx back then. Ever come across him?"

He studied it carefully and said, "No, but that doesn't mean he wasn't around. I was Homicide, not Narcotics."

"Speaking of which, does this guy look familiar? He worked Narco around then."

Eddie took the picture of Steljess and said, "Mad Dog."

"What do you know about him?"

"Total dipshit, that's all you needed to know. He was undercover but everyone knew he crossed over. Went native, you could smell it on him." He handed the picture back. "I hear they drummed him out. Good riddance."

"Well said," from Rook.

After Heat took back the pictures, she said, "One more question, if you don't mind, Eddie. Who was the big player then?"

"In drugs? Uptown and in the Bronx?" He chuckled. "One man, Alejandro Martinez."

———

On the flight back to LaGuardia Nikki said, "Nice one, thinking about Eddie."

"Not a problem. I am an investigative journalist, you know."

"Oh? And I understand you also have not one, but two Pulitzers." She drilled his ribs with her knuckle.

"Do I say that too often?"

"Not really. Maybe if you just carried the awards around it would be more subtle." She laughed and said, "But you did put your talents to good use. Even if we don't know all the answers to this yet, we do know one thing."

"If you're dyeing your hair black, keep out of direct sunlight?"

"Absolutely." Then she grew serious. "At least we know Captain Montrose was working on something and not . . . you know."

"Dirty?"

"And I knew it. And now that we've talked to Eddie, I truly know it. So thanks, times two, Pulitzer boy. For the idea and the plane ticket."

Rook turned to her and said, "I don't know who you're trying to redeem, Montrose or yourself, but I do know one thing. I'm with you on either."

———

Heat had multiple voice mails from Ochoa when they got off the plane. "What's up, Miguel?" she said in the taxi line.

"Where are you? I hear jets."

"At the airport. Rook and I just went to Florida." And then she couldn't resist adding, "For lunch."

"Man, my frostbite has frostbite. I want to get suspended."

"Oh, yeah," said Heat, "best week of my life."

"First off, Steljess did have his old cuff case and holster but no scrapes matching that leather bit. Same on Montrose's leathers. OK, more on the captain. Raley and I went to Forensics and personally checked out the questions you had about his weapon. He had a full magazine minus one bullet." Whatever relief Nikki had felt after meeting with Eddie Hawthorne flushed out of her. A deep sadness gripped her. Rook read it on her and mouthed a silent "what?" but she waved him off. Then Ochoa said, "But hang on. I checked his backup magazine from his belt and discovered something interesting."

Heat said it first. "One's missing."

"Even better. Not only is one missing, the top load in his gun's mag was the orphan from that spare clip." Nikki could feel her spirits rise back up while Detective Ochoa continued, "No prints on the cartridge, which is also strange—not even Montrose's."

"Not just strange," Heat said, "significant. I mean, come on, how does a dead man reload?"

———

Evening rush hour traffic back to Manhattan gave Rook an extra thirty minutes in the rear of the cab to work out a scenario to spin over Ochoa's revelation. "This is big. No disrespect to the vaunted Mr. le Carré, but this is bigger than *Call for the Dead*. This is a dead man's bullet. Hey, I think I have the title for my article. I should write it down. No, I'll remember, it's that good." Nikki didn't even bother trying to reel him in. He was not only more entertaining than the Taxi TV embedded in the driver's seat back—she had the Sam Champion promo memorized by now, anyway—Rook was like the broken clock that managed to be correct two times a day. For once he was thinking out loud about something she wanted to hear. Because she was sorting it out, too.

"OK, here's how it spools for me," he said. "Montrose is parked in the car and bad guy X, in the passenger seat, has got his gun somehow. Don't know how that happened but I say it did, otherwise this doesn't play."

Heat said, "We can sift the details later. Keep going."

"Fine, so Montrose's weapon is in the hands of his passenger, who has either been holding it on him or he takes the captain by surprise. Anyway, the passenger jams the gun under his chin, and pow. Which also explains why a chin shot and no eating the barrel."

Nikki agreed so far. "And why Lauren expressed reservations about the trajectory."

"Yes. Now, here is where we go a little *Mission: Impossible*, but stay with me because it's absolutely feasible. Montrose is dead. The issue for the shooter becomes how do you sell this as a suicide if the residue is on your hands, not the victim's? Answer: You hold the gun in the dead man's hand and fire another shot. Problem 2: Then the magazine is down not one, but two bullets, leaving a lot of messy questions to complicate things. So what the killer does is fit the gun into Montrose's hand, hold it out the car window, squeeze off the second shot to get residue on the captain, right? Then replace that second bullet by using gloved hands to take one of Montrose's own bullets—guaranteed to match his weapon— from the spare mag on his belt. The killer slides that round into the top of the clip. It looks like a perfect one-shot suicide, and he splits."

"You don't often hear me say this, Mr. Conspiracy Theory, but I think you're on to something."

Rook said, "Yes, but it's pure hypothesis, right? And that doesn't hold water."

"So leaky that if you took this theory to the Department, you'd need a mop."

"We could give it a try. I mean you do know a good water damage service, don't you, from the crime scene?"

They rode in silence a moment, Nikki staring at the silhouette of the Manhattan skyline in the greening sky of twilight. Then she pulled out her cell phone. "What?" asked Rook.

Heat didn't answer. She dialed 411 and asked for the number of On Call water damage restoration.

Rook said, "I was joking, you know."

————

DeWayne Powell from On Call met them in front of the Graestone Condominiums, where Heat had seen him parked the day of Montrose's shooting. "You got here fast," she said.

"When you're name's On Call, that's what you do. Besides, I have two brothers who are firefighters, so I like to do what I can to help out, you know?"

"Must be handy," said Rook, "having a few of the Bravest in the family when you're in the water clean-up business."

DeWayne beamed a sunny smile. "Know how lawyers chase ambulances? I do fire trucks."

"Tell me what you were doing here the other day," said Nikki.

"I'm happy to go through it with you again, but I already told those other detectives everything I saw. Not much to add when you saw nothing."

Heat shook her head. "I don't mean about the shooting. I mean, why were you called in?"

———

They needed flashlights by then, but DeWayne had three in his van and they took them up on the roof. He shined his at an array of orange safety cones connected together by yellow tape. "That's where I did my patching. Building's going to redo the whole roof, so that'll be it until spring."

"And any idea where the leak came from?" said Nikki.

"Oh, absolutely." DeWayne trained his light on the wooden water tank on stilts above them. It resembled the hundreds of cedar tanks atop all the buildings Heat had been looking at from the cab when she was checking out the skyline. "Folks on the top floor called and said they were getting flooded through the ceiling. With the freeze, we figured a busted pipe or whatever. But it was from the tank." He waggled his light beam over a fresh cedar plank. "Leak drained a few hundred gallons before we got here. By then, water level was low enough it stopped by itself."

"Don't know what caused it?" Rook was looking straight at Nikki when he asked it. Both were thinking the same thing.

"Nah," said DeWayne. "Water was done leaking by then, so it didn't matter to me. Figured that wood just split in the cold. The tank guy couldn't come till the next day, so I never heard what made the leak happen."

Rook leaned and whispered in Heat's ear. "My money's on a bullet hole from shot number two."

———

On the ride back to Rook's loft, Nikki speed-dialed Ochoa. "You'll be sure to let me know when I've depleted the favor bank, won't you?"

"Hey, no problem. The way it's going here at the Two-oh, it's nice to actually engage in some real police work."

"Iron Man?"

"Has no plan." She could hear Raley laughing in the background. Ochoa said, "Raley wants me to tell you that Captain Irons has set up eight A.M. tomorrow for desk inspection. For real. If we can't clean up the streets, at least we can tidy up our work areas."

Heat said, "It's probably best that this isn't sourced from me, so in about ten minutes, you're going to get a call from a DeWayne Powell. He's the guy who discovered Montrose's body. He's going to report that the more he thought about it, the water leak he got called in to clean up was from a bullet hole in the water tank on top of the building near the captain's car."

"Jeez," said Ochoa as he was struck by the implications. "Cap's bullet went straight up, so this one . . ."

"Right," said Nikki. "Could be the orphan slug from his backup magazine. Listen, my guess is if a slug punctured that cedar and got slowed by a twelve-foot-diameter tank of water, it probably didn't exit."

"We are all over it, trust me."

"Good, but wait for DeWayne's call. I just wanted to give you the heads-up so you took him seriously and had Forensics check out that tank."

"Will do," he said.

"And Miguel? This is all because of the job you and Rales did today double-checking his weapon and ammo. If we prove homicide instead of suicide, you've done this man a great service."

"Hey, I'll put on a mask and flippers myself, if I have to." And as she looked up at the CNN JumboTron above Columbus Circle and saw it was minus-three degrees, Nikki knew that was exactly what he would do if it came down to it.

———

Rook was hungry, but she was too amped to eat, so he zapped the scar-pariello that was left over from the night before while she pulled a dining room chair up to face Murder Board South and took a seat for her contemplation. "How was it?" she said when he ate his last bite.

"Even better as a leftover," he said. "And how did you know I was done, do you have eyes in the back of your head?"

"No, I have ears. You stopped moaning in ecstasy."

"Ah. So that's how you know when I'm done."

She turned to him wearing a sly smile. "I know when you're done, mister. You're done when I'm done."

"It's a beautiful thing," he said. She turned her attention back to the board, then rose with a red marker and drew circles around Rook's notation: "Montrose—What was he doing??" He said, "Guess we got the answer to that today, thanks to Eddie."

"No, we got half of it. We know what he was trying to do, but we don't know what investigative course he was following. And he kept it from me. Either because he had some pride thing about cracking it himself or he didn't want to admit it if he failed."

"Or . . . ," said Rook. "More likely, he knew it was dangerous and was trying to keep you out of it. Even at the expense of pissing you off."

She mulled that, then said, "Or any of the above. But what were his leads? Where was he going?"

"You could have Roach check his files, but, according to you, Internal Affairs beamed them up to the mother ship."

"I knew Montrose, and if he wanted secrecy he wouldn't have

kept anything at the office. Especially with IA all over him." Heat tapped the barrel of the marker against her lip and then tossed it on the tray, a decision made. "I want to break into his apartment."

––––––

It was nine-thirty, still early enough not to freak out Captain Mon-trose's next-door neighbor, although Penny the dachshund went on high alert on the other side of the door after they knocked. As the multiple locks snapped open, they heard Corrine Flaherty shushing and saying, "Relax, Pen, it's Nikki, you know Nikki." She opened the door and the two women hugged. Corrine, dowdy and late fifties, primped her hair and said, "I'm glad you called, it gave me a chance to chase the men out."

The long-haired mini dachshund turned absolutely inside out over Rook. She rolled onto her back in the living room, and he knelt on the carpet to administer a tummy rub while she melted, her caramel tail waving like a flag. "I'm next," said Corrine, followed by a smoker's laugh.

When she excused herself from the room, Rook stood and said to Heat, "So how are we going to do this, use her balcony to jump to Montrose's like Spider-Man? I mean the movie, not the musical; it's six floors down and I don't have my health insurance card on me."

"How would we get in the sliding door on his balcony if it's locked, which you know it must be?"

"Hmm," he said, "does Corrine have a hammer? I could break the glass with a mighty blow."

"Here ya go, Nikki," said Corrine as she came back from the kitchen with a key ring. "This one's the knob, this is the deadbolt."

Rook frowned as if deep in thought and said, "Spare keys. Very crafty."

––––––

At Montrose's front door Rook stepped in front of Heat, blocking her. "I'll do this part." He tore the police tape seals off the door and stepped back. "Wouldn't want you getting in any trouble with the cops, ha ha."

Once they were inside, Nikki felt a chill that had nothing to do with the low thermostat. They kicked up the temp and turned on all the lights, but it still felt like a place that would never be warm for her again. She kept her coat on and stood in the middle of the living room, turning a slow rotation, trying to put aside memories of the dinners she had enjoyed with the skip and Pauletta or the Super Bowl party the captain had invited her squad to three years before, after they got their citation for top case clearances. She shut those things out as best she could and simply observed.

On the way over the bridge to Queens, she had told Rook not to expect much, that Internal Affairs would have been over the apartment just like his office. She said to expect furniture but no files or anything like that. Those items would have been boxed and inventoried and shipped off for examination. When he asked her what she was looking for then, she told him whatever IA might have missed that she wouldn't. "They were only investigating him. I'm clearing him."

They worked together methodically, Rook following her lead and her instructions. The bathrooms were the first stops. Cops knew that's where most people hid their valuables because there was so much to look through. But when they opened the cabinets, they saw that clearly IA had had the same thought, because the shelves were bare in the medicine chests and under the sinks of both bathrooms. The kitchen was much the same. Although a few items were left on the pantry shelves, most items had been cleared out and were no doubt gone over by downtown.

The second bedroom, which had been converted to a study, had been picked clean, as Heat had predicted. They could see the gaps on the shelves where books and videos had been removed. The desk drawers were empty, and there were compression lines on the rug from the footprints of absent filing cabinets. The master bedroom was an easy search. The bed had been stripped and the frame was empty; the mattress and box spring were leaning neatly against a wall. "Not looking so promising," said Rook.

"It never does until it is." But she was feeling the futility as well. "Tell you what, I'll take the closet, you do the dresser, then let's call it a night."

Nikki was sliding suits on hangers along the wooden pole when Rook said, "Oh, Detective Heat?" When she stepped out of the walk-in, he was at the dresser. The top drawer was open.

"I'm not sure if this will be anything, but if it is, I figured you deserved the honors." She slowly crossed the room to join him, then followed his gaze down into the open drawer.

Captain Montrose's sock drawer. In it were about a dozen pairs of black and navy dress socks, folded and balled to marry the pairs. And toward the back of the drawer, a lone beige sock without a mate. Nikki looked up at Rook. Both were thinking it, but neither was saying it.

An odd sock.

Heat picked it up. Her heart raced when she did. "There's something in it."

"Come on, I'm gonna pee myself."

Nikki opened the sock and reached inside. "It's cardboard." She pulled it out. It was a business card. For a talent representative. "This is for Horst Meuller's agent."

When she turned it over her throat contracted and she stifled an involuntary wail. She covered her face with one hand and turned away as she handed the card to Rook. He flipped it over. The ballpoint handwriting read, "Nikki, just be careful."

SIXTEEN

At nine the next morning, when Heat and Rook climbed the subway steps up to 18th Street, a frozen mist was descending on Chelsea, wrapping the neighborhood in a harsh, woolen chill. They crossed Seventh, heading west, toward the agent's office, joining an eclectic sidewalk mix of tortured young artists and upstart dancers who might have been cast in a music-video salute to brooding. By the time they reached Eighth, Rook said he had stopped counting navy berets.

When they entered the third-floor walk-up office of the Step This Way Talent Agency, Phil Podemski was eating take-out oatmeal at his desk. As he swept old trade magazines and newspapers from his couch onto the floor so they could sit, the agent eyeballed Nikki and said he could really do something with her, considering her figure and looks. "You have to strip, of course. Not for me, I don't go for any funny business, I mean in the act."

"Much as I appreciate the offer," she said, "that's not why we're here."

"Oh . . ." Podemski sized up Rook and tugged at his orange Yosemite Sam mustache. "Sure, guess I could give you a bullwhip and a fedora. We'd market you as Indiana Bones. Or maybe go sci-fi. You sorta look like that guy who roamed outer space everybody's so crazy about."

"Malcolm Reynolds?" asked Rook.

"Who? . . . No, I'm thinking we give you a space helmet and some assless chaps and call you . . . Butt Rogers."

When Nikki jumped in and told him they were there to talk

about Horst Meuller, Podemski stuck the plastic spoon back in the wide-mouthed deli cup and frowned while he finished chewing. "You cops?"

Nikki dodged telling an outright lie by saying, "You already spoke to one of my squad members, a Detective Rhymer?" When that seemed enough of an answer, she pressed forward. Heat wasn't sure what she was looking for yet, but Captain Montrose had gone to great effort to leave her a posthumous clue leading to Podemski's agency. He had also told her to be careful, although her assessment of the agent himself was that he was more colorful than dangerous, a lovable schemer straight out of *Broadway Danny Rose*.

Nikki told Podemski she was with his client the day he got shot but that Horst had been uncooperative. "Do you have any idea why he won't speak to us?"

"That kid, I dunno. Since the boyfriend passed on, he hasn't been the same. His act as Hans Alloffur is my big draw. But he ducked out on me after his pal Alan died, didn't even tell me where he moved."

Nikki remembered that from Rhymer's report, which was why her plan with Phil Podemski was to drill down more on the dead lover, since that was driving Meuller's actions. She flipped up the cover of her notebook. "Tell me about the boyfriend. Alan who?"

"Barclay. Nice guy. Older than Horst, maybe fifty. In good shape but had one of those gray complexions with the hollow eyes and dark circles like you see on people in nursing homes."

Rook said, "And health food stores." Nikki shot him a look. "OK, tell me I'm wrong."

She turned back to Podemski. "He had some cardiac problems, right?"

"Yeah, that's how he kicked. Tragedy." The agent stirred his cold oatmeal and shook his head. "I never got that demo reel he said he'd make for my agency."

"Was he in advertising?"

"Nuh-uh. Cameraman." Phil held up both hands. "Videographer, pardon me."

"What sort of video, Mr. Podemski?"

"Reality TV. You ever watch that show *Payback Playback*?"

Rook sat upright. "I love that show." Nikki shrugged, unfamiliar with it. "You haven't seen it? It's great. Every week they have a different victim who has been screwed by someone—personal relationship, car mechanic, whatever—and they devise a hidden camera payback for the creep and play it back with him sitting right there in front of a nasty studio audience that yells, 'Playback's a bitch!' "

"My loss," she said. "So did this Alan Barclay do any other kind of video work? Anything like porn or maybe bondage videos?" It was a long shot, but she had to ask, given where the case started.

"Porn? No way. I'd bet the farm against that."

Nikki asked, "How come?"

"He was too religious. Strict Catholic. Alan was always trying to get Horst to give up the strip clubs and go legit. Maybe try out for Alvin Ailey or Juilliard. Messing with my income, that guy, may he rest in peace. Even tried to get his pastor to convert him."

Rook blurted the question before Nikki could. "Do you know who Alan Barclay's pastor was?"

"Sure I do. He's the one who got murdered. It was on the news the day after I met him."

Heat exchanged a glance with Rook and asked, "Where did you meet him?"

"Right here. The morning before he was killed. He was camped out in the hall when I came to open up. Said Horst Meuller told him to meet him here at nine sharp, so I let him in. All the while, I'm wondering how the hell do I entertain a priest? But Horst shows up pretty quick. Naturally, I ask him where he's been, and he says never mind—he's very nervous, freaked even. Then he and the priest take a walk. Last time I saw Horst till I heard he got shot."

Heat quickly ran the events of the the past week through her memory and asked, "How come you didn't tell any of this to Detective Rhymer when he interviewed you?"

"Hey, don't get mad at me, I was only doing what that other cop told me to do, which was not to tell anyone."

Heat felt her pulse flutter. "What other cop said that to you, Mr. Podemski?"

"He was a detective, too. The one who killed himself."

Heat said, "Captain Montrose?"

"Montrose, that's right." Podemski fished the captain's business card out of the slush pile atop his desk. "He showed up here a couple hours after Horst took off with that priest. Said he wanted to know where they went or if they left anything behind, you know, for me to hold or stash."

"Did he say what it was? Money, an object?" asked Rook.

Podemski shook no. "Just told me to call him if anybody else came looking and to tell nobody about any of it. Not even other cops."

"Has anybody else come by looking for whatever this is?" asked Rook.

"Nope."

Nikki said, "Mind if I ask why you're telling me?"

"Cuz I just realized that you're the lady cop from that magazine. I figured if I can't trust you, pack it in."

———

Rook hit the sidewalk ready to rock and roll. "We've got him now. I'm telling you, Nik, that German is in this up to his umlaut."

"How can you know that?" she asked.

"Come on, Meuller fights with Graf at the strip club, Meuller leads Graf away the morning he's murdered, Meuller runs from you . . . If you want to know why he hid out and quit those dancing jobs, I refer you to Mr. George Michael's theory about guilty feet and rhythm."

"Rook, think of our timeline and tell me this. Meuller left Podemski's agency with Father Graf just after nine A.M. How is it then that Graf shows up at *Justicia a Guarda* headquarters very much alive an hour and a half later?"

Rook shifted gears like nothing had happened. "Right. Alternate thought, that's good. Any other notions?"

"No, a question. I want to know what a male stripper could have with him that Montrose would want and that got so many people killed. I want to talk to Horst Meuller again."

"Great, let's go."

"Not yet."

"Absolutely not," said Rook, deftly flip-flopping. "Why not?"

"Because Meuller plays too close to the vest. I want to confront him, but I want to go in there knowing more than he thinks I do," said Heat. "So let's be smart and use the help Montrose gave us. He led us to that agent for a reason. Since we already knew about Meuller, I think it was to point us to his lover, the videographer. Let's see what we can find out about Alan Barclay."

Rook hailed a cab, and on the way to Gemstar Studios in Queens, where they produced *Payback Playback*, Heat called Mrs. Borelli at the rectory. The housekeeper not only confirmed that Alan Barclay was a parishioner at Our Lady of the Innocents but that Father Graf said his funeral Mass and delivered the eulogy two weeks earlier. "They knew each other very well, then? Were they friends?"

"I wouldn't exactly call them friends," said the woman. "Alan had some moral crisis he was dealing with, and Father was counseling him. The last days of poor Mr. Barclay's life, things got quite heated in Father Gerry's study."

"Did you hear what they were arguing about, Mrs. B?"

"Afraid not, Detective. I may be nosy but I'm not a snoop."

———

Heat told Security she and Rook would wait in the lobby for the producer, mainly so nobody would ask her to flash tin. If—as the giant poster on the studio wall said, "The Playback Is a Bitch!"—so was being a cop without a shield. The bearded man in the sport coat and jeans who came out of the double glass doors to meet them introduced himself as the line producer, which meant that Jim Steele's purview was the show's physical production, including hiring the camera crew. He asked if there had been some neighborhood complaint about damage or noise from their location shooting and relaxed measurably when she told him no.

"I just want to ask you a few questions about one of your former crew. Alan Barclay."

Steele closed his eyes momentarily and told her that the whole crew was still mourning him. "If you lead a good life, if you're fortunate enough, you get a chance to work with a guy like Alan. A lovely man. Very giving and an artist with that camera. Total pro."

Nikki said, "His name has come up related to a case we are investigating, and I'm really looking for some background on him."

"Not a lot to tell. He's been with me here since I hired him freelance on *Don't Forget to Duck*."

"Great effing show," said Rook.

The producer browsed him warily then continued, "That would have been 2005. Alan was so gifted I brought him onto *Playback* when we got our syndication order."

"What about before that," asked Heat, "had he worked another show?"

"No, in fact, he was sort of a risky hire for me because his background was news shooting."

Rook said, "Network or local stations?"

"Neither. He'd been a rover for one of the stringer companies that provide video footage to local stations that cut back on budgets. You know, stations can't justify the union crews to wait around on the overnight shift to shoot the occasional car accidents and robberies, so instead, they buy clips from the stringers on an as-needed basis."

"Do you know offhand who Alan Barclay worked for?" asked Heat.

"Gotham Outsource." Steele's smart phone buzzed and he checked the screen. "Listen, I've got to get back in there. Do you have all you need?"

"Sure do. Thanks," she said.

Before he left, the producer said, "Mind if I ask you a question? Do you guys ever compare notes?"

Nikki said, "I'm not sure what you mean."

"One of your detectives was here a little over a week ago asking the same questions."

———

The assignment manager of Gotham Outsource had the cranky demeanor of a taxi dispatcher. He half-swiveled from his computer monitor and, over the chatter and electronic noise of a few dozen scanners, said, "I already covered all this with your other suit a week, ten days ago, you know."

"Captain Montrose, right?"

"Yeah, same dude who ten-eightied himself," he said, using the police radio code for "Cancel."

Heat wanted to slap him hard enough for his headset to embed itself in his pea brain. Rook either sensed or shared her distaste and interceded. "Cover it again, it'll take you two minutes. How long did Alan Barclay work for you?"

"Started in 2001. We doubled our crews after 9/11, and he was part of the big hire."

"And you were happy with him?" asked Nikki, past her anger for the moment.

"I was until I wasn't."

She said, "Help me out there."

"Guy ended up being my best shooter. Great shots, hard worker, not afraid to get close to the action. Then he just flakes out on me. *Adios.* Doesn't even come in to quit or say kiss my royal red hinder. Just stops showing." He sucked his teeth. "Freelancers. These lowlifes are one rung above paparazzi."

Heat couldn't wait to get some distance from this goon, but she had one more thing to find out. "Do you remember the date he quit so suddenly?"

He gestured with both arms to the roomful of police radios and TV monitors. "Do I look like I'd remember the date?"

"Try," said Rook.

The man scoffed. "You're no cop. Not wearing a fancy watch like that. You got nothing over me."

Rook brushed past Nikki, ripped the headset off the guy, and spun his chair so he was nose-to-nose with him. "Hey, Ed Murrow, what would it cost your business if I called in a safety tip and some city inspections of your fleet of news vans stopped you from prowling for a night or three?" He paused. "I thought so." Then Rook wrote his phone number down and stuffed it in the man's shirt pocket. "Start remembering."

———

When Horst Meuller woke up from his nap, he gasped. Rook was lean-ing over his hospital bed holding a very large syringe in the German's face. "Don't worry, Herr Meuller," he said in a soft voice, "I won't hurt you." Yet he didn't move away, either. "But do you see how very easy it would be for someone else to kill you while you slept?" Rook gently swung the hypodermic back and forth; Meuller's eyes followed it, big and wide like a cat clock. "You're in a hospital, so there are so many ways. I've heard of contract killers who dress like nurses and inject poison into the IV drip of their victims." Meuller felt around for the call button, and Rook smiled and held it up with his other hand. "To live, press one now."

Horst's face wore a sheen of perspiration. Heat tapped Rook on the shoulder and said, "I think he got the message."

"True. No need to beat a dead . . . Oh, I want to say 'Horst' so bad. But it would be beneath even me."

"What are you trying to do?" asked Meuller.

Nikki pulled a chair bedside. "To get you to see that if you don't help us catch whoever you're so afraid of, I can't protect you from them. Nobody can. You will never be safe. Anywhere." She waited, watching him process. "So you have a choice. Wait for them to come or help me get them before they get you."

Meuller's eyes went from her to Rook, who stood behind Heat. He held up the syringe and winked. "All right," sighed the German. "Very well."

Out came the notebook. Heat said, "Who shot you?"

"I don't know, honestly."

"Was it the same people who tortured you?"

He pursed his lips. "I didn't see who shot me, and the others wore ski masks."

"How many were there?"

"Two. Two men."

"Why, Horst? What's this about?"

"Whoever it is wants something. Something they think I have, but I don't. Honestly, I don't."

She looked at his pleading eyes and believed him. For now. "Let's talk about what it is they want." He retreated into himself, and so she prompted him. "It has something to do with your boyfriend, doesn't it? With Alan?" When Nikki saw the dramatic change of expression, she was glad she'd waited to confront him until they had done some legwork.

"*Ja*, that is right."

"And what is it, Horst?" When he hesitated, she helped him along. She wanted to keep it moving while he was in the mood and also recognized he was in recovery from his wound and would fatigue shortly. "Is it money?" He shook no. "But it is something valuable." He nodded. Nikki got tiny head shakes for each item on her list: jewels, art, drugs. Then she arrived where she wanted to land. "It's a video, isn't it?"

He stirred and Heat knew she had been right. It made sense to her that something from Alan, a videographer, would be a fungible item, quite valuable to someone, depending what was on it. "Tell me what's on the video, Horst."

"You must believe me, I do not know. Alan would not tell me for the reasons we have seen. He said it was too dangerous for me to know. That is why he kept it secret all these years. He said people would kill to get it. And now . . ." His mouth was dry and Nikki held out the water cup so he could sip from the straw.

Heat asked, "Did someone kill Alan, is that how he died?"

"No, he had a bad heart. From birth defect. A few weeks ago he had an episode and had to be put in the hospital."

Nikki made a note. "And this episode, was there a cause for it?"

Something came over him. Acceptance? No, Heat had seen it in interrogation many times before. It was resignation. "You are going to make me tell it all, aren't you?" When she just waited, Meuller's eyes closed and opened. "OK. Yes, there was an inquiry made by a police detective. His name is Montrose."

Nikki caught his use of the present tense. "What was he asking about?"

"It was the video. Somehow this Montrose had traced it to Alan after all these years. Can you believe it? He said he had just talked to a security guard who saw Alan the night he made the video. He denied it and sent him away, but my Alan, dear Alan, he freaked. He was so upset. We went to bed, and a half hour later I have to call 911 because of his heart. It was bad. In the hospital they gave him last rites."

"Father Graf?"

He nodded. "That is when he made a confession about his sin of hiding the video. But the priest, he said, 'No, no, Alan, you must absolve yourself by coming forward with this to the police.' But Alan refused. I know they argued about this many times after he got out of the hospital. I guess the priest contacted the police detective to hypothetically explore delivering something to him on behalf of Alan, but my boyfriend refused to turn it over. He also refused to release Father Graf from his . . . what is it called . . ."

"Seal of confession?" said Rook.

"That, *ja*. The church law that makes a priest keep confession an absolute secret, no matter what. But when Alan was dying from his second heart failure, he told me to pass the video along to Father Graf to do as he wished."

Rook said, "Why didn't Father Graf just hand it over to Montrose?"

"That was the plan. But I had to get it to him first. I hesitated a few days because I, too, was scared. Finally, I met him at my agent's office and handed it to him then, thinking it was all done."

So now Nikki understood the phone calls between Montrose and Father Graf. And why the captain had searched the rectory. Once Graf told Montrose he was going to get the video from Meuller at the agent's office, the Cap was looking for it like everyone else. "After you gave Father Graf the video that morning, where did he go?"

"That I do not know. I was paranoid about my safety and boogied, you know?" His accent made it sound like "boo-geet."

"They found you, though, didn't they?" said Rook.

"I made the mistake of going back to the old apartment, the one Alan and I shared. I thought now that the video was finally gone, I could chance it. I had some photos of him I wanted not to leave behind. I miss him so." Nikki offered some more water, but he waved it off. "They were waiting."

"Are these the men who attacked you?" She held up the photos of Torres and Steljess.

"I cannot be sure. Both of them wore ski masks. They turned up my stereo and lashed me to my bed. There was a metal wand they used to torture me that shocked me and burned. You have to understand, it was a terrible pain. Terrible."

"Horst? How did you manage to get away?"

"When they left me to call someone in the next room, I slipped my restraints. You see, in Hamburg I was once a magician's assistant for Zalman *der Ausgezeichnet*. I used the fire escape out the window and ran for my life."

"Why did they stop the torture to make a call?" She closed her notebook and studied him. He grew uncomfortable under her gaze and said, "That electricity, it was the most awful thing in my life, ever. You can see, I still have scars."

Horst was still selling the pain. Nikki knew why. She didn't judge him, but she wasn't going to say it for him, either, so she waited.

"It hurt through and through, you see." Tears pooled in his eye sockets and Meuller slurped back mucus. "I am so very sorry but I . . . I told them. I told them I gave the video away. . . . To Father Graf."

Then he sobbed in shame.

———

Heat and Rook had a sober, contemplative ride across town to Tribeca. Halfway to his loft, Rook said, "Father Graf on his conscience. That's a big load to carry."

"I feel sorry for him. Truly, Rook, who knows what any of us would do under those circumstances." They rode in silence again. A block later her cell phone buzzed. "Raley," she reported when she did a screen check. "Hey, Rales, what's up?"

"Coupla things I know you'll be interested in. First, your man DeWayne did call. Forensics is draining and sieving the tank on top of the Graestone as we speak. Ochoa's there supervising."

"That's great. Let's hope there's a bullet in there somewhere."

"Now, I've got one more item in the breaking news category. In my spare time, when not focusing on maintaining an orderly work area, I ran a financial on Father Graf." God, thought Heat, how much she loved working with Roach. "Guess what kicked out. Remember that folder for Emma on his computer? I discovered that an Emma Carroll and Graf had a joint bank account. It's only got a few hundred in it now, but it's fluctuated as high as twenty, thirty grand over the past year."

"Rales, you're the best. At least you will be if you also have an address for Emma Carroll." Raley gave it to her, and when they hung up, Nikki leaned forward to the cabdriver. "Change of plans, if you don't mind. Park Avenue at Sixty-sixth."

———

From a high floor in any building in Manhattan you can scan the surrounding apartment rooftops and find a sunroom or two. Emma Carroll met them in hers, and Nikki was amazed at how warm and brilliant it was in there, even though it was near zero outside. The light did little to brighten the woman's face, however. Emma Carroll was quite attractive in what some would call a cougarish way, but the skin was swollen around her eyes, which had a dullness from medication or despondency, or both. "I'm still reeling," she told them as soon as they sat. "Father Gerry was a great priest and a great man."

"Were you close?" Heat surveyed her, wondering if there was any forbidden romance lurking, but she couldn't tell, which usually meant there wasn't any. Nikki prided herself on having finely tuned lay-dar.

"Yes but not like that, oh, please. What the father and I had was a shared vision for doing work through the church to foster human rights and social justice." She took a sip of whatever she had on ice on the coffee table. "Why spoil the fun with something tawdry?"

"I do see that you and Father Graf shared a bank account. An occasionally large bank account," said Nikki.

"Of course we did. I am not only a contributor, but also the treasurer of the account we held for donations to fund a human rights organization we believed in passionately."

Rook asked, "And that would be *Justicia a Garda*?"

Emma Collins perked up for the first time. "Why, yes. I'm so glad you know of them."

"Not so well, really." More for Heat's benefit, he said, "We have what I believe is more of an e-mail relationship."

Nikki ignored Rook's suspicions about Pascual Guzman and asked Collins, "So you would do both the fund-raising and banking for this cause?"

"Well, it began that way. But more recently, I do less administration and more of the development of new donors. I don't even use the bank account much anymore, but steer our patrons to give directly to the liaison for *Justicia*. They seem to enjoy the sense of hands-on funding and their capital administrator is a very charming man."

Nikki opened her notebook. "May I ask you his name?"

"Sure. It's Alejandro Martinez. Do you need me to spell that?"

"No," said Heat, "I've got it."

SEVENTEEN

Rook fortified his first cup of coffee of the morning with a shot of espresso and said, "Mother, are you sure you are up for this?"

"Up for playing the role of a wealthy socialite? Up for it isn't the phrase. Born to it would be more accurate, kiddo."

Nikki plucked the mug shot of Alejandro Martinez from Murder Board South and said, "Think it over, Margaret, this is the man you'd be meeting. He's a notorious drug dealer who's done prison time. He claims he's reformed, but he's also funneling drug money through a church. He may even be responsible for a priest's torture and murder."

"Look at that noble chin, will you?" said Margaret Rook. "And if you think I'm passing up a chance to have those eyes squeeze me across a mimosa, you're crazy."

When Rook had come up with this notion of asking Emma Carroll to set up a fake donor brunch meeting with Martinez, Heat was all for it as a way to bait him with some cash they could track and see where it ended up. By the time she realized the sting would be played out by his mother, the momentum was too strong and Emma had already made her call. "It's not too late to back out," Nikki cautioned. "If you have any worries, don't be proud."

"My greatest worry is which wealthy socialite from my Broadway career I shall reprise. Perhaps Elsa Schraeder from *Sound of Music*?"

"Isn't she the one von Trapp eighty-sixed for Maria?" said Rook.

"Oh . . ." Margaret made a sour face. "I've lost too many men to the nanny to endure that again. I know. I could bring back Vera

Simpson from *Pal Joey*." She examined the mug shot again. "No, he won't spark to her, too sulky. Let's see . . . Ah! I have it. Muriel Eubanks from *Dirty Rotten Scoundrels*. She got seduced by a con artist. Perfect."

"Whatever works for you, Mother, but you are doing the seduction."

"You bet I am."

"With this." Rook placed a Vuitton epi leather Keepall on the dining table. "There's ten thousand dollars of my movie option for the Chechnya article in here. Nikki and I spent all last night recording serial numbers, so no tipping, no dipping."

"Jameson, you are determined to spoil Mother's good time, aren't you."

They arrived in their rental car an hour early so they could claim a parking spot close to Cassis on Columbus Avenue. Heat and Rook had chosen it because it was small and the ambiance was quiet, so they could hear better from the car. "How's this going to work?" asked Margaret from the backseat. "On TV they always wear wires."

"Tada," said Rook. "From my new friends at the spy store, I got you this." He handed her a smart phone.

"That's it? Darling, I was hoping I could wear a wire."

"So *21 Jump Street*. This baby has state-of-the-art noise canceling and sound pickup. Just set it on the seat beside you and we'll hear everything. It also has a GPS. I had better not need to track you, but if something happens, I want to be able to."

"I approve," Nikki said in a British accent. "Very thorough, Q."

"You don't know half of it." He handed her a cell phone. "Since my e-mail got hacked, I've been worried about our phones, too. So while I was there, I got us new ones. I already did a GPS sync and programmed our speed dials."

Heat pressed a button on her new phone. Rook's rang. "Hello?"

"Nerd," she said. And then hung up.

———

From the front seat of their Camry they watched Mrs. Rook establish herself early at the window table they had told her to take. She also claimed the inside seat, as instructed by Nikki, so that from the curb they could keep an eye on Martinez and have a clear view of his hands. "I'll tell you now," came her voice through the speaker phone, "this blocking may work for you but it's far too drafty for me."

Rook made sure his phone was muted and said, "Actors."

While they waited in silence for the drug dealer to arrive, Heat's cell buzzed and Rook said, "You sure you still want to use your old phone instead of the new one I gave you?"

"It's the FBI, I think I can take this."

Her contact at the Violent Crime Unit in Quantico began with an apology for the delay. "It took me a while to get anything for you on Sergio Torres because I hit a firewall and had to get some approvals." A tingle of adrenaline stirred in Heat. "But it's for you, so I kept banging on it till I got clearance. Your man's records were classified because he was deep-cover law enforcement."

Nikki said, "Sergio Torres was a cop?" Rook stopped finger drumming the steering wheel and whipped his head to her.

"Affirm," said the FBI analyst. "Now, his whole jacket, the jail time he served, that was all real. Part of the legend that was built to give Torres street cred."

"What agency was he with?"

"Torres was in Narcotics, NYPD, assigned to the Forty-first Precinct. That's in—"

"—The Bronx," said Heat, "I'm familiar." Just then she saw the dapper figure of Alejandro Martinez walking down the sidewalk toward them. Nikki quickly thanked her NCAVC contact, hung up, and grabbed Rook. "Make out with me."

She pulled him to her and they kissed deeply, and then, just as abruptly, she pulled away. "I didn't want Martinez to clock me."

"No complaints here." Then while they watched Martinez kiss

Margaret's hand as he sat, Rook said, "Did I hear the human popsicle is actually a copsicle?"

The conversation in the restaurant was introductory small talk,
so Heat quickly filled him in on her Torres briefing. Then Nikki
said, "Whoa, whoa, I'm not liking this."

On the cell phone speaker, Martinez was saying he wanted to
move to a table toward the back. "I am not so comfortable sitting in
windows."

Heat said, "We should get her out of there."

"No." She had never seen Rook appear so cowed. "You don't
know Mother. If I intrude on her moment, I will pay dearly."

Margaret, savvy to the arrangement, took care of it herself—and
in character. "Oh, but you don't understand. This is my usual table,
where I like to see and be seen. Especially with you, Mr. Martinez."

"Very well then," came the smooth voice. "But only if you call
me Alejandro."

"It means Alexander, does it not? I'm fond of that name. I have a
son, his middle name is Alexander." Nikki gave Rook a teasing glance.

"You're right, Nikki, we should get her out of there."

"No, no," said Heat. "I'm learning all sorts of things."

Margaret and Alejandro's brunch continued like any first date,
which is to say replete with surface banter and feigned interest in the
mundane stories of each other. "I've always found it creepy to listen in
on my mother's private moments with men," Rook said. Then he immediately walked it back, saying, "Not that I ever do. Did." He
changed the subject. "I'm thinking this news that Torres was a narc in
the Forty-first makes perfect sense."

"This ought to be good."

"Hear me out," he said. "Then you can eviscerate my hypothesis." When she gestured like a game show model for him to continue,
he did. "One: Who else worked Narco in that precinct? Steljess. Two:
Who got killed in that precinct? Huddleston. Three: Who was the
drug kingpin in that precinct then? My mom's date. Same gentleman

whose DEA stash was in Father Graf's attic. So yes, Nikki Heat, I am seeing a connection or two."

Nikki smiled at him. "I'll hate myself for saying this, but go on. What are these connections pointing to?"

"I'm smelling some kind of highly organized narc bribery ring that's been operating in the Bronx. The way I see it, the drug dealers outsmarted the system and started funding crooked cops with DEA money so they wouldn't have to cut into their own profits. Elegant, I'd say. Hang on a sec." He listened to the table in Cassis. Martinez was laughing about the time Margaret went skinny dipping in the fountain at Lincoln Center. Rook said, "If only she had done it at night. . . ."

"Your theory's not totally ludicrous, Rook. But how does Graf figure in? And *Justicia a Garda*? . . . Or don't they?"

"Been thinking about both. Remember how my man in Colombia, T-Rex, said Pascual Guzman from *Justicia* received that secret shipment three weeks ago? What's the secret? Drugs? To quote Charlie Sheen, 'Duh.' And I'm thinking . . . just like our friend in there with his hand on my mother's knee . . . Guzman launders the drug money through Father Graf, who innocently thinks it's philanthropic donations for *la raza justicia*. He finds out it's drug money, and bye-bye padre."

Nikki stared into the middle distance, pondering. "OK. Then why bother with the Emma Carrolls and Margaret Rooks of the world?"

"Simple," Rook said. "First, it's more money to fund the bribes. And more importantly, it keeps up the façade. It's probably what prevented Father Graf from looking too deeply."

"Until?"

Rook frowned, willing the answer to come. Suddenly his face brightened. ". . . Until he heard about the video. That's it, I'll betcha. I bet that video they want so bad blows the lid off the bribery ring in the Forty-first."

"Possible," she allowed.

"You're not convinced?"

"I'm convinced we have a theory. And not a bad one—for once. But we still need something solid. I can't go to the department with a yarn. Especially with my disciplinary status."

"So what do we do?" he asked.

"I believe we are doing it. Waiting for some money to follow."

———

After a brunch of *moules frites* **and a** *frisée au lardon* **salad, which** Margaret proclaimed to be perfect, she paid the bill. Through her binoculars Heat noticed that Martinez made no effort to even pretend to grab it. After the waiter picked up the check folder, conversation dipped into that awkward lull that signals the transition to business. It didn't last long. Alejandro Martinez was not a shy man. "Emma tells me you are ready to support our cause."

"Oh, I am. Very interested. You believe in it strongly?"

"Of course. I am not myself Colombian, but as the great Charles Dickens once wrote, 'Charity begins at home and justice begins next door.'"

Rook turned to Heat. "Prison library."

Martinez continued, "But, as with all things valuable, this comes at a price." He paused. "It requires money." And then he said, "You brought the cash, right?"

Once they were on the sidewalk outside Cassis, Nikki said, "Smart. Your mother has the sense to stand so Martinez has to have his back to us to face her."

"Trust me, thirty years on Broadway, one thing my mother knows how to do is upstage the other person."

Martinez took the Louis Vuitton bag from Margaret, bent to kiss her hand, and the two parted. She walked south, as planned; Martinez hefted the strap over his shoulder and headed uptown. Nikki gave Mrs. Rook a thumbs-up as she passed, and Margaret gave a mild bow, her version of a curtain call.

They had decided on renting a car, figuring it would be the best way to tail his mother's date. They could split up on foot if he took a subway, but if a man like Alejandro Martinez felt vulnerable in windows, public transportation would be unlikely. Up at 72nd Street he got into the backseat of the black town car that was waiting for him, and the tail was on.

It was well before lunch hour, with just enough traffic to hide in but not so much to make it a difficult shadow. Approaching 112th Street, Martinez's driver gave plenty of right blinker for the turn east. Rook lagged before he made his right and kept a few cars between himself and the Lincoln all the way to First Avenue in Spanish Harlem. When the town car made a sharp right at Marin Boulevard and pulled over between a hubcap store and a funeral parlor, Rook drove past so they wouldn't get spotted. Halfway up the block, he pulled over and checked out the side mirror. Nikki unbuckled and knelt on her seat to watch out the rear window, and saw Martinez whisk across the sidewalk and into the doorway of *Justicia a Garda*, carrying the bag of cash.

A parking spot opened ahead of them right in front of a *taqueria*, and Rook eased into the space, which afforded a fine view of the sidewalk from both mirrors. As they waited and watched, Rook's cell vibrated. "Sure you want to answer that tainted phone instead of your new one?" Nikki teased.

"Shut up."

"No, you shut up."

"This is Rook," he said, answering his call. "Yeah? . . ." He mimed for a pen. She gave him one and held out her notebook for him. He jotted down a date. May 31, 2004. "Listen, thanks, I—" And then he held out his phone and stared at it. "Ass. Hung up on me."

"Your pal from Gotham Outsource?" Rook nodded and Heat said, "Huh. And here I thought you two hit it off."

They both did a mirror check. No sign of Martinez, although his driver was still idling, double-parked outside the building. Rook said, "May 31st of '04 was Memorial Day. Mr. Happy told me Alan Barclay quit and left him in the lurch on a legal holiday, when all the TV stations reduce their union crews and he's most busy."

Heat said, "Not insignificantly, the same day they discovered Huddleston's body in that Beemer."

"Here's what I've been trying to figure out." Rook made another mirror check and continued. "The TENS burns on Huddleston. When they zapped Horst Meuller and Father Graf, they were trying to get them to give up the video. Why torture Gene Huddleston, Jr.?"

Heat shrugged. "Maybe he was connected to the video?"

"I'm liking that," said Rook. "This was a Hollywood kid, right? Is it possible he and Alan Barclay made some secret gotcha video to bust the narcs who were on the take?" When she wagged her head side to side signaling doubt, he added, "Not for public service reasons. I mean for extortion. Trying to cut a better deal on product using the video as leverage."

"You don't leverage guys like that."

"My point," agreed Rook. "I think he found that out the hard way, and meanwhile, his videographer slipped away under the radar—with the video as his insurance policy if he was ever found out."

"I'm freaking out here," Heat said. "Either your theories are getting better, or working with you, I'm starting to lose it."

He cupped his hands and breathed like Darth Vader. "Nikki . . . Come to the Dark Side . . ."

She got out her phone and, while scrolling her address book, asked, "How confident are you that you can keep the tail on our friend?"

"Hey, that's my ten grand. Highly."

"And do you think you can resist getting yourself into trouble and call me when he starts to move?"

"Why," he said, "where are you going?"

"A little divide and conquer." She found the number she was looking for and pressed Send. "Hello, Petar? It's Nikki, how are you doing?" While she listened to her old boyfriend celebrate hearing from her, she watched the mirror. At one point Heat flashed a glance at Rook and met the eyes of fear and loathing. Ever since Rook crossed paths with her former college live-in on a recent case, he could barely keep a lid on his jealousy. Even though Nikki ultimately shut down Petar's attempt to rekindle, she could see that the green beast lived on in Rook. "Listen, Pet," she said, "I have a favor to ask. You were freelancing for the gossip mags back around 2004, 2005, right? If I took you to coffee today and picked your brain about Gene Huddleston, Jr., would you have any dirt to tell me?"

When she hung up, Rook said, "That Croatian reprobate doesn't know squat about Gene Huddleston, Jr., he just wants to have sex with you." When she got out of the car, he said, "Hey, you forgot this." He held out the new cell phone he got her and said, "Call me after?"

Heat leaned in the passenger door and took it from him. "Would it make you feel better if I had a chaperone? I could maybe ask Tam Svejda."

Nikki was still grinning when she set out for the subway.

———

Ninety minutes later Rook was still on stakeout in Spanish Harlem when his cell phone buzzed. "Any movement?" she asked.

"Nothing. Even his driver shut off his engine. Say, that was a quick coffee."

"I got what I needed and Petar had to get back to a production meeting." Her old boyfriend was a segment producer for *Later On*, one of the numerous desk-and-couch shows that fought over insomniacs after Dave and Jay and Jimmy.

"That's good," he said.

"Rook, you are so transparent. You don't even know what I learned from him, you're just relieved he went straight back to work."

"OK, fine. Tell me what you got from him."

"Something that connects Huddleston, I think."

"Tell me."

"I need one more piece, and to get that I need to take a little trip out of town."

"Now?" he said.

"If it weren't critical, I wouldn't go. This is why God invented homicide squads, so we could split up duties. You're my squad now, Rook; can you cover that base until I get back later this afternoon? With train time I should be back by four, four-thirty."

He paused. "Sure. But where are you going? And don't say Disney World."

"Ossining," said Heat.

"What's in Ossining, the prison?"

"Not what, Rook. Who."

———

There was a small blue plastic litter bag in the glove compartment, and Rook was calculating how much urine it could hold. Images of him kneeling above it in the driver's seat, trying to deal with the potential overflow made him chuckle, which only made his bladder press all the more. He thought, This must be what it's like for those middle-aged dudes in that commercial, missing the big play at the ball park having to get up and run to the can. He was seriously thinking about a dash into the *taqueria* when he spotted motion in the rearview.

Martinez stepped out of the door to *Justicia a Garda*. He was followed by a man in a cammy jacket with a Che Guevara beard, who was carrying the Vuitton money bag. Rook remembered the face from Murder Board South as Pascual Guzman's.

As before, Rook kept his tail loose, erring on the side of not being made, although their driver still didn't seem concerned about anything but his own ride. After he looped a few turns and headed south on Second Avenue, the blinker came on after crossing East 106th, and Rook eased back to a stop at the corner and waited as the town car stopped mid-block. Guzman got out without the black bag and trotted into a mom-and-pop *farmacia*. While he waited, Rook dialed Heat, got immediate voice mail, and left her an update. By the time he was done with the call, Pascual Guzman was back outside fisting a small white prescription bag. He got into the rear of the Lincoln without looking back and the journey resumed.

They convoyed down Second until the lead car worked a right at Eighty-fifth that eventually fed them into a Central Park transverse much like the one in which Nikki got ambushed days before. Coming out the other side, Rook almost lost them at Columbus when the taxi he was following as a buffer stopped short to pick up a fare. He jacked the wheel and sped around the cab, managing to catch up with the Lincoln at a red light at Amsterdam. The light changed to green, but the car didn't move. Instead Martinez and Guzman got out and entered a bar. Guzman had the black leather case with him. The town car left and Rook pulled into a loading zone around the corner from the pub.

He knew the Brass Harpoon for several reasons. First, it was one of those legendary writer's bars of old Manhattan. Booze-infused geniuses from Hemingway to Cheever to O'Hara to Exley left their condensation rings on the bar and on tabletops at the Harpoon over the decades. It was also a mythical survivor of prohibition, with its secret doors and underground tunnels, long since condemned, where alcohol could be smuggled in and drunks smuggled out blocks away. Rook knew this spot for another reason. He could picture its name in Nikki's neat block capitals on Murder Board South as the preferred hangout for Father Gerry Graf. He ruminated on the priest's missing hour and a half between getting the video from Meuller and showing up drunk at the *Justicia* headquarters and the math wasn't hard to do.

Rook was questioning what his next move should be. His bladder answered. On his way to the door he reasoned that neither Martinez nor Guzman had met him, so his chances of being recognized were slim. Unless he waited too long and walked in with wet khakis, he shouldn't attract any notice. But then, this was the Brass Harpoon, so wet trousers were probably the norm. Safe either way then.

It was just after four and there were only six customers in the place. All six swung their heads to check him out when he stepped in. The two he had followed were not in sight. "What can I do you?" asked the barkeep.

"Jameson," said Rook, eyeing the bottle of Cutty Sark on the top shelf under the small shrine that had been created in honor of Father Graf. His framed laughing photo was adorned in purple bunting, and a rocks tumbler with his name etched in the glass rested on a green velvet pillow underneath. Rook put some money down and said he'd be right back.

There were no feet under the stalls in the gents'. Rook hurried to his business, achieving blessed relief as he read the sampler hung above the urinal: " 'Write drunk; edit sober.' —Ernest Hemingway."

Then he heard the voice he had been listening to at brunch that morning. Alejandro Martinez was laughing and joking with someone. He zipped but didn't flush, instead roamed the restroom to hear which wall the voices were coming through. But they weren't coming through the wall.

They were coming through the floor.

Easing out the men's room door, Rook scoped the bar and saw a Jameson at his place, but nobody seemed interested in his whereabouts. He backed his way into the hall, and past the manager's office, coming to a brick wall. He had read the legends—what writer worth his or her hangover hadn't? He squared himself to that wall, scanning it, his fingers fluttering before him like a safecracker's. Sure enough, one of the bricks had a slight discoloration, a patina of finger grime on its edging.

He thought about calling Nikki, but someone was coming. Maybe to use the restroom, or perhaps the manager. Rook pinched the brick between his thumb and forefinger and pulled. The wall opened; its brickwork was just facing over a door. The air coming out was cool and smelled of must and stale beer. He slipped through the doorway and pushed the wall closed. In the murky light he could barely make out a flight of exposed wooden stairs. He tiptoed down, keeping his feet close to the side to minimize the chance of the steps creaking. At the bottom he paused to listen. Then his eyes were blinded by flashlights. He was grabbed by his jacket front and spun against a wall.

"You lost, buddy?" It was Martinez. And he could smell his mother's Chloé on him.

"Totally." Rook tried to laugh it off. "Were you looking for the men's room, too?"

"What the hell do you think you're doing?" came the voice of someone beside Martinez who Rook figured to be Guzman.

Rook squinted. "Think you could cool the high beams? They're killing me."

"Turn them off," said a third voice. The flashlights lowered from his eyes. He heard a switch thrown and the overheads came on. Rook was still blinking to adjust when the third man came into view like an apparition. Rook recognized him from the news and from his books.

There before him, standing in the middle of a makeshift apartment in the secret basement, among old kegs and cartons, was the exiled Colombian author Faustino Velez Arango.

"You know who I am; I can tell by the way you look at me," said Velez Arango.

"Nope, sorry. I'm just getting my vision back after your friends gave me the eye exam." Then he started backing toward the stairs. "I'm obviously the buzz killer at your little party, so don't let me intrude."

Guzman braced him by the shoulders against an old refrigerator and frisked him. "No weapons," he said.

Alejandro Martinez asked, "Who are you and why did you come here?"

"The truth? OK, at brunch this morning my mother gave you ten thousand dollars of my money in that black case over there and I want it back."

"Alejandro, he followed you?" Pascual Guzman's agitation manifested in scanning the basement as if their intruder had arrived with a platoon of ninjas.

It could have been a grave tactical error, but Rook gauged the author as the most powerful in the group and keyed off him for cues.

He took a chance and said, "Relax. There's nobody else, I came alone."

Guzman took Rook's wallet and opened it to his license. "Jameson A. Rook."

"The A is for Alexander," he said, eyeing Alejandro Martinez, hoping that would lend credibility to his story about following the money. "Nice name." But Rook's attention was drawn to Faustino Velez Arango, whose thick brow had lowered over a glare fixed on him. As he approached, working his jaw, Rook braced for a blow.

The exile stopped inches from him and said, "You are Jameson Rook, the writer?" Rook nodded tentatively. Faustino Velez Arango's hands came up at him, both suddenly clutching his right hand and shaking it with delight. "I have read everything you ever wrote." He turned to his companions and said, "This is one of the best living nonfiction writers in print today." Then back to Rook, he said, "An honor."

"Thanks. Coming from you, that's—well, I especially like the part about 'living' because, I plan to do a bit more of it."

There was an immediate sea change. Velez Arango gestured for Rook to sit in the easy chair, and he pulled up a wicker seat beside him. The other two were not yet aboard but seemed to relax a bit as they stood by. "I must say, Mr. Rook, that it takes courage not only to gain the access to a story as you do from all sides but then to overcome dangerous obstacles to get the hard truth into mainstream media."

"You're talking about my piece on Mick Jagger's birthday, right?"

Velez Arango laughed and said, "I was thinking more of the ones on Chechnya and also the Appalachian coal miners, but yes, Mick in Portofino was brilliant. Excuse me one moment." From the end table the novelist took a vial beside the white bag from the *farmacia* and shook out a pill. While he washed it back with some water, Rook noted the prescription label. Adefovir dipivoxil, the same drug unaccountably found in Father Graf's medicine chest. So now it was accountable. Graf was bearding for Velez Arango's meds. "Another bonus of being a guest of the government in prison," he said as he screwed the cap back on the bottle. "An inmate cut me with a blade and I contracted hepatitis-B."

"It must be hell to live the life of Salman Rushdie."

"I hope to write as well and live so long," he replied.

"How did you end up here?"

Pascual Guzman cleared his throat in an obvious manner. "Faustino, if he's a reporter . . ."

"Mr. Rook is more than that. A journalist. Which means he can be trusted. May I trust you not to reveal my secrets if I tell you about them, how is it said, off the record?"

Rook thought it over. "Sure, not for publication."

"Pascual and his heroic group at *Justicia a Garda* saved me from certain death. I was the target of a contract killer in prison—that was the man with the blade—and more were being recruited. As you know a rescue like mine was logistically complicated and quite expensive. Señor Martinez, who is a man of sincere reform, raised funds here in New York to mount human rights legal efforts in Colombia, as well as to gain safe passage for me here to my glorious exile." He chuckled and gestured to the basement he was living in.

"When did you get here?"

"Three weeks ago. I arrived in New Jersey after departing in a wooden cargo crate on a ship from Buenaventura, you know the place?" Rook nodded and thought of his tip from T-Rex in Colombia about the secret shipment sent to Guzman from there. But the secret shipment wasn't C4, after all—it was Faustino Velez Arango! "As confining and dismal as my basement life appears, it is a paradise compared to what I left. And I have been much helped by openhearted New Yorkers, especially the pastor and parishioners of one of your churches."

He reached into his shirt collar and pulled out a large religious medal on a thin metal chain. "This is St. Christopher, the patron saint of travelers. Just last Monday a wonderful man, a priest who championed our cause, came here just to give this to me." The author became drawn, creases appeared on his forehead. "I understand the poor man has since died, but what a kind gesture, don't you think?"

"Father Graf gave that to you Monday?" Rook knew it had to be soon after the priest met Horst Meuller at his agent's.

"*Sí.* The padre, he said to me, 'It is the perfect medal for hiding.'"

Rook didn't speak. He just repeated those words in his head as he watched the medal swing on its chain. His cell phone buzzed, startling him. It was Heat. "May I take this? It's my girlfriend and I know it's important. . . . Look, I won't say where I am."

Martinez and Guzman shook no, but Velez Arango overruled them. "All right, but use the speakerphone."

Rook answered just before she dropped to voice mail. "Hi, you," he said.

Nikki said, "Took you long enough. Where are you?"

Martinez moved a step closer. "You first," said Rook, and Martinez backed off a hair.

"Back at Grand Central trying to get a cab. Ossining was big, Rook. Huge." He was afraid to say the wrong thing in such a pressure situation, and as he thought, she said, "Rook, are you OK?"

"Yeah, just eager to talk to you. But let's do it in person."

"Truly, this is going to blow you away. Shall I come to you? Are you still following your money?" There was a rustling sound and she groaned. "Hey, what are you—?" Nikki started to scream.

And then her phone went dead.

EIGHTEEN

Rook bolted to his feet and finger stabbed the face of his phone, desperate to launch a callback. Heat's cell rang and rang as he took a step toward the stairs. Guzman blocked him. "Don't," said Rook, "I have to go." By then he was getting voice mail, "Nikki, it's me, call back, OK? Let me know what's happening. Soon as you can."

"Nikki . . ." Pascual Guzman sampled the name aloud and turned to Martinez. "I thought I knew her voice. That was the police detective who called me in."

"Me, too," Martinez said as he shouldered up to Guzman. Rook tried to slide around the pair, but Martinez pressed the palm of his wide, manicured hand flat on his chest and stopped him.

"Guys, I need to go help her, come on."

"And what's this about Ossining?" asked Martinez, who had done time there.

From moments before, when he discovered that his money trail surprisingly led to the exiled human rights novelist, Rook had been watching his narcotics bribe laundering theory come unstitched before his eyes. Combining that with the fact that nobody in that basement had drawn a weapon on him—not even Martinez—he took a chance out of urgency. "OK, here it is," he said, directing himself mainly to Faustino Velez Arango, who watched quietly from his chair. "My girlfriend is a cop who's working a murder case that I don't believe has anything to do with any of you."

"This is still the murder of Father Graf?" asked Guzman.

Rook thought it over and nodded. Guzman pulled at his thick beard and spoke to Velez Arango in Spanish. Rook couldn't understand all the words, but the tone was emotional. The exiled author nodded solemnly a few times. When they were done, Rook pleaded. "A life may be in danger. I can't believe you, of all people, Señor Velez Arango, would hold a writer captive against his will."

The man stood and crossed over to Rook. "I know that Father Graf did more than give me this holy medal. Pascual tells me that whoever killed the *padre* took away a saint on earth, devoted to our cause." Then a trace of a smile eased some of his gravity. "And, of course, I have read your profile of this Nikki Heat." He gestured to the steps. "Go. Do what you can to save her."

Rook started off, but Martinez blocked him again. "Faustino, he will give you up."

The novelist took his measure of the journalist and said, "No, he won't."

Rook dashed to the stairs and then, as an afterthought, said to Velez Arango, "One more favor?"

"*Qué?*"

"I'll need all the help I can get. Any chance I could carry that St. Christopher?"

Velez Arango folded his hand around the medal. "It is valuable to me."

Rook said, "Tell you what. Keep my ten grand, we'll call it even."

Nikki Heat ran up Vanderbilt Avenue, threading herself upstream between the tight flow of pedestrians making their way to Grand Central. She glanced over her shoulder and could see him coming, his black ski mask astonishing the late afternoon business commuters who stopped and turned to look at the man who rushed through them. Those who weren't stunned looked around, either for cops or to see if somebody was making a movie.

It had happened so quickly. Eager for a cab, Nikki had deployed her secret weapon in that neighborhood, which was to skip the organized taxi cue on Forty-second Street, a great place to make friends because the line is slow. Instead, she waited on Vanderbilt near the Yale Club, a favored drop-off spot and, therefore, an equally favored spot to snag a ride on the fly.

As she was on the phone to Rook, waiting out a suburbanite counting coins for the driver's tip, the guy came up behind her. Heat didn't notice where he came from. She only saw motion behind her reflected through the haze of road salt on the cab window. Before she could turn, one hand was stripping her of her cell phone while the other pulled her shoulder. The surprise of it took her off her game a beat, but Heat's combat sense kicked in, and she spun, going with the momentum of the grab and then using her shoulder to ram her assailant backward into the green light pole near the entrance of the club. Down on his ass on the sidewalk, her attacker started his hand toward the inside of his coat, and Nikki ran.

Half a block north now, he was closing in. Heat bolted across Vanderbilt, risking exposure in the open road, so she wove and dodged to present a poor target. Her goal was to turn the corner at 45th and get inside the lobby of the Met Life, where security guards could help. Beyond that, Grand Central was replete with cops and Homeland Security.

But then, the best of all worlds—an NYPD cruiser pulled up to the stop sign at 45th. "Hey!" she called. "Ten-thirteen!" Assist police officer.

The uniform at the wheel had his window open, and when she was ten yards from the car and closing, he turned to face Nikki. "Heat, get in." It was The Discourager. At first she wondered if Harvey still had her back—unlikely. Or if this was just luck—less likely; this wasn't his precinct. She started putting her brakes on as she reached the car and saw the gun on his lap, pointed out the window at her. "Get in," he said once more.

Heat was calculating the odds of outmaneuvering his aim by

bolting to the rear of his blue-and-white when a gloved hand came from behind her and clamped a rag over her mouth and nose.

Nikki tasted sweetness and then blacked out.

———

Raley came back on the line and told Rook that he checked, and sure enough, there had already been several 911s about a female being chased by a man in a ski mask outside Grand Central Terminal. Ochoa was getting it out on the air that the female was Nikki Heat. Raley expected the surrounding streets would be swarmed by units by the time Rook got there.

Translation: There wasn't much for Rook to accomplish there, but since it was the last place he had heard from her, he continued down Broadway. Waiting for the light at Columbus Circle, his heart raced as Rook drew the parallel to her pursuer in the ski mask and the crew that had tuned up Horst Meuller in his apartment. He relived Nikki's interrupted phone call: her excitement at what she had discovered upstate, then the suddenness of the assault, her cell probably taken or smashed.

Rook opened the Recents screen on his phone. Out of habit or spite, Nikki had used her old phone to call him. Which meant that, possibly, she still had the spy store phone he gave her to call for help. Rook wondered if she had it and, if so, whether she had it turned on. He got out his own new phone and began to figure out how the hell to enable the GPS.

———

Her temples were throbbing when she came out of it. Nikki was en-gulfed by a fog thick enough to make her feel underwater. Her head seemed too heavy for her neck, and she couldn't move her arms or legs. "Coming to," said the voice that seemed to drift in from another dimension. Heat tried to open her eyes, and the light, coming from unforgiving white-blue fluorescents in overhead tubes, pierced her so harshly that she closed them right away.

What had she seen in that little glimpse? She was somewhere industrial. A definite workshop or warehouse. Unfinished walls with exposed studs and metal storage racks full of boxes, and . . . tools and parts of some kind. Another look, that would tell her more, but not if she had to stare into those lamps again. She tried to turn over but couldn't and so lolled her head and peeked once more. Harvey, still in his uniform, leaned with his arms folded against a workbench, watching her. He was wearing blue plastic gloves. That disconcerting view pumped enough adrenaline to lift some of the haze. She rested her lids, chastising herself for not seeing the possibility before that The Discourager hadn't been tailing her for protection but to keep tabs on her. Harvey had been hiding in plain sight. Nikki remembered bringing him the pizzelles and felt an ache in her gut.

Someone else was moving around the room. With great effort, she rolled her eyes and recognized the jacket of the guy who had grabbed for her on Vanderbilt. He was wearing blue gloves, too, but not his ski mask anymore, which was even more distressing because it meant he was no longer concerned about Nikki's ability to ID him later. The other man turned and walked up to her and leaned his face into hers. Dutch Van Meter said, "Hey, Heat. Rise and shine."

She tried to turn away from him but couldn't, and then realized why. It wasn't from the chloroform hangover. She was lashed down. Both wrists and ankles were handcuffed. Heat struggled to lift her head. They had affixed her to a pair of wooden crossbeams, their own improvised St. Andrew's Cross. Van Meter must have seen the realization dawn on her. "That's right, cover girl. And you're such a hotshot detective, I'll bet you even know what comes next."

A switch clicked and there was a low electronic hum. She spun her head toward him. Dutch was holding up a stainless steel wand the size and shape of a dildo. It had an insulated grip with two corded jacks—one black and the other red—plugged into the handle. "Want to talk irony? These things were developed as a means to relieve pain. See?"

Heat flinched and turned away, bracing for the shock as he touched the TENS to her forearm. At contact, her skin buzzed slightly and the muscle underneath contracted only mildly. "Guess I don't need to tell you what else this can do." He removed it and switched the unit off. "So. Which way does this go, hard or easy?" Nikki was still turned from him. "OK, let's find out. First, easy. Where is the video?"

She swiveled her head back to face him. "That is easy. Because I don't know."

Van Meter nodded then turned over his shoulder to The Discourager. "They never make it easy, do they, Harv?"

Harvey said, "Detective, my advice? Just tell him, then we can make this quick."

"He's right. Pain or painless, you choose."

"I told you the truth. I don't know."

"Let's find out, shall we?" Dutch sat on a rolling work stool and flicked the switch. The hum, a little louder, returned. "We'll start small and give you a chance." He touched the same spot on her arm, only this time the vibration was greater and the muscle contracted involuntarily, forcing her elbow to bend against her will until he removed the wand. "And that was a low level," he said. "Any new thoughts?"

"Plenty," she said. "I'm thinking back to Central Park. When Harvey conveniently lost me. Who was driving the SUV?"

"Dave Ingram," said The Discourager from across the room. "Guy logs fifteen years on Emergency Services. A sharpshooter, and you waste him with a lucky shot."

Dutch swiveled his chair to Harvey. "He got sloppy."

"He underestimated me," said Heat. She gave Van Meter a look of defiance.

"Well, I haven't. That's why my little black box has so many settings." He twisted the knob and the humming increased.

Heat tried to ignore the awful sound and riveted Dutch with her gaze. "What did Alan Barclay record? What was on his video that was worth killing everybody?"

Detective Van Meter chuckled. "We're not talking, you are." Her eyes darted to the wand which was now inches from her face. "Harvey, do they all talk?"

"They all talk."

"They do," said Dutch. "All of them. The kraut dancer? He gave up the priest. The priest, he gave up Montrose." He paused. "Montrose, we didn't get a chance to stimulate. He got all heroic, so I gave him some Affirmative Action. Right here." He suddenly jabbed the tip of the wand under Nikki's chin. The jolt caused her head to shudder uncontrollably and her jaw muscles to tense, clenching her teeth together so hard they ground against one another. Just as quickly, he pulled it away.

Heat gasped for air and fought nausea. Salt from her own sweat stung her eyes. When she had gulped enough breath, she said, "It was you guys, wasn't it? You guys did something to the Huddleston boy. You were the ones who killed him." Nikki pulled in a deep lungful. God, she felt like she was drowning. "That was on the video, right?"

"Nikki Heat. Always the detective. You're handcuffed, we're torturing you, and you're asking the questions." Dutch waved the wand before her eyes and said, "I only have one question. I know what was on the video. All I want to know is one thing—where is it?"

He knew it was an exercise, but Rook left her one more voice mail. As he pressed End, he figured it was probably more for him and his need for contact, even if it was one-sided. No, he told himself. If he left her voice mail, maybe she would survive to hear it.

At Twelfth Avenue and West 59th Street, he gave up using the car. He pulled the Camry over into the nearest spot he could find, and even though the posted notice warned that it was an active driveway, he had bigger concerns than a ticket and a tow. The problem was that his phone GPS worked fine, but it only gave an approximate location within five hundred feet, roughly a tenth of a mile. He stood at the corner where the Westside Highway ramp elevated and watched the blip on the digital map as he turned in a circle. By his reckoning,

Nikki's phone could be in one of four buildings: the paint warehouse, the sign manufacturer, a nameless pale brick structure that looked like private storage, or across the highway at the City Sanitation dock on the Hudson.

A frozen drizzle started to fall. Rook pulled his collar up against the night. He began his search by walking the perimeters of the three buildings on his side of the street. After that, he'd cross over to the Sanitation pier.

———

"Tell me something," said Heat. Her throat was raspy, and when she ran her tongue along her teeth, she felt a new jagged chip on a molar. "You put three in Steljess to shut him up, didn't you?"

Van Meter adopted a pose of mock innocence. "Nonsense. I did it to save your life, Heat."

"Yuh, right. After you sent him to bomb my apartment. Where'd you get the C4?"

The Discourager started to speak, but Van Meter cut him off. "Shut up, Harvey. Enough."

"Military grade explosive is hard to get, even for cops," she continued. "Who's behind this? Somebody big, right? Is it somebody outside the force? Somebody big who has pull? Somebody down at City Hall? Somebody national?"

Dutch said, "You about done? 'Cause now it's time to light 'em up. Where is the video?" He twisted the red teardrop-shaped knob half a turn clockwise, and a buzz filled Nikki's ears like all the beehives in the world.

Behind him, Harv stood and turned his back, unwilling to watch. From that angle, Heat could see the deep fingernail gouge in his handcuff case, which was empty.

"Last chance," said Dutch. He paused. Then he rolled on his stool down toward her waist and out of her view. Heat felt her blouse being unbuttoned.

And then the lights went out and the buzzing stopped.

"Shit. Harvey, you said there was enough juice here for this thing."

"The fuck I know. Should be, but it's an old building, so shit happens. We need to find the circuit breakers, I guess."

The glow of the city against the clouds filtered through skylights and cast the workroom in a pale lunar radiance. At the door, Van Meter paused and said, "Don't go away." Then he and The Discourager left.

Nikki pulled against the handcuffs. All they did was bite her skin. She was resting, trying to suppress panic, when the door opened again. She lifted her head and saw Detective Feller. He wasn't wearing a ski mask, either.

"Your partner quit and gave up," she said.

Feller put a finger to his lips and whispered, "I screwed with the power to get them out of here." She felt the handcuff opening on one ankle, then the other. When he came up beside her to unlock her wrists, she saw the gun he held at his side. "Can you walk?" he asked.

"I think so," she whispered as she sat upright. "They must have taken my shoes."

"Deal with it," said Feller, who was already on his way to the door. He made a check outside and beckoned her forward. He slipped out ahead of her, and when she stepped out into the drizzle, she recognized immediately where she was. The building she had come out of, about the size and shape of a railroad freight car, was a work shed at the far end of the City Sanitation pier on the Hudson River. It was after hours, and all the parking spaces were empty except for Harvey's blue-and-white and Van Meter's taxi. Feller hand-signaled toward the other end of the pier and mimed a steering wheel.

They moved as quickly as they dared without making noise. Nikki was more silent crossing the icy concrete in her bare feet. After fifty yards they stopped suddenly. Just ahead of them voices were coming from one of the shacks that lined the wharf. "Try it again anyway." It was Van Meter barking at Harvey, his voice full of irritation. The door started to open.

Feller tugged her arm and they ran across the pier and ducked behind a Dumpster. He put his face to her ear and whispered, "That's the electrical closet. They'll never fix it." He craned to survey the distance to his car at the other end of the wharf. "I radioed for backup so we're probably better off sitting tight here till they show." They both turned to scope Twelfth Avenue, hoping to see red and white lights. None yet.

She whispered, "Sorry I accused you of being with them. I just figured you and Van Meter were attached at the hip."

"Were. But somehow he got on IA's radar and they asked me to mole. Shitty thing to do to a partner, I know, but . . ." He shrugged.

"No complaints here," she whispered. "How did you find me?"

"I was down at court when I heard the call go out about you at Grand Central. I tried to raise Dutch but got no reply. I wasn't sure, but thought—what the hell—and tracked the transponder from our cab here."

Nikki smiled. "What the hell."

Back up the pier there was a loud crack as the door to the work shack flew open against the wall. Van Meter must have slipped up there, and he was calling out, "Harv! She's loose!"

Feller cursed. The Discourager emerged from the electrical room and called back, "How?"

"Who cares, start looking. Now!" Across the parking lot a beam from Harvey's flashlight swept the buildings. Dutch called out again, "Check out that Dumpster."

Feller pressed his car keys in Nikki's palm. "Run." Without waiting, he bolted out from behind the bin and charged at Harvey with his gun up. As Heat ran for it, she heard two shots. She made a quick check over her shoulder. Feller was down. Harvey's flashlight scanned him. The beam came up, finding her. A shot followed and the slush exploded off the pavement a yard ahead of her.

And then the engine of the taxi roared to life. Van Meter fishtailed out of his spot, chasing Nikki down the pier.

There was no way she could outrun that cab. Heat shot desperate glances to both sides, searching in vain for a space between buildings she could slip through and dive into the river.

The police-modified engine rumbled, drawing ever closer, the tires swishing, kicking up the icy slop that had turned her feet numb.

Instead of running a zigzag, Nikki took a bold gamble and ran in a straight line, letting Van Meter gain speed, letting him forget the steering conditions. She sprinted, her lungs searing, toward the convoy of garbage trucks parked in a row outside the off-loading hangar. She held her course, waiting, waiting, as the high beams drew closer, bathing her back in hot light. When she could see her own shadow cast on the side of the first sanitation truck, Heat dove hard right, her body skimming prone across the water and ice accumulated on the concrete like it was a Slip 'n Slide.

Behind her, Dutch Van Meter, who had taken her bait, mashed his brake pedal and jerked his wheel, but the mix of precip that was icing that pier sent him hydroplaning. Traction gone, his cab floated into a sideways skid, slamming him broadside at top speed against the garbage truck. Nikki got up off the deck and saw him slumped motionless over the airbag on his steering wheel.

A gunshot cracked and hit the fender of the taxi beside her. Heat wanted Dutch's Smith & Wesson, but The Discourager was bearing down and his next shot might not miss. Nikki hurried into the open hangar door of the garbage receiving station and took cover behind the six-foot-tall bales stacked there for barging.

When she heard Harvey's feet slapping to a stop at the door, she crouched down and peered out between rows of compacted trash. He had turned off his six-cell so he wouldn't give himself away, but there was enough ambient light from the West Side that she could see him wince as he rubbed a tender spot on his chest. When he took his hand away, Nikki made out the puncture in his jacket just below his shield, where his Kevlar had stopped Feller's bullet.

Just as Heat renewed her plan to escape with a dive into the river, The Discourager worked his way around to her left flank, wittingly or unwittingly blocking her route to the open side of the hangar where they loaded bales onto barges bound for landfills. So Nikki crept to her right in the crevice between the stacks and made her way to the end of the row, where there was a small workbench.

Tools, she thought.

She studied the open distance to the workbench. It was risky exposure but better than waiting to become target practice. Heat was about to take a tentative step out of her hiding place when she heard his breathing. Immediately, she crouched low in the opening between the bales and made herself still.

Harvey was being quiet, too. Where the hell was he?

On a shelf above the workbench, among the girlie calendars and chipped coffee mugs, there sat some kind of trophy cup from the city or maybe the union. Nikki fixed her gaze on it and waited. Sure enough, after a few seconds, in the brass-plated reflection, she saw slow movement. The dark blue uniform was approaching the gap in which she was hunkered.

Detective Feller's car keys were still in her hand. Being careful not to jangle, Heat made a fist around them so that the two keys protruded from her knuckles. Not exactly Wolverine, but it would have to do.

Patience again, always patience. The cop tiptoed sideways to the opening, searching for her in the gap. But his mistake was to look eye-level. Heat was crouched low, and when he was centered in front of her she sprang up at him, driving the keys into his left cheek while she grabbed for his gun with her right hand. He cried out in shock and pain. She jerked his wrist upward and the gun fired. The bullet hit harmlessly, eaten by the garbage bale behind her.

Heat thrashed his face again with the keys and tried to wrest the weapon away. His grip was strong, and when, on her third try, she did manage to wrest the gun free, it flew and clattered on the floor.

Nikki bent to grab it, but he tackled her from behind. She twisted and used his momentum against him, ramming him back-first into the workbench. She elbowed him three times at the sore spot under his badge. He wailed with each blow, until he palmed the side of her head and shoved her into the wall, where her shoulder crashed, breaking glass. Heat looked up inside the shattered case and hauled out the fire ax.

Harvey was coming up from his stoop, the gun back in his hand. Heat quickly reared to swing. Mindful that he was wearing body armor, she went for his gun arm. And severed it at the elbow.

He writhed on the floor moaning and bleeding out. Spent, Heat dropped the ax and scanned the surrounding area for something to use as a tourniquet. Then she heard sudden movement beside her. Nikki spun, bringing her hands up.

Someone was diving at her, she braced herself for a blow, but in the same flash that she heard the gunshot, she recognized that the man pushing her aside was Rook. They both landed on the ground beside Harvey. Heat clapped a hand on his loose service weapon, came up with it, and put two rounds in Dutch Van Meter's forehead as he stood in the doorway holding his smoking S&W.

Nikki set the gun down and hugged Rook, who was still in her arms. "Oh, man, I don't know how you found me, Rook, but your timing did not suck."

But Rook didn't answer.

"Rook?" Nikki's heart stopped and her skin flushed with alarm. She shook him, but he didn't respond. When she rolled him over in her lap and touched his cheek, she smeared it with blood.

That's when she realized it was Rook's blood on her fingers.

Frantic, she ripped open his shirt, looking for the wound, and found it right away, a .9mm entry gushing red below his rib cage.

Sirens drew closer.

Nikki fought tears; coming around to kneel over Rook, she compressed the wound with one hand and stroked his face with the other. "Hang on, Rook, you hear me? Help's coming, you hang on. Please?"

The sirens stopped right outside and flashing lights filled the hangar. "In here!" shouted Nikki. "Hurry, I'm losing him." Verbalizing the thought crushed Heat, and she barked out an involuntary sob as his face lost more color.

The EMTs rushed in and took over. Nikki retreated in a daze and wept, her bloody hand covering her mouth. She watched, trembling, as they cut Rook's shirt off and went to work on him. That's when Heat saw something she had never seen on Rook before.

The big St. Christopher medal around his neck.

NINETEEN

"They're ready for you now." Nikki had been staring at nothing because that's what she needed, a glazed, checked-out, middle-distance fix on the posters and memos on the bulletin board across from her seat in the hallway at One Police Plaza. The administrative assistant came around to step into her line of sight, saw her swollen eyes, and gave her a tender smile. Sympathy. Please, no more sympathy. Nikki had had her fill of it in the last twelve sleepless hours and didn't know which was worse, the pitying faces or the consoling words.

But she stood and returned the woman's well-intended smile anyway. Then Nikki sealed the firewall once more. If she thought about Rook now, she couldn't hold her emotions. "Ready," she said. The aide opened the door for her. Heat drew a long breath and then stepped through it.

Rooms didn't come much more stony or intimidating than the tenth-floor conference room at 1PP that morning. The last time Nikki had been in there it had been just she and Zach Hamner—with the added attraction of the duo from Internal Affairs to confiscate her shield and piece. That had been frosty enough. Now she was being scrutinized by a full conference table of deputy commissioners, chiefs, and administrators, who halted their conversations to give her The Big Appraisal as she entered.

Zach had been waiting for her inside the door and led her to the empty chair at the head of the conference table. On her way along the row of weathered faces belonging to the NYPD's top brass, her eye caught a friendly wink from Phyllis Yarborough. Heat nodded her acknowledgment to the deputy commissioner and took the seat.

Todd Atkins, the deputy commissioner for legal matters, faced Heat from the opposite end. As soon as The Hammer perched on the folding chair behind his boss, Atkins began quietly, saying, "Thank you for coming in. I know this must be an awful time for you, and you have all our best thoughts."

Nikki fought away another wave of crushing sorrow and managed to say in her most professional voice, "Thank you, sir."

"We wanted you in to address this matter immediately," continued the Department's lawyer. "The commissioner would be here himself, but he is in a committee meeting on Capitol Hill about now and we felt it was important to remedy the miscalculation made by this body vis-à-vis your status." While he continued on, speaking in his coded language for their screwup, Nikki felt herself tumble into the kaleidoscopic tunnel that had swallowed her at Belvedere Castle in the aftermath of her attack. She held eye contact with Atkins, but all the while random images turntabled around him. Rook draped on her after the gunshot . . . Montrose cursing at his performance data printouts . . . Rook's ashen face . . . Van Meter pulse-checking Steljess in the auto salvage yard . . . Rook's blood in the sink when she finally washed her hands . . . the Murder Board after Captain Irons carelessly erased it, leaving red smears from her marker . . .

A wrap-up tone in Atkins's voice pulled her back to the moment. "It was a rush to judgment," he said, "and for that, we sincerely apologize."

"Accepted, sir." And then she added, "And appreciated." The Mount Rushmore of faces around the table relaxed. Some even smiled at her.

"It's our decision to reinstate you immediately to active status, Detective Heat," continued Atkins. "I should also say it's no secret that you had one major champion through this ordeal."

"No secret because she won't let us forget it," blurted the Personnel chief, with a laugh that lightened the mood around the room.

"And so," Atkins said, "I'm going to give the floor to the Deputy Commissioner of Technological Development. Phyllis?"

Midway up the mahogany, a beaming Phyllis Yarborough leaned forward, tilting her head for a better view of Nikki. "Detective Heat . . . Nice to be able to say that again, isn't it? Well, don't get used to it. I have been given the privilege and personal honor to inform you that you are not only reinstated as a detective, but today you will be given your gold bar and sworn in as a lieutenant in the NYPD." Nikki's heart galloped in her chest. Phyllis waited for the applause to settle. "Congratulations. And may I add that we have no doubt that this is just one rung on the ladder of your ascent within this department."

The applause grew louder and included a number of "hear, hear"s. When it died down, heads swiveled to Nikki, and it was clearly her moment.

Heat rose.

"I want to repeat what I told the Orals Board a few days ago. Police work—police work on the NYPD—is more than a job to me, it's my life's work. To whatever degree I am a professional, it is because I take it so personally. Which is why I wholeheartedly accept reinstatement and thank you for that." There was brief clapping, which she interrupted by holding her hands out. When they were quiet again, she said, "It is the same reason that I respectfully decline the promotion to lieutenant."

Astonishment hardly described the reactions before her. Sober, life-worn, career cops with poker faces were visibly stunned. Not the least of which was Phyllis Yarborough, who shook her head no to Nikki and then searched the others for some sort of understanding.

"So that I don't seem ungrateful—because I truly am thankful—I can help you understand why I made this decision by going back to what I said a moment ago. This is my life's work. I joined the NYPD to help victims of crime. And over time, I have grown to love it even more because of the proud association and friendship I have working with the finest cops in the world. But the process of gaining this promotion, as well as some insights I've gained over recent weeks, has made me realize that stepping up the ladder is a step away from the street. A step away from why I am a New York cop. Administrators do important work, but my heart is not in CompStat data, or scheduling, and all that. It's in doing what I'm born to do. Solve crimes. Out there. I thank you for your confidence and for hearing me out."

Nikki surveyed the table one by one and saw in most of their faces cops who knew all too well what she meant. They might not say it, but they admired the courage of her choice. And, to be honest, she also saw one or two who could not mask their bitter annoyance. "So," she asked, "am I really a cop again?"

Deputy Commissioner Atkins said, "I think I can speak for the group when I say, this isn't how we expected this to transpire, but yes, Detective Heat, yes, you are." He gestured to Zach Hamner, and the political cockroach who had so callously stripped her of her job and protection got up and strode to her end of the table to present Heat with her own shield and weapon, grinning as if they were gifts from him.

Nikki reached into her coat, pulled out her empty holster, and held it up for them to see. "I was hoping." That drew some chuckles. After she clipped her badge and her Sig Sauer to the old familiar places on her waist and adjusted them, Detective Heat said, "And now that I am officially a sworn officer, I would like to make an arrest."

TWENTY

A
t first they acted like Heat was joking. Maybe this was a follow-up to the quip about her empty holster. But one by one they absorbed the seriousness of her expression, and Nikki found herself with the rapt attention of the conference room of police brass she stood before.

"The murder of Father Graf was a case with numerous complications. I won't go into them all, you can read them in my report, but the essential obstacle we faced was an uncommon amount of resistance from within the Department." Zach Hamner leaned forward, trying to whisper something to his boss, but Atkins shooed him away. The Hammer sat back with a deep frown directed at Nikki, which she returned until he melted off and stared at the papers in his lap.

"I developed leads that eventually brought me to a solid theory that the priest's killing was tied to a narcotics bribery ring in the Forty-first.

"There's great credence for this idea. You all know the names of the five who not only tried to kill me in Central Park as I dug deeper, but are also implicated in the Graf killing, the Montrose murder . . . ," she paused to let the M-word sink in, then continued, ". . . as well as the sniper attack of Horst Meuller." Heat counted each on her fingers, "Sergio Torres, Tucker Steljess, Karl 'Dutch' Van Meter, Harvey Ballance, and Dave Ingram. At one time, all served in the Four-one. The key to my theory about Narco bribes to that group was the stash of DEA money in the pastor's attic.

"I was wrong." She paused. "The DEA cash turned out to be for a human rights group the priest was involved in—unrelated to the case. So then what was the connection to these bad cops? If it wasn't drugs, what was it? Well, it was another kind of conspiracy, and one that, sadly, reaches to the highest floors of this building."

The heat came on and the hissing of the vent filled her pause.

"Let's go back to Captain Montrose," she said. "In 2004, he worked a famous homicide, the son of the movie star, Gene Huddleston. When the case cleared as a sour drug deal, Montrose never bought it and recently started to dig in again on his own." Nikki turned to Hamner. "You know all about that, right, Zach? Did your pals in IA tell you he was sniffing around Huddleston when they checked him out?"

"Montrose lit up IA's radar by acting out of pattern. Their probe was legitimate due diligence." Hamner said it as if it was so SOP that it bored him.

"Clearly that's not the only radar my skipper got on." Heat turned back to the group. "I couldn't access the official Huddleston case files, but I did have an entertainment insider," she said, referring to Petar. "My source is highly credible and shared a number of secret rumors about this young man. The most strikingly relevant was that two years before his murder, Gene Huddleston, Jr., was in Bermuda on Spring Break and that he was one of the boys that raped your daughter, Phyllis."

Yarborough gasped and her hand flew up to cover her mouth. Tears welled in her eyes.

"Detective Heat," said Atkins, "this is feeling way out of line."

"I'm sorry, sir, but there's no easy way to go about this."

"But it's gossip," said the Personnel chief. He handed Phyllis a tissue.

"Which I have independently verified," Heat replied.

Deputy Commissioner Atkins said, "Go on."

"Jeremy Drew, who confessed to the assault and murder of Amy Yarborough, was extradited in 2002 and began a life sentence in Sing Sing, where I visited him yesterday. In our meeting Drew confirmed for me what I had heard from my source. That the Huddleston family had paid several million to his parents, who were on disability. All in exchange for his silence about the participation along with him by Gene Huddleston, Jr., in the gang rape on the beach that night."

"Why would he tell you?" asked the deputy commissioner of legal matters.

"His parents have passed away and he has had a religious conversion. This was his first opportunity to clear his conscience. By the way, I checked with Customs, and Huddleston's passport shows he was in Bermuda then and left the island on the first flight out the morning after the discovery of Amy's body in Dockyard.

"You know something, Phyllis? Even when I found out Jeremy Drew wasn't alone that night with your daughter, there was a part of me that didn't want to believe you were behind all this. But then I couldn't get past the cruise Montrose booked. A guy in mourning taking a singles cruise? And in the middle of a career crisis while he's also conducting a secret investigation? I called back the travel agent. The cruise was to Bermuda."

As a roomful of the best police minds in New York were doing the motive math, Phyllis Yarborough jarred them by speaking. "Nikki . . ." She shook her head mildly in disappointment. Her voice was hoarse and papery. "I can't believe this of you, overreaching like this. And so hurtful. Are you trying to make me twice a victim with some tabloid conspiracy theory about me?"

"I am sorry for the loss of your daughter, you know that. But this is not a theory anymore. The leather fragment from under Graf's fingernail matches Harvey Ballance's cuff case, and the button fragment from the crime scene is from one of his shirts. Harvey is in the hospital and he is talking. About you. And all the money you offered five cops in 2004 to take care of Huddleston."

"Detective, come on," said Yarborough, trying to reclaim her composure and distance, positioning herself as judge rather than the accused, "let's stop all this, please? You know criminals talk all sorts of bull to cut deals. This is hearsay and conjecture. Whatever happened to the Nikki Heat who deals in proof?"

"Proof," said Heat. She crossed to the door and rapped lightly. Lovell and DeLongpre entered. While the Internal Affairs detectives rounded the table toward the flat-screen on the side wall, Nikki swallowed thickly, revisiting her grim memory of the paramedics cutting Rook's shirt off. Spotting the holy medal she had never seen before. And after, listening to his final, pleading voice mail urging her to call him back and saying that he had the video on him. Nikki saved that call, his last words before he was shot. Then she examined the St. Christopher, which was not just a medal but a locket. And hidden inside—a black microSD video chip about the size of a pinkie nail.

Lovell stood, having finished his DVD setup, and waited.

"Let me set the stage," resumed Heat. "Memorial Day weekend, 2004, Alan Barclay, a news video shooter, followed Gene Huddleston, Jr., from a nightclub in the Meat Packing District. Huddleston was just out of rehab—again—and Barclay trailed him to the Bronx, hoping to score some salable footage of the bad boy making a drug purchase. Both he and Huddleston got more than they bargained for. Watch." Lovell started the DVD as DeLongpre dimmed the lights.

The video began with the camera in motion. Jerky footage of a dashboard and then a blur as the videographer got out of his car—still rolling video—and crossed a dark street. This was the raw stuff they edited out of *Cops*.

A block later, the lens moved to a hiding place behind a low wall. The shaky picture settled as the shooter rested his camera on the top cinder block, using it as a brace. The lens zoomed in and focused on a car parked about thirty yards away in front of a warehouse. Under the orange sodium lamps it was easy to make out a man Heat recognized as Sergio Torres approaching the M5. Huddleston got out and they chatted. Their voices were too low to understand but their conversation was easy; Huddleston seemed familiar with Torres. Then everything changed.

Headlights approached from both ends of the block as two cars with police lights flashing roared in and screeched to a halt, sandwiching the BMW. One was a blue-and-white, the other a plain-wrap

Crown Victoria. Huddleston shouted for Torres to run, but he didn't. Instead, he grabbed the kid by his shirt and slammed him facedown over the hood of his M5, cuffing him while The Discourager approached from his cruiser and Van Meter and Steljess joined the party from the undercover vehicle.

Nobody seemed in a hurry. It had the menacing feel of something that had been worked out. Huddleston was the only one agitated, whining, "Aw, come on, don't bust me, my dad'll kill me," and "Do you have any idea who my dad is?"

Steljess could be heard now, "Shut the fuck up," right before he kicked him in the ass as he bent over the car. Huddleston shouted curses that were ignored as they hauled him upright by the cuffs and started to lead him toward the warehouse.

The bravado of privilege turned on a dime to fear. Huddleston freaked. "Hey, where are you—? Just take me to jail then . . . What are you doing?" He tried to make a break. "Hey?!" But the four cops held him in check easily.

The video shook as the camera adjusted its angle to track the group. When it settled again, they were nearing the warehouse under the graffiti-tagged sign for the uniform rental company that once operated there. The door opened from the inside and a man held it wide for them. Nikki didn't recognize him but figured he completed the set of five—Ingram, the SUV driver she killed in the Transverse.

When Ingram pulled the warehouse door shut, Barclay kept rolling, but there was a lull. Heat used the interval to assess the room. Eyes were transfixed. Nobody made a sound. Phyllis Yarborough was the only one not staring. Her head was bowed to her lap.

Huddleston's screams burst into the night, jarring everyone in the conference room. Bodies shifted, leaning in toward the flat-screen. In its own way, this point of view of a desolate industrial zone in the middle of the night, whose solitude was cut by shrieks and cries, seemed more chilling than watching his actual torture. But everyone there had heard about the TENS. And they all knew what was happening to the kid in there. And as bad as it sounded to them, it had to have been hell on earth inside. The uncomfortable minutes they endured as the electrocution continued must have seemed eternal to the howling victim.

In the eerie quiet when it was done, a dog barked in the distance. The door opened, and a sobbing Huddleston, limp and spent, was carried out. They bore him upright by the armpits with his toes dragging the ground behind him. Van Meter broke off from the pack and held a walkie-talkie up to his mouth. His words didn't pick up, but there was a squelch when he was done. Seconds later another metallic Crown Victoria pulled up.

And Phyllis Yarborough got out.

They had him inside his car by then, Torres even using his gloved hands to buckle the seat belt. He stepped aside to let her stand facing Huddleston, who was beseeching her, "Please, help me, please . . ."

"Do you know who I am?" she said.

He peered at her and became suddenly animated. "Oh, fuck me, oh no . . ."

"Good, you do." He cried and muttered drooling pleas, and when his words degenerated into quiet sobs, she said, "Take this moment to hell, you filthy son of a bitch."

She stepped away, and Sergio Torres slammed the car door. They both joined the others on the other side of the car. "Kill him," said Phyllis Yarborough.

Steljess opened the passenger door and leaned inside. Soon *American Idiot* came blasting hot from the car speakers. Under the blare of Green Day, the interior was illuminated by a muzzle flash and the glass blew out of the driver's side window.

The video jostled as the camera moved from its perch on the wall. The next shot was a blur of motion as Barclay slowly backed away from his hideout. His foot must have knocked over a bottle. After the glass *tink* and roll came a shout from the cops. "Somebody's there!"

Barclay didn't hesitate but ran full-bore up the street, the video whooshing and shaking like earthquake footage as he sprinted. In the distance came their voices, blending together: "Street . . ." "Camera!" and "Stop!"

But Alan Barclay didn't stop. The last of his video was the camera flying onto his passenger seat and rolling onto the floor as rubber squealed and the videographer escaped. He got away that night carrying the deadly secret he would hide until years later when Captain Montrose canvassed the old crime scene and an elderly night watchman at a bakery told him about the man he'd seen running away with the camera.

———

The lights came up and Yarborough was glaring at Heat.

"There's your proof, Deputy Commissioner. Proof that you waited two years for the dust to settle before you got your revenge. Proof that you paid off those cops and then conspired all these years to keep a lid on it. And I'm going to make an educated guess that, along the way, you utilized your job as tech czar to monitor for any signs of discovery. Like Montrose reopening the old case; like me pulling Huddleston's computer file; like hacking Jameson Rook's e-mail and sending it to that reporter to get me suspended when I was getting too close. . . . After your boys weren't up to the job of killing me." Heat shrugged. "That part I don't have to prove.

"You know, the first time I met you, I remember we talked about revenge and justice. And do you recall telling me that all your accounts were settled? I think we just got confirmation."

"Damn you for this." To Phyllis Yarborough it was as if she and Nikki were the only two in the room. Her indignation had been stripped away, leaving only the raw hurt and a wound, a decade old and still open. Her face was composed, but tears fell down both cheeks. "You, of all people, should know how it feels to be a victim, Nikki."

Heat felt her own ache, sadly present every day. "I do, Phyllis," she said softly. "That's why I'm sending you to jail."

———

A searing blue sky freshened Manhattan as a brilliant rising sun warmed the city for the first time in a week. It reflected on row upon row of badges facing the cathedral on Fifth Avenue, making the thousands of chests that wore them sparkle like a single vast treasure of radiant diamonds. New York's Finest—plus cops from Port Authority and New York State—stood shoulder to shoulder, filling both sidewalk and street, their numbers obscuring pavement, windows, and walls.

When Detective Nikki Heat emerged at the top of the steps, bearing the front corner of the casket, there was nothing to see that morning outside St. Patrick's but an ocean of dress blue and white gloves in salute. A lone bagpipe played the opening notes of the sober, joyful "Amazing Grace" and was soon joined by the full pipes and muffled drums of the NYPD's Emerald Society. The only thing missing that morning was Rook. As Heat beheld the spectacle, she could only imagine how Jameson Rook would have captured it. And made it live beyond the day.

She and the other pallbearers, including Detectives Raley and Ochoa, and Eddie Hawthorne, descended slowly, carrying the fallen commander under the traditional flag of green and white stripes.

Once his body was in the hearse, Heat, Raley, Ochoa, and Hawthorne moved across the avenue to fall in with the grim block of detectives in their tan overcoats. Nikki chose the spot beside Detective Feller, who had stubbornly abandoned his wheelchair for the moment to stand out of respect.

The mayor, the commissioner, and all the other top brass descended from the cathedral to the curb and stood, either saluting or with hands over hearts, before the remains of Captain Charles Montrose at the Full Honors funeral Nikki had attained.

At the conclusion of "Amazing Grace," the elite motorcycle brigade formed up for escort at the front of the car while the band made two columns behind the vehicle. The muffled drums began their somber cadence, the motorcycles rolled slowly, and the hearse followed.

Then Nikki heard them coming. The low drone sounded just like the pipes at first, but the sound grew, expanding until the thundering vibration shook the concrete canyons of Midtown. Discipline wavered as all eyes ascended to see four NYPD helicopters zoom up Fifth Avenue. The instant they were above the cathedral, one of the choppers pulled up and broke away. The other three continued on in Missing Man Formation.

As soon as they were gone, she returned her attention to the passing hearse, saluting her captain, mentor, and friend. As it moved by the dignitaries, the police commissioner caught Heat's eye and gave her an approving nod. At least that's what it looked like through the haze of her tears.

———

The first thing Nikki did when she entered Rook's room in ICU was to check the screen for activity. Heartened to see regular green spikes, she stood over him and took his hand. She squeezed lightly and waited, hoping, but her only feedback was his warmth, which was something, anyway. Leaning carefully over his breathing tubes, she kissed his forehead, which felt dry to her lips. His eyes were closed, but when the lids fluttered, she took his fingers in hers again. Nothing. One of them must have been dreaming.

Exhausted from the day, she pulled the plastic guest chair bedside and sat, resting her eyes. She awoke with a start an hour later when her cell phone vibrated. It was a text from Ochoa, who had just gotten confirmation from Ballistics that the bullet he had recovered from the water tower checked out as Montrose's, matching the reloads from the belt mag. She had just texted back to congratulate him when the nurse came in to hang a fresh bag on the IV tree. The nurse stepped out, only to return a moment later. She placed a container of orange juice and a chewy granola bar on the tray for Nikki and left again.

Heat sat there for another hour, simply watching the rise and fall of Rook's chest, glad for that miracle and knowing that she would so never hear the end of this.

If he pulled through.

During the eleven o'clock news she ate her snack, and when it ended, she muted the TV. With the report that steam service had been fully restored to all of Manhattan by now, she could finally go back to her apartment. Nikki thought of her own bed . . . of the bubble bath that awaited her. She got up and picked up her coat, but didn't put it on. Instead, she pulled out the paperback from the side pocket and sat back down.

"Are you ready for some cultural stimulation, Mr. Rook?" Heat glanced up at him and then back to the cover of the novel. " '*Castle of Her Endless Longing*, by Victoria St. Clair.' Like the title. . . ." She turned to the first chapter and began to read aloud, " 'Lady Kate Sackett stared forlornly out of the carriage as it bounced along the muddy, rutted byway outside her ancestral village in the northland. She was contemplating the brooding form of the castle built into the cliffs when a young man on horseback cantered up to her window and kept pace. He was handsome in a roguish way, the sort of rascal who would charm a more naïve woman for his own sport and be gone. "Pleasant, morning, m' lady," he said. "These are dangerous woods just ahead. Could I offer to ride along?" ' "

Heat reached out and gently laced her fingers between Rook's, watched his breathing once more, and then returned to the book. Happy to read to him endlessly.

ACKNOWLEDGMENTS

A chef never makes a meal alone. I learned this the hard way as a latchkey kid, bored and hungry with a craving for cherries flambé. Who knew cognac could take off like that? Or that my mother wouldn't appreciate the irony of coming home from her triumphant Broadway performance in *Burn This* to charred walls and a disapproving hook-and-ladder crew?

Much like cuisine, you need help making a book (although there's less risk of fire—unless you count the unfortunate book burning of one of my early Derrick Storm novels). So these pages are reserved for me to tip my big, tall, chef's toque to the many cooks who actually improved the broth.

As ever, I am in the debt of the top professionals at the 12th Precinct who tolerate me still. Detective Kate Beckett has shown me the ropes of homicide investigation, not to mention how to make sense of songs. Her colleagues, Javier Esposito and Kevin Ryan, have welcomed me like the brothers I never had. And the late Captain Roy Montgomery, to whom this book is dedicated, was a great mentor to all who worked under him and an even greater man to all who knew him.

Dr. Lanie Parish at the Office of Chief Medical Examiner has given me almost as many insights as she has eye rolls. I may be a pain in the ass sometimes, but I do like to think I break up a day when you work in a refrigerated environment.

While my thoughts are on 30th Street, let me give special thanks to Ellen Borakove, the Director of Public Affairs for the Office of Chief Medical Examiner in Manhattan, who gave generously of her time while I researched this book. She is a shining example of the compassion, dignity, and respect evident throughout the staff there. I am grateful to Ellen for all she taught me on my guided tour of the facility—especially how to breathe.

The folks in the Clinton Building at Raleigh remain my heroes. You amaze, surprise, and keep it fresh always. And Terri Edda Miller, ever by my side, thank you for choosing the title. So much better than *Heat, Heat, Heat.*

The lovely Jennifer Allen continues to teach me the secret o' life. May it be a long lesson.

To Nathan, Stana, Seamus, Jon, Ruben, Molly, Susan, and Tamala— you remain the embodiment of dreams that come true relentlessly and tirelessly. You always bring the heat.

I have gone too long without mentioning my darling Alexis, whose every glowing, beautiful, pure, and wise moment causes me to soar with pride and to recheck the birth certificate. Yes, thankfully, she is my daughter. And let me also celebrate my mother, Martha Rodgers, who taught me that a story can be performance, that life can be art, and that the cognac goes in the pan when it's off the burner.

Thanks to Black Pawn Publishing and, especially, to Gina Cowell for giving me the space to follow my bliss. Gretchen Young, my editor, continues to be a staunch ally and cherished colleague. A shout out to her, Elizabeth Sabo Morick, and to everyone at Hyperion for believing. Melissa Harling-Walendy and her team at ABC continue to make this a dream association.

My agent, Sloan Harris at ICM, has been in my corner since our first handshake years ago. He deserves my deepest gratitude for the unwavering support and faith he has shown.

There is an empty chair at my weekly poker game. Connelly, Lehane, and I decided to keep dealing you in, Mr. Cannell, and somehow you keep winning. As it was in life, my friend and mentor. You had me at Rockford.

Andrew Marlowe is a gift. He inspires, he guides, he creates, he performs, he simply makes it all work. How many people are you glad to hear on the other end of your phone when it rings? Andrew, for your talent, bravery, and, mostly, your friendship, thank you. And Tom, you had a hand in this one again, too. Like I said, bad things can happen when the chef's alone in the kitchen. Thanks for working the line, braving the burners, and pulling your share of late shifts along the way.

Finally, to the fans, please know how you are admired and honored. You are the reason for it all.

RC
New York City, June 2011

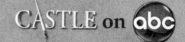